LIGHTSTORM!

Where there had been only endless blue, now there were pulsations of intense green and purple growing rapidly across the sky. They distorted her vision with colors so vibrant that they burned themselves into her mind.

The noise began as a barely audible rumble, rising in broken waves until it seemed to Rifkind that every sound she had ever heard was infinitely repeated in dissonant chorus. She stood for a few moments, supported only by the sensory overload she was absorbing.

'I am a warrior. I am a healer. I will not be conquered by this!'

A figure approached them, clothed in a shining emerald cape that rippled with iridescent crimson as he walked over the magenta sands. His skin was black ebony, his eyes glittered like diamonds; a third gemlike spot glowed on his cheek. He hailed her, and the sound resonated from the horizons.

Rifkind felt her eyes to see if they were open. They were not.

DAUGHTER OF THE BRIGHT MOON

DAUGHTER OF THE BRIGHT MOON

LYNN ABBEY

SF
ace books

A Division of Charter Communications Inc.
A GROSSET & DUNLAP COMPANY
51 Madison Avenue
New York, New York 10010

DAUGHTER OF THE BRIGHT MOON

An ACE Book

Cover art by Bob Adragna

First Ace printing; July 1979
First mass market printing: February 1980

2 4 6 8 0 9 7 5 3
Manufactured in the United States of America

For Bob, without whom all of
this would have been much
more difficult.

guards I left them to their doom, still my dream-spirit hoped ardently that I was wrong. That the cloud was just a dust devil or a mirage, not my clan's fate.

'I did not—do not—honor you. My blind, crippled, dishonored father, my perfumed, cowardly brother ... the rest of you ... but I am a healer. I did not wish you dead. I had come back to you with my knowledge, but you spurned my healing just as you had spurned my sword.'

Rifkind leaned over and wrenched a splintered tent pole from the hard dry ground, used it to probe the smoldering mounds without dismounting. The few loyal warriors formed a sparse ring of corpses around the pavillion wherein her father had lain a cripple—and her brother had lain with his harem of captive women.

"*Halim!*" She shouted her brother's name as she savagely thrust the stake into the felt and mohair of the ruined pavillion. 'I know you're here, damn you. *You* did not fight. They found you cowering behind the silks of your women. There is no knowledge in your entrails; they killed you where they found you.'

The bloody corpse of the blue-eyed slave who had most pleased Halim tumbled down from the pile of debris, revealing the fat, headless, castrated corpse of her brother.

'Fitting: they took your head, which you never used, and your manhood, which Chala died defending. Did you recognize your slayers, or did the other chiefs of the Gathering send faceless assassins to kill one who living was a dishonor to them all?

'You were weak and loved luxury like a Wet-Lander. Yet even so when I returned from my years with Muroa I offered to heal our differences. I

would have left you the women—what use to me?
And you never cared for fighting; you would have
had to challenge Father. And blind crippled wreck
that he was, you loved him ... Or did you fear that
despite everything he would rise from that pallet
and wield a sword more effectively than you? I
would have lifted that load from you. But no—'

Her arm snapped forward, releasing the tent pole
with such force that it drove through the silk-
swathed belly and into the ground beneath. Though
small even for an Asheeran, Rifkind had driven her
body to a physical perfection that let her claim a
warrior's sword in a society that sold its women
into marriage once they had proven their woman-
hood.

The defiled well made it clear to her that the raiding party had been from her own Gathering. She
had been a child when the Gathering had last
swooped down to annihilate a member clan. They'd
burned the clan's blood leaders alive and read their
charred entrails at the subsequent feast. Her father
had been hetman then, and she'd hidden in her
own tent frightened as much by the wild sputtering
fires themselves as by the yowls of torment. Her
mind filled with the memories of that night—only
now it was her father's sightless eyes that stared out
of the flames, whose unbound arms reached out for
her.

Rifkind fought the remorse and grief with her bitter hatred.

'You lingered untimely long. When neither Muroa
nor I could heal you, you ought to have *begged* for
death, rather than let us all come to this! Who would
think that the man who led our Gathering so proudly in his youth would cling to life so piteously!

'Had it not meant fighting every warrior left to the clan I would have challenged you myself ... In the end, it has made no difference—either way, the clan is destroyed. I am alone.'

She dismounted and led Turin to the fringes of the camp where her own tent had stood. An outcast, she had been distrusted by her own clan—but still clan-blood; they could not send her away, yet the doorway of her small russet tent had always faced the open steppes of the Asheera. And now the dogs were adding their own dishonor to that of the Gathering.

Whirling a scrap of cloth that trailed smoke and ashes, she chased the dogs away and returned to stand in the still-warm ashes of her home. Those boxes and sacks that had survived the burning had been pillaged. Imagining their reactions to the piles of sand and stone they had found, Rifkind gave a short, vindictive bark of laughter. A healer, she had a small secret cave in the barren rocks not too far from the encampment. Distrusting those of her own clan as much as any possible raider she had kept her possessions of value hidden there.

They had destroyed her clan—but everything she cherished was safe: her gold, the consecrated objects she'd received from Muroa at her initiation, the moon-stones and her ruby pendant—suddenly she clutched the neck of her tunic. The evening before, Vernta had taken the necklace to tighten one of the links, and had not returned it before Rifkind had stormed out of her father's tent. Panic stricken, she plunged into the debris with her bare hands while Turin made anxious noises outside the charred perimeter of her tent.

"Rifkind?"

A weak voice came from the debris. She lifted the heavy felt and found her manservant.

Unable to speak she touched his shoulder gently. His eyes opened, but did not focus on her.

"I knew you'd come back ... Tahrman called for you when they took him. 'Rifkind. Avenge me, daughter! Avenge the clan!' He called on you. Then —the fire!"

The man struggled for breath, his charred face filled with agony and remembered horror. Rifkind took his outstretched hand in her own. She had left them to their deaths.

"Vernta? Where's Vernta?" His voice was weakening, but his grip was strengthened by impending death.

"Can you see her?"

Rifkind looked about for the man's wife, found her. Her right arm had been slashed off and her skull split open. A dog had claimed the body as its own.

"She's gone. A battle death. You can be proud."

"She fought to the end ... The ruby? ... She had the ruby ... It was your mother's, you know ... She always wore it around her neck on a big gold chain. ... Ah, princess, you're so beautiful ..."

His grip loosened and he reached out, seeming to find something. Rifkind did not need the intense focus of a healer to know he had passed from the reality of the living to that of the dead. His last broken words were addressed to the ghost of her mother. His hand dropped a final time, the gurgling in his chest ceased. After a moment, Rifkind pressed the lids down over the dead, staring eyes.

The man wore three gold neck chains that somehow the raiders had missed. She broke them off and stuffed them into a tunic pocket. His other ornaments were not valuable. She stepped over his body to squat by the mangled body of his wife. Vernta clutched a bloody dagger in her remaining hand. Rifkind had no doubt that the woman had fought to the end.

"I knew you too well, Vernta. You would never have fought for this clan; you befriended me only because I reminded you of her. There was never any doubt where your loyalty lay."

Rifkind slipped her own dagger from its sheath and began slitting the corpse's clothing.

"You wouldn't die until that stone was safe."

When the heavy chain and its ruby pendant did not appear in the cloth folds, Rifkind plunged the knife deep into Vernta's abdomen, making an S-shaped slash. She enlarged the gash until her knife grazed something harder than bone. For reasons of her own, the old woman had pried the thumbnail-sized stone from its setting and swallowed it. Rifkind wondered if her mother's nurse had intended to keep the stone herself, but that no longer mattered. After wiping the stone free of gore, she slipped it into the suede pouch which held her oracle moon-stones.

Turin thrust his muzzle at her cheek. She looked up and absently scratched his nose.

"Yes, Turin, I see the sun. The dark moon is behind us; the Bright One not yet full. We're not likely to have lightstorms today, but still it's time to get to shelter."

The dogs were back in the camp before Rifkind's feet had found the stirrups of her saddle. She had seen packs of them follow a raiding party and lingering for a week or more to feast on an un-

fortunate caravan plundered by her clan. But that
had been in the days when they were victors; now
the dogs fed on them. It was too much to endure.
She dug her heels into Turin's flanks and urged the
war-horse to battle frenzy. She drew her sword, and
he lowered his horns. They trampled the ruins in
their mutual rage, but only old or injured dogs fell to
their fury. The rest retreated to the rocks to out-wait
her.

Battle frenzy gone, she was drained of her over-
wrought emotions. She looked down at the grey-
muzzled dogs—both slashed and gored. But there
would be other dogs, even if she had slain the whole
pack. It was the Asheera's way of reclaiming its
own.

Woman and steed turned away, Turin choosing
his own path out of the camp and toward her cave.
He took them by a devious, circular route, in case
raiders might still be nearby, yet made sure they
reached the rocks well before the sun reached mid-
heaven. Rifkind dismounted and relieved Turin of
his saddle, then left him to a peaceful afternoon
cropping the bitter greenish-white grass of the
Asheera while she crept into the small cave.

The dark shadows of the rocks provided shelter
from the heat of the midday sun and from the terrors of lightstorms, which disrupted visible light and
the minds of anyone who did not take shelter. The
Asheeran nomads traditionally slept the dangerous
and uncomfortable days away, conducting their
business in the cool safety of the night air.

Rifkind sat, cushioned by a heavy embroidered
riding-cloak, in the darkness of the cave, unable to
sleep.

Her thoughts ran first toward redeeming her selfing too long as it is. Leave. Search for your own fate. It's no good to have that destiny stalking the Asheera."

"Where else would I go?"

"You've cast the moon-stones. Go where they tell you."

Rifkind's gaze returned to the stones. If glorious vengeance was difficult to attain, winning an argument with Muroa was impossible.

"They make no sense."

The old woman laughed. "You go too deep, girl. Look at them! All in a line like that. Follow the line, and by morning, the Bright One will set at your feet."

"It's not like the Bright One to move from behind. ... If it's a line, it's a line to moonrise."

"It leads out of the cave, child, toward moonset."

"If I followed that, I'd wind up in the Death-Wastes, alone, with no extra animals, no food or water. And no tent for protection against the light-storms! It is not a line to moonset. That isn't the Bright One's way: the Wet-Lands are only ten nights' journey the other way. There are rocks and wells."

"Go away from the cave. Toward moonset ... ah, never matter. You'll leave now—either way."

Muroa sprang to the back of her war-horse with an agility which belied her sixty-odd years in the steppes.

"Wait, I'll go with you."

"No, not tonight, Rifkind. I go to Kerdal's camp." The old woman saw the questions in Rifkind's eyes and laughed again before digging her heels into the war-horse's flanks. "Someone has to read your father's entrails; it can't very well be you, can it?"

Muroa's final words seemed to echo in the night

"I have a duty to the clan. I must claim vengeance." Rifkind protested with more determination than she felt.

"You're more than able with a sword, and you've more skill in the Art than I'd got at your age; but girl, you'll get no vengeance riding alone into that nest. Or don't you know? No, I can see in your face you don't. Your brother-in-law Kerdal rounded up the whole Gathering to make that raid. He could have done it alone, but he shared the glory and honor, and now everyone is sitting peacefully at his feet."

"It will be a vengeance in spirit. My clan has died! I must have vengeance or die with it."

Rifkind began to pace the ground before her cave.

"You have a destiny to fulfill!" Muroa's voice rose in anger.

"My clan is my destiny!" Rifkind answered in kind, turning on her heels, her hand resting lightly, absently, on the sword hilt.

"Your clan lies out there eating the bitter dust it so richly deserved. Your destiny is as your mother's was. Take that stone and leave the Asheera!"

The two women glared at each other. Then Rifkind dropped her stare and looked off at the scattered moon-stones.

"Of all our treasure, that alone remains. Vernta saved the ruby for me."

"Vernta!" Muroa spat for emphasis. "That she-jackal. No doubts of her loyalty. She'd keep the stone —for eternity if she could. . . . No matter—you've got it safe?"

"I cut it out of her stomach."

"Then begone. Finish your destiny—it's been wait-

keep the bowl from overflowing. There must be less of the spirit of water in the air here to be called by the ritual. Still, it is strange we did not try this before —in droughts we fled our wells and fought bloody battles over mudholes—even our clan ... we could have avoided our dishonored end. ...

'But I didn't know then, either. My tal has strengthened daily since I put the Bright One at my back, though the Lost Gods know it is a hard, unpleasant journey. Muroa misread the signs and I mistrusted her. It is said that the Wet-Lands are called Dro Daria, and Dro Daria surrounds the Asheera, and that the center of Dro Daria is called Dro Daria. Anyplace which can surround the Asheera and also be at the center of itself will not be difficult to find. Even if Muroa sent me in the wrong direction.'

A thin line of water appeared at the rim of the bowl. Rifkind smiled with satisfaction. She had devised the water ritual when their journey led them into the Death-Wastes of the Asheera, a place far more barren than she had believed possible. The wells which had marked the change from the steppes to the desert had been marked only by small mud bricks and were often dry. The clans they stealthily passed seemed more desperate and ragged than her own had at its worst. Hospitality was risky even among the clans she knew; she did not risk it with strangers near the Death-Wastes.

The water ritual was only one of several innovations the journey had necessitated. Rifkind had become proficient with a bow; a weapon she had always considered suitable only for those who could not or would not wield a blade. The journey had left her no time for leisurely contests with aggressive beasts; the game they found was small and wary, and they were hungry. The clans on whose lands they trespassed maintained guards by night, so they had reversed the traditional patterns and traveled by day. As a healer, with a highly developed tal ability, Rifkind feared the power of lightstorms; as a warrior, she refused to fight the unreasonable odds the wary night guards presented. There were no clans in the Death-Wastes themselves, nor were there shelters from the light and heat of midday. Again the warrior in her won out; if there was danger from the burning sun, she would face it squarely rather than cower under the heavy folds of her riding cloak.

She had waited until the relatively safe period after the waning of the Dark Moon before entering the Death-Wastes, using the water ritual to sustain them both. The blistering rock-and-sand desert was vast beyond her expectations. She drove herself and Turin with the knowledge that the reddish-gold presence of the Dark One was crescented in the night sky again, and the Bright One ebbed quickly.

Turin had the first bowl of water; she repeated the process for herself. The ritual took even longer the second time. The entire crossing was taking too long. Neither she nor Turin had eaten since they had left the last dry well. Water enabled them to keep going but she knew no ritual to heal the hollowness in their stomachs.

Rifkind took Turin's reins while she checked their course by the sun. It was no more difficult than following the Bright One, though she shot only brief sidelong glances toward the fiery hot yellow star.

They traveled the hard-baked yellow stone for two days more, each day covering less territory than the day before. Turin's unshod hooves were bruised and battered by the uneven, windswept ground. Rifkind walked along beside him, carrying much of her own gear. She too was footsore. They tried the dunes, but found the soft, powdery sand gave way beneath them. Their empathy was narrowed to a shared desperate desire to be out of this blinding place and back to the familiarity of the steppes.

Rifkind unbraided her hair and let it fall across her face. Her night-sensitive eyes were swollen and painful from the continual desert glare. Turin walked with his head down, rarely looking toward the glistening horizon. Rifkind didn't sense danger in the first darkening of the sky, only relief that her eyes hurt less. Despite her half-numbed senses she finally realized that the sky did not darken at mid-day and that the darkening was not the reddish hues of sunset, but improbable combinations of green and purple.

Lightstorm!

Where there had been only endless blue, now there were pulsating blotches of intense greens and purples growing rapidly across the sky. They distorted her vision with colors so vibrant they burned themselves into her mind. The blotches divided, becoming reds, blues, and yellows as well, until the whole sky was blazing with color.

The sound had been there from the beginning; Rifkind noticed it only when the colors reached a plateau of sustained brilliance. The noise began as a barely audible rumble, rising in broken waves until it seemed to Rifkind that every sound she had ever heard was infinitely repeated in dissonant chorus. She stood for a few moments, supported only by the sensory overload she was absorbing. To Turin,

standing beside her, she seemed to collapse from
within, her eyes still open, low, agonized moans
strangling in her throat.

The war-horse looked around them. He saw only
a darkened landscape caused by the appearance of
a black disk which was slipping quickly across the
sun. Stars should not replace the sun in such untimely ways—he was angered by this disruption, but not
afraid of it.

A sliver of natural sunlight emerged at the edge of
the black disk. Turin understood the ending of the
eclipse no better than he had understood its beginning; but once normality was restored, he wanted
only to forget the interruption. His Rider should
stand once again so they might resume their difficult
journey. Only when she continued to lie on the barren rock did he become anxious. Gingerly he probed
her mind with his own, and was driven back by the
dazzling lights and sounds he found there.

Rifkind felt his inquiring presence, but its reality
was lost in the aftermath of the throbbing sounds
and colors. She knew that her mind and senses had
been damaged by the storm, but was unable to
gauge the severity of her injury. She opened and
closed her eyes, cupped and uncupped her hands
over her ears. Kinetic sensations remained true, but
everything else was distorted. There was no difference if her eyes were open or closed. Her screams
of anger and fear brought white-rimmed panic to
Turin's eyes, but she could not hear herself.

'I am a warrior. I am a healer. I will not be conquered by this!'

Rifkind mustered her reserves of will, ascended
into the meditative state of tal-mind, which the

The figure stepped forward, well within range of the snaking sword. He reached for her; she slashed, still awkward and unbalanced. The blade passed harmlessly through his cape. Rifkind fell hard to her left side from her own clumsiness. She scrambled to her feet again. Twice more she struck, and though each stroke caused the figure to hesitate, none harmed him.

Within her tal, Rifkind pieced together the knowledge that she was fighting a chimera; a projection from the body and mind of a powerful ritual master. She tried to recall what Muroa had told her about chimerae, remembered that she could prevail against it only if she struck in the direction of the projecting mind.

The tal-concentration lasted too long. A cold hand clamped down on the back of her neck. Leaping up with the sword, she struck reflexively. The figure retreated. Her fighting instincts had never depended on seeing the ground to know it was there. Rifkind relived her training and gathered strength from it. Her conscious mind and memory remained bedazzled by the effects of the lightstorm, but her body snapped into a reflexive readiness for battle. Muroa had taught her how to locate a person's center-most thoughts for the healing rituals. Long years of practice with a sword in Gathering melees and personal duels had taught her what else could be done with an adversary's centered thoughts.

Turin's solid presence was easy to locate. She ordered him to remain motionless while she sought the physical origin of the chimera. The emerald-and-black figure had stepped out of sword's range; his diamondlike eyes narrowed to slits while he watched Rifkind make a methodical search of the horizon. The mind which projected the chimera had made no mistakes. The double barrier of her own disorientation and the immateriality of the chimera did not yield or reveal a true direction. She reluctantly dropped into a defensive posture and waited.

The black face smiled, the diamond eyes glowing with painful intensity, as the chimera advanced again. Rifkind, holding herself motionless within the tal, felt the advance first from a point on the horizon just in front of her right shoulder. She focused her own mind there, but contrived to keep her gaze fixed before her.

The figure's fingers tapered to long nails the color of the vermilion sands. Rifkind waited, her sword gripped tightly, until those nails were inches from her. Then, with the warbling shriek that was her battle cry, she spun toward it, moving the sword in powerful figure-eight arcs as she did. The chimera staggered back. She had felt no resistance to the blade, but the strike had been true and an ebony arm lay momentarily on the blood-red sands before vanishing.

"You who wear a silver crescent on your cheek and can project a chimera of your tal, hear me. I am Rifkind, survivor and exile, master of the sword, mistress of the rituals. I will never give you the ruby; even if you dare to face me yourself, you will not take it from me."

"You speak too loudly and foolishly."

The chimera was unaffected by the loss of its arm. It advanced again into sword range. Once more Rifkind waited until the hand was almost at her throat before striking. At the very instant when the magician had to place something of his physical self into the chimera she swung the sword in another double arc, severing the other arm and slicing through the neck.

Rifkind stepped back, still wary, yet satisfied that she had damaged the chimera beyond any use to its creator. She had no delusions that she had touched the mind which had projected it or in any way diminished the magician's desire for the stone she wore at her neck.

"Tell me your name!" she demanded of the dissolving chimera.

"You have been lucky, witch. You will not win by luck again. I will not be tricked into giving you my name as you've given me yours. Next time, Rifkind, I shall take the ruby at once. I've waited too long to be merciful."

The figure shrank to nothing, as if inhaled by its creator.

Rifkind let her weight rest heavily on the sword. Her eyes were closed now, and her muscles trembled with weariness and suppressed fear. She hoped her senses would clear with the passing of the chimera, but was not surprised that her challenger had only taken advantage of the weakness the light-storm itself had caused, and which remained after his departure.

The ruby was still in the pouch around her neck. It was a precious thing of beauty, a treasure she had worn with no small insolence in the impoverished clan. The ruby was hers; passed to her from her mother, who had not belonged to the clan, but to another several Gatherings away. Once it had belonged to her brother Halim, but a slow-moving fifteen-year-old had lost it to his swift, aggressive younger sister after an ill-timed challenge.

"Turin," she whispered. The chestnut war-horse thrust his muzzle against her cheek. In her distorted vision, he seemed a brilliant, blue-winged beast without horns.

'Turin, I curse old Muroa for luring us to our deaths, though I know it was my decision as much as hers. Will he return to pluck the stone when our bones are bleached? Should I take it now and bury it? It will do us no good—why should we surrender it in death? Vernta made a mistake leaving it where I would think to look.

'No, I'll keep it to the end, and beyond. It is not within my pride to hide my ruby. Muroa always scolded me for my pride. I ought not to have given him my name like that. She always said a name is power! She's never told anyone her true name; Muroa's only what we agreed to call her. But I'm a fighter before I'm a ritualist. My name is my pride, my power.'

"By the Lost Gods, I've little left of either. In one afternoon I've been nearly defeated by a chimera, and my senses have been destroyed by a lightstorm that I ought to have had enough sense to avoid—and certainly should have known not to watch like some gaping clod. Today I earned death, not life."

Turin snorted. Rifkind scratched his forehead between the horns. He recognized sounds and thoughts of death in her conversation and reflexively rejected them.

"I've been punished for my stupidity. I'm a lot worse off than the other time I wandered out into a lightstorm. But then I was too afraid to look up. This time . . ."

She had survived three lightstorms: the one which had claimed her mother moments before her birth, one as a child of nine winters brazenly defying the elders and tradition to stride out of the tent when even her father prudently pulled a cloak over his eyes, and today's, which had almost brought her death at the cold ethereal hands of a chimera.

The muscles in her legs trembled despite her determination to stand firm. Although her eyes saw a gaudy landscape and her ears were filled with the sound of thousands of half-heard conversations, Rifkind could feel the desert's heat and the dryness of thirst in her throat. Ringing Turin's neck with her arms she hid her face in his mane and shuddered.

'We're going to die here, both of us. I can't contrive water now, not any that'd be safe to drink. Ritual needs empathy, I'm out of empathy with everything. The power of the warrior! By the Bright One, I should have given him the damnable stone—then had him pull us out of here into his power. We've no better place to go.'

Rifkind's thoughts were for herself alone, but pressed against his neck as she was, they poured into Turin's mind with a clarity that struck deeply at his reality; the chaos of her mind threatened his own carefully ordered world. He pushed the chaos back, knowing instinctively that the world could never be anything but what long experience said it was and would always be. With the same willful and simple knowledge, he crossed the barriers into her mind to pursue the chaos.

The sky was blue, the sand yellow, the air still and quiet. The wild distortions of the lightstorm faded from Rifkind's mind, replaced by a measure of Turin's insistent faith that things were as they should be.

Rifkind lifted her head and stepped away from

the war-horse. She was fully aware of what he had accomplished and was grateful. Her body was an aching mass of strained muscles, her head throbbed, but when she cautiously opened her eyes it was Turin's world she saw from horizon to horizon.

She was tired, and curled up on the heavy cloak to rest while Turin waited with his usual enduring patience. It was hot; the sun beat down on her dark clothing. She ignored it. The lightstorm and the chimera had done their worst, and still she had survived. Come evening, when she was rested, she would think of a way to make water appear in the enamel bowl again—and perhaps food as well. Her mind was filled with possibilities for turning sand into meat and grass when she finally fell asleep.

CHAPTER 3

Dro Daria. The Wet-Lands.

Rifkind had always known that the Asheera was surrounded by an alien land where water was so plentiful that people there immersed their whole bodies in it. She had heard the homesick mewlings of women captured from caravans crossing the steppes, or in occasional forays by border clans into the alien exterior. But still she was unprepared for the heavy, verdant land which suddenly revealed itself on the far side of low hills scarcely distinguishable from the hundreds of other serpentine formations which laced the Asheeran steppes.

This was green—lush, moisture-laden, not the pale waxy shade of grasses Turin had always cropped. She had gathered handfuls to stuff into her sacks of ritual herbs, fearing the phenomenon was limited to only a small part of the universe, but the green grew more prominent with each step of the journey. She saw trees, recognizing them as the source of the wood the clans prized only slightly less than gold or water. Then she felt rain.

Rain.

It had been an odor in the heavy air until it became a frightening presence. Water, sheets of it falling in incomprehensible quantities from the heavens, driving into her face and clothes until, absurdly, she needed to take shelter from it. Discomfort from water—a contradiction even the refined perceptions of her tal could not comprehend—or ignore. She had jumped from Turin's back, splashing through the mud to sink her hands into the soft oozing life-rich ground of the Wet-Lands. The abundance of energy in the soil made her sensitive fingers tingle. She forgot the terrors of the journey and held the rich sweet-smelling earth close to her face.

Every day brought new sensations, but nothing equaled the strangeness of water falling from the sky. Even the half-awed, half-hating peasants who now watched them pass were ordinary by comparison. She hunted with ease and impunity, avoiding only those animals penned or otherwise obviously domesticated by the Wet-Landers.

'This land is too easy. I eat meat every night. I cannot always find an animal small enough to feed only myself. I have forgotten what it is to be thirsty already. The people are weak and without leaders, they let me pass through their lands without a challenge. When I get to Dro Daria, the center of itself, I will have no trouble gathering a clan around myself. These people need strong direction, and I will provide it. I may even guide their caravans across the Asheera for them.'

Rifkind's mind filled with grand schemes for survival and even prosperity in her new home, yet she was not completely deceived by the idyllic land they crossed. Turin was anxious. His empathic senses found more than passive curiosity in the peasants they passed. Some recognized them as Asheeran nomads and radiated fear; but as they left the steppes farther behind, Turin felt a resentment he could not comprehend—he conveyed it to his Rider, whose mind encompassed colors and tones that his did not.

'The hornless horses do not respond when Turin greets them—he has no language—it can be only that these horses lack his empathy and intelligence. They endure having bits of metal or leather drawn through their mouths and they haul heavy wagons without complaint. And the people, if Turin is right, endure what no clansman would tolerate—yet at the same time they look at us as we ride down these wide, smooth trails and hate us not because we are exiles, or from the Asheera, but because I *do* ride, and carry a sword.

'Yet what are these trails for if not to make the way clear and fast for a war-horse? There is too much life for us to travel in any direction we desire. ... Where are the clans who cut these trails, if those who live along them hate those who ride by?'

"Turin!"

Rifkind's voice cut through the jangle of their gear. She had resorted to a verbal command when other methods had failed to compel his attention. He had lowered his horns at a youth who had the courage to stand on the road in front of them; faced with the stallion's martial display, the youth had dived back through the hedgerows.

'That will be enough. We are not a raiding party. We are going to live in this land. They may act afraid of us, but we are outnumbered, on strange soil. I, for one, do not want to examine at first hand their fighting ability just yet. Their fear is too consistent and exaggerated. They cower as if we were demons; if we are so feared, then we must also be hated. So far we have met only those whose fear is stronger than their hate; we are not ready to meet men of the other kind. We are going to that city in the distance. We are going as quickly and quietly as possible. There will be no more battle displays.'

The chestnut war-horse did not break stride as her thoughts drove home. Even this far out he could feel the emotional vortices of the vast numbers of Walkers pressed together in that vast grey place. It did not strike him as the proper place for a war-horse and Rider.

Rifkind felt and shared Turin's discomfort. The grey mass had to be a city if only because she'd never felt anything like the psychic surges of the jagged silhouette before them. It projected a wall of emotions twisted and contorted almost beyond recognition. In the clans it was said that the strongest of the chiefs and healers could sense the approach of another clan and identify it by its group thoughts. The city sat like a gaping psychic wound, spilling raw uncensored emotion and thought toward every horizon.

Though Muroa claimed to sense her surface emo-

tions, Rifkind strove to keep her private thoughts and
deeper feelings hidden and protected by the energies
of her tal. Turin alone could enter her mind, and he
was limited to her surface. She quickly increased
her resistance to the emanations of the city, then set
Turin to an easy canter. Unaided instinct urged her
to reach the city before sunset—the first time she ever
recalled wanting to face the unknown in full light.

The approaching sunset was marred by a gathering of low black clouds which advanced rapidly toward them. Rifkind waited for rain, but instead
found herself enveloped by increasing darkness and
ground mist. Turin slowed to a prudent walk.

'These roads twist and turn; the land itself is
rutted and crossed with free water; the air is never
clear enough to judge distance properly. We had
enough trouble traveling when the water actually
fell from the sky; now the air simply thickens into a
visible wall. I can't see. I can't breathe. It's no wonder Dro Darians do not travel much by night. Lightstorms wouldn't occur in such thick air, and it is too
easy to become lost in air such as this.'

They followed the shrouded road. The fog muf-
fled the sounds of Turin's hoofbeats and the jangling
of the ornaments on his horns. Rifkind drew the
damp cloak tightly around her until she was completely concealed in its folds. The walls of the city
reared high above them before they noted a change
in the texture of the air, and recognized this greyness
as stone rather than fog.

Rifkind needed no special knowledge of the Wet-
Lands or the city to know that its inhabitants had
planned their defenses carefully; the trail widened
into a broad avenue; any archer on the walls would
have had an easy target as they approached. A deep,

dry moat separated them from the walls except at one point, where a causeway funneled into a high-walled passageway which led—she hoped—into the city itself.

Turin flattened his ears and worked up a rapid lather in silent protest at their entering the passage. His instincts told him the close-walled thing was certain death. He could not clear the walls, nor was there enough room for a running attack. His more acute senses also told them that there was at least one Walker hidden in the darkness.

Rifkind accepted his warnings and slowed their pace to a stealthy walk, but did not alter their course. Her destination was the center of Dro Daria, the city itself. She held his reins tightly as they entered the dark passageway.

"Halt! Who goes?" A man's voice, followed by the diffuse beam of a lantern, emerged from the far end. Rifkind guessed the distance to be not much more than ten paces.

"A traveler, seeking shelter in Dro Daria."

'Best not to say from where, I think. His accent is almost incomprehensible; mine is not likely to be less so to him. He'll know I'm not from here.'

"Traveler? Alone on a night like this? Ye must be mad. Come into the light so as I can see you. You sound like a woman, though Mohamdru alone could tell from the way you speak."

They advanced slowly. Rifkind still put most of her concentration into controlling Turin. She forbade him to attack the stranger, but acknowledged his belligerence and beneath the cover of her cloak withdrew her sword from its scabbard. They stopped at a good defensive distance: an unmounted man could not move more than a pace before Turin would have leaped the distance and Rifkind's sword was at his throat.

"Asheeran bitch ... Seeking shelter! Your kind doesn't take to shelter," the Wet-Lander snarled as the lantern light fell on her face.

Rifkind was unprepared for the intensity of his hatred, so great that it made her physically uncomfortable.

"The law of Dro Daria is that no one may be refused the sanctuary of its walls."

'That's what the captives always said. It hasn't ever made much sense to me; they always rattled on about Wet-Land laws, though we never paid any attention to it.'

"Darius can do as he likes in his stinkin' city. This ain't Dro Daria, it's Isinglas, an' we don't take in Asheerans. Go tell your friends out there that this isn't one of Darius's border forts. This is Isinglas, and we've our own garrison. Our own men. She's our city, and we'll defend her to the last."

'I have the feeling he would, too. Isinglas? Not Dro Daria? After all this I've come to the wrong city? I've never even heard of this Isinglas. ... They may not have sent caravans through the Asheera. Perhaps they are smarter. It is a city—he says that much. I can make my way here as well as anywhere else. If I can conquer their hatred.'

"By the stones, there is no one with me but Turin here. We are seeking shelter, nothing more."

The conciliatory words and tone came with difficulty. Turin did not understand what she said, only that it was hard for her to say it. He shook his horns menacingly, flinging bits of foam into the fog.

"Come to kill us all. Probably hired by Darius himself ..."

He backed toward the sentry box, a malicious, determined gleam in his eyes.

"Do you think you can play games with us, Wet-Lander? I travel alone, but yes I am Asheeran; I know your intentions."

'Not as well as I'd like, but he radiates a confidence—that means he has some plan he believes is beyond failure. He can't intend to fight us himself; he carries the lantern in his sword hand. He thinks he can sound an alarm?'

She registered the rope just as the guard reached for it. Alone it meant nothing, but as the object of his attention, she guessed it was a way of calling or warning others. Turin needed no signal to begin his attack-leap, only the relaxation of the willful control she'd held on him. Accustomed to the bone-wrenching suddenness of his movements, Rifkind bared her sword. The guard froze, the rope to the great alarm bell within the walls just beyond his grasp. Turin's horns quivered at his chest; Rifkind's blade was poised a hairsbreadth over his extended wrist. She held the blade motionless at full arm's length, betraying no strain from its weight.

"I know your intentions."

"The gate. To open the gate, I must call for help."

"You look strong enough to me. You can do it alone this once."

Rifkind prodded his shoulder gently with the sword while Turin backed away slightly to let him move toward the gate. The war-horse was easier to control once he was given an opportunity to display his feelings.

Instead the guard reached again for the rope. Rifkind flicked the sword-tip across his wrist and palm, laying skin open to the bone. Beads of sweat

broke out on his forehead; he leaned against the
sentry-box, shaking, all courage fled. Rifkind waited
impassively while the wounded man struggled with
the pulleys which controlled the heavy gates. When
she had seen enough to understand their operation,
she leaned forward and slashed the man's throat.

'He died honorably, defending his clan. If there is
dishonor, it is mine—that he was not armed.'

They passed between the barely parted gates.

'There was more blood than necessary. If there
had been witnesses, I'd be ashamed. He died noise-
lessly enough from a wound which could have been
from any sword or knife.

'It would not have been wise to leave him to tell
his fellows. If Isinglas needs walls and guards I'll
venture it has enemies enough; with luck they'll
merely think that he was stupid and careless—
which he was.'

Rifkind's feelings of satisfaction and confidence
vanished when they stood in the pitch-black of the
gate tunnel. Surrounded by thick permanent walls,
Rifkind realized what would have been obvious
long before if her determination to reach the Wet-
Land cities had not blocked all other thoughts—she
had no idea of life within walls. The Dro Darian
countryside, for all its strangeness, was still open
and free. Within walls, nothing in her past could
guide her; some habits could prove to be downright
dangerous, and she might not know which ones until too late.

Belatedly, Rifkind gave some hard thought to her
idea of guiding or guarding caravans, admitted to
herself that there was no chance that the Dro
Darians would hire her. Her people had always
taken their wealth from the Wet-Land caravans; it

was not likely that they would forget this when she told them she was a wandering exile.

Rifkind sank into her thoughts, let Turin find his way out of the tunnel and into the open square. She didn't look up when he stopped, unwilling to choose among the dark, anonymous streets. His anxiety flowed into her mind where it mixed so completely with her own thoughts that she did not notice anything until he turned his head and nipped her knee.

Her thoughts transmuted into shame in an instant: her self-indulgent despair was eroding her warrior's alertness; had she been so absorbed in a strange part of the Asheera, her life would have been worthless. That fine-tuned awareness pushed out the shame as she focused on the square and the streets, again resuming her proper role as survivor and decision maker.

'They all look alike. Dark, narrow, treacherous paths to—where? We can't stay here in the open, so we'll take the path that seems least traveled. I'd prefer, I think, to meet those whom the Dro Darians avoid.'

They walked the edge of the square, doubling back to a narrow street which had grass forcing its way between a few of the paving stones and a smell reminiscent of the burned-out camp. Following the random twist of streets into the maze, even Turin's senses were soon satisfied that the buildings were empty rather than filled with sleeping citizens. Rifkind dismounted to explore an abandoned building more closely. The wooden door was charred, but still sturdy.

She guessed the purpose of hinges, located a weak point in the structure, and after a few shoves broke into the ground floor of what had once been a fash-

ionable residence. A scurrying of small animals
enabled her to guess the size of the room. On the far
side was a stone area in which she could make a
fire. Turin waited in the street, radiating disbelief
that she actually expected him to follow. When less
blunt forms of encouragement failed, she grasped
his reins and led him forcefully through the
doorway.

'We have been lucky and would be fools to think
anything else. It is not a question of leaving the
Asheera and living in the cities of the Wet-Lands. I
knew it would be somewhat different, but never
thought how much I would be ashamed for being
so blind.

'We can't hunt here. There's no ready meat except
these little animals, and less grass. They live in these
solid boxes, and though I don't like the idea, if I
stayed here I don't think I could keep Turin with me
in one. The Dro Darians keep their hornless beasts in
separate boxes, if the air is any measure.

'Already the press of people affects me; I'm nervous and careless—I'll get myself killed dis-
honorably, or worse. It's too soon to come into the
cities. We will rest, steal some food and water, then
go back to the open country. We can survive out
there. I'll consider our next moves more carefully.'

Turin shifted his weight from side to side as he
rested in the far corner. The rattling of his coins pro-
voked another decision. The shining display of coins
and banding which represented at least half her
ready wealth, not counting the ruby, would be more
useful tucked into a pouch at her waist than hanging
openly, however well Turin could defend them. The
Dro Darians, she knew, used gold not for ornament
but for business, and preferred small disks marked

by weight and stamped with the likeness of some forgotten princeling. Reminding herself to attend to the coins when they were both rested, Rifkind settled into a corner for a sequence of short naps.

Before the next day's sunset, Rifkind had secured the coins in her pouch. Unadorned, the war-horse was still impressive; his horns frightful weapons, each nearly as long as her forearm and black except for an ivory streak on the right one. In the Gathering, they had said the ivory meant his blood was mixed with that of the immortal war-horses of the gods. It was a legend, but she repeated it until she half-believed it again herself, and the wild look had left his eyes.

It had rained during the day, turning the streets to swamps, but the skies had cleared by sunset and the Bright One provided ample light. Having forsaken their dubious haven, they watched for a sign of the walls which bounded the city and separated them from green freedom as they prowled the streets of Isinglas. By day their task would have been difficult; now, in the growing darkness, the narrow-angled streets never offered a clear view.

As they wandered into a populated part of the town, Rifkind thought of food. She had not eaten for two days. The unfriendly stares of the townsfolk as they edged away from their path kept her alert and expecting attack from any direction.

'People—or rather, Wet-Landers—by the Lost Gods, they unnerve me! Of course, I've never been around so many before. We've been followed by the corners of everyone's eyes since we left the burned area. They distrust each other as much as they suspect us, or I'd be expecting an ambush at every corner. We've passed four places which offered food inside; the fifth is just ahead. Five is lucky. There are several of the local beasts tied in front which look as though they've been ridden hard. We'll try our skill at getting food by the customs of the Wet-Lands.'

The mounts already tied to the rail shied nervously when Rifkind led Turin into their midst. She did not tie his reins to the rail; he would not leave unless he had a good reason, and if he had one, she didn't want him hampered.

Rifkind stood for a moment watching him before broaching the entrance to the dark, noisy tavern. With no small discomfort she absorbed some of the confusion in his mind: she had changed since they had entered the Wet-Lands, and if many of the changes had forced Turin to become more like the dumb beasts the Dro Darians rode or drove before them—what had she done to herself?

Her future was clouded; she could grasp only that life was not yet as different as it was to become. The Wet-Land tavern was a place filled with danger. Months before, she would not have considered entering it without a full raiding party behind her, or at least Turin's ready horns. She gripped the heavy iron handle to pull the door open: now not only would she enter the place, but attempt to live by the customs of her traditional enemies.

Turin's gaze bored into the back of her head. He did not approve. Nothing could shake his notion of the natural order of things. She betrayed generations of breeding and trust by leaving her faithful protector to scrounge grain from beneath the feet of the other beasts while she faced the unknown dangers alone. There was no choice. She had followed the Bright One out of the Asheera and now dealt with her destiny as best she could.

A Wet-Lander burst out the door, nearly knocking her over in his haste to reach his mount and leave the tavern area at a recklessly fast canter. No others came out, and despite Turin's echoing snorts of disapproval, Rifkind stepped into the tavern.

CHAPTER 4

The smoky, dark atmosphere of the room brought Rifkind to instant wariness, though precious moments passed before her senses could adjust to the strange atmosphere. Rifkind was used to moonless nights and windowless tents, not to the thick, rancid air of a tavern. The sound of the door closing had drawn every eye in the room to her. Her healer's empathy was awash with the general suspicion and vague animosity directed at her for no reason except that she was a stranger. Had the noise level not quickly returned to its normal din, she would have turned and fled.

Berating the Dro Darians for the foul practice of cooking within walls, where the cooking odors would quickly permeate everything, Rifkind studied the room contemptuously—then realized the irony of expecting Wet-Landers to behave like Asheerans. The filth did not seem to bother anyone else; she resolved not to let it bother or betray her.

'Be with me, Bright One! I have never seen such a place as this. The captives always spoke of Dro Daria as a land fit for the gods. Liars! No gods of the Asheerans would abide in such filth, unless it is true that the Wet-Landers do not worship in light and air.'

Rifkind's thoughts did not mar the expression on her face. Clan diplomacy taught children to mask emotion behind an unmoving countenance or face severe discipline.

'There is no choice now but to go on with it. Perhaps I will not be so noticeable as I feel. These Dro Darians are ... are so unlike each other, of all sizes and complexions. But for all their variety, no one is Asheeran; none has hair as black as mine, nor skin as golden. If they see my face, they will know I am not one of them. If they need to see my face. It's enough—most likely—that I wear tunic and trousers unlike theirs, and probably forbidden to women altogether.'

Her fingers lingered over the warm metal of the silent crescent.

'Forgive me, Goddess, but it is your talisman most of all which would doom me. Some Wet-Landers might chance to have eyes as black as mine, or a face which is more long than round—but none would have received the mark of your favor. They reserve their longest and least honorable deaths for those they call "witch."'

Suddenly the size of the city was brought home to her as she realized that in this, the fifth tavern they had passed, there were more people than had been in all the tents of her clan. At one table, a little separated from the rest, a woman of obvious quality sat surrounded by similarly dressed men, all eating in conspicuous silence.

Rifkind watched her carefully, realized that the other woman was even more uneasy than she was herself. There were other women in the tavern; serving girls, servants, slaves. They were a part of the inn itself, and uninteresting. She noted that they were all younger than she was, despite most being taller.

The boisterous, often crude, way in which the men treated the wenches neither surprised nor shocked her. The clan had had its share of captive females. She herself had had personal servants all her life, though in the Asheera she'd had little use for them except as beasts of burden—but she'd always known why they had no quarters of their own. When she'd grown older, she had became shrewder in the uses of the captives and more than once had ordered a terrified girl to the side of a guest or relative whose attentions she'd found annoying. But her own tastes did not run toward women, and the clans never took men captive.

"Don't stand there, boy! If you've got a message to deliver, do it and begone!"

One of the tired-looking wenches had spotted her standing in the corner and was elbowing her way across the room. It was uncomfortably obvious to Rifkind that the braying creature had not only mistaken her for a boy, but had every intention of flinging the filthy rag she held in her hand. It was a threatening gesture, but not of a type she knew. Her fingers clutched the dagger hilt nervously, but left it in its sheath.

"I'm no camp herald. You have food—I want a meal. I can pay if you wish."

"Wish?" The wench laughed, and the rag dropped to her side. "You pay before you sit down. Rodiger!"

The last was bellowed to a drawn-faced man across the room, but the wench failed to turn her head, and Rifkind caught the full force of both volume and malodorous breath. She held her ground, focusing her attention on the middle-aged man hobbling toward her on a crudely bandaged foot.

"A meal?" he said with a smile which obscured his eyes completely.

"Yes, I think so."

"Ah, a lady?" Her voice had given her away. "Traveling alone ... and ... ah ... in secret? You wish a supper? And perhaps a room ... with breakfast tomorrow? You've chosen well, milady, the Golden Bull's a most respectable place. Our food's the best, and all the rooms are vermin-free."

Rodiger's smile faded slightly. "Ten korli." He held out his hand.

'Korli, korli? Korli are the little gold coins, I think. I'm not sure. Ten gold coins for this? An outrage. He takes me for a fool or worse. I'll give him but one of mine and for that Turin gets fed, too.'

She dropped a coin into his hand without revealing the location or fullness of her purse. Rodiger stared at it a moment, bit it, then slipped it as masterfully into a fold of his oily vest.

"I've a war-horse outside. Feed him, too."

Rodiger opened his mouth, but left without saying anything. The wench who'd been waiting led her to an empty table, and after much protest, allowed Rifkind to sit facing the door with her back to the wall.

Rifkind mimicked the others in the tavern, approaching the chair, sitting in it, breaking off a handful of the dark brown bread which sat out on the table, but she had never sat in a chair at a table or eaten bread. As both a healer and fighter, she was accustomed to feeling competent; now in the smoky crowded room she felt like an awkward child.

Her meal arrived in a wooden bowl holding a portion of stew nearly hidden beneath a tide of greasy gravy. She swallowed hard when the bowl was set rudely down in front of her and visibly recoiled when the rocking bowl released some of its contents onto the none-too-clean table. Eating standards in the Asheera were not elegant, but meals were prepared with a mind to the fact that no water could be spared to clean away mistakes. Rifkind noticed belatedly that all the other diners had their own eating utensils: knives large and small, and a multipronged device which snared the meat from the liquid. The latter was the first sign she'd seen that intelligence and cleverness had not completely bypassed Dro Daria.

Rifkind reached into the hem of her cloak and felt for the handle of her least-valued knife. In the Asheera, she had eaten with her fingers or with small skewers which the women provided with the meal. She did not wish to mar one of her good knives with whatever floated in the stew gravy; likewise she had no intention of plunging her fingers into the bowl. The hovering serving wench stepped back suddenly—surprising Rifkind, who had not considered her gesture a threat.

"Sorry, milady. It's the table. S'not even."

"Seems even enough to me." Rifkind's voice confirmed her discomfort.

"You're not from these parts?"

"No."

"You're from the Asheera, aren't you."

The girl peered intently into the shadows of Rifkind's still-raised hood.

"The Asheera! I may not be from Isinglas, wench, but I'm not from the Asheera!" she hissed as if insulted.

"You needn't worry about me, milady. I'm not from Isinglas either."

Rifkind stared hard at the girl from the concealment of her cloak hood. 'By the stones, this girl knows what I am. Whether she means to betray me or ask for help, I'll have to find out carefully—but she knows.'

"It's no small matter to call a lady an Asheeran."

The girl seemed suddenly frightened, unsure of herself.

"Your voice—when I was a child, the Asheerans camped in the fields beyond our village one winter. They had dark cloaks with all the workin' done on the inside—so it wouldn't wear, they said. Like yours, milady ... Your lord must have given you that, then. He must be a bold warrior."

"No, it's mine."

The girl paused; the dull, ignorant expression of her face faded as she assessed her next move. The stew rocked again as she thrust her hip suddenly into the table edge.

"Dark Vitivar protect me, I'm so clumsy. Sorry,

milady, did it spill on you?" The girl moved closer
and added in a whisper, "Best not to linger here,
milady. I remember the healers from my village
days; no one else would know what you are. . . . But
they don't trust strangers. No one'd think you'd be
from the Asheera an' this far seaward, but they'll
think you're one of Darius's spies. An' that's none
safer for you."

"If the healers taught you, why do you remain
here?" Rifkind questioned softly, curiosity overcom-
ing caution. It was not unknown for one of the older
healers to teach the arts to a captive, if she had natural talents, much as Muroa had taken Rifkind from
her clan for four years to teach her a lifetime's worth
of experience and secrets.

"Oh, no, milady, not taught anything. When the
Asheerans wished to exchange hostages for their
safety that winter, my father sent me. I saw a lot, but
learned very little," she sighed. "Enough, though, to
be called a witch and driven from the village. It is no
small thing to call anyone an Asheeran, milady."

"You are unable to return to your clan?"

"My family will not have me."

The need to trust the girl—or someone—to get her
out of the city weighed heavily on Rifkind's mind.
Her life had always been based on predictability,
never on trust. The girl's intense eyes peered into the
shadows of Rifkind's hood. Rifkind let the hood slip
back far enough for their eyes to meet clearly.

"I must leave Isinglas. Asheeran, spy, whatever
they think I am, it is not safe for me here. I've never
been within walls before; I cannot find my way to
the gate."

"Not the gates, milady. They'll never let you pass.
Follow this street 'til you reach Tanners' Street;

you'll know it by the smell of the hides and vats. Go along that to its end. Don't mind the turns and corners—just follow the slurry-trough down the middle. It's a foul journey, but there's a break in the wall at the barber's hospice. The guards never stand their posts there, and any that do won't stop you."

A final swipe and the last of the spilled stew was caught in the corner of her apron. Without another glance or word, she moved back into the din of the tavern. Rifkind gave no indication of the importance of the information she had just received. Tactics of intrigue came naturally to the only unmarried daughter of a fractious Asheeran clan chief. Her alertness turned immediately back to the greater scope of the room.

'No, it is not that I sit here with my knife stabbing at this bowl of spoiled meat. There are eyes watching me.'

A shiver raced up her spine.

'Not everyone, but a few whose glances are frequent but short. I am not supposed to know I am being watched. The girl is right; whatever they think I am, I'd best leave quickly.'

Rifkind wiped her hands carefully and inconspicuously, letting her left hand move to the reassuring handle of a throwing knife in a forearm sheath. She always wore at least two.

Her mind reached through the crowd and roused the resting war-horse. Rodiger had already begun to walk toward her, closely followed by a younger, more robust looking individual.

"You've scarcely eaten a copper's worth. Food not to your taste?" Rodiger's final words conveyed more threat than concern.

"Perhaps the Asheeran prefers her meat raw?"

The second man smiled, revealing a mouth of broken, dirty teeth.

"I find I'm not hungry after all."

She stood up, but before she had taken a second step her path was blocked. Rifkind held her ground against the physical intimidation, noting to herself that the closer the man pressed, the greater her ease in killing him with a swift plunge of her now-drawn but still-concealed dagger.

"It's said you're going to Dro Daria itself. An Asheeran going to the king's city. Plannin' to talk to the king himself, no doubt. He could use your help against Hogarth and the queen. 'Course, maybe you're not an Asheeran at all . . ."

Broken-tooth threw the hood away from her face even as the knife bore deeply into his heart. He stared, blankly disbelieving his own death, while the rest of the room gaped at her thick black hair, golden-toned skin, and mostly at the silver crescent healer's mark on her right cheek. Rifkind did not need to know what they were staring at to take advantage of the lull. Pushing Rodiger and his already dead companion aside, she bolted for the door.

"Stop her!"

The anonymous shout broke the spell over the room. Arms reached toward her. She slashed a wrist with the bloody knife, then drew her slightly curved sword, prepared to hack her way to Turin, if necessary, or die in the tavern, rather than let them lay hands on her. A few more prepared attackers drew knives of their own; the rest advanced with their eating utensils. Rifkind backed to the wall, using it as a guide as she inched her way backwards toward the door. From the outside she heard the sounds of approaching horses at a gallop and Turin sounding his own battle challenge. Without further thought to the hopelessness of the situation, she narrowed her attention to the grasping hands and knives, ignoring all else.

There were no individuals—only bodies, armed and unarmed, nearer or farther. Someone had grabbed her cloak—she swung the sword blade in a swift S-loop without turning. A severed hand arced over the heads of her other attackers, its owner's screams hardly audible in the general furor. A chair leg spun through the air, grazing her shoulder. She stepped back, her timing momentarily broken, while she absorbed the knowledge that objects could be thrown in this battle. She slashed to her right with the sword while she came on guard again, knowing without need of confirmation that at least one of the men would have taken advantage of her weakness. The sword was in her right hand; she'd switched the throwing knife to her left. The long belt knife would have been a better *main gauche*, but there was not time to change knives, and she had long since learned to fight with whatever was in her hand. She was used to undisciplined combat; it was not unlike fighting with her brothers as a child, except that there would be no punishment for killing one of these. She found a rhythm to the disorder: slash, cut, then step back, steadily moving to the door and the fracas in the street. Almost half the men had fallen back; the ones who still fought were well-armed and cautious. The joy of battle without regard to its start or finish filled her face, giving her the look which had made the Asheerans hated and feared.

"Milady!"

An urgent whisper, combined with a tug at the

edge of her cloak, almost resulted in the death of the one person in Dro Daria whom Rifkind trusted.

"Milady, they've called the garrison. They're outside with your horse. I'll run out, pretending I'm you. Follow me, then remember, right 'til Tanners' Street."

The girl scrambled away and Rifkind lost track of her as she dealt with the taverners; it was apparent that now they only hoped to detain her until the garrison troops arrived with swords, but they would be quick to take advantage if she were careless. She caught a glimpse of a dark cloak and the clatter of the girl's sabots as she went out the door, leaving it open by accident or design. There were screams and shouts. Rifkind waited a few heartbeats then called Turin with her mind and brought him to the doorway. With a final flourish of swordwork, she backed through the doorway.

Turin was there, but faced with a mounted soldier who was swinging mightily at the black horns with his sword, and she lost precious moments timing her movements to the war-horse's before leaping into his saddle. Faced with the horns, the skittishness of his own mount, and now a blood-crazy woman with a sword in one hand and a knife in the other, the soldier gave ground. Three of his companions had chased the serving wench into a nearby alley, leaving him and another whose horse had been gored by Turin's horns to face what was obviously the true cause of the alarm they had received. The soldier called into the alley but made no move to close with Rifkind again without help.

His dismounted companion made a heroic attempt to haul her out of the saddle as they passed him. Turin lost his balance from the sudden added weight; his full attention was on escape and he had not observed the man at his side. He kept his footing, twisting in mid-gallop, but Rifkind slipped precariously to the side of the saddle as the soldier wrestled with her. She had sheathed her sword before mounting, and had had to stab across her own body to plunge the dagger into his neck. It refused to come out cleanly.

In his death throes he kept his hold on her arm and clothing. She was dangerously close to losing balance and stirrups and falling to the cobblestones in front of the pursuing soldiers. The dagger still protruded from the dead man's neck as he fell to the pavement. She had lost her left stirrup in the scuffle and held herself on Turin's back with the right, and a handful of saddle. Swinging with her head upside-down against Turin's flank, she saw the soldiers' horses advancing over the body of the fallen man; they were too close behind for her to see the riders.

Turin was slowing down, fearing for her. Rifkind poured her frantic energy into a command for him to gain ground. She was close enough to his hindquarters to feel his muscles bunch for a sudden powerful leap. One hoof barely missed her face, filling her with visions of being killed by her only loyal servant. Arching her back, gaining force from a heartfelt scream, Rifkind threw her body upward into the saddle.

She overcompensated, her head hitting Turin's, and the high pommel pushed cruelly into her stomach, but her weight was over the stirrups and she settled back into the saddle with an ungraceful thud. The soldiers maintained their pursuit. Rifkind watched for Tanners' Street as she pelted along.

The tavern girl had bolted into an alley to the left

of the tavern; in the confusion, Turin had headed
down the nearest street; Rifkind hoped it was the
correct one . . . already the pungent aroma of curing
leather filled the air. Turin's practiced ability to corner at full speed regained the lengths lost to un-
familiarity with street-travel on the straight passages. Tanners' Street was littered with barrels and
racks of leather in every stage of cure. She and Turin
crashed through many of the racks and heard a
pursuer downed by one of the vats.

The slurry-trough picked up the reflected light of
the Bright One, becoming an easily-followed path
through the sloping, twisted street. In the moonlight,
Rifkind watched the ribbon widen into a silver pool
stretching from one side of the narrow street to the
other. Turin needed no urging from her to adjust his
stride and leap over the muck before them. She reinforced his instincts with reminders that distance, not
height, would be demanded, and blocked her own
knowledge that a false step on the slippery surface
would surely break his legs. He cleared the morass
by half a length, his speed scarcely faltering.

Rifkind risked a backward glance and saw that
two of the remaining horses floundered in fetlock-
deep mud, while the third had thrown his rider
rather than enter the morass. She leaned back in the
saddle and laughed triumphantly as war-horse and
Rider galloped on. The dark mass of the wall soon
loomed in front of them, and the odor of curing
leather was challenged by the smells of the barber's
hospice and the slaughterhouse. People stood in the
doorways of the always-open death-houses, but as
she had been assured, no one moved to stop her.

The slurry-trough widened into a stagnant offal-
filled ditch. They would have to wade into it and

follow it into the darkness under the walls. Turin slowed to a walk before entering the ditch. She pressed her heels hard against his flanks when he hesitated to descend the slippery banks, at the same time holding a corner of her cloak over her nose against the stench. The Bright One was visible at the far end of the tunnel. They slogged on as fast as the sludge would allow.

CHAPTER 5

'Rain.

'I would never have believed there was so much water in the world. All the leaves have been washed down from the trees, and the pleasant warm smells of the harvests are replaced by the reek of damp fur and clothing. There's more water in my cloak than ever there was in our best well. We killed for water; now I could kill for dry clothes. Turin doesn't mind so much. His winter coat is in now, and the water just rolls off. I'm not so lucky. We'll have to find a better shelter than abandoned forest chapels if I'm to see this winter through.'

Rifkind sat motionless in the downpour. Turin occasionally shook the water from his eyes, but otherwise he rested also. They had traveled steadily since escaping the city of Isinglas. Moving slowly and with greater caution than she had displayed in entering the walled city, Rifkind had begun to frequent village market-days and wayside inns. She had disguised her accent and acquired local clothing in the two months since their escape through the tanners' sewer. They were in a large isolated mountain area a good distance from the district which had been their goal. She had no hope of reaching the city of Dro Daria before snow sealed the mountain passes, but she did hope to escape the mountains themselves.

They stood in the lee of a large evergreen that provided little in the way of shelter but did serve to slightly obscure them from passing eyes on the muddy road downhill from them. Down there a young couple was trying to right an awkward canvas-topped wagon that had mired at the edge of a sharp curve. The rear wheels were hub-deep in mud, Rifkind did not think that the pair had much hope of regaining the somewhat more solid footing of the road, especially with the tired, mismatched team of horses they had pulling with them. The man and woman were oblivious to the approach of a half-dozen mounted men who stopped just within Rifkind's line of sight on the far part of the curve.

Though the mounted men had a clear view of Rifkind as they advanced on the wagon, they did not give the hillside and its lone evergreen a second glance. She would not have expected them to, even if the wagon had not been holding their attention. Unlike the always-wary Asheerans, the Dro Darians

did not seem to see anything which they were not
expecting. The man and woman did not look up
from their work until the riders had formed a semi-
circle around the wagon. Despite the distance and
the weather, which served to distort empathic sensibilities, Turin reacted strongly to their complete terror on discovering the visitors. Rifkind used Turin's
more acute emotional receptiveness to study the situation.

'They fear for their own lives, and more. It is as if
they have something more valuable than their lives
to protect. Turin detects the same intensity of feeling
in the man and woman as he's found in all the
peasants we passed on the road to Isinglas. Yet the
overall content emotion of the riders is cruelty—they
are not Asheeran.'

She couldn't hear the conversations at the wagon,
even using Turin's senses. But from what she could
see and feel, the confrontation was becoming dangerously heated. Without thought or hesitation,
Rifkind reached behind her, drew out the short,
heavy hunting bow, and began absently to string it.
She had no clear thoughts of using it. In the Asheera,
bows were the defense of the weak; they were not
fighting weapons. There was no honor in killing a
foe who couldn't strike back. Still, she had a vague
sense she might need it and let it lie ready in her lap.

The riders first bullied the man, and when he was
tired and bruised from being pushed about and
dropped into the mud, they turned to his wife.
Rifkind could hear the shouts and screams now. She
held the bow upright, still resting, but more ready
than before. None of the riders were so armed, and
she did not feel threatened herself. It was a reaction
to the emotional currents distorted by the rain. The

muddied man rose to his feet to wrench a pole off the side of the wagon and strike the rider who had lifted his woman onto his saddle. The others closed around the man. Rifkind noted they had drawn their swords. There was no need to see more; she and Turin felt the emotional changes which meant someone was unconscious or badly injured and dying.

Still she resisted betraying her presence. The quarrel did not concern her, and neither side possessed anything which interested her. The woman screamed, slipping into hysterical shock at the sight of her man's mangled body lying in the mire. With her repeated screams, the canvas flaps of the wagon cover parted and a girl's head emerged.

'Ah, so that's what it was. They were protecting a child. The Dro Darians place great importance on their children, even before they can think of testing their mettle. It is foolish. They and the child will likely die because of it. Though perhaps there is some reason for this attachment which I have not yet learned . . .'

The girl jumped from the wagon, moving with surprising speed toward the brigand who held her mother. From her size, Rifkind judged her to be about the age of the serving wench who had risked her life for her in Isinglas. The man backhanded the girl, sending her sprawling on the ground. Again the woman screamed. The brigand backhanded her also, and she was silent. The girl was motionless, face down in the mud. The brigand nearest the wagon unhooked the oil lantern and threw it into the interior.

The memory of destruction by fire—more than

the thought that there might be other children in the wagon—brought Rifkind to quick, unreflective action. The men were large and slow compared to the elusive game animals of the Asheera. The one who had tossed the lantern fell from his horse, clutching his chest. A second arrow found its mark before the surprised brigands sorted out the hillside and located the source of the attack. The remaining four fled with their captive.

Rifkind did not pursue them; her own impulsive actions puzzled her. Despite her speed, she had acted deliberately; without the rashness that had characterized her early efforts at dealing with the Dro Darians. She had not realized how deeply the memory of the burning tents and mutilated bodies was etched in her mind, nor her still-ready desire for vengeance. A clanless exile could not afford such uncensored emotions.

Turin started down the hill on his own accord. His disdain for the adults of this new land did not extend to their young. His affection for children was not surprising since the Asheerans raised their prized war-horses and less-prized children together —it was often many years before the two groups learned they were not kin.

Flames licked the top of the canvas covering. The rain had kept the wagon from becoming an inferno, but the unburned canvas kept the rain from extinguishing the fire. The flames continued to hold Rifkind's thoughts as Turin made concerned noises over the child.

'Yes, the man is dead. Dead many times over. The girl has a break in a bone of her head. She struck a rock, or the man wore a heavy ring. There is fever

also, but that is older than the wound. I would need
sweet flower oils and leeching herbs and a warm
place . . . .'

Rifkind snapped into focus with a shudder. Turin
stood over the girl, protecting her from much of the
rain with his body. He had nudged the girl's body so
her face was no longer in the mud.

'The head wound is not as serious as the fever.
There is no separation or damage to the substances
under the skull. She was unlucky to have fallen so,
but, for that sort of injury, she is not badly hurt.'

Rifkind, with her healer's instincts, studied the
girl; her conscious mind was seeing only the small
cut above the fracture and noting that she was unnaturally pale and thin.

Turin's rising impatience and her own years of
training overcame her reluctance to deal with any of
the Dro Darians. She crouched by the girl and ran
her fingers lightly around the wound.

Grimacing, she took off her oiled leather outer-
cloak and wrapped the girl in it.

The fever's the worst, she thought to Turin, *as I
thought. She has no resiliance either. I don't think
she'll survive the healing. But I'll try, so stop fuss-
ing.*

Turin stood patiently while Rifkind secured the
wrapped body to the saddle in front of her. There
had been no inns along the road they had been following; she would have to follow the brigands' trail
in hopes of finding a dry place to spend the night.
She took the reins of the better of the dead brigands'
horses and guided Turin down the road.

The war-horse chose a slow pace, both for the
comfort of the injured girl and to allow his Rider to
watch for ambushes.

They were not long out of sight of the wagon when Rifkind spotted a woman's body in the run-off ditch by the side of the road. There were no life-signs in the woman, although no wound was visible. They continued on their way without stopping. Rifkind doubted that the brigands had intended murder, but could understand that once begun, they could not afford to leave witnesses.

The girl writhed occasionally against the thongs Rifkind had used to secure her. Even through the leather cape, she could sense the girl's worsening condition. If they did not find an inn soon the whole venture would become pointless.

Rifkind spotted a smoke curl shortly before night. It was almost invisible against the darkening sky, and the inn was set back from the road. She regarded it as a good omen and relaxed slightly.

Rifkind took Turin and the other horse off the road to conceal her preparations for entering Dro Darian society. She adjusted the voluminous folds of the peasant skirt she'd bought at a village a few weeks back, making sure the slits she'd made in its seams aligned with the knife sheaths she wore low on her thighs. The sword and bow she quickly coated with light oil and wrapped in cloth before lashing them to Turin's saddle. He could protect them as well as she could, and they were impossible to explain in the Dro Darian clothes she now wore. Using a brown powder from one of her herb sacks and the ready rainwater, she made a paste which in turn became a dark, irregular scar concealing the healer's mark on her cheek.

While she transferred her unconscious patient from Turin's back to the brigand's horse she rehearsed the phrases she would use on entering the inn. Her accent was already disappearing, and her gestures, when she concentrated on them, no longer seemed awkward or uncertain. Mimicking was only empathy without understanding, and as a healer, she was adept at attuning herself to her surroundings.

Turin wandered deeper into the forest, where he would wait until her mind reached out to touch his. Then Rifkind mounted the brigand's horse and headed for the inn at a trot. She believed her own story enough to make it convincing no matter what or who she found at the inn, but within her tal she knew the deception she forced on her conscious mind, and what she must do to help the injured girl and keep herself alive.

There were a few horses standing in the rain, but none of them belonged to her brigands, and she doubted they were the type who would put their mounts in the stable. She left the horse with the yard-boy and carried the child into the inn. Quickly singling out the innkeeper from the others in the large open room she called to him with a sense of urgency bordering on frenzy.

"Bandits, brigands! They've killed my sister, her husband! Our wagon went off the road three miles back. They came up while we were righting it."

Rifkind shook her head, forced a convincing display of tears and sobs while she supported the unconscious girl, pretending the task was almost beyond her. With her free hand she blotted away the tears before they were stained by the false scar.

"Where? Toward Barraclough?" The innkeeper moved quickly to her side and placed a hand on her shoulder.

Rifkind nodded through her tears, wondering as she did whether Barraclough was the village they had passed or the one they were approaching.

"Your sister, her husband, you're sure they're . . ."

With a loud sob Rifkind nodded again. She had watched the whining terror displays of the captives and had practiced at other inns along the way. The innkeeper looked questioningly at the leather-swathed figure leaning against her.

"Their child, she—she ran to her mother—the bandits struck her into the mud." Rifkind forced sobs and released the straps of the cape, letting it fall open and reveal the girl's bloody and dirty face, though she almost lost her grip on the unconscious girl and staggered to keep them both upright.

"Havvy! Cort! Take the post-horses and head up the road. Find their wagon and take care of it. Then go to the bailiff in the village and tell him. Mara, help the woman, there! You! Tess! Ready one of the upper rooms. Light the fire and put water on to heat."

The innkeeper, typical of the better of his breed—short, robust, loud and amiable—spewed orders around the room. He passed enough information to his other patrons to ensure that they would remain until the situation cleared. He oversaw his servants' clearing a table and laying the girl on it, at the same time he handed Rifkind a foaming mug of the dark local ale.

Rifkind swallowed the heavy, sweetish liquor gratefully and allowed the serving girls to remove her soggy cloak. Reluctantly she'd removed the bold embroidery, so that now it was only a serviceable garment—but a garment incapable of betraying her. She stood in the heavy skirts she'd acquired, every inch the scarred, plain, unmarried peasant woman she affected to be. No one suspected the slits in the

seams of her skirts or the knives she had strapped to
her thighs.

The innkeeper stood between her and most of the
others in the room. He blocked prying glances and
gossipy questions, and was otherwise protective of
his new guests. Rifkind relaxed enough to enjoy the
second half of her ale. She found the Dro Darian
streak of generosity and trust to be unwarranted and
risky, but without it she could not have treated the
girl. In the Asheera she would not have survived so
unceremonious an approach to a strange clan's
camp alive, even as a healer.

She leaned over and felt the girl's pulse; it had
weakened considerably. She made worried noises
until the innkeeper noticed and began ordering the
serving girls around again. At last Tess appeared at
the top of the stairs and announced that the room
was ready. Correctly judging Rifkind too small and
exhausted to carry the girl up the steep stairs, the
innkeeper took her in his arms and led the way to
the upstairs room.

As she followed him, Rifkind realized that his
concern meant that she would not likely be left
alone with the child, and various rumors she had
heard about witches and spirits made it seem unlikely she would be allowed to conduct a semi-
public healing. An older woman, apparently the
innkeeper's wife, waited for them in the room. Together they washed the child and laid her in the
large, freshly prepared bed.

Tess returned with a platter heaped with cold
sliced meat, chunks of bread, and fruit preserves.
With unconcealed delight Rifkind accepted another
mug of ale. The innkeeper's apologies that there
were no surgeons in the area, and that they could do
nothing for the child but keep her warm and dry

until the morning when a local priest might be available, was a source of even greater, if less blatant, satisfaction. They left, shutting the door. Rifkind bolted it shut and wolfed down a third of the meat before planning the healing itself.

The girl seemed impossibly thin and weak, her bandaged head blending into the fresh linens, her body a hardly noticeable lump in the mattress. She didn't move at all as Rifkind unwound the bandage from her head. Had Muroa been there, the unwrapping would have been unnecessary; the old woman could work through bandages and blankets, but Rifkind did not trust herself unless she could actually see the wound or the focus of the fever. After touching the girl lightly in several places, Rifkind got her herb sack and set up a small tripod and brazier in the open fireplace.

Her art was sympathetic rather than precise. The healers had to work with whatever was at hand; their patients rarely got ill when all the necessary ingredients were available. Like a cook who knows a hundred ways to prepare a meal, Rifkind fixed the final essence in her mind and proceeded to mix Asheeran powders, Dro Darian leaves and herbs, and a fingerful of the fruit preserves, haphazardly creating an aromatic mixture in the brazier. When she was satisfied with the dried substances, she poured the rest of the ale and some water into the brazier as well, and set it over the fire to simmer. While the aromas intertwined and matured toward the essence she had fixed in her mind she sprinkled other powders on the wicks of the three fat candles which burned in the room.

When all was right she extinguished the candles and removed the tripod from the fire. Her chant began in the common dialect spoken by Dro

Darians and Asheerans alike, but as she was swept
into the rhythms of her own keening, the familiar
words were replaced by more ancient and exotic
syllables. Even Muroa did not know the grammar of
the Old Language. Rifkind, pacing between the bed
and the fireplace, was not aware how many new
phrases had crept into her own knowledge since she
last used her arts.

She watched the girl, still unconscious, but now,
to Rifkind's eyes, marked by glowing streams of life-
energy. The streams moved toward the wound and
the focus points of the fever, where they seemed to
evaporate into steamy wisps. Unmindful of—and for
the moment immune to—the red-hot metal of the
brazier, Rifkind removed it from the tripod and
bathed the head-wound and fever points with the
near-boiling liquid. She worked in silence. Once her
invocation had been answered there was no need
for further communion with the powers. The
healers did not turn to the strong but fickle deities of
the earth, or to the dark, binding power of the
copper-dark moon, Vitivar.

Rifkind returned to the sideboard for the rest of
the meat. Some healers grew lustful halfway
through a healing; others demanded water or wine.
Rifkind had learned from experience that she grew
ravenous. The patterns around the child grew
stronger while Rifkind ate, but there was still life-
force escaping at the fever points. She returned the
brazier to the tripod and let it heat again, then repeated the anointing. This time the girl moaned as
the steaming liquid touched her skin. Rifkind set the
brazier aside and held her icy hand tightly.

"The pain will pass. The herbs draw the death-
essence to the surface; the sweet oils carry it away.

You are very weak, little one; the fever alone kept you alive, feeding on the last of your strength. There was little to replace the death essence when I drew it away. But it is gone, and I've eaten for you. You are so thin that I'm sure I have strength enough for both of us. I won't let you die now."

The energy streams faded, the girl's moaning ceased, and her breathing became deeper and slower. She was asleep. After lighting the candles Rifkind began to rewind the head bandage. There was no sign of a scald near the wound, and the edges had already drawn tightly together. As the ritual-induced numbness and cold passed from the child's body, the fever returned. But it was not so strong as before. Rifkind hoped they had defeated it.

The child continued to sleep, and Rifkind turned her attention to cleaning the brazier before falling into near-exhaustion herself. She sat by the fireplace throwing the infusion into the fire drop by drop. She did not so much fear discovery as she desired that a consecrated infusion be properly disposed of.

"So you're the fearsome witch we've been waiting for!"

The brazier flew to one side, leaving a damp trail. Rifkind thrust her hands into the skirt slits and drew her knives even as she spun around to face the voice. Despite rising panic, she took time to notice that the bolt was in place on the door and the window was still shuttered—both from the inside. But there by the bed stood a young man, better dressed than most she had seen in her journeys. No one could have entered the room, but the young man did not seem about to disappear on that account. He raised his arms away from his sides, palms open and forward, apparently unarmed.

CHAPTER 6

They faced each other in silence. Since she and Turin had left Isinglas, Rifkind's greatest fear had been the penetration of the disguise on which she had lavished so much care and attention. In the nightmare scenarios she had envisioned, the confrontation took place on a road, in a village square, or in the public rooms of an inn. The young man who stood disarmingly in front of her had evaded the heavy bolts and locks the Dro Darians placed on their doors and windows. With bitter irony, she realized she had never doubted the solidity of the walls themselves—a mistake she would never have made in a tent.

'The walls seem solid enough—but here he is. And if he is here, there are probably more like him nearby, and I'm not so curious as to want to meet any more people appearing out of walls or thin air. There is no good reason for him to be here. The Dro Darians would kill me if they knew I was Asheeran; from what I've heard, they'd do worse if they thought I was a witch. Only the priests in the temples have any dealings with the gods—they have no tolerance for a woman who can heal the sick with herbs or water.'

"Explain yourself—quickly!" Rifkind demanded, withdrawing one knife slowly until its blade was visible to her visitor.

"This is not what it seems: I am no threat to you. I too have a knife, but I don't mean to use it. I hid away in your room to find out if you were the witch Father sent me to find. I've no doubt of your skills now, and no desire to remain under the bed if the child needs more witching. My purpose is to offer you my family's protection while you are in Glascardy—if you are the Asheeran witch An-Soren fears."

"Then you—and others—have been following me. For how long?" Rifkind thought of many other questions to ask, and her mind swirled heavily around the name "An-Soren," which dredged the image of the chimera and the ruby from her memory, the thought of which left her far more uneasy than the handsome intruder before her.

"In truth, not nearly so long or far as I ought to have been; it's been many weeks since I had the message from Father telling me to seek after you, but I felt that pursuing Mountain Men and brigands was more important than chasing a witch, until this afternoon."

"I'm no witch—be clear on that. I am a master of empathic ritual, but I know nothing of this witchcraft that is so feared in these parts. Since I arrived in your lands until this evening, I made no use of my arts."

"Among us we make no difference between such as you and sorcerers like An-Soren. Sorcery or witchery, it is a double-bladed weapon. Though I believe you have healed the child, I do not doubt you could have slain her just as easily."

"I could not! To use ritual for evil would draw the wrath of the Bright One."

Rifkind's tone was all the more emphatic from the memories and stories of ritualists who had been tempted away from the teachings of the Bright One by another god or personal demon—only to be found grotesquely dead in the moonlight.

"Milady, I did not mean to imply that you *would* have killed the girl, or would ever desire to do so; only that in Dro Daria it is believed that the powers that heal can also harm. All I know of witchery or sorcery are the displays that An-Soren put on at the court when I was a child, and what I have seen you do this night."

Again the name "An-Soren" brought a shudder of apprehension. But she ignored it to deal with the increasing puzzle of the young man.

'This one is different. I have seen taller men since I arrived in Dro Daria, though not many. And I have learned that such fair pink skin and sunset-bright hair is not an affliction to be healed, but a trait common in some clans. He is different. He neither drops those sky-colored eyes as many do if I look directly at them, nor does he make crude attempts to penetrate my consciousness.

'His hands are strong, but not gnarled or weathered as those of peasants are, even though they be as young as he seems to be. He is a man accustomed to the sword. He knows it is an artist's weapon, not a club with an edge. By his hands he is a horseman, too, one who could command a war-horse. But his hands do not belong to the rest of him. There is too little flesh on all those bones. His arms hang loosely at his sides, though his back is erect. And his face . . . His eyes meet mine, yet his mouth gapes open. He is neither bearded nor clean-shaven. His impression is of one who is uncertain whether he is man or boy.

'If he were all of a piece, I would want to start my clan with him.'

"You spoke of this afternoon. What did you see this afternoon that led you to me? By your clothes, you are not like those I saw on the road or at the wagon. Yet might you be their clan-chief?"

"Milady, I am Ejord Overnmont, sworn enemy of the Mountain Men you slew this afternoon. I pursued and harried the ones who escaped you; before the last of them grew intimate with my blade, he spoke of a gold-skinned woman who rode out of the mists on a horned horse, loosing a magic bow.

"The Mountain Men know nothing of the Asheerans, but I have heard of your horses and your short hunting bows. It seemed possible that if there was an Asheeran woman wandering the area, she might also be the witch Father had mentioned."

Rifkind felt the muscles in her back and neck grow steadily tighter. Ejord was still not a threat, though he knew who and what she was and any violation of her disguise was itself dangerous.

"The reasons I have left the Asheera do not concern you; that I have come to the Wet-Lands to make
my life here is enough. I intend to make my way to
the capital, which I have learned is a long journey
from here. I will pass quickly and quietly through
your lands, hetman Overnmont. I have found nothing here to dissuade me."

Ejord frowned before replying. "I do not offer the
protection of the Overnmonts lightly. It is a dangerous
course you would follow, milady; the nearer you get
to the capital, the greater the chance An-Soren or the
others will find you. Dro Daria is no place for a lady
alone. Your skills may protect you, but each time
you use them you will draw attention to yourself.
The Overnmonts are honorable and loyal, but at
times I think we are mostly alone ourselves."

'There is something different in this one. Not
merely in his clothes, which are clean and well-
fitted, but in his assurance—which covers even his
awkwardness. He is a person accustomed to the
ways of strength and power—the first I have seen
since leaving the Asheera. Oh, I wish Turin were
here. His sense of these things is so much better than
mine. I see what I want or need; he measures only
what is there.'

"Certainly honor and loyalty are important, but I
would hesitate to ally myself with a clan that is
alone against all others. I would do better on my
own, I think."

"You are not on your own, milady; I do not think
you will abandon the girl."

"I shall find her clan and return her to it."

"Then you will be taking her to the capital itself.
That wagon had traveled far, probably bearing a

farmer ruined by the troubles around Daria. It would be a long, hard journey at any time, but unthinkable in winter. Even if you will not accept my family's protection, at least accept our hospitality until spring comes. Come to Chatelgard with me. Father will winter there as always; he might be there now. Perhaps you can strike a bargain with him."

'He makes sense. I can scarcely imagine what this land will be like if there is still so much water in the air when· winter comes, but I do not think I'll like it very much. And there is the girl. I could leave her here or give her to him to buy his silence, but I don't think I'll do either. If the girl survives, I'll keep her with me.

'Muroa was there when my mother died birthing me and claimed me as hers. This girl will be my first pupil in the Wet-Lands; perhaps my destiny is to bring the Ritual Arts and adoration of the Bright One to the Wet-Lands, where now she is scarcely known and less honored.'

Ejord had not moved while Rifkind was absorbed in her thoughts. His sense of timing and distance seemed perfectly matched to her own, though when he spoke his words aggravated or disturbed her.

"You are too eager. In the Asheera, such would be a sure sign of betrayal or conspiracy."

"Then the Asheera is not so unlike Dro Daria as I've always been told. I lack the skills and arts of diplomacy. I tend to our estates while Father and the others are at court. But Glascardy has been the domain of the Overnmonts for eight generations; we protect it and its people. You have fought our enemies, slain two of them, and saved a child whose family was seeking shelter in our lands.

"Our winters are harsh and deadly, especially for someone like you who is used to the dry air of the Asheera. I give you my word—not my family's— that you will be welcome at Chatelgard."

Slowly Rifkind relaxed her grip on the knife hilt.

Ejord had the fair skin and large stature of most of the Wet-Landers, but she did not find him as strange-looking as other men she'd looked at closely since her arrival in Dro Daria. He was a full head-and-shoulders taller than she was, with sandy red hair unusual even in the Wet-Lands, and clear blue eyes which neither pried into her own nor avoided her stare when she met them. She had already acquired a student; she was prepared to accept the serendipity of her goddess's sending her a second member for her new clan.

"I accept your offer to go to Chatelgard because of your word."

Ejord smiled and extended his hand farther toward her, a gesture she ignored.

"Will you leave with me in the morning?" he asked.

"Depends on the girl. I believe the healing was successful, but it will be some time before I can tell for sure. She was ill with fever, aside from her wounds."

She looked over to the bed. The thin, blonde girl had recovered consciousness far more quickly than Rifkind had expected. She was pale and unsteady, but there was no sign of fever in her wide, staring eyes.

"Where're Ma and Da?" she asked hesitantly.

"They aren't with us anymore."

Rifkind's voice was firm but not hostile. Many times she'd come back from a raid or hunt to tell of a warrior's death. The Asheera gave its people little enough time to live and no time to mourn or grieve.

The girl looked from Rifkind to Ejord, then bunched the bed linens in her hands and stared downward.

"They're dead, aren't they?"

Rifkind nodded. The girl didn't look up, the question was a formality, the answer already known to her. She hid her face in the bedcovers and began to cry.

A sobbing child was beyond the range of Rifkind's skills. Children, with their awkwardness, fears, and questions, had never interested her. She had ignored them with a callousness exceptional even in the Gathering—but she had never been responsible for a child before.

"It's not so bad," Rifkind said after a moment. "I'll be taking care of you until you're ready to go off on your own."

Her abrupt tone did little to reassure the girl, whose restrained sobs quickly became loud gasps of despair as she glanced quickly at the strange young woman who would care for her. Rifkind watched helplessly while the child curled up in the covers and shut out the world in her intense grief.

Turin! Where are you?

Rifkind's mind reached out in search of the warhorse. He was dozing, but she woke him summarily.

The child retreats from the knowledge that her parents have died! Surely even before she asked the question she knew that they were gone. Her mind is not impaired, yet she will not put the past behind her. I will make a link—do something with her!

Rifkind felt Turin absorb her imperatives, sensing

the translating process. She felt the mind of the war-horse study her with puzzlement. He did not understand her problem. He filled her mind with images of abandoned younglings, of his kind and hers, then with thoughts of warm, gentle things. Rifkind broke the contact and looked at the girl.

There could be no mistaking Turin's advice, but she could not bring herself to sit on the bed beside her or place her arms around the girl's shoulders. Affection had played no role in her own childhood, and she had not missed it.

"It is unfortunate about your parents, child. But there was nothing you could do to stop it, nor anything you can do now. There is no reason to continue thinking about it."

Ejord stared harshly at her, then sat down on the bed, still watching Rifkind.

"With all your knives and magic, you've never taken the time to learn about people, have you?"

Rifkind glared at him, but he had turned to the child and was oblivious to her anger.

'I have survived because I know people, she wanted to say to him. I don't rush to them or swoon over their every injury, any more than was ever done for me. What would you know—you are like Halim!'

She refrained from answering him. The girl was only sniffling now, twisting the bedcovers with her hands rather than rolling her body in them. She and Ejord spoke in tones too soft for Rifkind to hear without stepping closer, but there was no doubt that the girl was quieter for Ejord's compassion. Rifkind's fierce determination never to be bested at anything warred with her belief that comfort and concern were the inevitable precursors of disaster for all involved. Unable to resolve her own emotions, she retrieved the brazier and began to clean it carefully.

"Linette, here, would like to know your name."

Rifkind jumped, but not nearly so much as when Ejord had first appeared in the room.

"Rifkind."

"Jordie says you're a witch, an' that you saved my life. He says you tried to save Ma and Da, but couldn't, but you kilt the Mountain Men. He says we're not for Isinglas anymore, but Chatelgard, where he lives. An' I'll have a room of my own with a hearth, an' someone to light it every night, an' a pony come spring."

"Jordie"—Rifkind emphasized the diminutive—"talks too much."

She'd meant the remark for Ejord, but the girl reacted to it far more than Ejord did. Her wide blue eyes glistened again with tears, and her lips began to tremble. Rifkind silently appealed to the Lost Gods for insight into the minds of Wet-Landers.

"Now Rifkind here, being not merely a witch and a feisty mistress of the sword, is from the Asheera, where words and manners aren't very important. As a result, she's a bit mean-tempered and hard to understand. But in her own way she means you well."

Rifkind looked at Ejord's smiling face and held her peace. A weak smile crossed Linette's face, and the moment of tension faded.

"If we are to travel to your father's camp in the morning, Linette will need her rest. I've a war-horse in the forest near here. He'll find you and lead you to a meeting place."

"As I said, more than a bit rough about the edges

—but I have it on good authority that even Asheerans
don't bite."

Ejord patted Linette's head and settled her beneath the bed-linens before returning his attention to
Rifkind.

"I've heard of these war-horses of yours. Then it's
true that the Asheerans use their magic on
animals?"

"All animals sense emotions. We've bred ours to
be especially sensitive and especially loyal to one
person. There's no magic—just patience, generations of breeding, and good training. You can trust
Turin to find you."

"I'm not about to go looking for him on a night
like this. The garrison at Isinglas is still talking about
the damage you both did."

"We were fighting for our lives. I was not well
pleased with that place."

"Who is?"

"Isn't it part of your clan's territory?"

"In name only . They've a charter saying they owe
allegiance to us in return for protection and the like,
but the burghers and the garrison officers say that
was made worthless when my great-grandfather
swore fealty to Handro the Great when he united all
of the fertile lands and named them Dro Daria."

"If the Overnmonts are truly the more powerful,
why can they not control that place. Or if Isinglas is
more powerful, why do they allow you to continue
the farce?"

"That's politics and diplomacy, and I'll leave that
to Father. After three generations of hard feelings, it
really doesn't make much difference to me or anyone else in Glascardy or Isinglas itself. Except, I sup-

pose, I'd rather Isinglas were closer to the capital and the king."

"But you just said they reject your authority because you do acknowledge this king?"

"It's really much more confusing than it seems. We're loyal to the king, but the capital itself favors the queen, since she's Hogarth's sister—and Hogarth's lands surround Daria. But the queen spends her time with An-Soren, who is supposed to be the king's seer, but is actually the queen's lover. And even that doesn't account for Hogarth and his party—or Father himself, for that matter." Ejord paused, while Rifkind stared blankly at him. "It's all politics, not worth worrying about, unless you're determined to go to the capital."

'He thinks he frightens me with all those names. He thinks because we don't have cities that we live like herds of animals. I don't need to be told about rivalries or alliances—the only reason I'm even in this forsaken place is because I came out an extra body in our own struggles.'

Ejord walked to the door and put his hand on the bolt.

"Not that way!" Rifkind called sharply. "If it truly is as dangerous as you've claimed, it would not do for you to be seen just walking out of this room. Use the window, and then the roof."

Sighing audibly, but not arguing with her, Ejord crossed to the window and unbolted it. The rain was still falling, though it had tapered off somewhat, and the air was much colder. Without further words, he dropped from the window ledge to the muddy stableyard below. Rifkind heard him slip and curse softly, then the sounds of a lone horse moving off in the night. She listened until she could hear nothing but the rain and echoes of the inn below, then rebolted the window.

Linette was sitting up again. Her eyes never left Rifkind, and she looked ready to slip back into hysteria.

"What will happen to me now, you bein' a witch an' all?"

"As we said. If you're strong enough, tomorrow we leave here. If Ejord is to be trusted, we go to his father's camp for a time. If he's not to be trusted, Turin will warn us and we'll head for Daria at once." Rifkind had tentatively concluded that Dro Daria was the entire land, and Daria the city she wished to approach.

"We'd left Daria for Isinglas. Da said it was the only safe place left."

"I didn't find it to be very safe. And neither did he."

Rifkind watched the now-familiar clouding of the girl's eyes and the course of a large tear as it moved down her cheek.

'By the Nameless Gods! I had not meant to upset her!

'These Dro Darians, *Wet-Landers!* Parents die protecting children, and children mourn and cower as if their own lives end when their blood-parents die!'

"Child—Linette. I don't mean to be so harsh with the truth. Still, at your age, you must be able to tell that these are not the most friendly of parts."

Rifkind sat down on the bed and abruptly took Linette's hand in her own. For a moment, while she waited for some inspired thing to say to the child, she looked at their two hands. Her own was several shades darker than the child's, and marked not only with the callouses and scars of nomadic life, but with long practice sessions with knife and sword, and her first attempts at healing. The hand of someone who had learned to take care of herself, but could not possibly care for a child.

"We left Daria 'cause Da said a family couldn'a live by honest farmin' with the soldiers an' An-Soren so near. The soldiers wasn't the worse of it. Mos' time they'd pay somethin' for what they'd taken. But An-Soren . . . When the crops didn'a come up, they'd all go out in the fields an' look at Daria an' say, 'An-Soren's work.'

"They said it'd be better around Isinglas. But there'd be no farmin' here. You won't be for farmin' anyway, an' you can fight back—I seen that. An' Ejord says I can have a pony, an' a room that'll always be warm . . ."

Rifkind sat silently until the child talked herself to sleep. She blew out the candles and sat down by the hearth, staring at the embers, until, one by one, they went out.

CHAPTER 7

The sun broke through the heavy grey clouds, throwing shafts of light into the small forest clearing where Rifkind had cast her moon-stones. A raw wind was blowing; it was much colder than it had been the day before, and despite the brief spells of sunlight, the storm clouds still hung low over them.

'Six patterns from five stones! I give up.'

Rifkind grimaced, then turned away from the stones. Shadows were as important to the interpretation of the pattern as the actual position of the stones. Each time the sun had broken through the clouds the shafts of light had cast radically different shadows. A peculiar and unpleasant sensation buzzed in her head—even the intense, yet mediating, focus of her tal could not digest the shifting patterns.

'Two would have been one too many, but I could have dealt with that. But sir, I fear the gods are playing with me. It is probably an offense to one of them to use the stones before anyone but the Bright One. With all the rain and clouds, I haven't seen the Bright One in over a week! Next time I'll use a hearth—at least then I'll be dry. These layers and layers of skirts are always getting soaked through. When Turin gets here with Ejord, I'll switch back to my own clothes. I'm not making a long journey in this sort of weather in half-frozen borrowed clothing.

'Ejord should be here by now. Turin kept track of him all night, and Turin knows this place. He seemed very reluctant to travel with an adult Wet-Lander, as opposed to Linette. The images in his mind seem to indicate more that he fears he will be less important to me than that he has any real concern for our safety with the Overnmonts. It has all been very hard for him. Poor Turin; his loyalty and empathy so far exceed his intelligence. . . .'

"Milady Rifkind?"

Linette's voice interrupted her thoughts.

Rifkind looked up at the girl, who to all outward appearances had made a complete recovery.

"Just Rifkind. What do you want?"

"Can we eat now? I'm hungry and Ejord's late." She handed Rifkind the heavy parcel the innkeeper had prepared for them when Rifkind had told him they were leaving. "Has Turin gotten lost? You said he'd bring Ejord right away after we stopped here. You don't think they met up with the Mountain Men

again and had to fight, or something like that? Or
that the innkeeper stopped them? He didn't look so
happy when we left."

Rifkind unwrapped the bundle and began slicing
a sausage.

"Would be hard to say if he was suspicious or just
concerned. You were near death yesterday and, as
everyone's so fond of telling me, my healing is considered a questionable practice in Glascardy.

"Either I healed you, and am therefore a witch—
or you were healed by the gods directly—which is a
miracle and involves priests. Or we were both fool-
ing the innkeeper—though he was paid handsomely
enough."

They had taken no chances. They left the main
road as soon as they were out of sight of the inn and
traveled overland in case the jovial innkeeper had
spoken his mind to someone less easygoing than
himself.

"What're they for?" Linette asked, picking up one
of the moon-stones.

"Seeing."

Rifkind took the stone from her hand, putting it
and the others back in the suede pouch.

"Seeing *what*? Anybody could tell they're jus'
stones w'thout starin' at them so long."

"Not seeing the stones, child, *seeing*—like seeing
how the journey will go, or if Ejord is to be trusted."

Linette looked hard at the ground where the
stones had lain.

"Wha'd'ya see?"

Rifkind shook her head. "Nothing much, and
nothing certain—except Ejord is coming, and so is
bad weather. We'll be leaving at once after he ar-
rives, I think, so you'd best eat well now. I'll be sur-

prised if we stop again before nightfall."

Even as they ate, the clouds grew thicker and greyer. Rifkind probed again for Turin's mind. The war-horse was leading Ejord all around the countryside instead of bringing him directly to the clearing. She chastised him and made sure he would lead Ejord to them, regardless of the war-horse's own reservations about the Dro Darian. They continued waiting and eating. A few snowflakes fell, but the storm did not start.

"Your horse, here, either takes me for a fool, or he has no desire for us to get through High Tor before the storm closes it."

Ejord's cheerful voice announced his entry to the clearing.

"Twice we crossed the Barraclough road, and the Umouth River more times than I or Blackthorn, here, care to remember."

He patted his big black horse on the shoulder and jumped to the ground.

"I did not tell him how to bring you—only that you should be brought here; this is carelessness on my part. Turin has a mind of his own."

'A very mixed mind, I would guess to look at him. He doesn't want to trust Ejord, yet he likes him. I've seen him try to gore a stranger who made the mistake of touching him—but he lets Ejord thump him soundly on the shoulder without flinching.'

Ejord sliced some of the sausage while Rifkind quickly shed the heavy peasant skirts she had used as a disguise and replaced them with the quilted felt and leather of an Asheeran warrior. After carefully adjusting her knives and sword, she threw the heavy black cloak around her shoulders. Its weight and drape reassured her, and she adjusted it with a flourish before realizing that both Ejord and Linette were watching her with rapt attention.

"I hadn't realized we were expecting *that* much trouble," Ejord said when her eyes met his.

"Unless I miss my guess, it is several days' ride to Chatelgard through mountain passes which are at best unfamiliar to me, and quite possibly dangerous from weather or these Mountain Men. I'm not expecting trouble—I simply prefer not to be surprised by it. Or would you suggest I ride unarmed?" Rifkind replied, the edge of her voice as sharp as her sword.

"No, you're being reasonable. Eminently reasonable. And would you be surprised if I suggested we leave here at once? Turin's meanderings have tired neither him nor Blackthorn; but that storm is going to start soon, and we've lost time."

"I was expecting we would."

"Linette—is she well enough to take a fast pace? There are shelters along the way that the mountain cults erected, but they expect their pilgrims to set a harsh pace."

Rifkind ripped one of the discarded skirts in half as she answered. "We'll use a lead line from you to her pony, then back to me. I'll wrap her in these— I've no further use for them—and we'll lash her to the saddle. She can watch or sleep as she wishes. As for the pace—I know little of your Wet-Land winters, but a healthy man or war-horse can die in one night of an Asheeran winter, if the wind blows wrong.

"The innkeeper was suspicious; it would be impossible to return there. She must withstand the pace."

"Mmm? For someone so unfamiliar with us 'Wet-Landers,' you seem to have thought things out fairly carefully. Did I hear you say that I would be leading the way?" He spoke with mock incredulity.

"Of course. I have no idea where Chatelgard is."

But casual humor was more alien to Rifkind than rainstorms in the Asheera; though with her refined sense of empathy and timing, she was beginning to learn that some of her responses were jarringly out of step. An Asheeran might laugh at someone else making a fool of himself, or a well-told and embarrassing anecdote, but never at himself. Rifkind, who had fought harder than most to create the life she wanted to lead, saw very little that was amusing in the world around her.

True to his words, Ejord set a fast, steady pace along roads which became narrower and steeper after each fork. The forest continued to surround them, and it was only occasionally that Rifkind had any idea of how high they had climbed. The clouds remained a solid steel-grey mass, with little wind to either usher in the storm or clear the sky. The ominous sense of the impending blizzard remained when, shortly before darkness, Ejord turned off the narrow road and led them to a small stone structure camouflaged by the surrounding rocks.

"The mountain cults have temples atop the various mountains here in Glascardy. Each peak has a different cult, but all the cultists have made common cause against the Mountain Men, who don't worship or respect any of them. These chapels can be secured from the inside and have ample food and water within."

· Ejord dismounted and led her into a surprisingly clean room, pointing out the barrels of provisions along one wall.

"Because the Overnmonts also fight the Mountain

Men, the cults give us use of the chapels so long as we don't disturb the altars."

He gestured toward a ferocious demi-beast carved out of stone that crouched in the opposite corner.

"We're going to spend the night with *that!*" Rifkind asked, approaching the idol with outward disdain and inward caution.

'I've no desire to be buried in the snows of that storm, but that contains no small power—and no great compassion, if my measure of these things is at all accurate.'

"I don't bother the cults or their idols and they've never bothered me. And I've been roaming these mountains alone since I was Linette's size."

"But you do not know anything about ritual or empathy," Rifkind countered with nervous frustration.

"That's important?"

Her anger was blunted by Ejord's openness. She shrugged her shoulders, deciding against explaining her concerns to him. The little chapel was as defensible as Ejord had claimed, and there was no need to bring up possible dangers from within the walls if indeed the powers behind the idol had never bothered the Overnmonts.

Rifkind was investigating the barrels when Ejord led the three horses into the room, cutting the living space in half. Turin's satisfaction at having found someone who understood that a war-horse's place was on the same side of any wall as his Rider was a warm glow of contentment which impressed Rifkind. She noted that any reservations he had been harboring about the Dro Darian had disappeared, and he now classified Ejord as a Rider rather than a Walker like the rest of the Wet-Landers.

The idol stared impassively at the chaos as Linette and Ejord busied themselves with civilizing the shelter. Rifkind settled in a spot where she could watch the people, the animals, and the idol without turning her head, and withdrew into thoughtless reverie.

It grew colder during the night, and the wind increased; somewhat past midnight, the wind loosened particles of ice from the storm and drove them against the shelter. Rifkind knew this because she remained awake, unable to sleep in the same room as the idol.

Before dawn, the power behind the idol investigated the room, touching the minds of the occupants.

Turin detected the presence first, and Rifkind admitted to them both that she was grateful he'd been within the walls to warn her. The idol's guardian was not a benign, gentle power like the Bright One; neither was it as malevolent as the carving implied. Rifkind protected her own mind and asked it its name. It made no response, but withdrew as subtly as it had come.

One of the Nameless Gods?

Rifkind's thoughts wandered idly as she continued to fight the need for sleep.

'We invoke their powers in hopeless situations, since they are said to be from times long before us and are not our gods at all. Yet the idol is new; the sense of its maker still clings to it. I would like to explore further to see if the Nameless Ones are real and still with us. There are so many things we never needed to know in the Asheéra, but that are interesting and might be useful to me if I'm to live out my life here. Perhaps I shall stay at this Chatelgard, if, as it would seem, it is near these mountains. I do not know what my destiny is in this land. I believe it involves Linette and the ruby, but I do not know if it involves Daria—the capital—at all.'

The storm drove a wall of snow and ice against the heavy wooden door of the shelter, coating its iron hinges with ice. It took all their strength, and coals from the fire, to loosen the frozen door in the morning. It swung open into the shelter, releasing a cascade of snow into the room. Linette leaped into the instantly created snowdrift; Turin withdrew nervously from a substance he could neither eat nor fight; Rifkind and Ejord stared into the wind for a moment.

"Can we travel in this?" Rifkind asked, throwing her weight against the door in an effort to close it.

"It's an Ystra-storm if it's anything. There's not much snow yet, at least along the passes where the wind blows; it's all being blown into these sheltered spots. That wind won't die for another day, at least. When it does, it'll snow for about another three days."

Ejord continued. "It's the first of the season, so the passes should open up again. But maybe it's stronger than it looks, and the passes will stay closed until spring. It will be rugged traveling in the wind and ice, but I'd be inclined to try it. I know the passes will be clear until that wind dies down, and we can always hope that the storm is this side of the crest instead of on both sides, and that we can outride it."

"Is that likely?" Rifkind asked.

"It's possible. It's the first storm of the season."

Rifkind looked at the provision barrels, which were abundant for an overnight stay, but woefully inadequate for the winter. She didn't have a clear grasp of the exact location of the shelter, but they were far enough above the forest that she doubted there would be much hunting. Without enthusiasm, she concluded that they had to go on despite the storm.

Rifkind took some of the straw from the floor of the shelter and padded Linette's legs with it before wrapping them in strips of cloth torn from the peasant skirts. Ejord packed the horses.

When Linette complained that she couldn't walk, they carried her to the pony and lashed her to its back. Though they had not used any of the shelter's provisions, Rifkind felt it necessary to leave a token offering to the idol and the nameless power which watched over it. There wasn't the time for a trance which could give her insight into what other travelers had left or the god's preferences, so she left a small gold pin inlaid in silver with the image of a fighting war-horse. It was an object she had treasured for a long time, and she reasoned that something valuable to her would be important to any god.

They were at the mercy of the ice and wind. The passes were clear but treacherous with ice where the tiny particles had been driven into the small cracks and pockets of the trails. They moved slowly and silently. Twice they stopped to wrap Linette more tightly in her cloak, until Rifkind worried as much that the girl would be unable to breathe as that her fever would return.

Turin's coat had come in as thickly as Blackthorn's, but the big black was used to the twisting narrow pathways. Despite Rifkind's almost constant reassurances, the war-horse's nervousness left him a cold miserable shadow of his usual self.

'There is really little difference between this and the Death-Wastes. Cold, wet, and unpleasant, against hot, dry, and unpleasant. Both are easy to die in.'

No, Turin, easy . . . relax. We will survive this, just as we survived the Death-Wastes.

'This is the second time in as many journeys that I've acted on the advice or inclination of others, and wound up considering the possibility of death. In each case, though, I have been unprepared for the advice I've tried to follow.

'If I'd had the time to line the cloak with pelts, properly, or even asked Ejord more closely about this journey, it would not seem so bad. I can tell from the steady way he sits astride Blackthorn that this is far from the worst he's encountered. But the Dro Darian horses, with their thick legs and heavy bodies—though they cannot run so well as Turin, they are more suited to these places than he.'

No, Turin, I do not intend at all to replace you with a hornless, dull-minded Dro Darian beast.

The sun never penetrated the storm. It left the mountains in a near-dawn greyness. At each branching of the trail, Rifkind wondered how Ejord knew which one to take, but had the sense not to ask. The monotony and cold numbed her mind; she used her tal to block any sense of time. She thought of little—and very slowly—as they forged on.

"Rifkind!"

The sound of Ejord's voice above the noise of the storm penetrated her tal, startling her. The trail had widened somewhat; cautiously she guided Turin past Linette's pony to Ejord's side.

"Mountain Men," he said simply, pointing to a

mound of rubbled stones and masonry.

"That was to be our shelter for tonight?"

"Unfortunately so. There'll still be some shelter from the wind, if we pile up the stones again, but not enough for a fire or to keep out the snow if the wind breaks.

"My sincere—and worthless—apologies, milady. Until now I had expected our journey to be difficult, but not truly dangerous. In all the years I've been traveling this trail, I've never known them to destroy a shelter. We'll need considerable luck. If the storm holds, neither worsening nor letting up, we might survive until morning—if the Mountain Men do not find us here. I should warn you that I've never been considered lucky."

"But *I am*. I've not come all this way to freeze in these forsaken mountains when I could just as easily have died in the Asheera months ago." Rifkind paused, and Muroa's words came back to her. "Besides, I have a destiny."

"Oh, one of the lesser-known benefits of witchery, no doubt? Up to now, I've been glad enough to be an unimportant son of an important family; but if your destiny will give me vengeance on the Mountain Men for this ..." He paused but did not finish his thought. "Let's not waste time!"

Ejord jumped down from Blackthorn, dislodging numerous icicles from them both as he did. They quickly cleared one section of the rubble and tucked Linette down into it, then built as much of a shelter as they could around her. The strain of the day's journey had taken a toll on the girl; her fever had returned. Once they had a semblance of shelter, Rifkind devoted her attention to the child while Ejord secured Turin, Blackthorn, and the pony.

"How is she?" Ejord asked as he squatted down into the rough windbreak. "Can you do anything for her?"

"Nothing useful in this weather. The fever she had when I found her has returned; the other injuries seem well-healed now. But the fever was seated deeply within her, and I was not sure I had reached it all at the inn. I would risk too much if I tried anything here. I guess we shall simply have to rely on more luck."

"You seem more confident than I that one can rely on luck."

"Perhaps."

There was nothing more they could do. Linette lay still, uninterested in the half-frozen chunks of bread and sausage Rifkind offered her. Blackthorn stood windward of Linette's pony, and Turin blocked much of the wind with his shaggy bulk. The three were motionless; in the fading light and blowing ice particles, they disappeared into the formless mass of the mountain. Rifkind chewed the sausage slowly—letting each mouthful thaw before chewing or swallowing it. She overturned a few of the nearest stones, looking for the idol of the place, but without any luck.

"These Mountain Men you speak of . . . they are like the brigands I killed three days ago?"

"Some of them are. The Mountain Men here are a breed apart from the rest of us, the legends say, though it's not true—they were all born in the valleys there. The best of them are like your brigands—cold, vicious and cruel—the worse are less than animals and should be hunted out."

"That is a description I could apply to most of Isinglas, and one most of Dro Daria applies to us."

"Well, the Mountain Men aren't really like the Isinglaziers, but they have some things in common with the Asheerans—at least the legends of the Asheerans.

"The stories say that a normal man or woman goes to the mountains to escape persecution in the lowlands. After a few years, he may return with special powers. He can make himself invisible, he can talk to animals, and he is abnormally strong. Legends, just like the stories of the Asheerans—but I believe there is some truth at the bottom of it."

"Someday you will have to tell me your stories about my people. For now, why do you think there is some truth to these stories?"

"For some ten years I've been coming into the mountains here, trying to keep the passes safe. I sometimes chase the same band for two or three seasons, and I know something happens to them. I wouldn't say it makes them anything more than the rest of us; I know a raiding band rarely has the same members more than a few years. There are always a few from the valleys to replace the old ones who go up farther into the mountains.

"If a man returns to the valleys before a winter up here, he's much as he was, but if he's gone through winter, then he's different for all time," Ejord concluded.

"It all sounds very peculiar to me," Rifkind agreed. "There are powers in these mountains; I felt them last night in the idol, but even the Dark One who absorbs all who worship him does not affect men that way."

"I've never suspected witchery or religion, milady. I've figured that running wild here in the mountains does something to them. The cult priests who spend all their time up in the mountains don't run around in uncured hides eating raw meat as I've seen some of the Mountain Men do after they've left the bands to go up even farther into the peaks."

"It is enough to know that they fight and die like other men, and I know that from before."

"Die, yes, but this far into the Mountains we're as apt to be up against ones who've been here for years and not the valley-raiders."

"There is a style to men's fighting, just as there is a style to animals'."

"This far into the mountains, we'll fight animals who look like men."

There was a decisive note in his voice, and a sensation of concern from Turin, who, as always, was eavesdropping. Rifkind looked across in the rapidly dying light and met Ejord's stare.

'There is more to this than idle belief. Turin senses on Ejord's part more disgust and hatred toward these Mountain Men than bears antagonizing. Men are men, and the ones I killed when I saved Linette were beyond any doubt men—cruel and vicious beyond any I've known, but nothing other than men.

'But, by the Bright One, there is something uneasy in this destruction. The idol is gone—I'm sure of that somehow. This was something violent beyond necessity or reason.'

"I'll take the first watch, until about midnight. You rest; your luck might not work if you're too tired," Ejord suggested.

Rifkind made no false show of equality by insisting on watching with him. Their lives were dependent on each other, and until that situation changed, she could trust him. Ignoring the cold, aching numbness in her hands and feet, she forced herself to sleep.

CHAPTER 8

"Ejord!"

Rifkind leaned across Linette's sleeping form and whispered urgently in Ejord's ear.

"Wake up! There's something out there."

"When? How many?"

To his credit, Rifkind noted, Ejord woke up quietly and generally alert.

"Turin's sensed them. I can't tell anything about them yet, and he can't get a very clear vision of them."

'Can't, or won't,' she added to herself. 'He will not focus clearly on whatever's out there—he cannot understand it or face it directly—though he's plainly convinced we're in danger.'

"No idea how many?" Ejord asked, carefully replacing the cloaks around Linette as he moved toward his pack.

"Not too many, apparently, although there could be more he can't sense. Sometimes the distance is too great for the empathy."

"Mountain Men? Crag-wolves?"

"I don't know. He's acting very strange. I don't think he can ... well, fit an image to what he sees ... if I want to know what's there, I'll have to enter his mind and see what he sees."

Rifkind drew her own sword from its scabbard, carefully examining its edge in the darkness for traces of oil or ice.

"Then we'll call them Mountain Men, if he can't tell if they're man or beast."

Rifkind pushed harder against Turin's mind until she felt what he felt and saw what he saw. There were six of them lurking at the edge of his senses, and the dark, seething thoughts they produced reminded her of no man or animal she had ever encountered before. One advanced closer to their shelter, and Rifkind took advantage of the movement to probe more deeply into its emotions until she collapsed backward against the stones of their windbreak in exhaustion and horror.

"Rifkind!"

Ejord reached across the still-sleeping Linette and took Rifkind's hand. She withdrew her hand and recovered from the shock at once.

"They are Mountain Men, as you said they would be. Not Turin's mind raised to the intelligence of men, but our own minds constricted and diseased. . . Ejord, this is a trap they've prepared for hunting food. They intend to eat us!" She shook her head, denying the image of gaping hunger which she had absorbed from the mind of the Mountain Man.

"And they're all the same?"

"Yes . . ." She touched Turin's mind again, cautiously testing each thought center. "Yes, they are all the same, all the ones we can find—all hungry, all waiting." She broke the mental contact. "I cannot bear touching them longer. I can't fight something like that if I can feel its mind. It makes me feel that we could become like that if we stayed here too long."

"No, you're like the cult-priests. You could never be animals. The only way you could become like them is to be eaten by them." He spoke in a tone she found oddly reassuring.

Ejord yanked a great ax from his pack, testing the head lashings before sitting down again.

"You'll fight with that? That's for trees, not battle!" Rifkind exclaimed.

"When my enemy intends to make dinner from my still-warm body, I'll fight with whatever will best keep me alive. I'm sure you will, too."

Ejord stood up, buckled his sword-belt on, and headed, ax in hand, for a small, clear space midway between their shelter and where the horses were tethered. Rifkind shook her head and returned to the ritual of polishing her sword. The Mountain Men were still clear in her mind, and in Turin's. Their unnatural appetites unnerved her as no other opponent had been able to do. Though she would lose the advantage Turin's foreknowledge gave her, she shut her mind to the war-horse and the Mountain Men he envisioned, knowing that her survival depended on an ability to stay calm and sane in battle.

Rifkind tested the footing on the crude ramparts of their shelter and chose her fighting position. Months of daylight journeying had not completely ruined her night vision, and she knew tricks to improve what remained. Glancing out of the corners of her eyes, she saw the grey hulks which were Turin and Blackthorn, both pawing nervously at the ice and snow. She had time to wonder whether Blackthorn was under Turin's influence or was a fighter of his own volition. Time to wonder about the question, but no time to find an answer.

"Ejord, they're coming!"

Black shapes flowed out of the darkness. Rifkind heard the swish of the ax as Ejord made one practice swing. Then, with a final glance at the loose stones and icy patches around her, she shut out everything but her own private battle.

Rifkind lifted the sword to meet the first attack, but the Mountain Man lunged at her unmindful of the weapon she held, a short knife clutched awkwardly in his hand. She had no trouble in dealing him a fatal neck wound, even though her mind recoiled from an opponent demented enough to ignore a drawn sword. She dealt with the second as she had dealt with the first.

'I should have known at once that any creature which sought to make a meal of men would not likely be a very clever fighter.'

When no third leaped out of the darkness at her, Rifkind stepped off the rampart and wiped her blade on one of the corpses. The wind and ice still whistled in the air, and the encounter had not been enough to lift her above awareness of the numbing cold in her hands and feet. She listened and watched a few moments more, then sheathed her sword.

"That wasn't so bad," she said softly, as she limped toward Ejord.

"No . . . wait, you're limping—did one of them get you?" His voice was filled with proper gentlemanly concern.

"No crazed animal of a knife-fighter is going to get past my sword—even if my boots were damp this morning and now my foot is numbed with cold."

"Then you rest . . . I'll finish the watch."

"I can finish anything I start."

Rifkind pushed past him and stood defiantly at the perimeter of their shelter.

Through the sounds of the storm, they both heard the scrabbling sounds of men climbing over the rocks. Then Turin squealed and Rifkind's mind burned with the image of a sword flashing but being blocked by the steel-hard black horns; no empathic block could resist Turin's ultimate battle-warnings. Her sword was out, the pain in her foot forgotten.

They had an advantage in the narrowness of the ledge in front of the shelter; the Mountain Men could approach no more than two at a time, though she could see more eyes waiting in the rocks should the first not be successful. Their swords were heavier than hers and wielded by men inherently stronger than herself. Her hard-learned evasive tactics were nullified by the cramped space and the uncertain footing of the rocks.

Rifkind had to meet each swing squarely—a tactic she knew would fail in the end, if only because she was outnumbered. The Mountain Men fought as a team, never interfering with each other. Rifkind tried to vary the timing of her parries in a futile effort to break their rhythm. The battle assumed a precise flow as Rifkind grimly realized that it was not enough to be a far superior sword-handler than either of her opponents. Together, even though she could anticipate their every move, they had a decisive advantage over her. Each blocked swing jarred her arms and shoulders—it would only be a matter of time until fatigue caused an error on her part.

In desperation, Rifkind dropped her left hand to one of the throwing knives lodged in her belt, lifting it out of its sheath without breaking her rhythm or concentration. The left was not her stronger or more accurate hand, but it would have to be good enough for a blind throw at her left-side opponent. If her knife broke their pattern for only one beat, it would be enough.

She waited precious moments until her instinct told her that a double blow would come from the right; then, relying only on reflex and luck, she flung the knife into the darkness on her left while she parried the sword-strokes—the second close enough to cut the thick quilting on her forearm, far enough to glance off without serious injury.

There was a gasp. The next swing from the left was delayed long enough for her to get under it with her blade. She couldn't guess where the knife had struck, but watched her sword edge cut deeply into the Mountain Man's rib cage. He dropped his sword. The weapon was too heavy to be of any use to her; she kicked it aside and turned on the second enemy with renewed energy.

Rifkind had room now. She could use her speed

and finesse with the lighter sword to advantage. A quick small arc under the other's weapon, cutting up, severing the ligaments in his wrist, if not the hand itself. The second sword clattered to the ground. She thrust forward, pushing the tip of her sword deeply into the soft spot below his ribs.

There should have been more. She was alone, wary, perplexed. There had been more pairs of eyes waiting—she searched the periphery of her vision to find them. Ejord had fought well, but only two bodies lay at his feet and he was also searching for the rest. Turin and Blackthorn were quiet.

Where were they?

Rifkind began the risky maneuver of raising her consciousness to the tal-state where she would be able to see the thought centers of the Mountain Men —and expose herself to the full impact of their demented thoughts.

"Rifkind! Behind you, Linette!"

She spun around, centering back into battle alertness, mind and eyes straining. They'd circled around, fighting like men but with the same diseased hunger of the others; they had grabbed the bundle of cloth and fur which contained Linette.

'No!'

Myriad thoughts welled through her mind, all converging and focusing into one.

'No! That shall not be!'

Rifkind's feet were anchored to the ground; not in shock, but tapping into the great stores of energy which were the mountains themselves.

'She is mine! My student, my responsibility! She is me!'

There were none of the mild sensations of ritual empathy, but a paralyzing, ecstatic surge of raw elemental power flowing up through her body. Power which was now hers to use as she willed. She did not notice the golden aura which surrounded her as she lifted her right arm and pointed it, sword extended, at the panicky Mountain Men whom she could now see with surreal clarity.

'That shall not be!'

A sharp, hard sensation which was almost pain struck at her side. Her will faltered a moment—it *was* pain. Then she extended her arm again at the retreating figures. The pain was gone.

'You shall not be! Leave her!'

The energy of the mountains leapt out from the point of the sword. With steely satisfaction she saw the handful of men carrying Linette drop their burden and flatten themselves against the mountainside.

'You shall not be!'

Rifkind felt the power she controlled press against them, squeezing the life-forces out of them until there was nothing left to hold the bodies upright and they slumped to the ground. A second almost-painful distraction struck at her arm. She looked down and saw a sword-blade still thrust into the flesh of her upper arm, now resting against the bone. Her offended stare moved up the sword; her eyes met the crazed eyes of the sword-fighter she had first disarmed.

"None of you shall be!"

His eyes rolled back from the forces she directed at them. He fell backward, and though she could not see them she felt the life-force leave another four who had hung back in the shadows. The sword balanced a second on her arm bone, then fell to the ground.

Rifkind relaxed. The contact with the mountain was broken and the wave of reality crashed over her. She dropped her own sword and gasped as the first true awareness of the wounds in her arm and side reached her.

"My arm!"

She fell forward, but Ejord had gotten to her side and caught her before she completely lost her balance. He lifted her up and carried her to the shelter.

"My sword . . . don't leave my sword . . ."

"Don't mind the sword. Be quiet and don't move. Do you even know that you're hurt?"

"Hurt?"

Ejord worked quickly, bandaging her arm and side before retrieving Linette from the ledge where the Mountain Men had dropped her. He glanced down once at the bodies, then turned quickly away.

Ejord had been awed by Rifkind's display of power, but not enough to miss the wounds she took for them all. Once it was safe to approach her, he had been ready to take charge of her. His competence and concern surprised Rifkind far more than her mastery over the elements had. Turin had entered the shelter area and refused to move from her side.

The wind had died down, and instead of ice particles, large snowflakes were quickly covering the grotesque remains of the Mountain Men. Behind the clouds, the sun was rising. The inky blackness of the night was giving way to a softer grey.

Rifkind opened her eyes as Ejord knelt down. She struggled to raise an arm from the tightly wrapped bandages and cloak.

"My sword—did you get my sword?"

"Yes, I put in your pack. Turin's guarding it and

you very carefully ... exceedingly carefully."

Rifkind smiled weakly.

"He's worried about me."

"He's not the only one. I'm going to have to move both you and Linette when it gets brighter."

"Linette!"

The girl's name brought back the battle, and Rifkind twisted within her confinement to see her.

"She's all right. The Mountain Men dropped her carefully, everything considered. Your witchery didn't seem to affect any of us."

"Witchery ..." she repeated slowly, remembering the power sensations she had felt and the painlessness of the sword-blows which now tormented her.

"Get some rest. You seem to have some sort of self-healing abilities along with everything else; those cuts stopped bleeding almost as soon as you came out of that trance. But don't go tempting your fates again. I'll believe in your luck, your destiny, and your witcheries now—you don't have to show me anything else tonight. Just get some sleep."

"Witchery ... you were right, Ejord; what can heal can also kill. ..."

There was more. A whole new dimension of knowledge encountered and mastered within the space of a few seconds. But Turin's empathic concern and Ejord's good advice overrode her desire to talk. It was easy to close her eyes and almost impossible to open them again. It was certainly not worth the effort.

CHAPTER 9

There was only a cold, agonizing pain where her arm had been, and a searing stab in her side every time she breathed. Her wounds had been bound—she couldn't remember when—and now she was being lifted onto Turin's back. The guiding hands tried to be gentle, but the effort was too much for her. She fell forward.

There was sand in her mouth, in her eyes, ground under her fingernails and inside the felt lining of her boots. Her small fingers closed upon a rock and she staggered to her feet clutching it tightly.

"Halim, I hate you!"

Rifkind, a child again in her dreams, screamed, throwing the rock into her brother's face.

He was easily twice her size, and half again her age. But everyone in the camp seemed bigger, older, or stronger than she was, and she had the bruises to prove it.

The stone drew blood from Halim's cheek and he lunged for her with a berserker's anger. He caught her snarled hair, and they crashed into the sandy ground of the camp together. Halim was stronger, but Rifkind writhed in desperation until she could sink her teeth and fingernails into bare flesh. She hung on until Halim's screams made up for the battering she took.

Rough hands, larger even than Halim's, gripped her shoulder, pulling her upright with an authority which could not be challenged.

Her father! But even his angry face did not dim her satisfaction at seeing Halim's bloody shoulder. She had left a mark. She hurt—there were more cuts and bruises—and Halim would have his revenge. But he'd pay for it again. She was smaller, weaker, but she had a stubbornness and will that only their father could match.

"What is the meaning of this, brawling through the camp like dogs!"

"She started it!"

"He called me names. He said I was born in a lightstorm. He said my mother died when she saw me."

"Halim!"

"I remember what happened. It's all Rifkind's fault. Even Muroa said it was a curse." Halim stood defiantly, ignoring the blood which trickled down his cheek.

"Rifkind, come with me."

She followed the towering figure into the central tent, making a rude face at her brother as she passed him. The slaves and captives were dismissed as she sat on the carpets. Her father paced before her, as was his custom when disturbed.

"Daughter, it is not seemly that you are always fighting with your brothers. You will not be a child much longer, and we shall have to find a suitable marriage for you."

"I'm not going to marry someone like Halim. I'll have my own sword and make my own life. And if he calls me names, I'll kill him."

"Rifkind, you will do nothing of the sort. You've run wild without a woman to tame you, and I've gone beyond myself letting you behave like this. But you are not a warrior. There will be no sword for you at the next Gathering. By then you will dress and behave properly, and I will arrange your marriage."

"But I'm more of a warrior than Halim or the others, even if I am smaller and younger. Halim will never win a sword. Even Adijan says so."

Her father paused in his pacings to stare at her. She cringed for a moment, then, secure in the sword-master's confidence in her, she met his stare. The anger melted from his eyes. He squatted down on the carpets before her, taking her hands in his.

"After you were born, I thought I would protect you and raise you up to the image of your mother. I did not send you as an infant to one of my brother's clans to be raised as a first wife for one of their sons. I kept you near me and watched you grow in the directions Halim has always scorned. But now you are becoming a woman, and I know I cannot protect you forever. You cannot take up a sword, you cannot think to take my place—though I would go to the Death-Wastes tomorrow if I thought that your claim would be honored. You must understand and accept being a woman."

"I could do that, and fight, too."

"Yes, I'm sure that if you believe you could, then you could. But what is important is that no one else will believe you, and you will not have the time to convince them otherwise. It is one thing for a woman to be adept with a knife, as you are; it is another if she carries a sword. For your own safety, I will forbid you to fight for a sword at the next Gathering."

Rifkind pulled her hands away from him.

"You can't do that! I've got to have a sword... *that* sword!" She stood up, ran to the sword-rack which stood near the tent entrance, and laid her hand gently on the hilt of a gleaming, unadorned sword.

"Why, that's your grandfather's sword. It's longer than you are tall; you'll never grow tall enough to wield a blade like that," her father said with a smile intended to end their conversation.

"With that sword—if I learned to use it, if I never stopped practicing—I wouldn't need to be as tall as Halim; my arms would be as long as his then. I've tested it; the steel is good—and light. Of all the swords in the Gathering, that is the one I will fight for."

Her father shook his head. "You know too much," he sighed in a voice she was not supposed to hear. "Come, I'll forbid Halim and the others to tease you unless they want to fight me also. And I'll give you *this* instead of the sword."

He reached into an ornate chest and lifted out a heavy gold necklace with a massive pendant which held the large ruby.

"That was my mother's," Rifkind said slowly.

"And, before that, your grandfather's."

"The same grandfather?"

"The same."

She stared at her father with cunning which belied her eleven years. "If you forbid Halim to hit me, and he does, and you aren't there to stop him right away, what happens to me?"

"I will punish him."

"But what happens to me—can I hit back?"

He smiled slightly. "You might fight to defend yourself, or run away. Whatever suited you."

"I'll take the necklace." She reached out for it.

"And no sword?"

"No sword."

He hung the necklace around her, the pendant clanking against the buckle of her belt. She looked down at it and strode proudly out of the tent.

"Where'd you get that?" Halim grabbed her arm.

"From Father—an' you let go of me."

"Why?"

" 'Cause he said so."

"Just like he gave you that."

Halim was as soft and unmuscled as an Asheeran could be, but he was large enough to be a threat even without being competent. He reached for the ruby with his free hand and she shoved him aside, forgetting for a moment that he held her tunic. They fell, and Halim, with more luck than he usually had, improved his hold as they fell, landing on top of her and twisting her arm behind her as he forced one knee into the small of her back.

Her other hand was trapped holding the pendant and her legs were twisted so she could not writhe them about and free herself. The pain in her back and arm became excruciating. She gripped the pendant tighter, using self-caused pain to offset the other. She refused to scream since a scream would relax her and the pendant would be hers only so long as she didn't relax. Halim twisted her arm tighter, she held her breath and bit her tongue. He twisted again and the strained muscles began to tear. He twisted a final time, and then she felt nothing.

She was older and taller, but Adijan had still made a special sword-belt to keep her sword from dragging on the ground. She had practiced until her draw was as smooth as any of the others' despite its awkward angle. Adijan rushed at her on his grey war-horse, his drawn blade gleaming in the morning sun. She held her ground until he was committed to his attack, then darted quickly to one side, dodging the gilded horns, parrying the sword-stroke and delivering a return attack which would have slashed through Adijan's leg if he had not carefully padded both himself and his war-horse.

"Well done! Well done! You nearly unseated me anyway." Adijan dismounted and walked back to her.

"Next time I'll have a war-horse of my own."

"First you must train him carefully. Did he come in with the herd?"

"Yes, an' bigger and stronger than the others now, just as I knew he would be. Halim's didn't, and he says he'll have Turin instead of me; but my mark is still there from last Gathering."

She sheathed her sword and walked with Adijan from the practice field. She saw, but ignored, Halim and her half-brothers and cousins who stood near the tents watching her. They hated her, adding an extra intensity to their hatred when they saw her practicing with Adijan. But they had never wanted to practice with her since she had beaten Halim for her sword, and Adijan was always eager to teach her more.

Her father and uncles sat by the well. They conducted the business of the clans at the annual Gatherings. Rifkind spied them pausing and watching her as she walked by. That afternoon the elders would separate the two-year-olds from the great herd and award them to the youths who had claimed them the previous year. There had been dissent then, when she had moved into the herd to select a war-horse. But no one had expected the spindly chestnut to survive a year, and no one had expected her to win her grandfather's sword two days later.

"Rifkind!"

She stopped, annoyed that she hadn't gotten by them.

"Do you still intend to claim your war-horse?" an uncle she barely knew demanded when she approached their circle.

"That is my right as a warrior."

"You aren't still thinking of yourself as a warrior?" another asked wearily.

"I *am* a warrior."

"Her mind is made up. I've told you that," her father reminded the others.

"Halim challenges your right," the uncle who had called her said.

"Halim always challenges me. I've beaten him before; eventually he'll learn."

"You will meet after the matching this afternoon. It will be a fight until the other yields."

"I understand."

She walked away. Turin would never belong to Halim so long as she lived, so it would be a fight to the death unless he yielded first. It was not her fault that his choice had not survived the winter, or that he still fought with a borrowed sword. He could always challenge someone less skillful or more willing to lose than herself, and there were always the mares. But Turin would be hers.

The two-year-olds milled about nervously, separated from the rest of the herd for the first time in their lives. Their eyes showed white, and they lowered their new, long horns at their new masters. Rifkind moved quickly, not trusting Halim to wait until Turin was hers and out of the enclosure before making his attack. Adijan had told her to radiate confidence and trust as she approached the colt. She put thoughts of Halim out of her mind when she located the chestnut near the center of the small herd.

Turin? Turin? Can you sense me? You're Turin; you will be both fast and strong. I am Rifkind. I will teach you.

He pawed the ground but did not lower his head, and the white ring around his bulging eyes receded as he listened to her voice and mind. While the others were frightening their choices with frustration or eagerness, Rifkind slipped a soft old rope around Turin's neck and led him out of the enclosure toward her tent.

Halim met her, his sword already drawn.

"The matching is not over," she said evenly, still flush with the confidence she had used to approach Turin.

"It is for you. That's enough."

"We must wait for Father and the others."

"I will tell them what happened."

He advanced. She looped the rope over a nearby tent pole and drew her own sword. It was lighter than Halim's, but Adijan had taught her well. Before Halim could pin her into the narrow rope-ridden tent areas, she leaped into the clearing by the well. He had been practicing, and settled into a battle-mind more resolved than she thought possible. Still, he was used to fighting with all his strength against others who also matched strength for strength. Halim was unprepared for her deflecting defense. His heavy sword and powerful style were ill-suited against a more agile opponent. He battered down on her expecting each blow to hit home and end his sister forever, only to find his sword sliding down hers and far past its target.

"Do you understand now? You cannot hurt me. Forget this—take another colt or a mare and breed your own war-horse. Father will give you one of his until yours is grown. Challenge Orikan; he is a coward and will let you win your sword."

Halim shook his head. "I will take what is mine, and I'll take it from you since you've stolen it from me anyway. I'm not going to beg Father or fight Orikan."

He swung again, a powerful, angry blow. She blocked it and left him a deep gash along his forearm. He dropped his sword from the shock. She placed her foot on the blade and held her own sword at his neck.

"Turin is mine. Long ago I was forbidden to fight with you unless you attacked me. I won't kill you now and risk Father's wrath. But I can always defend myself. It will be a month before you can fight again; and if you challenge me then, I will cut you again. Cut and cut until you learn that Turin and the sword are mine.

"I do not hate you the way you hate me. There is no need to fight; I will never challenge you for the clan. I want only what is mine. Do you understand? Will you yield?"

Halim looked around him. They had attracted a crowd, their father among them. He looked again at her sword, still dripping with his blood.

"I will yield."

She lowered the sword; he stepped back, turned, and walked through the crowd. Now she felt all the eyes upon her and realized that she had won her war-horse, her sword, and the enmity of all her people for humiliating the logical successor to her father. Her father would not meet her gaze; she realized that he had been the one who had trained Halim for this battle. Only Adijan smiled and nodded as she looked at his face. But he was a Wet-Lander captured years ago by her father and spared the usual fate of male prisoners because of his martial skills. Then she saw Turin, alone and waiting. Wordlessly she left the crowd and walked to her war-horse. It had been worth it, but there was a dull ache in her heart where the clan had been.

"You have nothing."

"I have Turin, wealth, and my weapons."

She was older, and despite the oiled leather straps which held her sword and knives, a woman. She sat in her own tent talking to an ancient weathered crone who wore only one knife, yet commanded the respect of even her father, who was the most powerful man in the Gathering and rarely spoke to her anymore. He was also lying gravely ill in his own tent.

"There is no clan which will have you—especially your own. Your freedom was bought with your father's strength. Now he will be a cripple, and they will destroy you."

"They know I am wiser and stronger than Halim."

"And that is why they will kill you. You will not get what you want with a sword, child."

"I am not a child, Muroa. I am a warrior of this clan; though they wish me to the Dark One and back, they know I am a warrior and respect that."

"You are ignorant and willful. Come with me now. I'll take you to the caves and teach you what I know. I'll give you the silver crescent of the Bright One, and no one will touch you with or without a sword. You will have this miserable clan if you want it."

"It is no miserable clan; it is the strongest in the Gathering, as well you know since you travel so much."

"It is not the power of time and numbers; it is the power of your father's mind, and when that is gone, this clan will be like so much meat left to rot in the sun. I have seen that. Come with me. Let me teach you."

"If what you have seen is true, then my place is here. I am a warrior, not a healer. I will not see this clan and our wealth carved up among vultures."

"You were born in a lightstorm. Unless you turn

to the Bright One, your powers will surely destroy you. I've never suggested putting aside your knives or that sword, only come with me and learn."

"My place is here. You yourself say that Father will never see or ride again. I must stay, even if it is only to die."

"I will leave at midnight."

Muroa left the tent with a silent agility that few suspected she possessed. Rifkind watched her go, then walked to the central tent. Her father lay on the carpets. His swollen leg was supported by pillows, his eyes covered with a silk bandage. Returning from their last caravan raid, he had fallen from his war-horse, unconscious but not wounded. The clan healer could not help him, and they had called for Muroa. The old healer had come from the depths of her caves to cure his disease, but not the damage it had caused. Halim sat silently at his father's feet. He looked up as Rifkind entered.

"Is he awake?" she asked.

"No, they gave him draughts. He'll sleep a while longer."

"Muroa says he won't see or ride again. Do the others know?"

"Yes, she saw to that; you were the last. I didn't want to make the announcement." Halim shuddered as he spoke.

He had grown closer to his father since the day a year and a half before when she had won Turin from him.

"Do you intend to challenge him, or simply forbid his treatment?"

"Neither. The old healer says his mind will be clear. He can still guide us. I could never challenge him."

"A clan without a strong leader to plan raids for them will be a target of raids itself!"

"Do not tell me what to do, sister. I know your mind, your hatred of me, of him, of all of us. You want to see us fight to the death; even blinded and one-footed, you think he is beyond me. With both of us gone, you would claim to be the only one of full blood and with that slinking Wet-Lander Adijan at your side, you'll try to rule the clan and the Gathering. But you won't. Even if they don't like or respect me, they'll stay behind me if it means getting rid of you. As long as you both are alive, I'm safe."

She glared at him in impotent rage. He was weak, but he knew how to survive. There was a commotion outside the tent and three of her half-brothers burst in with a mutilated head on the end of a tent-pole.

"We caught him poisoning the water for your father."

"You did well." Halim nodded.

She studied the head; its face was bloody beyond recognition, but the blond hair was certainly Adijan's. She turned to Halim.

"It is the proper punishment, is it not, Rifkind?" the pole carrier sneered.

"This will not be forgotten."

She pushed past them headed for her own tent. They attacked when she entered the dark stretch which separated her tent from the others. There were two, and one fled when she did not go down at once but shrugged off the thrown knife. The second ran when she drew her sword and advanced on him. The knife had made a shallow wound in her side, but the blade was poisoned, and she was quivering in shock even as she lifted up her tent flap.

Vernta and Amorn were gone; she tried to call out
for them, but a hand closed over her mouth.
Thrown back on her sleeping silks, she lay motionless but conscious while Muroa chanted and drew
symbols in the air over her wound. The weakness
passed; she slept and woke to find her belongings
packed and herself dressed for a long journey. She
stared at Muroa, who stood at the tent entrance,
holding up the loose flap.

"It is midnight."

Rifkind nodded and stood up. Her knives were in
place, and the sword. Turin was saddled and waiting behind her tent next to Muroa's bent-horned
war-horse. There was some activity in the camp, but
it was all centered on her father's tent. She was briefly curious, then vaulted into the saddle. The Bright
One had not yet risen; no one would see her leaving.
She felt the vaguely tender spot in her side.

"I will be back," she whispered to the camp. Then
she followed Muroa into the darkness.

"It is really quite remarkable she survived at all."

A long-robed man stepped back from the bed
where he had just examined Rifkind.

"No fault of mine, though. The wounds were well
toward healing when you brought her down from
the mountains. In fact, if I didn't know you better,
Ejord, I'd say you made the story out of your imagination."

"She's both an Asheeran and a witch."

"So Lord Humphry delights in reminding me. I
haven't seen him this excited since old Hogarth got
thrown from his horse and died. Your father seems
to think she'll be able to defeat An-Soren, disrupt the
queen's forces and make Dro Daria safe for his kind

of monarchy. I doubt even An-Soren could take all that on."

"That's his plan? He never confided it to me, though that's not unusual. I don't think Rifkind here's had much experience taking orders before. I've a mind to sit back and enjoy them match wits now that he's half-satisfied I've done my part of the job."

"This little lady matching wits with the lord himself? She's an unschooled barbarian!"

"Five korli says my father's met his match."

"Five korli, eh? Five korli and a keg of cider and it's set."

"Either you're feeling rich, or giving up cider this winter."

CHAPTER 10

Rifkind regained consciousness slowly. Her first impressions were that her surroundings were strange and unfamiliar. She remained motionless until she was fully alert. A fire crackled in one corner, warming the room despite a stiff and doubtless cold wind which beat against the shutters. Except for herself, the room was reassuringly empty. Her side and arm were healed, and though definitely weaker, she felt no worse for the ordeal which seemed in her memory to have lasted hours instead of days.

She flexed the muscles in her arm and the soft

contraption in which she lay shifted under her as no
sleeping silk had ever done. As she moved, a faint
odor of spices and flowers was released from the
depths of the softness. Her arm was encased in a
cloth tube which ended in an uncomfortable ruffled
feeling at her wrist. She froze again and cautiously
opened her eyes.

Tapestries and furs decorated the walls of the
stone and plastered room. Straw mats covered the
floor, and the windows were sealed with a substance which let in sunlight but shut out the wind. A
heavy canopy covered the bed, reminding her of a
tent. A heavy covering similar to the canopy lay over
the contraption which she now realized was an ex-
ceptionally large and well-made bed. She threw the
covering back.

"By the Nameless Ones!"

She looked in disbelief at the long lace-trimmed
nightgown which covered her. Her hair had been
unbraided and hung loosely to her waist as she
jerked upright.

She missed her knives. *Turin! Turin? Where are
you, where am I?*

Rifkind blasted her thoughts in all directions until
she found him. His total enthusiasm at discovering
she was well again made it impossible to learn anything from him until he had calmed down. At her
insistence, he relived his memories of the hazardous
journey to Chatelgard with her lashed to his back.
She saw the warm, comfortable stable he shared
with Blackthorn and several other Dro Darian
beasts. Ejord visited him frequently, and there were
others he thought of as Riders who took care of him.
His memory for faces was not such that she could
recognize anyone but Ejord in the image he pressed

into her mind. He was content, well-fed, and un-
afraid.

Relieved that he was all right and not suspicious
of Chatelgard, she withdrew from his mind. His
time sense had never been particularly reliable, but
if Ejord had visited him once a day, then they had
been at the castle for six days. That seemed reasonable to her.

Her immediate concerns taken care of, Rifkind
wondered about Linette. Turin had no notion of the
girl's location and had not seen her since their arrival. If Linette had been close by her room, Rifkind
thought she might have been able to detect her presence, but the thickness of the walls and her own
limitations defeated her. She would have to venture
beyond the room to find her pupil. With that
thought, she directed her attention to finding accept-
able clothing, and, of course, her weapons.

Her knives and sword had not been deliberately
hidden, but carefully placed in an unlocked chest
near the bed. Her clothes had been cleaned and
mended, then placed below the knives in the chest.
Throwing the nightgown onto the bed, she dressed
quickly, and after testing each blade, opened the
door of her room.

The corridor was darker and cooler, but also the
way to the nearest stairway. She wandered without
losing her sense of direction. She could tell one heap
of grey boulders from another in the Asheera; the
corridors with their doors and tapestries were no
great challenge. Linette's voice came softly from an
open door. The girl was sitting on the floor of a
room not unlike her own, dressed in a rich gown
and playing with a small striped cat.

"Milady Rifkind!"

Linette jumped to her feet. The kitten darted under the bed, and before Rifkind had quite surveyed the room, the girl ran to her, hugging her with an enthusiasm not unlike Turin's.

"Oh, Rifkind, it's everything Ejord said it would be! A fireplace all of my own. A kitten, 'cause I can't really have a pony 'til spring. More food than Da'd grow inna year. An' three gowns all my own, not made for anyone but me!"

Rifkind was still wondering how to respond to Linette's greeting when the child released her and led her to a wardrobe which contained the three gowns. Despite her distaste for traditional women's clothing, Rifkind retained her nomad's taste for bright colors. Linette's gowns intrigued her; she was about to examine one closely when a loud gong shattered the silence of the corridors and rooms.

"Dinner!" Linette beamed. "Will you come to dinner with me, Rifkind? There's so much food, they'll never notice if there's someone extra. Half the chairs're empty anyway, an' I've been storin' some food up here every night, in case I ever need it. An' Ejord'll be there, an' Lor' Humphry. Lors, will they be surprised to see you!"

"Yes, I guess I'll come to dinner. I'm hungry and I should meet my hosts."

Linette scooped up the kitten and whispered something to it before leading Rifkind out of the room.

"You seem to have recovered well. Last I remember you, the Mountain Men had you," Rifkind commented as they walked.

"There's so much food, I'd had to be dead not to get better. An' ol' Bainbrose, he's a healer too, not like you, but he mixes these funny things an' makes me drink one every morning. An' there's no wagon, or rain, or pushin' the wagon outta the mud."

"No headaches, or chills?"

"You sound like Bainbrose. I'm fine, I've found a good place to live, better'n anything I coulda hoped for before."

"Food and fireplaces—that's a good place?"

"Why not?"

Rifkind remained silent the rest of their walk. The frail, ill girl she had carried in the rain had disappeared, replaced by a young woman who, though totally different from what she had been at that age, was no longer a child. It was none too soon to begin to train Linette in empathic arts, but the Wet-Lander was going to be no more pliant than she herself had been when Muroa had first approached her.

They passed little groups of liveried servants who whispered in the thick Glascardy dialect as they passed. Rifkind doubted that she would be at all inconspicuous when they reached their destination. Her fears were realized when they reached the great hall with its vast horseshoe table. She spotted Ejord's face, and taking Linette's hand, made haste for him.

"Rifkind!"

The voice reverberated through the hall, silencing all the others. Rifkind needed nothing else to know that Lord Humphry had noticed her. She turned, looking for a tall, commanding figure like her father; then, seeing none, began to study the crowd more closely for other clues, since the voice had not repeated itself.

Ejord came up beside her.

"You should have warned me you'd be at dinner. Follow me," he whispered and led her to an older man of average height, somewhat overweight, with a florid complexion. "Father, may I present Rifkind, our guest here from the Asheera."

"My witch! At long last! We had begun to doubt if you would recover."

Lord Humphry put an arm around her shoulder, separating her quickly from Ejord.

"Foolish boy, risking your life in the passes like that. I understand if it hadn't been for you he'd have been killed and eaten. It would have been no great loss—I've better sons—but I'm grateful."

"Ejord fought well enough on his own, and I could never have found my way without him."

"If he had found you at once, there would have been no problem getting you here safely. Bungling that way—he should have sent for help."

"He had no one he could send," Rifkind said, growing quickly uncomfortable with Lord Humphry's tone and manner.

"He could have found someone, or come himself."

Lord Humphry allowed no further discussion of the topic and clapped his hands once to signal the meal had begun. He indicated a space next to his own great chair, and another chair was brought from the shadows around the edge of the room.

"You'll sit next to me."

He gestured again to his left, and the servant carrying the chair came perilously close to crashing into Rifkind in his efforts at immediate obedience.

Lord Humphry bent over with complete confidence that the servant would have his chair beneath him before he unbalanced himself. Her own talents for mimicry did not include that much trust of a stranger, but there was little choice—the man obviously feared the wrath of his master more than he feared her warning stare. He swept her up and pushed the chair to the edge of the table.

Her sword, which could be comfortably accommodated at an open air Asheeran feast, rattled noisily against the side of the chair as she wriggled forward to reach the table. Her legs were too short to reach the floor or the rungs of the chair. She reached for a joint of meat; the sword caught in the chair and jerked hard into her waist. Her appetite had vanished.

"The walls of Chatelgard are strong, milady, and those within are all sworn to me. It is not our habit to come armed to the table."

Rifkind shifted the sword again and faced him.

"This may be so, but I am from the Asheera. Our Gatherings would be poor feasts if we limited them to our sworn families or disarmed our guests." She paused. "And though I am a grateful guest of your clan, I am sworn to none but the Bright One."

"Ah, yes, Ejord had mentioned something to that effect. Nonetheless, you'd agree there is no need to go armed within these walls?" He stared at her sword and knives.

"Do you fear I lack the honor or skill to care for my weapons properly?" Rifkind intercepted his stare with an equally cold look of her own.

"It is only that others might think—"

"Lord Humphry, Ejord came searching for a witch, not a warrior. If you expect me to be able to help you, it is not my knives which you should fear."

Lord Humphry's face turned a deeper shade of red. He clapped his hands twice, and a procession of kitchen servants bearing more heavy trays wound its way through the hall. Her appetite had returned. She took out the small carved-ivory eating utensils she'd acquired in her months in the lowlands and took advantage of her nearness to Lord Humphry to fill her plate.

"Excuse me, milady, but I had not thought forks were common in the Asheera."

She turned to the grey-bearded man seated to her left.

"They are not uncommon, they are unknown. I got these from a careless traveler not far from Is-inglas."

"Careless, you say? Ah, well. Permit me. I'm Bainbrose. I'd kiss your hand, but my beard has already encountered the grease from the kitchen, and I've heard the custom is frowned upon in your lands."

"You're a healer? I have seen Linette; she is better than I'd expected. I am pleased to find competence where none was expected."

"Not a healer such as yourself. Only a scholar who knows when to leave well enough alone—a rare art in itself—and enough of the appearances of medicine to keep other meddlers away."

Rifkind smiled and began to relax. He had caught her off-guard, and her first questions had been abrupt, but he'd reacted with humor and dignity. Bainbrose would have had no place in the world of the Gathering, but she found she liked him anyway.

"Have you been to the Asheera?" she asked after a moment.

"No, my travels have taken me to many places, but neither the border provinces nor your clans have much use for a man who can fight only with his tongue."

She nodded. "You are a most pleasant warrior. You seem to know more of the Asheera than anyone else I've met in Dro Daria. You were perhaps with the caravans, or a spy?"

"I have been a spy; it is a career well suited to a man of no other apparent talents. But I would never spy against an Asheeran, especially, you'll excuse me, a healer like yourself. By the mark on your face, I've known you were a healer, not a witch—though the distinction is meaningless in these lands. If you became suspicious of me, either you or your warhorse in the stables could well determine the nature of any threats I could make. And the Bright One has never forbidden self-defense?"

"We survive."

"I've imagined that. When I was a young man, I was obsessed by the menace of the Asheeran hordes. I poured the best years of my life into studying the Asheerans. Know what I learned?"

He leaned forward in a gesture of confidence.

"What?" The sword clanked again; she hoped it didn't strike him in the knees.

"The Asheerans never were or will be a threat to Dro Daria. The kings keep their armies tied up in garrisons at the edge of the Asheera, wreaking havoc among the provinces, and occasionally, I suppose, annihilating an unlucky clan or two far away from court politics. Everyone believes the Asheerans want to conquer us, but the clans don't want the Wet-Lands, only the caravans. They let enough of those through to keep overland travel a bit safer than ocean voyages, which, of course, the clans know nothing about. It's remarkable how these things always balance each other."

Bainbrose sat back in his chair.

"Of course, no one wanted to hear that sort of heresy. We've been hating the Asheerans for generations; if we stopped now, we'd start fighting among ourselves. It's a fact, if you read the Chronicles, do you read?—well, never mind, no one else does here either, and I'm honest. They show a clear coincidence in the growth of the king's land, the army's size, and the rumored strength of the Asheeran horde. This all began with Darius Primus, who, surprisingly enough, was a caravaneer plying the Asheeran trade before he decided to unite all of Dro Daria. His parentage is a bit obscure—might have been a bit of an Asheeran himself, but that's all been hidden away, you know."

"I think these things took place too long ago to be of use to us now," Rifkind replied.

"You don't read—I can tell for certain now. Of course, you're right. Oh, well—but there are some things in the present I think you should know. Overnmont wants you to eliminate An-Soren for him."

"That I already know; Ejord told me. I have nothing better to do. I can't go back to the Asheera, and I've discovered I'm ill-suited to the life of a peasant."

"You talk as if An-Soren were some hedge-fox to be run down of a fine afternoon and eaten with a Lambeth wine for dinner. Milady, do you know who, or what, An-Soren is?"

"Well, I've heard he's a sorcerer." She paused, wondering how seriously to take Bainbrose.

"Yes, but in a land where sorcerors are either charlatans, incompetents, or puppets of this or that godling, An-Soren is an Asheeran like yourself."

"Your eyes fairly glow with this knowledge, but it

is meaningless to me." And Rifkind hoped her eyes did not betray her reaction to the information that An-Soren was a renegade healer.

"Oh." Bainbrose paused to drain his wineglass before continuing. "Where to start? Rumor or fact? Fact first, I think: An-Soren has a black scar on his cheekbone, far too regular to be a birthmark—it's a diamond shape, I believe."

"Diamond?" Rifkind sat back searching her memory, there had been something in Muroa's lessons about a diamond mark.

"Yes, definitely a diamond. Is that particularly important?"

"Long ago there was a healer; his name has been forgotten, but it must have been long ago. Men haven't been healers for many generations. He abandoned the Bright One for the forces of the Dark One, Vitivar. He hid himself where the rays of the Bright One couldn't reach him; in time, the other healers sworn to the Bright One banded together and went after him.

"It was said they found him in the caves not far from my own clan-wells. They fought and the healers—the true healers, sworn to the Bright One— were nearly defeated. The sun rose, but the Bright One stayed in the sky until they brought all the renegades into the open."

"That is interesting. I love legends and stories, but they're even further from the present. What does that story have to do with An-Soren who's likely dining this evening just as we are."

"Their teaching mark was a silver diamond; the Bright One, of course, took it back. But it was said that a few escaped."

"And perpetuated the heresy? Branding their pupils with a black diamond instead of a silver one?"

"Unlikely. I doubt they could find followers in the Asheera without us knowing it."

"Us?"

"The ones who remained after the battle."

"I'm getting completely confused, milady. One moment you're talking a legend from 'long ago', the next, you're speaking as if you were at the battle."

"There were bearers of the silver crescent there, though their names are mostly lost, too. Many lines of healers died that day, but mine survived. I have some limited memories of it from the time of my initiation. I would know if the diamond was alive again; nothing has changed in my lifetime, or my teacher's lifetime. I'm guessing that he is a survivor of that battle."

"Isn't that just a bit unlikely?"

"No, it is possible the Dark Brethren had made a pact for eternal life before the final battle. Is he old? Does anyone remember knowing him when he was younger?"

"Hmm? There is a certain consistency about the man that has been remarked upon. You may be right. But if he survived your ancestors, can you overcome him now?"

"I shall have to try."

"Healer's ethics?"

"In a way. I cannot suspect who he is and do nothing. Perhaps it is just coincidence, but there is something in this which seems to be of a pattern I've been studying. Excuse me, I must think this through."

Rifkind rose to move her chair from the table.

Bainbrose caught her eye and shook his head.

"Here at Chatelgard we eat when the lord eats; we leave when he leaves. I, myself, have composed four sonnets on winter just since we have returned from the court. I wouldn't repeat them aloud; I mean only to indicate the concentration which is possible in a noisy, unpleasant room."

Rifkind nodded. Lord Humphry was engaged in a loud conversation on the merits of game over domestic meats, and Bainbrose quickly and politely immersed himself in his own thoughts.

'*An odd fellow.* Turin might have to find a whole new category for him, neither Walker nor Rider. My own inclination is to accept him on his own terms; scholar and observer.

'By the Nameless Gods, I wish Muroa's tales had not bored me so. Even when she used the fire to illustrate them, I could barely keep awake. Now I can't remember anything useful. But Bainbrose has touched patterns and rhythms in my mind. The only surprising thing is that I've taken so long to see them myself.

'Muroa has told me I am cursed, yet I have a destiny to fulfill. I have met a scarred chimera in the Death-Wastes ... I should have recognized the Brethren then but I was distracted by the effects of the lightstorm itself. Who else—what else—but the Dark Brethren of Vitivar? It is all so clear now ... no, that's not true either. As a pattern, there are too many empty spaces; and worse, there is too much that doesn't fit anywhere. The ruby obviously belongs, but I don't know where—damn! What did the chimera call it? And Linette—Muroa said a pupil was always a gift.

'I'll make new stones. That's what Muroa'd tell

me to do. New patterns, new stones ... I'll go back
to those mountains and make new stones.'

"Milady?"

It was Lord Humphry's voice. Rifkind looked up,
startled to realize that the meal was nearly over and
a ragged group of minstrels was singing in the central court.

By the Bright One, I've been lost in tal-mind! "Yes,
Lord Humphry?"

"It would seem our supper has tired you. I had
hoped to have a word with you in private. Perhaps
I should wait until morning?"

"No, after your hospitality and my rudeness, the
least I can do is talk with you."

She expected that he would clap his hands and
the entire room would rise to leave them alone. Instead, he merely raised one hand, and servants
rushed to pull both their chairs from the table. She
looked around the room for a moment, surprised
that no one appeared to notice their leaving, then
hurried to the curtained doorway where Lord Humphry was waiting for her.

CHAPTER II

The narrow tapestried hallway sloped upward to a small private chamber whose fireplace and candles had already been lit. Two massive wooden chairs had been pushed toward the fireplace. Lord Humphry selected the more ornate of the pair, then motioned Rifkind to the other. She discovered it was larger than the dining chairs and tucked her legs into a more comfortable position.

"Well, now, Rifkind, I hadn't expected I would have to explain myself, the court, and the dangers of An-Soren to you. But nothing that involves Ejord ever goes the way I expect. And now he tells me that you

see no need of the benefits and protection of the Overnmont name and arms. He doubts you'd swear
allegiance to me, or to anyone else, and says my
only hope is to convince you that you want to help
me in my fight against An-Soren."

"In the Asheera we would not offer the name of
the clan to someone not born to it unless he had
something the clan needed desperately. I have
always been wary of a clan or person who is desperate," Rifkind stated firmly, testing Lord
Humphry's resolve and responses.

"Ah, it's very plain you do not feel the least sense
of awe toward us or our problems. But is this because my son has failed to explain all things properly to you? All of Dro Daria is on the verge of civil and
religious war. Even my remote land of Glascardy is
affected. Families like Linette's flee the lands around
the court. The king's forces are divided into impotent
factions, everywhere outmaneuvered by Hogarth
and his men. And behind Hogarth is An-Soren and
the priests of Vitivar.

"An-Soren, sitting in his tower rooms watching
everything, using Dro Daria to play a monstrous
game in which he alone will be a winner and all the
rest will lose."

Rifkind remained silent long after Lord Humphry
ceased talking. His eyes never left hers; she knew
they were taking each other's measure. She doubted
that he could guess that her mind was already made
up. The information she had received from Bainbrose over supper left her with an obligation to seek
out An-Soren and complete the vengeance of the
Bright One if the sorcerer was indeed a survivor of
the Dark Brethren. The combined strengths of her
Goddess and healers from all over the Asheera had

not been enough to eliminate the Brethren; she knew better than to confront An-Soren without the best support she could inveigle from the Wet-Landers.

"What exactly will you lose?" she asked after a moment.

"Everything! For generations the Overnmonts have stood behind the kings. Darius Primus gave my family the title of King's Defender, and by the gods, we've done that! We've struggled for a strong monarchy to keep the countryside at peace. When fertile lands are carved up into hostile kingdoms, there is constant war or famine. Here in the mountains we have meat aplenty, wood and stone for our homes, and great buildings everywhere—but barely enough grain and no iron or steel. Time and time again our lands were threatened by those who had what we did not and desired what we did.

"I oversaw the regency of young Darius. I blocked the influence of An-Soren then, even though he was already too strong at court for me to remove him as regent. I negotiated the marriage between Darius and Gratielle. The feud was ended. Hogarth placed the hand of his youngest sister in mine. I gave it to the king; there was peace!"

Lord Humphry stabbed at the air with his hands, impressing Rifkind more with the force of his will than his logic—if simple desire could affect life-energies, then Lord Humphry would not have lost the peace he had sought after.

"But Gratielle—she was too much woman for Darius, and he lost her to An-Soren before a month had past. Now the queen stands opposed to her husband, and Hogarth and An-Soren conspire with scandal and innuendo to destroy not merely the king, but all Dro Daria!"

Rifkind studied a scar on her knuckle. "A man who could do all you say you have done should have no trouble with your king or queen; you made them, you can unmake them. An-Soren is only a man. I could use ritual to create a drink so subtle that all but the one it is intended for might drink safely of it. But if An-Soren were a ritualist himself, he would see the art in the drink and not touch it. Surely somewhere in Dro Daria there is one skilled in more direct means of assassination? Could you not have found someone before this to kill him?" She looked straight into his eyes as she finished, then quickly stared at the fireplace.

"No. He fears you. I have never known him to fear anyone before. There have been attempts, but nothing succeeds and no one survives. I myself, of course, have not conspired before; I looked the other way when my more reckless peers threw their might against the magician. Always failure. Even when the rebellion came from within the ranks of Hogarth's forces, still failure.

"But An-Soren fears you. Feared you enough to try to stop you some time ago by means I could not discover. Feared you even more when that failed, enough to tell the Border Lords that his own attempts had failed and that you were the witch vanguard of all the clans massing to destroy Dro Daria itself."

"And you believed that?" Rifkind asked raising one eyebrow.

"Of course not, and he knew that; he didn't tell me, though I'm a Border Lord myself. He expected you to approach Dro Daria from the west, near the court, where Hogarth and he are the strongest. Yes, it is what he said, and the others believed it. They have not had Bainbrose nattering at them these past twenty years that the danger is not from the Asheera, but from those who say it is from the Asheera.

"Nonetheless, I have spies and informants within Hogarth's forces."

"An-Soren has never spoken of how I eluded him, or the type of danger I am to him?"

"No, he has no advisers or confidants, except perhaps Gratielle. All he has ever said is that you are Asheeran and have great powers which can harm Dro Daria."

"I don't have any of these 'great powers.' I'm a healer: no more, no less. I can see life-forces, and at times control them. I can change the nature of things according to ritual laws. But I certainly cannot walk into a room and enchant or kill a man by looking at him."

"But in the mountains!" Lord Humphry protested. "Ejord told me about your fight with the Mountain Men." His face darkened. "Did my son lie to me?"

"No, but I don't think I could do that again. I have no idea where that power came from. It wasn't from the Bright One who is slow and subtle, the river of all our knowledge."

Lord Humphry looked at her, and a dark furrow of concern crossed his face. He rose from the chair, pacing the length of the room without looking up or speaking.

"An-Soren fears you; you must have these powers. He would not fear you unless he knew that you did. Perhaps you had never tried before. There is no worship of the Bright Moon in Dro Daria; perhaps you receive your strengths now from some stronger deity. You're our last hope. If An-Soren isn't stopped, the country will fall into ruin. The legions Hogarth has been training will sweep out of the Eastern Mountains, and all we have worked for will be lost. I could keep them out of Glascardy, but only because we will have nothing they need.

"We need everyone working together, and government—not religion—in charge. Too long has the countryside been carved up into little fiefdoms, each with its own gods and wars. The priests never care except for their own treasure, and how to get their neighbors'.

"Since Darius united the land, we've built ships and roads. A farmer in Daria itself can take his grain to a royal depot, watch it weighed and loaded. He is paid in royal coin, good for everything anywhere. From the depot the grain goes to the ports to be put on ships and sent to places like Glascardy, where the ships were built and paid for the same way.

"Do you understand why we have to protect this?"

"No."

Rifkind watched the stout man pull himself up to his full height and prepare to explain his vision of the future of his land. If she had not been growing more tired, she would have let him retell the story several times; not for her own understanding, but to impress upon him that the ways of Dro Daria meant little to her, despite her presence in Chatelgard. But, being tired, she lifted a hand to stop him.

"Much of Dro Daria is beyond my understanding. My problem has nothing to do with ships or depots, only with An-Soren. Why should I risk myself to challenge him when he has done nothing to me?

Though he fears me, why should I fear him? I don't want to know about roads; I want to know why I should risk my life for you."

"Because I will protect you. You will risk nothing."

"If you could protect me so well, you would not need my help. I have no great hunger for your protection, Lord Humphry. I have been in Dro Daria long enough to know I can survive here."

"An-Soren will find you. If you need a reason to fight him, the reason you should have fear of him, let it be simply that he fears you—and he hates what he fears. He destroys it. He knew you were coming and tried in some arcane way to intercept you, but he failed. He will not allow himself to fail again."

Rifkind paused.

"If he is as vengeful and powerful as you say, then, good lord, I doubt that all your walls, sworn men, or your personal skill could protect me."

"Our mountains will."

Rifkind looked up, her eyes betraying questions and curiosity.

"An-Soren has never moved against the mountain cults. The gods of our cults are dark, cursed beings, but apparently they are feared by the denizens of Vitivar. Though we at Chatelgard have nothing to do with the worship, we protect the pilgrims as they go up to the temples. An-Soren knows this and has never moved against this family. Old Hanju says he won't."

"Hanju?"

"One of the ancients up in the mountains. Sends us messages now and again."

"And one of those messages was that I was coming to Glascardy?"

Rifkind had guessed wildly on instinct, but the pattern she was building required a manipulator in Dro Daria, and An-Soren did not seem to be the one. Humphry denied her question several times, convincing her only that she wanted to meet Hanju when she returned to the mountains to make her new stones.

Lord Humphry rambled on about the future of Dro Daria and An-Soren's threat to it. She imagined the king to look like Halim, struggling weakly against the Dark Brethren and the strength of the clan chiefs. She felt no pity for the monarch, only further proof of the danger of weak men. She watched Lord Humphry rather than listening to him. His short, sharp and decisive gestures marked him as a man of action in his own specialty, which she quickly understood to be rivalry not unlike that both within and without her family. She also judged the Overnmont lord too old to do his own fighting.

The fire was dying down, and the drafts from the open slit windows became apparent despite her heavy cloak. Rifkind pulled her cloak tighter and sank farther into her chair.

"I see it is futile," Lord Humphry commented bleakly, seeing her retreat. "You do not want to understand our problem. I have nothing that will entice a barbarian such as you into my service. You see no immediate danger from An-Soren, and therefore no need to do anything about him. That is why you and your people will always be wandering.

"I can only hope that when you do find a reason to challenge him, it will not be too late for both of us. I could get you into the court—into his presence, where you could study him, learn of his habits.

Then you'll be able to strike successfully in your own time.

"But it would be foolishness to lure you to him. You do not feel equal to the challenge."

Lord Humphry pulled the bell-rope to summon the servants. He had made his final move against her pride and her people. Rifkind knew she had his limits, and it was time to reveal her own intentions.

"I could perhaps disguise my tal from him. Perhaps I could conceal the crescent completely. But, as you point out, I am an Asheeran. Anyone can tell this from the moment they see me. I have an Asheeran accent; I walk and eat like someone who has never been in your walled buildings. I am a warrior and a healer, two things which you discourage in your women. If you took me as I am to this grand court you speak of, nothing could protect or conceal me."

"You agree to try though?"

Rifkind nodded slightly. Lord Humphry's face brightened into a smile; he pulled the bell-rope violently several more times before returning to his chair. He twisted his beard through his fingers in obvious delight at having a concrete problem to work with, instead of the task of convincing a reluctant ally.

A servant entered the room.

"Attend to the fire. Bring a bottle of wine—a good one this time—and a tray of sweetmeats. Don't just stand there. Idiot, fool!"

The servant raced mutely away.

"Incompetents! Glascardy, I love you, but your clear air leads to empty heads!" Lord Humphry gazed up at the ceiling and continued to mutter to

himself before looking again at Rifkind, who'd been
watching him carefully. "It is the start of winter.
There are five months until we would have to be
back at the royal court. Yes, yes, even if I did go back
now to prepare things, Bainbrose and Anelda
would stay here. They can teach you everything in
that time; you must be able to learn things, though
you are Asheeran.

"We will say you are a distant relative. My wife,
rest her soul, had family in the valley. They were a
dark, swarthy lot, all of them. That's it! You'll be one
of my wife's cousins, I'll say I'm going to marry
Ejord off to you, in a gesture of friendship."

Rifkind raised an eyebrow.

"Oh, I don't expect you to take that seriously. Even
my wife's family wouldn't have Ejord—I don't expect you to. It's merely an excuse—a way to account
for your being at the court, attached to the Overnmont family, but not to me. It's a way of getting you
more freedom . . . I will have to bring Ejord along;
it's a risk we'll have to take."

Three servants entered the room; one rekindled
the fire, the second carried a small table, and the
third brought food and wine. The sweetmeats reminded Rifkind of the rich fermented meat deserts
of the Gathering feasts. The wine was full-bodied,
but she drank little while Humphry rambled on
about his plans for her reeducation.

The fire had died down again. Humphry had
called for maps and given her a first inkling of the
shape of the world. Their land was almost round;
the Asheera took up most of the interior of an immense island Lord Humphry called Dro Daria. A
ring of mountains separated the Wet-Lands from the
steppes she had known. Only in the area he said

was Glascardy did the fertilizing rains extend past
the mountain ring and ever so slightly into the
Asheera.

He named all the other territories which made up
the great kingdom of Dro Daria and Rifkind repeated them dutifully much as she had once repeated Muroa's first lessons. Her mind was
elsewhere, noting that noplace on the entire island
could be farther away from her original destination
of the capital of Dro Daria than the small dot Lord
Humphry assured her was Chatelgard.

When his discourses began to include the lesser
rivers and cities, Rifkind stopped him, saying she
was too tired to understand anything he was telling
her. She yawned broadly while he looked at her. He
called for the servants to escort her to her room for
the night. Her tiredness had sharpened her insistence that she would go to her room alone, and
thankfully Lord Humphry did not disagree.

The dining hall was dark and deserted except for
the ever-present servants. The table had been separated into sections, then pushed against the walls.
She took her bearings from the banners hung from
the ceiling and headed across the floor. Many of the
candles and lamps in the hallways had been extinguished, although the sound of talk and music in
various closed rooms told her the castle was still
very much awake. She heard voices at the top of the
staircase which connected to the corridor directly
outside her room. Out of habit, she slowed to a
stealthy walk.

The voices sounded familiar, but to her ears, most
Dro Darians sounded alike. Her newly formed al-
liance with Lord Humphry kept her from drawing

her sword, but not from slipping one of her small throwing knives into the palm of her hand. The sword itself, which had been a noisy encumbrance at dinner, swung silently at her side as she mounted the stairway, her body long accustomed to its every movement.

The conversation she could hear was meaningless gossip which gave her no clues to the identity of the speakers. She bolted around the last corner, clearing a half-flight of stairs in two leaps and had taken a long step down the corridor before recognizing the speakers as Ejord and Bainbrose. She had stopped almost before they had realized she was approaching them. The energies she would have used to meet the imagined danger left her in short, deep gasps.

Bainbrose had frozen in terror, his mouth wide open and one hand raised in a dramatic gesture. Ejord was surprised for a moment, but guessed what had happened and recovered first.

"I get the distinct impression you still don't trust all of us here."

Rifkind slipped the knife back into its sheath in a deft movement the pair did not seem to notice. Her heart still pounded; she remained silent. The weakness of her recent injuries had not fully left her. She had no desire to reveal it to anyone.

"I didn't know who you were. It's hard to get used to these twisting and turning halls. I guess I really don't need this." She gestured with her hand, letting the wrist-knife drop into her hand again.

Bainbrose had recovered enough to mumble "A knife—she has a knife. Just like that, out of thin air. I'm getting old, Ejord; I can't see things anymore."

Ejord laughed. "When I brought you here eight

days ago, the whole household was alive with tales that you carried seven knives. All anyone could talk about was where you carried them."

"Only seven? Your house servants are not the most careful people," Rifkind said with a meaningful smile.

"I think you will find we haven't advanced to the state where people bother to conceal their weapons. If it's not visible, it's not there. If you can see it, it'll be used."

Rifkind wrinkled her nose. "Only a fool would do that—a young fool; there aren't many old ones. There're always the last weapons. Everyone in the clans carries at least one, to be sure you don't die alone. I've never used mine—if I do, and I live afterward, I'll devise another."

Leaning against the wall, she set the knife in its sheath. Her legs seemed like heavy, yet unstable, posts beneath her; she wanted only to go to her room, lock the door, and sleep.

"Father took off with you after dinner; he was convinced he could bring you into the Overnmont household once he explained our problems to you. I feel bad for you, facing him so soon after you recovered, but I'm also curious. Has he convinced you to join him?"

"Before I talked to Lord Humphry, Bainbrose told me things which convinced me that as a healer and ritualist sworn to the Bright One I will have to approach An-Soren and think of him as an enemy.

"Your father's arguments are so much Wet-Land babble. He will teach me to act like a Dro Darian. I will approach An-Soren in secrecy. That is all that matters to me. I must see An-Soren; I must know what he is. If he is a renegade, I will destroy him for the Bright One, not for Dro Daria, not for Glascardy, nor the Overnmonts—you or your father." Weariness put an edge on her voice she made no effort to conceal.

Ejord shuffled awkwardly on his feet. "You're tired," he said at last. "Your eyes are red and you're shaking. Father's been after you all evening, and now me. I don't blame you for being angry. This won't mean much to you, but no one's ever stood up to him before. He's always right around here. Everyone jumps to his commands. I don't want to see Glascardy overrun or starved out. But if you do help us, I'm glad it will be by coincidence and not because he bent your will."

Rifkind nodded and walked past him; he stopped her with a touch on her arm.

"If there's anything I can do for you?" His voice was strained; a vague hint of his father's complexion appeared in his face.

"I just want to get some sleep."

Ejord dropped his hand. She headed into the shadowed corridor toward her room.

"I think I owe you some cider," she heard Bainbrose say to Ejord as they disappeared down the stairway, and she pushed open the door to her room.

The fireplace glowed with a recently kindled fire, and a stout candle burned on the table by the bed. Unlike the rooms at the inns she had visited in the valley, the castle rooms had no locks on them. She shoved the heavy clothing chest against the door. Even if she slept deeply, the sound of the wood scraping across the stone would awaken her. The bed coverings had been straightened, the nightgown folded and laid carefully across the pillow. She picked it up.

'I am to become a Dro Darian. I'll speak like them, dress like them; if I'm not careful, I'll think like them. I will do all this to spy on a man who might be a renegade from a revolt that took place generations ago. Is this the destiny Muroa saw for me? I have had no choice! No choice whether to leave the Asheera or to imitate these women!

'I do not want to give up my sword and wear a gown with sleeves that touch the floor. I fought for that sword; I don't think Lord Humphry has ever had a hand laid on him. I fought for that sword—if I hadn't . . . if I hadn't, I'd still be in the Asheera. And now tonight, without planning, I put all that behind me without a struggle. Lord Humphry didn't have to bargain with me—if he knew what I know, or what Bainbrose knows, he could simply have waited until I asked him. I will need his help to get into that court and make plans.

'No, not yet though. One last night I'll sleep properly, in furs, on the floor, by the fire. Tomorrow will be soon enough to become a Wet-Lander.'

Rifkind put the nightgown back on the pillow, then carefully lifted one of the furs from its place on the wall. The sword lay easily within her reach, the knives settled comfortably against her. The heavy black cloak was the only pillow or blanket she needed.

CHAPTER 12

"Right, right, skip, hop, hop, left. Lift your feet! Smile, Rifkind!"

Obediently Rifkind bared her teeth. Lady Anelda said it was a simple country dance, but Rifkind found it a meaningless jumble of movement. Her natural agility enabled her to wind up on the proper foot most of the time, but, as Lady Anelda constantly pointed out to her, she lacked spirit and enthusiasm.

Linette whirled around the room, singing the tune's nonsense lyrics. She had learned the steps as a simple country child and was obviously enjoying her advantage over the children of the castle.

Rifkind's own growing sense of frustration and anger was not eased by the knowledge that she was by far the oldest of the students.

"Rifkind! Left, left, hop, hop, *hop!* You're dreaming!"

'Right, right, left ... by the gods is there no end to this? First they got me a gown with a skirt that drags on the floor. I cut it to the proper length, and they told me I was supposed to be a "lady" and a lady's skirt has to be too long—the sleeves, too—or people will think I do something ... wound up tying thongs to the bottom of the wretched thing so I could get up the stairs by myself without tripping.

'Now this insanity. And if this is one of their simple dances, I dread what else they do to amuse themselves. Every night I've had to rerig my knives. I'm not going to jump around like this and not have my knives with me, or have them crashing to the floor. It's not healthy to whirl around for no good reason. If it wasn't for Bainbrose and the pattern, I'd probably think An-Soren was the only sensible person at the court.

'Bainbrose has been useful; he's got no concept of tal, or any knowledge of patterns, but he's got a good memory. The chant he remembered An-Soren using when he made the fire images was definitely in the Old Tongue. I don't doubt anymore that An-Soren is one of the Dark Brethren, but if he can use our rituals without the wrath of the Bright One reaching him ... well, the man is most likely more powerful than I am.'

The music ended, and brought Rifkind back to the present. Linette bounded out of the warm solarium with the other students; the musicians left almost as quickly. Lady Anelda picked up her needlework

while Rifkind looked out the window. An Ystra-
storm was blowing itself into oblivion. The second
of the season it had all but closed the passes until
spring.

"You seemed very distracted today, milady. It
must be very difficult for you—you don't have
amenities in the Asheera, do you?"

Rifkind turned to stare at Lady Anelda.
"Amenities?"

"Manners, arts, music, and the like."

"If you mean this dancing and singing—we don't
waste time on them. There are more important
things to learn or practice besides twirling around to
music."

Anelda shook her head with a sigh. Rifkind let the
subject drop. Lady Anelda was Humphry's younger
sister, a spinster who ran Chatelgard or whatever
other place Humphry called home. She had not re-
linquished her control while the lord's wife was
alive, and in the five years since her death, Lady
Anelda had assumed subtle—but total—authority
in domestic matters. Because of this, and because
Rifkind generally enjoyed conversation with the
older woman, she humored her. Humoring people
was a Dro Darian art almost unknown in the
Asheera, but one in which Rifkind was developing a
conscious proficiency.

"Lord Humphry has called for a dance this sennight. He has determined to go back to the court and
wished to see how much you've learned."

"He sees me at dinner every night. I thrash about
like any proper lady and sit calmly in a chair while
some stranger thrusts me toward the table. What
more does he want to see?"

"Much more, milady, if you are to convince anyone you've lived anyplace other than the Asheera. You are an accomplished mime, but your attention is easily diverted, and once that happens you become some Asheeran ger-cat again."

Rifkind smiled at the unintentional use of her childhood nickname. Folding her skirt carefully, she sat on the cushions near Lady Anelda's chair. The latest fashion at the court dictated that young women would sit demurely on cushions and wear their hair in thick braids. Lady Anelda decried the style as barbaric. Rifkind did not look closely into the good fortune which decreed that the otherwise-incomprehensible royal court would adopt the style of the Asheeran witch An-Soren had frightened them with.

"Very well then, a dance on sennight. How long does that give me? I can't get used to days that have no relation to the phases of the Bright One."

"Two more lessons ... it will be strange not having the lord here at midwinter," Lady Anelda mumbled almost to herself.

"I thought the passes were closed by now. Why would he want to go anywhere in weather like this?"

"Humphry feels An-Soren will tell Hogarth to move his armies in the spring. When we left for Chatelgard this autumn, we did not expect to return to Daria in the spring. No one had heard from you, or Ejord. Even An-Soren had stopped raving about a witch-menace. Here at Chatelgard, or anywhere in Glascardy itself, we can hold out. Oh, there's rabble in Isinglas and the other cities who support Hogarth or An-Soren. But rabble will support anything which promises them something they don't already have."

"Pretty strong rabble—a quarter of Isinglas was

ashes when I was there."

Anelda twisted her hands together. "Isinglas is a free city—it has its own garrisons of creatures they call citizens. Our word is powerless there. It is unpleasant for us, but Hogarth could never defend or supply Isinglas—a fact that rabble will discover if we ever have to prove their dependence on us to them."

Lady Anelda seemed to lack her brother's theoretical visions, but Rifkind found her grasp of the practical applications of power to be even more shrewd and ruthless than Humphry's or her own.

"Your brother's dreams for Dro Daria do not seem well-omened. An-Soren and Hogarth appear to have much ready strength by your own admissions."

"If we can defeat An-Soren, Hogarth will fade like a whipped dog. He should have met with an accident as a child. A loud vain braggart then, he's grown into a conspiring troublemaker. An-Soren needed a bitter fool from a good family, and nothing was more available than Hogarth—that his sister was married to the king sweetened the taste a bit more. If we destroy Hogarth, An-Soren will eventually find another to recruit and train his armies. But without An-Soren to control him, Hogarth is nothing."

"Why do you assume An-Soren needs someone like Hogarth. I would think the man's flaws, as you describe them, would not recommend him to anyone."

"As I said yesterday, An-Soren rarely leaves his tower at the castle in Daria. When a plague swept through the city and everyone else fled to the countryside, An-Soren locked himself up in the tower. It's not openly discussed, but I don't think the man likes open air very much. He's certainly not the type who'd travel through the countryside making speeches and reviewing the troops."

'Another piece in the pattern. Not a surprise, really. An-Soren may somehow be able to use our rituals, but he lives as they lived in the caves, without natural light. If he came into free air too often ... The Bright One knows no time; she cannot forget.'

" ... if Humphry can intercept the messages between Hogarth and An-Soren," Lady Anelda continued, not noticing that Rifkind's attention had wandered for a moment, "he can keep the king's forces as prepared as they can be. Oh, Darius himself is little help. He whines and moans that Gratielle spurns him. He hasn't even the sense to take a mistress. If he'd treat that bitch and her family the way they deserved, there'd be fewer problems. But Darius thinks kings have nothing better to do than be worshiped by their subjects. He doesn't understand that he must set an example, no matter what."

"Why don't you just get a new king? You're having nothing but trouble with this one. In the clans we'd challenge and kill anyone as incompetent as he is—or at least some of us would. You wouldn't have trouble with Hogarth if your chieftains were strong—as you said, he'd have had an accident long ago. An-Soren might still be a problem, but not as much. I don't know why you aren't planning to get rid of all three of them."

"Barbarians! All you Asheerans—you're all barbarians!" Lady Anelda snarled, breaking the silk thread of her embroidery. "No respect for the true blood. Darius is the king; he was born to it. There can be no other way. Darius has the noblest blood in all Dro Daria. It is his responsibility to be king and to get the queen with child. It is our duty to defend the king."

"Unless it protects him from death when he is wounded, the king's blood is no nobler than anyone else's. Rulers have to fight and stay strong. Darius is a spoiled child. My brother was like that; he's dead now. Humphry is probably too old—why not this Roubleard? Everyone seems to think a lot of him . . ."

"We're Overnmonts, not traitors!"

'And you're doing things the hard and dangerous way,' Rifkind thought angrily. 'If this Darius is the puff-flower you say he is, getting rid of An-Soren or Hogarth isn't going to solve the problem. Halim should have been born here; he would have liked the idea that being born assured him the right to rule the clan. Everyone here would apparently agree with him. I'd kill myself before I'd believe such nonsense.'

Rifkind kept her thoughts to herself with difficulty while she fumbled with the sewing which followed the women of Dro Daria wherever they went. Sewing, cooking, and children—all the things Rifkind had avoided whenever possible now surrounded her. The silence in the room became annoying—Rifkind knew she had offended the proud Overnmont woman, but resisted the Wet-Land habit of making peace at any cost. Without offering an explanation, she got up and left the room.

The Ystra-storm was abating—but a trek to the stables to see Turin, whom she had not seen since awaking in the castle, would still mean braving a powerful blinding wind. During the storm, she had had to content herself with tal-mind contact with the war-horse. She had made a promise to herself not to wear her Asheeran clothes again until the long gown felt comfortable. A walk to the stables or anywhere outside the castle was unthinkable in her old clothing in such weather.

She had discovered that people in the castle never argued with her except with stony silence, as Lady Anelda had done. They seemed firmly convinced she was both a nasty fighter and a powerful witch, and none wanted to cross her openly. The servants, especially, disappeared into the shadows as she wandered the corridors of Chatelgard. She wandered near the library where Lord Humphry spent most of his time planning the downfall of his enemies. The lord and Bainbrose were deep in a discussion of supply lines.

If she had not been aggravated by the thought that all their maneuvering was going to protect a weak and incompetent chief, Rifkind would have interrupted their discussion. They both listened eagerly when she talked about the swift-mounted harrying attacks the clans launched on each other and on unfortunate caravans.

Rifkind roamed toward Ejord's favorite haunts; the eyrie where the falcons were kept, the lesser dining hall and the out-of-the-way room where servants and Overnmonts alike gathered to wager on the outcome of cards or dice away from the prying eyes of Lady Anelda, who disapproved of all gambling. Rifkind had always liked gold and jewelry for its inherent wealth and had eagerly joined in the games, though all told her that ladies did not do such things. She added her winnings to a carefully concealed hoard behind a loose stone in her fireplace.

But the room was empty for the first time since

she had discovered it. Intrigued by any mystery which broke the boredom of life in the castle, she searched for Ejord down every hallway or staircase, opening each door she found unlocked, and a few that weren't. In a short time, Ejord was forgotten as she pressed her way down increasingly dusty passages.

'I should have brought a candle. Most of Chatelgard is actually empty, and has been for a long time if the smell and dust around here is any measure. They have so many rooms, they can't possibly use them all. Ejord said something about every generation building its own living quarters away from the rest of the castle. The Wet-Landers are perverse.'

Abused by months of daylight activity, her night vision was little use to her. Rifkind crept along the walls, feeling her way with her fingertips, remembering precisely the location of the few doors she did pass, but in the darkness she no longer bothered to open them. The murky atmosphere did not bother her, but a sense of uneasiness arose in her anyway as she went deeper into the unused portions of Chatelgard. She pushed it into the recesses of her consciousness, intending to ignore it.

But her uneasiness returned. The hallway branched to her right and left; a door lay directly in front of her. Without thinking, she grasped the handle and pulled it open.

There was no dust or cobwebs in the windowless room, but four braziers of burning oil, one in each corner. In the center of the room there was a statue similar enough to the one she had seen in the wayside shelter that she knew she had found a functioning altar of the mountain cults.

'The Overnmonts do not worship the mountain gods!'

Her mind's voice mimicked Lord Humphry's announcement.

'Ha! And what other lies has he told me, if this isn't an altar? Those bowls can't hold more than a day's worth of oil, and unless I've missed my guess entirely, that's fresh blood in the gutters there by the altar itself!'

Her uneasiness had leveled off since finding the statue; it did not increase when she took a step closer to it. She stood motionless for several moments, reaching into the dimensions with her tal. There was nothing, not even Turin. She was filled with a sense of soil and mountains. The room was deep beneath the rest of the fortress. The Bright One did not extend her rays into the bowels of the mountains; that was how An-Soren had survived—if he was a renegade. The mountain gods were part of the pattern she was building.

Rifkind pulled her arms into the full sleeves of her gown, finding the small pouch which held the moon-stones and the ruby. She knelt down, and, watching the stone eyes of the god, cast them onto the smooth floor.

Their clatter offended the stillness of the place. The flames flickered with their fall, but her tal still felt only the emptiness of the place. She stared at the god, waiting, then looked down at the stones. Nothing. She pushed out further from her consciousness and into her tal.

Cool dark silence. She moved deeper into the earth. Only the uninformed called them the mountain gods; those who knew better knew they were old gods of the earth. Mountains—the greatest visible extension of the earth—were their most sacred places. Deep within the stones the gods met their remaining worshipers. Those who knew—who had been initiated to the mysteries—knew that the source of greatest power lay not in the air, or the heavens, or even in the waters which covered most of the world, but in the soil which supported everything. The gods were old; they had greeted the first men at the dawning of time. They had been forgotten by those who remained.

She felt them watching her and prepared to withdraw.

He was tall, naked with a bronze-black skin that glistened as though coated with sweet oils. His eyes were large and luminous amber with split pupils. He was hairless but not withered, ancient but not old. His tal radiated from a point somewhere above his head. Rifkind lowered her head and shrank back from him. He smiled, slowly extending his hands to her. He intended no harm; he was welcoming her to his home. His thoughts wafted gently toward her, but she resisted them, centering deep within her own tal.

The glistening afterimage remained in her consciousness even after she had opened her eyes. She looked down. Two of the stones were his eyes, two his hands and the fifth his tal. With a shudder, she brushed her hand over the stones, gathering them into a small pile. He disappeared from her hand.

There were others now in the room with her. She recognized several of the faces as servants in the castle, but they wore long robes instead of the Overnmont livery and did not retreat from her. She drew her hands back into the long, draping sleeves of her gown, assuming the submissive hands-hidden posture of Dro Darian ladies while she stuffed the stones into her sleeve-hem and palmed a throwing knife.

"Rifkind, daughter of the Asheera, sworn to the Bright One of the night, why have you come to the altar of the Mountain God?"

Her questioner was behind her. She rose to one knee and began to pivot toward him.

"Do no move. You have stepped into the God's eye, offending him. Explain yourself!"

She froze, noticing for the first time an oval of thin brass that had been pounded into the stone floor near the altar. All the robed figures stood outside the marking; only she was within it.

"She has defiled the eye!" a woman sneered from her right.

"Witch or not, she is not one of us. She does not belong here. It is sacrilege," a man added.

"Her gods have no power here; she must be punished like the rest. Kill her!" another man added in a deep whisper.

"Silence. Explain yourself, Rifkind!"

"I explored the castle and found this room; it was not locked or barred in any way. There was a presence within it which I did not know. I cast the stones to learn about it. I have known the mountain gods before when Ejord led me through the passes. They know me; there was no offense taken by your gods."

Rifkind felt the certainty of her own words after she spoke them. Knowledge that the ageless, nameless gods of the earth had accepted her was as certain as her own initiation to the Bright One. The tingling sense of power swirled around her feet— waiting for her to direct it. The other initiates were arguing among themselves. She saw them as if they were tiny creatures far below her. She did not hear their words; their arguments were meaningless to her. The energies surged within her.

From the full strength of her energy, Rifkind stared back at them—they shrank back to the walls of the chamber. Slowly, deliberately, she turned to face her interrogator. He was as small as the rest—but different. She saw him as an equal. Unlike the others, he wore more regular clothes: soft leather breeches and boots, at his side a long, curving Asheeran sword.

An Asheeran sword! The curiosity which was Rifkind pulled back from the tal and the power of the mountain gods, to her own memories and consciousness. The energies dispersed with a sigh. With her own eyes she stared at the man, not believing what she saw.

The long blond hair, fair skin, blue eyes and the Asheeran sword worn as only a true sword-master could wear it.

"Adijan!"

"Ger-cat!"

CHAPTER 13

Her carefully palmed knife clattered to the stone floor; she bounded out of the oval eye and threw her arms around her old sword-teacher. He responded with a bear hug which lifted her off her feet.

"All these years, I thought you were dead! Halim had your head on a pole!" she gasped.

"I'm surprised at you, Ger-cat, as if Halim and all his friends could separate me from my worthless head."

He released her, pushing her to an arm's length away.

"You haven't grown any. That sword's still a good

hand span too long for you, and you still need that extra strap to keep it off the ground. But they've made you into a woman! My Ger-cat in a fine woolen gown."

He embraced her again, no longer with the soldierly embrace of comrades-at-arms or even master and pupil. Rifkind knew the difference and squirmed in his arms. She denied the knowledge or memory that the sword-master had been a young man when he had taught her to fight and was not old now.

The stunned cultists recovered, murmuring nervously. Adijan kept his hand around her shoulder as he led her out of the shrine.

"How did you find this place?" he asked when they were some distance from the other cultists.

"Just as I said. I was exploring the castle."

"There's no way to the castle from here. This path comes up in the stables; the other leads to a cave higher up in the mountain."

"I came straightaway from the castle. The corridor stopped in front of the door. The way was dark and unused, but unblocked."

"That straight passage comes to a dead end twenty paces back from the room. It's a false exit."

"I don't walk through walls, Adijan."

She followed him up a narrow, steep staircase which seemed deliberately treacherous. Turin's nearness bored excitedly into her mind. Adijan opened a hidden door, and they emerged into an unused stall. The chestnut stuck his head out of his own stall and whistled his welcome. Rifkind ran to him, and despite trailing sleeves and skirts, vaulted onto the top ledge of the half-door to his stall.

Yes, Turin, I missed you. How could I not miss

you? Do I have a truer or more loyal friend in the world? No, I couldn't visit you because of the snow and wind ... yes, the same as we traveled through up in the mountains. That's what you hear, that noise—that's the sound of snow and wind.

She felt his questions and distress, answering them in her own thought patterns, knowing that he would understand them as the emotional tones and shades of her mind. His soft brown eyes never left her face as she rubbed his muzzle and scratched the wide forehead between his horns. His sense of self restored itself in her presence. She felt him absorbing her, and in return basked in his loyalty and strength.

Adijan stayed a distance away from them until the excitement of reunion had been replaced with calmer emotions.

"I knew when they brought him in it had to be you. I'd been hearing about the witch. I never thought it would be you. Never knew if Muroa'd convinced you," he said, still standing a respectful distance from her.

"I left with her the night you ..." She paused at the irony of her memory. "The night Halim convinced me that you were dead."

"Those puppies? Five of them set on me; if one survived, it was my own carelessness and not their skill. You Asheerans—you can fight one another, or the unarmed caravaneers; but against anyone who knows what he's doing, you lack discipline and style. At your best you alone would have been a challenge, but your brother's minions? It was an insult."

"If I had known! Without you to back me, I was afraid. When they caught me on my way to my tent,

I realized I'd always be fighting and there would never be anyone to cover my back. Without you there was no one I could trust except Muroa."

"It was time for me to leave anyway. I'd certainly have been gone before winter. Couldn't take another season there. I took your father's war-horse and some of Halim's gold. Left that night. I'd talked to Muroa before; she'd always known what I was. She was the only person I could talk to for years.

"I'd told her to get you out of that camp if she had to drug you or tie you up to do it. She never thought the Bright One would accept you as an initiate.

"Guess she did; you've got the crescent. Wouldn't have made any difference. Once the tal rises, some god or another would have noticed you before long."

A vague sense of anger filled Rifkind as she sat holding Turin's head in her lap. The thrill of seeing Adijan was being eroded by a feeling of betrayal; he spoke of her as if she were little more than one of the horses he now seemed to take care of. Her hand slid absently up and down Turin's striped horn.

"You wouldn't have stayed with me?"

"Ah, Rifkind, you were a great fighter—smart, careful. I was proud to have taught you, but you didn't have a chance with that clan of yours. Maybe if you'd been a couple years older, but at your age—if you hadn't gone off with Muroa, they'd have killed you or married you off to some other clan. I took the war-horse and came back to Glascardy and the cults. I never intended to stay as long as I had anyway. Your father was an interesting man, until his accident.

"Muroa must have kept you with her until she got a notion that An-Soren was trying to raise Vitivar again. Always told her that you ritualists out there needed an internal defense or Vitivar would come back. You can't bring the power of one of the moons down without riling the other one. She finally came to believe me. I'll wager the two of you could take care of yourselves."

"I left Muroa right after I was initiated. I went back to the clan. The healer had gone back to her own clan, and Father needed help often."

"That old bastard held on for four years? What did you live on—dung and urine?"

Her sense of anger sharpened. Turin laid his ears against his head in sympathy with her.

"I stayed with my clan until the end. It was bad, and they'd done much that was wrong and foolish —but they were my clan, and I owed them that much. When the time came, I did not die with them, and I left the Asheera right afterward."

"Muroa didn't send you?"

"If she knew of An-Soren, she never told me," Rifkind said firmly. "When there was nothing left for me in the Asheera, I left."

"Word in the castle is that Humphry's sworn you to rid Daria of the old sorceror for him."

"I'm not sworn to anything or anyone except the Bright One. I'll go because An-Soren's one of the Dark Brethren, and as one of them, he is my enemy. I take what I need or what I can get from the noble Overnmonts."

"Why? An-Soren's no threat to you. Even if he takes a part of Daria for the worship of Vitivar, that won't affect you. Why get involved in the god's affairs? The only thing you'll accomplish if you defeat An-Soren is giving Humphry and his ideas a free rein in Daria. The struggle between the Bright Moon and the dark is eternal. But without An-Soren, there'll be taxes on everything—the royal finger in every pot. If Humphry wants his Daria so much, let him fight for it. Don't spare his hands the blood. Take Turin here and go up into the mountains. There's a lot of room for you in the cults. We could cleanse you of that vow you made to the Bright One —you didn't know better—and you could dedicate yourself to a god with some real power."

"No."

Rifkind shook her head while she stared at the stall floor collecting her thoughts. Finally she looked up and met Adijan's stare without flinching.

"The Bright One has been true to me; that's all the power I need behind me. I'll remain faithful to Her. When Vitivar rose, She was the one who cast him back—not your gods 'with real power.' "

"Rifkind, you know the ways of the sword. You're a fighter, not a mumble-mouthed chanter. The Bright One doesn't have the power or style for you."

"Perhaps you've changed too much since you returned to the Wet-Lands, Sword-Master. At least now I've been here long enough to know that you're one of them. Your temptations of power mean nothing to me, any more than Lord Humphry's did. I am not surprised at Humphry—he knows nothing of the Asheera—but you lived with us for most of my life. You should not bend so low.

"I have my own destiny—I'm secure and happy with it, and if I weren't, it would make no difference. If you had what I wanted, you would not have to tempt me.

"Of course you're right—I've killed in anger and pettiness as well as in just cause. I've even known your mountain gods, but that doesn't mean I'll turn my back on the Bright One or my own fate. I'll do what I have to do. For now I understand that I will find An-Soren. I'm told he knows of me already, so that should not be too difficult. If I am going to fight him and win, I'll need the help of the Bright One— not some nameless power which is a stranger to me."

Rifkind spoke with grim determination, convincing herself as much as the scowling Adijan. He called her a blind, stupid child, a toady of the Overnmonts. The sword-master drew himself to his full height, glaring at her disapprovingly. She had the sensation of another mind pressing against hers, encircling her tal, pushing her toward something she did not want.

For a moment, the idea of using tal to influence another surprised her; but when she recognized the purpose of his attack, she was repelled. The technique was not so different from controlling Turin's emotions or desires. She studied the constraints a moment. Indeed, he was trying to treat her like a war-horse, and now she was more amused than angry. She retreated before the pressure until Adijan, certain of his victory, dropped the curtain of subtlety and smiled triumphantly. With a shrug of her shoulders, she cast his presence across the stable. They stared at each other for several heartbeats before Adijan fully realized what had happened and looked away.

"Ger-cat, I had no idea!" He stepped back from her. "Rifkind, I'm sorry."

She looked at him impassively; his attempts had ultimately been too feeble to take seriously.

'He is no longer my teacher—any more than Muroa would be if I went back to the Asheera. Not because he did not stay with me at the clan-well when I thought I needed him. He did what he thought he had to do to survive. Now, though, he's trying to tell me what to do as if I were a six-year-old child again, begging him to convince my father to help me. I thought everything of him. He was different in his own way, and because I was an outcast, I idolized him. I've seen him again, and he is no different from anyone else—certainly no better. He looks so forlorn standing there.

'It must be hard to realize that you do not have the strength or influence you once did.'

"Adijan!" she announced, forcing a broad smile onto her face. "Ejord has said there was an arena in the stables where one could exercise and ride the horses in the winter season. Can we ride there? It's been too long since I've raised a sword against my betters."

"Ah, well . . . yes, there is; but milady, you're hardly attired for battle."

"I can run back through the tunnels to my room and get dressed. I'll be back here as soon as you can be ready."

"Milady, it has been a long time since I have used my sword. In Lord Overnmont's house I am not the sword-master, only the keeper of the stables. I have not fought in the Asheeran style since I left your clan."

"It has been longer for me; healers do not often go on raids. But, if you would rather not, I would not force you."

Though she would have enjoyed crossing swords with the master for its own sake, her only purpose in suggesting the match had been to break the mood of the stable. Adijan was still uneasy and embarrassed, but the tension was no longer building.

"No, I could not miss the opportunity to see my finest pupil. I'll ready myself and Blackthorn. He's the best of the lot, and Ejord's already been down to the stables today."

"I won't be long."

The skirts slowed her on the narrow staircase and the passageway was no longer deserted but patrolled by cultists who watched her pass with forced politeness. The entrance she had found to the mountain sanctuary was being bricked up. Rifkind overheard them whisper that she had walked through their spell-warded illusion-wall, and that the real one they were now building would cause the Chatelgard cultists considerable inconvenience.

Rifkind ignored their suspicions as she forged past them on her way back to the castle. Their suspicion hardened to distrust when she told them not to block her return; but it was a distrust of greater power, and that did not bother her.

The initiates were still muttering in the hallways when she returned in the supremely practical gear of a warrior. Though they might have tried to intimidate a tiny woman from the castle, they parted silently before the easy confidence of a woman who was both witch and warrior.

She entered the stable to find Adijan waiting for her. The sword-master's scabbard was dirty, and there was rust on the hilt of his blade. Averting her eyes from the disillusioning signs of her teacher's laxness, Rifkind walked by him and saddled Turin. The war-horse was excited by the prospect of the mock-battle; even Blackthorn seemed to have caught some of the excitement. Adijan spoke harshly to the big black as he led him out of the stable. Rifkind heard his tone and became unsure of the wisdom of the match.

They followed a wide torchlit corridor to the large dusky arena. The few torches lit along the sides of the arena gave Rifkind an idea of the size of the exercise ground, but the middle was completely dark. Such blackness lent an air of realism to their practice; most duels had been fought in darkness, preferably during the nights the Bright One hid her face from the sky. Rifkind vaulted onto Turin's back, claiming the far side of the arena as her own.

"To first blood!" Adijan called after her.

She stiffened at his challenge. Not that she had not fought to first blood before, or more often death itself—but never against her teacher. He had disappeared before he considered her training complete and she had never had the traditional graduation fight to first blood against him.

'He knows he has lost something. He thinks he can get it back if he can prove to both of us that he is still better than me. I've admitted that I haven't fought well for some time now, but that is different from letting my sword grow rusty; he must know that—he taught me how to rank my enemies.

'He can't be certain he will win, and he must be desperate for something. I never could read him well. Of course that doesn't surprise me now that I know he's an initiate of his own gods. I've proved he can't influence me now, but he can keep me away from his tal just as easily.'

Adijan was a torchlit silhouette slowly mounting the big charger. They paused a moment; then Blackthorn moved forward, and they were lost in the shadows of the central arena. Rifkind listened carefully, as she'd been taught, and used her ears to guide Turin into position. With a final thought to Turin that the battle was only a practice and he was not to use his horns against Blackthorn, who would have no defense against them, she set him on a collision course with the big black.

The war-horse's timing was instinctive and unaffected by practice or the lack of it. The instant the swords clanged above him, he pivoted on his hindquarters and propelled Rifkind and himself away from the others.

Adijan shouted that he had not been touched. They circled back to their sides again. In the twilight darkness, they swept past each other three times, each accompanied with a ringing collision of steel, and each to no avail. On the fourth pass, Rifkind had Turin hold his ground instead of leaping away. Long years of lessons returned to her, but not the split-second timing of the Asheera. If Adijan had not been more unprepared than she, her defense would have fallen and the bout been over. But she lured him into a broadly slashing attack that she deflected easily off the edge of her lighter sword—a parrying move Adijan had taught her—and forgotten.

He circled short of his side and drew a long dagger into his other hand. She saw it in the torchlight and drew hers. Turin could be trusted to respond smoothly to her tal-commands; Blackthorn could not be used to such things. She questioned Adijan's judgment even as Blackthorn charged down on them.

She held her war-cry until Adijan was committed to the attack. It was only a collection of meaningless Old-Tongue syllables, but it had the desired effect of terrifying Blackthorn. While Adijan struggled to control his mount, she pressed her advantage. She wanted first blood, and slid the razor-sharp sword along Adijan's sleeve. The sound of cloth ripping was audible even over Blackthorn's frantic squeals. She dropped back.

Adijan did not immediately acknowledge the mark, but then he had no small difficulty controlling the horse. He favored the arm—even cradled it—as they moved toward the arena exit on their side. Rifkind slipped the sword into its scabbard and took Turin's reins with her right hand, the parrying dagger still in her left. Adijan was not moving; she approached cautiously, but with her healer's duty to aid the injured foremost in her mind.

Blackthorn whirled around to face them as Adijan filled the arena with his familiar war-cry. Rifkind saw the sword-blade catch the light of the torches as Adijan raised it for a powerful and deadly cut. With disbelieving numbness, she knew the foolishness of her own trusting moves. Adijan had caught her, but his sword was aimed for more than first blood.

Turin was fast, but speed was only so much of the battle. It would not be enough this time to get them out from under the curving blade. The air itself seemed to restrain her arm as she lifted the parrying dagger into the best of the poor parrying positions available to her. The blades met; hers weakly near its hilt, Adijan's with full strength halfway up the blade.

The great bulk of the black horse crashed into the smaller Turin; he staggered back, struggling to maintain his footing in the soft dirt of the arena. The swords slipped for a moment. Adijan leaned forward, bringing his greater strength and heavier blade to bear on her awkwardly held parrying dagger.

Turin found his balance; she could feel the tensing of his hindquarters through the saddle. He would not need to be told what to do; she poured all her strength and concentration into keeping her arm in the agonizing position, raised high, bent and already quivering from the strain. As he bolted away, she threw her last strength into a desperate backswinging arc with the dagger. She ducked, Adijan's sword swished wide of her back, and they were clear.

Rifkind's time sense snapped back to normal. She laughed silently; there was no other way to celebrate her luck. Turin turned around in their corner; she reached across for her sword. Her right hand was moist and black in the torchlight. Her fingers moved, but she was not surprised to find that she had been marked during the encounter. She had been maneuvering to save her life, not the skin on her hand. Without being able to remember how the wound had come, she accepted it.

"Halt!" she called across the arena.

"First lesson—a fight's not won until your enemy's vanquished. You've forgotten everything I taught you, Ger-cat."

There was a coldness in his voice and he did not wait for her to cross the arena before riding Blackthorn up the corridor to the stables.

It was just as well. Angry thoughts, defeat and the pain of injured pride clamored for her attention. She was just as glad to ignore him in the numbness of battle fatigue.

Turin reached around and nuzzled her leg.

"But I fought well, even if I was stupid," she whispered to him. "He wasn't coming for first blood, and that's all he got—there's no defeat in that. He be-

lieved I was dead; I don't think he was very happy
to find out that he was wrong. I should have guessed
that there would be no going back."

Rifkind reached down to scratch Turin's muzzle.
The blood was still sticky on her hand. An old
blanket hung by the doorway across the arena, and
they made their way toward it. The wound had
brought no pain or stiffness, only blood. She wiped
her hands on the blanket; there was no sign of a cut
on her hand. Stunned, she looked at her sword scabbard; there were traces of red at its top. Withdrawing the sword itself, she saw the line of red left on its
blade.

There was no sense of victory in her discovery,
only a deeper sense of loss. She could not even get
angry with the sword-master. The unanswered
questions about his duplicity were shoved into the
locked corners of her mind before they could be
asked. It was sufficient that she had conceded the
match. He would have no desire to see her again.
She had no desire to see him either.

After she heard his footsteps leaving the stable,
Rifkind led Turin back to his stall. She sat quietly in
the manger staring blankly at the walls in front of
her. For once she did not retreat into the tal-mind
which would reveal everything in cold, abstract patterns, but remained in the confusion of her own
emotions.

Reddish rays of sunlight filtered through the
cracks in the stable walls before she stood up again.
The storm had ended; the sun was setting in a
cloudless sky. She was tired to the depths of her
being, but in the end she had found her own victory.
She didn't need Adijan to confirm her graduation.

She avoided the passageways to the castle,

marching instead across the fresh snow to the kitch-
en. The servants looked at her in silent curiosity.

The dinner courses were in their various stages of
preparation. She was hungry; she looked forward to
the rich foods, the intricacies of dinner conversation.
She hadn't seen Ejord or Bainbrose all day. And
Linette. Rifkind chided herself for neglecting the
pupil the Bright One had given her. As she mounted
the steps to her room, she resolved that after talking
to Ejord and Bainbrose about her discoveries of the
day, she would begin Linette's education.

CHAPTER 14

Rifkind bounded up the final flight of stairs to her room.

'By the Nameless Gods, I'm late! Linette's been waiting for me half the evening. But Ejord wanted to hear about my sword-training in the clan, and Bainbrose got Lord Humphry out of the way, so there was no after-dinner lecture on Darius the this, or Darius the that. I didn't tell Ejord about Adijan, or the altar beneath the stables, but it was pleasant, in a way, to talk about the Asheera to someone.'

The deep green dress she wore was her favorite among the new clothes Lady Anelda had had the

castle seamstresses refit for her from Lord
Humphry's deceased wife's wardrobe. Lady Anelda
had chosen it because it set off her exotic golden
complexion. Rifkind liked it because green was a
color she had seldom seen in the Asheera, especially
not the rich lush green of the wool dress. She had
loosened the severe braids she normally wore and
had twisted her hair in several soft loops held in
place with one spectacular gold comb. It was the
style of an Asheeran noblewoman, and the envy of
all the Chatelgard ladies, who looked properly civilized no matter what they did.

The elegantly molded Asheeran antelope crest of
the comb lifted out of the base to reveal a row of
envenomed teeth. It was too obvious to be a true
final weapon—that was the smaller plain spike she
wore in her braids. No one in the clans would have
doubted the true function of the comb, but the wom-
en of the castle had held it in their hands without
noticing the small pin which would release the
crest—and the venom.

Once in her room, she removed it carefully.
Linette knocked softly on her door as she slipped it
into the cache behind the loose stones of the fireplace.

"I came earlier, but you weren't here, so I waited
until I heard you in the hallway."

"I hadn't expected to be so long at dinner. It
seemed that Ejord suddenly developed an interest in
sword techniques that wouldn't wait until tomorrow, when I could have shown him."

"It seemed to everyone else that you'd developed
an interest in talking to Jordie."

Linette's habit of sounding and acting far older
than she was again startled Rifkind; she was grate-

ful that her Asheeran skin was not susceptible to the local custom of blushing.

"Why do you always call him Jordie? He's a man, a warrior in your own customs. You don't make up names for *me*, do you? Jordie—a name like that and you'd think him a child or an idiot."

"Well, it's certain that you don't!" Linette said with a teasing smile.

Rifkind's efforts at relaxation and contentment stopped short of a tolerance for any sort of teasing.

"Ejord is the only one in this castle who handles a sword well and practices with it daily. He hunted down the bandits who killed your parents, he fought to save both of us in the passes, and of all the Overnmonts roaming about this place, he's the only one the servants respect rather than fear."

Linette faced her squarely for a moment, then looked toward the window.

"What did you want to see me about?" she asked awkwardly, a girl again rather than a woman.

"Ah, well, in the Asheera, people like me—once we're on our own and finished with our own educations, we're expected to pass what we've learned on to others so the line will stay alive." She had not been sure how she would broach the subject. Linette's precocious comments, coming at the end of an already revealing day, left her feeling tongue-tied. "I'm not going back to the Asheera, and if I did, there's no one there—"

"You mean you'd teach me how to do all the things you do?"

Rifkind hesitated as Linette finished her speech for her. Her pause upset Linette.

"I'm sorry, Rifkind . . . I didn't mean to say that. I just got all excited thinking . . . You know so many

things no one else does. I thought for a moment that
if you'd teach me ..."

"No, you thought right. Even though the healing
arts are outlawed here in Dro Daria, all anyone can
talk about is magic of one sort or another. You've got
the intelligence—and I think the talent—to make
your way in the arts."

"If I do good, will I get that silver thing you have?
An' a sword?"

"The crescent won't come from me—if you merit
it, the Bright One will place it on your cheek at your
initiation. The sword is something else. I can teach
you how to read the life-forces; if I tried to teach you
how to handle a sword, I'd only be responsible for
getting you killed."

"Oh, you're wrong, milady. I learn quick. I'll
learn anything you teach me. I even learned how to
throw a knife back in Goat's-tail."

"Then that's enough. I probably wouldn't teach
you the sword if I could, but I'm completely serious
when I tell you I can't. You'd need a sword-master
for that." She paused again, remembering her life in
the clan after she'd won her sword. "The price of a
sword is something I wouldn't ask you to pay."

"But people step aside for you; no one dares to tell
you to do something they don't think you'd like to
do," Linette protested.

"If you watch carefully, you'll see they avoid me
whether I've got the sword or not. You can be
avoided as much as you like once you master the
rituals."

Linette thought a moment, then brightened. "I
want to be like you, Rifkind. You can't carry a knife,
much less a sword dressed like this, can you?"

"Of course not." Rifkind slipped a knife out of the

sheath she wore slung between the heavy wool out-
er dress and the lighter linen underdress—where
more traditional ladies kept their embroidery
needles.

Linette had never noticed the deeper slits in
Rifkind's skirts before. While the girl's attention was
fixed on the one knife, Rifkind slid the wrist knife
down into her other hand. Linette gasped with delight.

"You can carry a knife almost anywhere. But
don't ever let me catch you carrying something you
can't use—and I know what to look for, so don't
think you can fool me. I've seen my brothers get
killed the night they were awarded their sword. If
you carry a weapon, your enemies will assume you
can use it—and if you carry a weapon you'll get enemies sooner or later."

Linette nodded silently.

"I understand, I think. I don't think I'd ever want
to use a sword to fight with. Even a knife—except to
cut meat."

"Then I'll teach you the rituals and we'll leave the
blade-work to those of us who don't use our good
knives to cut our food."

Linette nodded again.

"Do I have to do anything special—like spend a
night naked in the forest?"

Rifkind tried not to laugh. "No, that's certainly not
necessary. I should be with you when you learn,
and I certainly couldn't teach you anything exposed
like that."

"That's good! I can learn right here in Chatelgard,
until you go away to the court in the spring?"

"We'll start whenever you're ready. It'll take a
while for you to get comfortable with the idea, I

think. I grew up with healers and ritualists all around. Every clan had at least a minor healer. We were lucky; Muroa was a full ritualist as well as a healer and my teacher. You'll have to get used to the idea that ritual empathy is powerful and controllable."

"Like you have to get used to dancin'?"

Rifkind grimaced. "I hope that dancing is nowhere near as powerful as ritual."

"It's not powerful, it's fun. Back in Goat's-tail, that's where Da's farm was—in Goat's-tail, until An-Soren came through and put his curse on the fields. When we weren't working at something, we danced or sang. Didn't do a whole lot of it, but they couldn't put a tax on't. It's fun. You never laugh or sing. Is that going to happen to me when I learn the rituals?" Linette hesitated, seeming to have sudden doubts about her education.

"I've never really seen anything much to laugh or sing about."

Linette was dumbfounded. "With all the things you can do? You can go anywhere you want because of Turin. You're not afraid of anything. You're rich. That thing in your hair tonight—I bet it was all gold. Even if it was gold 'n' lead, I'd be happy with it."

"Perhaps someday you can show me the 'fun' in this dancing and singing. Not tonight—I'm too stiff to enjoy this 'fun' of yours. I'll show you your tal."

Rifkind spoke in a tone that was intended to end the discussion. She reached for the pouch with the moon-stones in it, intending to lay them out in the tal-pattern. She expected her pupil to be properly awed and impressed by the impending ritual. Linette ignored her, far more interested in knowing how Rifkind had become too stiff to dance or sing.

Rather than talk about her encounter with the cultists or her duel with Adijan, Rifkind ascribed her discomfort to the morning's dance lesson itself. Again she expected the explanation to satisfy and end the conversation—again it didn't. While she hurriedly stuffed the moon-stones back into their pouch, her pupil began yet another round of instructions for the simple country dance.

"Ol' Anelda doesn't know anything 'bout dancin'!" Linette quickly reverted to her old speech habits when she was excited. "All that ol' bat knows is where ta put your feet. 'Smile,' she says, 'lift yer feet, ladies' an' all that rot. We don't do it like that. My sister an' brothers—they made things *move* when they hopped up an' down that ol' Anelda don't know she has."

Rifkind paced through the steps as Linette described the randier possibilities of the simple country dance. She had no subtle or polite way to deal with minor inconveniences like Linette's stubborn enthusiasm. Her strongest inclination was to tell the child to be still and pay attention to the ritual lessons. She could also remember showing Muroa the proper way to mount a war-horse, how to dismont from a gallop, and insisting that the considerably older woman try both.

As Linette reached further into what Rifkind found to be a surprisingly sophisticated vocabulary, Rifkind continued her faltering imitations of hops and turns. They went through the sequence of steps again. Rifkind could feel the girl's frustration and growing sense of failure as a physical presence.

"It's not working—I guess you *are* too stiff. Maybe

you should just show me those stones you got out before, huh?"

Rifkind nodded, relieved that it had not taken more than a slight pressure from her tal to enlighten Linette. She felt a twinge of conscience for using Adijan's technique, and for having gotten away with it. The twinge disappeared quickly as she reminded herself that another round of dance steps would have necessitated more drastic or permanent measures.

With Linette watching quietly, Rifkind drew back the drapes from the window and looked at the sky. The physical source of her power would rise sometime during the night—she could feel that much. But living within walls had dulled the delicate senses which would have told her when, or if, the moon's light would be reflected into her room. Besides, the sky was cloudy. She decided not to wait, although the results she'd been getting by firelight or sunlight were considerably less predictable than those from the Bright One herself; she wasn't trying to perform an intricate ritual, only to show Linette her own tal.

Rifkind laid the stones out at the points of a pentagram she drew in her own mind, its peak toward the fire. Linette knelt at its base. Rifkind knelt behind her, and realized she could no longer see the stones she had carefully laid out. Muroa had never told her how she would teach her own students, only that she would. As she closed her eyes, concentrated on the pattern that remained in her mind, and laid her fingertips over Linette's eyes, Rifkind doubted the wisdom of not waiting for the Bright One.

'Nothing. Not even a faint aura around the stones. It doesn't make any sense. I'm sure she's supposed to be my pupil—even Turin felt the attraction. He wouldn't have reacted to someone who didn't have any empathy.'

Puzzled, yet committed to teaching and learning, Rifkind brought her own tal forward. It appeared in a shadow image before the fireplace. Linette began to tremble. Whatever the girl was seeing, it was not her own vague tal. The only image within the pentagram was Rifkind's own, with her own clearly defined tal glowing above the eye-level of the shadow.

'She doesn't even have an aura!'

Rifkind fought a wave of panic. Even plants had an aura, and animals like Turin had a bright tal over their stomachs.

'I should go back. Something is wrong—totally wrong. I know what she is—I can't be wrong about that. She had to be a student . . . I should wait until I can examine her before the Bright One who sent her. If I was wrong about Linette—then I've been wrong about almost everything that has happened since I found her. I've got to be right.

'I can feel her eyes darting around. She's acting just like I did when I first saw my tal; maybe I shouldn't give up. I could move into my tal and look back this way . . . I could get trapped out there, too.'

Linette jumped, surprised by something Rifkind could not see or feel. The girl placed her own hands over Rifkind's, pressing hard against her eyes.

'There is an aura; Linette has a tal. The Bright One would not lie to me, even if walls and clouds keep us apart and the firelight plays games with me. I'm to be her teacher—I must not run away from this. I have to see what she is seeing.'

Having convinced herself, Rifkind made the ritual

transfer to her tal-mind inside the pentagram. Waves of distortion swept around her as they had in the lightstorm. Transfer to an externalized tal always brought confusion and risk. Other than at her own initiation, Rifkind could think of only three times she had been out of her body for any length of time, and each time then she'd had Muroa near to guide her back. Now she was Muroa to Linette.

Her body was visibly tense; she forced it to relax. Calmed, dressed in the Dro Darian gown and with her hair loose around her shoulders, Rifkind found herself to be a far different person than she had remembered. It was not a matter of recognition, but a sudden rediscovery of something she had not realized she had. She had always been a warrior first, even before she was a healer; the thought of being a woman as well had never been natural to her.

'Enough of this staring at myself as if I were some beautiful lady. I'm here to find out what is happening to Linette. I can always stare at myself.'

"Linette?" She whispered through the dimensions. There was no answer.

"Can you hear me?"

Still no response.

"Are you here?"

"I'm here."

The answering tal was not Linette's but some strange omnidirectional entity without a true focus. Rifkind had to commit herself totally to her own tal in order to know what had surprised her, and perhaps endangered Linette. She would not have been surprised to see the lightstorm chimera, nor was she surprised to find the bronze-black figure from her afternoon's adventure lingering just within the farthest reaches of her tal's knowledge.

"Where have you taken her?" Rifkind demanded with considerably more force than she felt.

"Her?"

"Linette, the one over there."

Rifkind, her mind now located behind and above her body, pointed down to the humming and swaying figure in the room.

"Her? She is where she is—I've taken you."

Rifkind felt a rising panic. She could not span the gap between her mind and her physical body. The distance was too great, and she lacked the necessary subtlety to avoid the stranger who was moving closer as they spoke. She knew she had been trapped.

"An-Soren?" she whispered.

"Do I truly seem like An-Soren to you?" the stranger said almost gently.

"Seem? Seeming means nothing. You say you've taken me. I have only one enemy who would do this. You must be he."

"But you already know An-Soren!"

"*You're* An-Soren," she said, retreating farther from her body as he occupied more of the room.

He smiled patiently, shaking his head. "No, you met him back in the place you call the Death-Wastes. He corrupted all the energies to get the ruby from you."

"That was An-Soren? That was how he knew I was coming?" The new information fit the pattern she had in her mind, but the stranger was still unknown, and she kept moving back, edging slightly for the fireplace and its chimney.

"For now."

"That's not an answer."

"That is true. If you want an answer, you must

come to the Mountain. Adijan is not the one now. Ejord, or some other, will lead you. Or you could come alone, if that was your desire. Then, you might not come at all. You don't need to have an answer. There are many paths; you are the one to choose."

"Choose what. Choose how to find you? Who—or rather what—are you?"

"Do not bring the child. She cannot choose your paths with you."

The clear detailed image faded back to the hard-edged tal-shadow, with the shimmering glow of his tal suspended above it. Then that faded, and she felt Linette in front of her. Her mind had returned to her body once the path was clear again. Skillfully she centered herself within her body and recalled the tal. The tal-shadow of Linette was apparent within the pentagram, its small, immature tal pulsing strongly above her heart.

Emotionally drained, Rifkind dropped her hands to her sides. The visions vanished.

"Oh, Rifkind, it was beautiful," Linette half-crawled out of the pentagram and grasped her teacher's hands.

"What was?"

"Oh ... I understand—I'm to tell you what I saw, so you can tell if I'm right for this or not?

"First I saw me, or my shadow, with a candle flame in the middle of it. Everything else was the same, so I concentrated on the flame. I saw a lot of me at different times. When I was back in Goat's-tail, now, and even a lot of me when I'll be grown. There was this beautiful music when I was grown up, and I was in another room with everyone watching me. I'm going to be a great lady—a lot more important than old Anelda!"

"Did you see yourself with an 'initiate mark'?"

"A what?"

Rifkind shuddered despite herself. "A mark. A crescent like I used to have. A sign of the Bright One, or the other gods?"

"No. I was always me."

CHAPTER 15

The window casement was tucked away in a hidden corner of the great dining hall. During the day, it let light into the cavernous room; at night, especially on nights when the great hall was being used for dancing or listening to music, the wide-ledged casement was Rifkind's escape. There had been nine dances so far; only the first, while Lord Humphry was still at Chatelgard, had been at all difficult for her. Since then she had perfected her imitation of the Dro Darian style and could whirl about the floor with any partner who dared to ask her. She had learned most of their more popular songs, and found among the more sober melodies several which stayed with her, filling the empty times in her mind with stories and legends of times she guessed would have been far more suited to a warrior-maiden.

Squirreled away in her hideout, Rifkind could listen to the sounds of the dance without anyone noticing her. Ejord, and more intolerably his innumerable brothers and cousins, sought to gain her attention at these affairs. If she would submit to it, she could dance each dance with a different Overnmont—each bent on demonstrating to his fellows, if not to her, that he was her best partner. She tolerated their attentions while she learned the very definite limits of her own sociability. She had learned that she enjoyed the company of Bainbrose, who had declined to make the arduous trip across the mountains in winter, and Ejord, who asked questions rather than talk about himself. But both of them were trapped in other conversations, and so she hid in her window casement.

"Your moon risen yet?"

Ejord stood at the entrance to her hideaway, blocking the exit. She looked up at him with undisguised anger—no one had ever interrupted her privacy before.

"Didn't really mean to disturb you. I've been watching you hide back in here for a few weeks, but now the rest are catching on. Harkness was on his way over. It seemed that, well . . ."

"You're right, I *do* prefer your company to his."

She noticed that he seemed surprised by what she had considered to be the appropriate "polite" response.

"—That is, when I can't be by myself." She turned

away, staring out the window, when he smiled again. "When will it be over?"

"Anelda's starting to look tired. Not much longer."

"No, not this, the winter. It's been so long since I've been outside. I'm tired of walls, I'm tired of all that snow, I'm tired of doing the same silly things day after day—up in the morning, dancing lessons, singing lessons, how-to-act-like-a-lady lessons. All with Anelda, which makes them seem longer, now that all she does is worry about Lord Humphry. By the afternoons, when I don't *have* to do *anything*, I don't *want* to do anything."

"You could spend more time in the stables. Anelda would never know. She has the same problem you do, and solves it by sleeping the entire afternoon. Keeping us up half the night with these amusements."

Rifkind didn't answer him. She had avoided the stables since her bout with Adijan. After that first day, she had found the passages blocked with fresh mortar and stone. The few times she had seen Adijan, they had passed each other with stiff formality. Turin protested and suffered in his neglect—his mind becoming more like the Dro Darian horses' because she was not there to constantly remind him of what he was.

"You're unhappy here, aren't you?" Ejord interrupted her thoughts again. "I've watched the others Father has prepared for the court—and you're not like them. You don't know, or probably care, that half the women of the castle would climb High Tor barefoot to look like you, since way more than half the men here would kill each other or themselves if you would single them out as your favorite.

"Anelda has worked a miracle of sorts. She's

found colors and cloth to suit you, and then led you into a compromise with yourself. You aren't the sword-carrying witch I brought here, but the proper image of an exotic sorceress ...

"But this bores you, doesn't it? You don't notice your beauty, only the walls. Have you ever been in one place this long?"

She decided not to tell him how long her clan had been pinned down to its last well.

"It's the walls—not just the ones here, but the mountains themselves. They seem to get higher each day. One morning I'll look up to find the sun, and there will be only mountains."

Ejord shook his head sympathetically, though Rifkind was certain he did not vaguely understand the feeling of vulnerability the double enclosure of Chatelgard and the mountains gave her. The Dro Darians measured their security in the thickness of their walls, while her security had always been the knowledge that she could travel beyond the horizon in any direction.

"What should I be watching for? A change in the winds? Anything that will tell me I could take Turin and get away from here for a day, at least?"

"It's going to be a while yet. When there's no snow in the keep, the downside passes are probably open again. When the vines by the kitchen put out flowers, then the high passes should be open."

Rifkind looked down at the rectangular keep with its hip-deep accumulation of snow and sighed.

"I'm a fool. I thought if I'd mastered those ridiculous dances and songs, Lord Humphry would take me with him when he left these forsaken mountains."

"Father has a plan, and not even you could

change his course," Ejord said with a bitterness which caught her attention away from thoughts of warm, open spaces.

"And you?" she asked. "Can you change your father's course?"

"I don't know—it's been so long since I tried.... I'm the fool." He laughed. "I thought if I taught myself to fight and hunt he'd notice me and see I wasn't a sickly boy anymore. But Father doesn't believe he has the time to look at something more than once. I was weak from colds and fevers—I would be a scholar. He didn't think I would be fit for anything more ... manly. He hired Bainbrose to teach me things which didn't interest him and refused to notice when I grew taller than my brothers....

"I don't know why I'm speaking like this."

"I had a brother, Halim—one of many. The gods should have delivered him to your mother's birthing couch, and you to ours."

"Perhaps, but the gods delivered me to Glascardy. Bainbrose knows I'm no student, but Father no longer even asks of my progress. I don't think he realizes that I run all the estates we have here. He creeps back here each winter to plot his moves and listen to his spies. He no doubt knows what the queen wore to bed last week, but nothing about our own harvest."

"Why don't you tell him? He is growing old. His face turns a violent color whenever his will is challenged. If he would look up, he would see the marks of his time on the stars. If you do not claim your rights from him now, who will speak for you?" Rifkind surprised herself with her hastily outspoken concern for Ejord and his future.

He shook his head. "No, I'm my father's son, too.

Perhaps it is just as well I was born here. My fortunes and his cross only here in Glascardy. He may wander where he wishes, and take my brothers with him, but I will remain here in Glascardy. When the people here think of Overnmont, they think of me.

"He left me nothing else, so I learned to love this land with its wild people and impossible mountains. He never gave me anything else, and he'll never take this away."

"And yet he's asked you to come to court and play the role of my betrothed?"

"It remains to be seen how long I remain in Daria."

Rifkind nodded, sensing that the brief moment of candor had spent itself and Ejord would quickly become the smiling, willing, open-faced young nobleman again.

"When do we leave for Daria?" she asked after a moment.

"Once the lower passes open up."

"I'd like to go up into the mountains again before we leave here," she said without facing him.

"We'll be leaving before it would be safe to go up there."

"Your father mentioned a magus named Hanju. I think I would learn much about An-Soren if I talked to him."

Ejord's face was transparently surprised.

"Hanju? What'd you want to go off and see Hanju for?"

"It just seems like a good idea. I think he has things to tell me."

Ejord thought quietly a moment. "Well, it might not be so unreasonable. Hanju did send Father the message that you were coming this way. He might have an interest in this, though it's hard to guess what it would be. I can arrange some sort of contact, probably nothing in person.

"There're people here in Chatelgard who have some dealings with the cults. If you come down to the gaming room sometime, I'll point them out to you. If it's possible for you to get up to see Hanju, they could tell you how."

"No, I specifically want you to guide me."

Ejord did not answer her, and after a few moments she realized that she was feeling the tingle of earth-energies rising through the stones of the castle. She had the strength, and more, to force the will of her desire upon him.

"Milady, Rifkind ... I don't know the way to the cult-temples. You could go there—but me, I'm no member of any cult. They will not trust me with the pathway to their sanctuaries. The cults are powerful and well-known, but they do not admit strangers."

Rikfind checked the energies of her mind and spoke calmly to him.

"You've said before that the shelters were for their pilgrims. Can't we just follow the regular trail?"

He shook his head. "There is no guarantee that they would meet us when we arrived at the last shelter; and if they did, even less chance we'd be welcome."

"I know we'd be both met and welcome."

There was another long silence in which Rifkind noticed that Ejord was unnaturally centered within himself and apparently unaffected by the forces which surged around her almost out of control.

"If you say that is so, I won't argue. Even without the crescent, you are a—you're far more than an innocent healer, milady."

Rifkind impulsively raised her hand to touch her cheek. The warm metal was still there, but hidden now beneath ritually induced skin. She had improvised the ritual and by the light of the Bright One, presumably with her patroness's permission, had brought scar tissue over the mark. It would not fool anyone who knew what to look for—but it was not intended to. She meant only to avoid the curiosity of the court, and hoped An-Soren would not suspect what he did not see.

"When could we leave?" Rifkind asked after a moment.

Ejord shook his head. "Not before the snow has begun to melt. If we went now, even if you had assurance we would be met at the shelter and guided on the last part of the journey, the lower trails would be too treacherous to travel. As it is, the paths will be unrepaired and dangerous."

"Then I'll wait until you tell me we can leave."

"There is a man here. I don't know him well; he stays in the stables, mostly, training our horses and avoiding us. He's said to have some connection with the cults ... some think he is actually the one who carries the messages. I'm sure if you spoke with him he could get a message up to Hanju, and a reply back, long before we could think of leaving."

"No, that's not the way I'm to go. I'll wait until a thaw, and then you will lead me through these mountains."

"As you wish, milady."

His formal tone cut deeply into Rifkind's conscience; she reined her near-rampant willpower again.

"You're talking to me as if you were one of the

servants. You can say no."

"Just now, here, you've been like An-Soren for the first time since I met you. I would not risk refusing you."

"There is no risk."

Rifkind had been absently watching the great hall gradually empty. Anelda had announced that there would be one more dance before the evening was brought to an end. Uncomfortable under Ejord's steady accusing stare, she jumped down from the window-ledge and headed for the center of the room.

"One last dance."

She thrust her hand into his in a spirit completely contrary to custom. Silently, radiating both confusion and anger, Ejord led her to the serpentine chain forming for the final dance of the evening.

In her seemingly endless lessons from both Linette and Anelda, Rifkind had eventually mastered all the court dances. She merged a number of her sword-arm exercises into the movements to create a personal style which passed for enthusiasm. All those who watched openly marveled at such skill in a barbarian. Ejord, who would play his part as her supposed fiancé at the court, shuffled clumsily through a dance he barely knew and plainly disliked. His face remained impassive. Rifkind discovered that he was as unaffected by her more gentle empathic overtures as he had been by her unsubtle pressures.

Her room was in a different wing of the castle than the family suites—Ejord made no effort to accompany her to her room when they finally left the great hall, although it was not unusual for them to continue a discussion of tactics until she reached her own door. Disturbed without knowing why, she followed him down the hallways toward his quarters.

"I am sorry, Ejord. I had no right to pressure you like that."

"There was no pressure."

"I have pursued a pattern I imagined. It is possible for me to bend others to my purposes. I fear I tried with you, and you saw it for what it was. You are the only one who has always treated me honestly; I am sorry to have betrayed your trust."

"There's nothing to apologize for, milady; whatever your intent, I assure you that I'm as untouched by your witchery as I am by An-Soren's."

Ejord opened a doorway, revealing a steep staircase. She had never been able to explore the personal quarters of the Overnmonts, and was curious about this part of the castle, but prudence overcame curiosity, and she waited at the bottom of the stairs. Halfway up the stairs, he turned to face her.

"It is a natural part of being what you are. You should accept that. I couldn't expect you to act differently and have any hope of surviving when you face An-Soren."

His voice was tired and made Rifkind frantic. She started up the staircase.

"It is not the way I have to be. It is not the way I am at all, Ejord. It is an ability I have discovered only recently—and one I would rather not have. Empathy requires that I feel what others feel, not that I force my desires on them. I will lose my ability to heal this way."

"No doubt empathy is necessary for what you call a healer. No doubt it's a good quality for any person. But you are not like other people, nor other healers. Whether or not you overcome An-Soren, you are more like him than you know; and I doubt you could be anything else, with or without the pretty fancies of the Bright One."

"You can't truly think that there is no difference between An-Soren and myself." Rifkind was more subdued than angry, but determined to hear all he might have to say.

He hesitated, then shook his head. "No, I don't expect you to send ghouls or specters through the night to suck the blood of your enemies, or make a spectacle of cursing some poor wretch whose shadow happened to cross yours—both of which An-Soren has done. But you could do it—and the reasons you don't have nothing to do with the reasons why *I* wouldn't."

"I wouldn't do any of those things," Rifkind answered. "I'm a healer; I don't bring suffering to others. I've sworn my life to the Bright One!"

"But it's always the Bright One—and never your own conscience—who determines whether or not you've brought healing or suffering."

"She is more knowledgeable in these things than any of us. Of course I listen to Her. Her voice is more powerful than my own. I would be wrong to ignore Her."

"And if she said to force me to take you to Hanju tonight—what would you do then?"

"She would never ask me to force someone against his will."

"*Something* did."

"No!"

"I felt it, Rifkind. If you did not summon the energies from the ground yourself, milady, then you should learn quickly to control them, or they will surely control you."

They had reached the top of the stairs, and Ejord had opened another door leading to an open porch on the top of one of the castle towers. Despite the cold, Rifkind paced the length of it, fighting the conclusions Ejord had forced on her.

"Ejord," she said softly, "how do you know about the energies from the ground?"

"I felt them surround you, just as they did in the mountains. I thought, both times, that you could summon them deliberately; now you say they came to you unbidden. I fear for you."

"Does An-Soren have this power?"

"To call energy from the ground? No, I don't think so. But it's been many years since I've been to court, and it's not likely I've seen all of his powers. I scarcely remember An-Soren. As I recall, he did not seem to have the ebbing and flowing of energy which marks you. He was always surrounded with something cold and dark, and always staring at me. I avoided him, as everyone else at the court did. Now I'm aware of him only when Father and the others return to Chatelgard each fall."

"How is that?"

He laughed. "It is not unlike meeting someone who has put on clean clothes without having first washed the odor of the stables off his hands and feet."

"And you feel this way with me—as if I were of the stables?" She was uncomfortable, cold, and did not like what she was hearing; but she pressed the conversation, hoping he would say something which would set her back at ease.

"If I did I would have left you at the inn, or in the mountains; I would certainly not be standing in this cold talking to you. At times you radiate a force which is similar to An-Soren's. Even so, you could not compel me to aid you—any more than An-Soren could. I agreed to help you because I think you are going to need a good deal of help."

Rifkind thanked him awkwardly and backed down the stairs.

The castle was quiet as she walked toward her own room in the far wing of the castle. The dual knowledge that Ejord considered her to be more like An-Soren than unlike him, and that he described himself as immune to both of them, vied unpleasantly in her mind. She knew she wasn't going to sleep that night. Her faith in her own rituals and patterns had been severely shaken. Even the Bright One's shining clearly through the unshuttered windows only made her more anxious.

Linette was waiting for her in her room. Their rapport had advanced to the stage where Rifkind could sense her pupil's enthusiasm for her next lesson several rooms away. The sky was clear and cold, the first night of the waxing phase of the Bright One. Rifkind back-tracked down the corridors to a different concealed staircase and reemerged onto the cold roof.

The wind had started blowing. Rifkind wished for her heavy Asheeran cloak, but had no intention of returning to her room to get it. Stuffing her arms into the long, trailing sleeves of her gown, she crouched in the shadow of the wall, her back to the moon. The place on her cheek where the silver crescent had been placed against the bone in an ecstatic moment of initiation burned with the cold. For one terrifying moment, she feared the Goddess had come to reclaim her. Then she realized that the new skin which covered the silver mark was simply—and normally—reacting to the cold.

Rifkind thought primarily about Linette, who still waited in the room some distance below the porch. The girl had taken to the Ritual Arts more readily than Rifkind had expected. Linette had developed an empathic capacity which exceeded that of many of the clan healers. Rifkind still found it difficult to observe her pupil's tal as it shifted and strengthened, and Linette continued learning explorations which excluded her mentor and from which she invariably returned saying that she was never anyone but herself.

Until Ejord had brought her to face the essential sameness of all the ritual energy sources, Rifkind had been excited by Linette's unusual progress. Now, as she shivered in the darkness, she doubted all the experiences and teaching she had absorbed since Muroa had spirited her away from her clan.

'The patterns, everything. I've always been so sure that there were such clear differences. That because I'd been sworn to the Bright One anything I saw had to be true and just, because she was showing it to me. I did not want to question whether what I saw was the truth, nor if she was the one showing it to me; now Ejord throws both into doubt with a few simple words. I've had an odd feeling about Linette all along; perhaps she was given to me as a pupil, but I can no longer guess by whom, or for what.

'Yet things can't really be different. The patterns are real—they don't change; only my understanding of them changes. Though now I no longer trust what I think I understand.'

Rifkind stood up, walking about in the pale moonlight, still with her back to the Bright One. She looked across the castle yard and saw another lone figure pacing the porch roof of a different tower. Ejord. As she watched him, she was aware of a solution to her dilemma. Ejord claimed to be unaffected by the forces which threatened to dominate and confuse her. As she walked downstairs, she decided that he would be for her what he had said she had lacked: a conscience.

CHAPTER 16

The single golden bellflower blossomed brazenly over the still-solid blanket of snow outside the castle kitchen door. The days were longer, if not appreciably warmer, and the wind did not cut so close. Linette reached for the flower and broke it from the stem.

"There was no need to do that," Rifkind grumbled, surprising herself with such sudden ill humor over a mere flower.

"I wanted it for myself—the first flower of the new year."

They stared at each other. Although Linette's lessons continued to progress smoothly, their empathic bond had weakened since Rifkind had resolved to have Ejord as her conscience. More than once Rifkind had threatened to discontinue the lessons, only to go back on her word when Linette made a temporary effort to appreciate those things Rifkind now insisted were important. It was a lost cause, and in a silent, brooding part of her mind Rifkind knew that Linette learned only what pleased her and was unconcerned with anything else. Rifkind feared that Linette was pleased by the powers that now tormented her.

"The first flower of the new year, and you pick it just like that."

Ejord strode out of the stables where he and Bainbrose had been looking over the new foals.

"No sense of the moment. Of course there will be more, but that was the first—you should have let the others see it growing. The Lost Gods know we've all seen enough of the winter," Bainbrose chided as he joined them.

Linette let the flower drop, then crushed it into the muddy snow. Rifkind grasped the young woman's wrist harshly, bending it backward with a subtle and excruciating twist.

"Put it back!" she snarled, releasing the hold.

Linette glowered, but picked up the remains of the blossom and held it gently between her palms. She breathed onto the now-concealed flower; when she opened her hands the blossom was whole. Holding the blossom in one hand and the stem in the other Linette brought the two together, again obscuring their union; she closed her eyes, seemed to hold her breath, and the flower was restored. With a black glance at Rifkind, Linette then turned her back on them all and half-ran into the stables.

"An interesting trick," Bainbrose muttered, studying the flower without daring to touch it. "I've seen all manner of dancing fires and talking animals, but that is most impressive."

"That was not a trick, Bainbrose," Ejord responded before Rifkind could. "That little demonstration of true witchery would get us all hanged back in the valleys."

"Oh." Bainbrose pulled back his hand entirely. "She's quite good, isn't she?"

"You're teaching her, aren't you?" Ejord turned to Rifkind.

"Yes, I show her how to do some things, if that is what you mean. She learns quickly, and no two adepts perform the rituals the same way—but I am as much a teacher to her as anyone is."

"You're a priestess, or something, of the Bright Moon?" Bainbrose questioned. "You folk have an apprentice system of sorts?"

"I attempt to guide Linette and hope that she will develop a devotion to the things which I believe. I would like to see her bound to the Bright One at her initiation. But I do not bind her to anything, and the Bright One does not reveal her choice until the initiation."

"A bit risky, isn't it? Teaching her all these things, when it seems that you already resort to physical force to control her, and cannot count on your own goddess for help. Oh, I'm sure you can handle her, but what about the rest of us when you aren't around to watch her?" Bainbrose said solemnly.

His question hit deeply into an area which was tormenting Rifkind. A torment aggravated by her own conviction that Linette did not spend her time in the stables grooming her new pony. Turin had already confirmed that Linette spent little time with the pony, criticizing her in his own way for neglecting one of his kind. Turin had no certain knowledge of where Linette *did* spend her time, but Rifkind attributed much of the girl's precocity to additional lessons which Adijan was supplying at the underground cult-altar.

"If I stopped teaching her there would be no way at all for me to influence her development. Rituals are not the fixed set of rules and lines which the priests repeat for the people in the temples. They are a way of seeing and thinking. A person who has the ability needs only to imagine that something is possible to develop the ritual to do it."

"And in Linette's case, you tell her what is not possible?"

Rifkind nodded reluctantly.

The sun had retreated behind the clouds, and the brief spell of spring was replaced with the familiar cold of winter storms. They headed back to the castle.

"When will we be leaving for court?" Rifkind asked.

"Maybe a week, probably a bit longer; this is an early thaw. It's hard to say. We're still waiting for Father's signal," Ejord replied.

"Oh, we got that in the last message," Bainbrose corrected him.

"That?" Ejord grimaced in disbelief.

"What?" Rifkind added.

"Oh, Father's last message was filled with the court menus. He told us everything he'd eaten for the past three days, how much, and whether it had set well in his stomach afterward."

"It was a cipher, Ejord," Bainbrose said with strained patience. "Lord Humphry suspected no one would guess. We'd worked it out between us before us before he left; he was very worried about getting any important information out of Daria."

Ejord's features tightened. "Why wasn't I told?"

His voice had an unfamiliar icy tone to it. Bainbrose stepped backward, visibly at a loss for words in the face of Ejord's anger. Rifkind had long suspected there was more to the easygoing Ejord than met the eye. She watched, waiting and measuring.

"We didn't think you'd be interested," Bainbrose stammered after a too-long hesitation.

"Who thought—you, Anelda, my father? Why doesn't anyone ask *me*? When I ask to be kept informed, who is to say I am not interested in these ciphers you and Father have made up. With Father gone, and my brothers going to the armies instead of court—I'm going to be responsible for getting you, Anelda, and Rifkind to Daria safely. Don't you think I should know whether or not it is someone's considered opinion that I haven't the mind to understand these subtleties!"

"It was an honest mistake, milord."

Ejord's anger vanished almost as quickly as it had surfaced. His face began to relax; the white-knuckled tension in his hands eased.

"I know, Bainbrose—it's not your fault—it's not even Anelda's.... Can you tell me what all those meals meant?"

"We made up a sort of alphabet based on food. I take certain of the foods Lord Humphry mentioned and construct the true message."

"And the true message was?"

"That we are to come as soon as possible. Your

father feels that Hogarth is already moving his armies toward the capital despite the winter, which is apparently mild this year. He feels that everything will be over by arbortide, and unless he is able to stop Hogarth and An-Soren by then . . . well, there will be little any of us can look forward to."

"What has the magician been up to this winter?" Ejord asked casually.

"No word in this message, but in the last one—we used women for that code, if you recall—the lord reported that An-Soren has been connected with particularly violent storms which have all but isolated several parts of the realm for some months. He is also suspected of causing a virulent disease to break out among the king's soldiers, killing many of them and hindering their proper training."

"That sounds like Lord Humphry. It also sounds like the sort of excuses everyone makes when the uncontrollable disappoints them," Rifkind interrupted. "I have yet to hear anything about An-Soren which demonstrates more than an ability to ride with his own luck."

"The storms are no doubt natural, but the pestilence is his, I think, milady. The lord described it a madness which struck of a single evening and caused normally brave men to run naked from their beds and rip themselves apart in the moonlight. Those few who survived that first night have been passing the disease along to their fellows. It was only by total isolation of the regiments that the plague was contained. I'm no healer, as you are; but I've earned my keep with potions often enough, and I know of no mortal sickness which moves so."

Rifkind nodded slowly.

They had reached the great hall, the fireplace

blazing with the afternoon fire though the room was empty. They dragged chairs from along the walls where they had been pushed for the evening dances and set them near the fire.

"When will we be leaving then?" Rifkind asked.

"Oh, most likely in about two weeks. There could be one last Ystra-storm even now. The snow wouldn't last, but I wouldn't suggest we leave before the Bright Moon reaches full phase. Would be nothing but folly to leave early and get trapped in the southern passes, or worse," Ejord answered.

"Have you told Anelda? I believe she expects we'll leave this fifth-day," Bainbrose questioned.

"No. I'll tell her at dinner then. She could never be ready in four days, Bainbrose; it will take her a week at least to prepare herself and leave instructions for everyone. I know my aunt."

"Not this time, Jordie. Lord Humphry insisted we leave as much behind as possible, for speed on the roads and to conceal our departure as long as possible. She will have little to prepare for herself, and I believe she has long since given instructions to the majordomo for the house in our absence. Her mind is already in Daria."

"Ejord, don't we have a journey to take sometime soon?" Rifkind raised one eyebrow for emphasis.

Bainbrose saw the gesture, interpreted it as a request for privacy, and discreetly left the room as Ejord answered, "You still want to see Hanju?"

"More so now than when I first asked you."

"Linette? Do you think it would be wise to introduce her to the Old Man in the mountains?"

"No, I'm not planning for her to accompany us. I don't think she would even if I asked her to, and if I insisted it would only be another battle the whole journey—with no predicting how she would act once we got there. In fact, I don't plan to tell her at all. If Adijan knows, he can tell her."

"What happened between you and Linette anyway? Back before midwinter, she all but idolized you; and now, well, it appears that you are locked in some sort of struggle. Is this the way apprentices are usually taught?"

"I'm not sure. Muroa and I argued often, but always about such things as why I had to lay the fire and catch our game. Perhaps that's what I did wrong. I thought I should treat Linette more as an equal than Muroa ever did me. Now she doesn't want to listen when I tell her how things have to be."

"Linette's not surrounded by the same things you are. I should have told you this before—I've known it since the night we fought the Mountain Men. I don't think it's your fault or hers. I'll wager she doesn't need to know the things you do—and you wouldn't have the vaguest idea how to teach her if she did ask you for what she'll need."

Rifkind got out of the chair and began dragging it back to the wall. "For someone who knows nothing of the Ritual Arts, you speak rather presumptuously."

"Too close to the mark, there, eh? I said I was immune to your so-called arts. But I'm very much aware of them. Think about it—do you think there's anyone else here, including my father, who is sincerely convinced that you are what you claim to be and not some sort of fraud? The others do not know what 'magic' is real and what is not. I can see some things far more clearly than you—simply because they can't affect me."

Rifkind looked back over her shoulder at him.

"I dislike these large rooms—give me the open sky or a small tent, but nothing like this. There're several hours until dinner—can we find someplace else to talk?"

Ejord appraised her slowly. "The library, perhaps. It has only one entrance and is almost cramped by these standards."

She nodded and they went up the narrow stairway to the room where she had first talked to Lord Humphry. Rifkind shut the door and slid the heavy bolt into place.

"There is no point to all this. It's all false security —either there's nothing to worry about, or there's nothing to be done about it."

She walked around the edge of the room once before sitting in the large leather chair, aware that Ejord was watching her every move. "When I asked you to guide me to Hanju, you suggested I speak to a man in the stables—whom did you have in mind?"

"Adijan."

"What do you know of him?"

"He is an incomparable trainer of horses. When I was a child, our riding stock were little more than groomed plow-horses. Adijan came back a few years ago and now it's no boast that the Overnmont herd is one of our most valuable possessions. We can sell a good stud for more than we collect in a year in taxes from the valley. You've seen Blackthorn: he's one of the first—but in all of Dro Daria there's no finer mount."

"I'd take Turin any day," she replied testily, thinking of her bored, fretting war-horse, who had not enjoyed his long winter confinement at all.

"Of course—Turin is attuned to you as none of our horses could be, and your whole mounted style depends on his abilities as well as your own, but if you could use Blackthorn's strength as you use Turin's quickness and agility, I think you'd find the differences minimal."

"But Turin was bred for empathy, it would be impossible to establish empathy with Blackthorn— no disgrace to him."

"Not impossible, just difficult. Turin was also bred to trust one person above all, was he not?"

Rifkind nodded in agreement.

"Blackthorn was bred and trained by Adijan. I've seen what amounts to your empathic bond between them."

Ejord spoke as if that settled the matter without raising any other questions. Rifkind found the new questions sufficient to press for more information.

"What else do you know about Adijan?"

"I've always guessed he spent some of the time he was gone in the Asheera to learn how your people bred your horses. But I don't know what he did before he showed up here to supervise the stables, nor what he did to learn his secrets. He came back, and the next year, the brood mares produced foals like we'd never seen before."

Ejord looked up at her. "Yes, and I know he's a priest of the cults and has a following and an altar set up somewhere around here. He's got all manner of designs and purposes—but as I've said, the mountain cults won't bother us."

It was a phrase he'd used before, but not since she had learned of his unique gift. What had once seemed the idle over-confidence of an independent youth now hung in the air with implied import and power.

"I think Adijan is influencing Linette away from me and the Bright One."

Ejord chuckled. "Why would he do that?"

"Adijan knew me as a child. At first I was over-joyed to find him here; he was surprised, but not overjoyed. We had a practice duel, Asheeran style, and he tried to kill me—I think because I refused to abandon the Bright One for his cults."

Ejord stared into the empty fireplace while Rifkind experienced the frustration of knowing he was thinking about her, but without being able to get any empathic handle on those thoughts.

"Our Adijan, here, fought an Asheeran-style duel with you. Now that is interesting—not particularly useful or important, but interesting. Adijan, who adamantly refuses to carry even a short sword when he goes into the mountains to tend the herds, fought well enough to give you the impression that he was trying to kill you . . . well, Adijan's a mystery that's existed all my life—surely it will wait until next year when we get back from court. He's taken more than a passing interest in Linette—you're right there. I can see his influence over her."

Rifkind pounded her fist into her palm.

"Now, milady, you can't control Linette; but we all agree that she's got to be controlled and taught how to control herself—so why feel defeated if Adi-jan can provide the control and guidance you can't. And anyway, you won't be having much time for apprentices once we reach the palace."

"I worry about her, she's my responsibility. I started her along this path."

"If Linette is going to have a measure of greatness, she'll have it no matter who teaches her—all anyone really has to teach her, according to you, is control; the rest she'll learn on her own. You and An-Soren play with forces that dwarf Adijan's best efforts with the horses, but even he could put a stop to her if she needed to be stopped. I've watched him cull the herds."

"You don't think there's any danger in leaving Linette here with him?"

"I don't know what his personal feelings are toward you, as a woman or as a ritualist, but Adijan answers directly to Hanju. Hanju up there in the mountains could organize the cults, and the likes of An-Soren, or you, would fall like autumn leaves. For some reason though, the Old Man never leaves the mountains or gets involved in what happens beyond them. No one can begin to understand him, and apparently no one has seen him in generations. I know the mountains better than Adijan or any ten other cultists put together. There is nothing to fear from Hanju, and as long as Hanju is in the mountains, there is nothing to fear from Adijan or Linette."

"Do you fear An-Soren?" Rifkind asked.

"Or you? Yes, because the essence of your energy is very different. Were it not that I feel you will need help, I would not go to Daria for this confrontation."

"Will you take me to see Hanju before we go to Daria?"

"I said I would."

"Tonight?"

"If that is when you want to leave."

Rifkind nodded.

CHAPTER 17

Turin was nervous. Winter in the quiet, darkened stable had left him anxious and easily excited. His neck was streaked with foam and sweat even before they were out of sight of Chatelgard. He tossed his head and shied at every rock or shadow.

Rifkind could easily have forced her emotions and intelligence into his mind and calmed him. In his eight winters in the Asheera, he had never become so nervous. She had delayed their departure until morning rather than take him onto the treacherous mountain trail at night. Without thinking, she laid her hand on his neck to calm him. She had always let him readapt to movement at his own speed. She left him alone now.

Ejord was having similar problems with Blackthorn, compounded by the black's greater size and strength, and the absence of tal-control altogether. There was no conversation as Ejord led the way along the narrow and still icy mountain trail.

The sky was clear though the air was more like winter than spring. Great icicles still hung down from the tall rocks, and the shadowed crannies of the trail were deep with snow. The sense of danger settled both horses and riders quickly. Rifkind forgot her worries about Linette in her constant watch for the one ice-filled crevasse which would send them careering down the mountainside when they crossed it.

"We left too soon, milady—another few days," Ejord called back over his shoulder as Turin's rear hoof dislodged a head-sized rock that clattered down the slope, gathering companions as it fell.

"We've waited half the winter; we'll get through this."

Rifkind had forced an extra note of assurance and casualness into her voice. Turin was openly disturbed by the unsteady footing. He was no longer skittish but would have refused to go one step farther if Rifkind had not insisted on it.

"We'll get through all right—will we get back? These high trails change from year to year. The cults have some secret way of repairing them. If we miss the sanctuaries, or are not welcome, we'll have made a fair disaster of our escape route."

"If the clans haven't been down to fix the trails yet, we have a better chance of finding Hanju in his tent," Rifkind replied determinedly.

"Aha, you *are* nervous! Tents, clans. Hanju's probably never seen a tent in all his life!"

Rifkind stiffened silently. She had not expected her anxiety to be betrayed by a lapse into Asheeran idiom or logic. The treacherous pathway and their uncertain reception by Hanju had served as a welcome distraction from her concern with Linette, Adijan, and An-Soren, but neither set of cares relaxed her.

Ejord had meant only a sort of grim levity, but she found that his triumphant tone reminded her of the quarrel she had had with Linette after her decision not to leave Chatelgard until morning.

"I can make anything I want," Linette had sneered.

"You are working with life-forces—do you understand that? It is forbidden to destroy or pervert an existing life-force to create another. We can transform lower existences to higher ones, or restore things to their proper form—that is the only way."

"Or what? I'll be shriveled up by the light of some moon goddess? You don't understand anything about power, Rifkind; you don't have any imagination. You just do what you've been told, like all the Asheerans do. The cults know better than that."

"Does Adijan tell you about the cults and the Asheera?" Rifkind had demanded. "Do you find what he has to teach more interesting?"

With that comment, Linette had drawn a long, slim knife from a concealed placket in her dress. She held it carelessly. The girl was a menace to herself and anyone near her, as well as a dishonor to a finely wrought blade.

"He says I'll make an excellent swordswoman. I'm as big and strong as any youth my age. He says I'll be a ger-cat."

Rifkind forced herself to maintain control, even though her supposed pupil stared at her with a hard defiance which Rifkind felt was certain proof that Adijan had revealed some, if not all, of his experience with her clan. It was over. Adijan's indiscretions were disturbing, but if Linette believed them, Rifkind could not justify arguing with her. Any attempt to dispel Adijan's influence over her would only jeopardize the girl's future with the gods more than it had been already. Her mind was settled, but her pride did not quiet so easily.

"A ger-cat does not waste its time showing off its claws and fangs. Its strongest weapon is its intelligence—that is why even the other hunters fear it."

With that she had left Linette, and spent the night in one of the chairs in the library. Her weaponry and ritual articles were guarded by wards she had devised since she no longer wore her Asheeran clothes and could not carry many of the things she once had.

'It was the only way.'

Rifkind spoke softly to herself as her thoughts returned to the icy trail.

'Adijan has only the personal flaws of any man. If his teachings lead her to the mountain cults rather than the Bright One—well, it is far better than having her as a battleground between us. Linette is not a child, nor even the sick and frightened orphan I found upon the road. She is as much a woman as I was when I left to study with Muroa—Adijan will not dominate her any more than Muroa ruled me.

'And as Ejord said, it is for the best. I won't have time for her; I can't divide my attentions now that it's time to deal with An-Soren. This task of teaching has been more difficult than I had imagined. I know

I was headstrong and stubborn, but I do not remember Muroa ever looking as tired as I feel.

'Ger-cat! Damn that, though; you can't make a warrior out of a woman who has herded pigs and goats all her life. I am the ger-cat.'

The force of her determination had caused Turin to halt suddenly. The sun had begun to sink in the sky. With a certain sense of embarrassment, Rifkind realized she had spent the greater part of the day's journey lost in her own thoughts, totally ignoring Ejord, who was now looking back at her with concern.

"Something wrong, there?" he asked, preparing to turn Blackthorn on the narrow trail.

"No."

"Worried about Linette? You're taking that too hard, milady. I know little of what is needed to make a good healer like yourself, but Linette's a Darian farm-girl. She'll never develop the subtlety or skill that you, An-Soren, Hanju, and the others have. Whatever there once was between you and Adijan, don't let it blind you to Linette. Besides, she's a fair wench; Father would not have lavished such attention on her unless he had a place in mind for her at court."

"I have no dealing with Adijan, except to know he is a priest of the mountain cults," Rifkind retorted while noting Ejord's implication that Linette would be accompanying them to court.

"He's been heard to brag of late that he taught you what you know about swords and knives. He's well into his cups when he says things like that, so no one much believes him. There are a lot of rumors and mysteries about our stableman, and there's no doubt he's been a changed man since your arrival."

"He remembers, that's all. He used to ride with the caravans. I suspect he left a part of himself in the Asheera. It would not be surprising."

"You would know better than I. He's become grim and haunted, as if an old wound had turned septic. I think he takes little comfort in us or the cult. You may just remind him of something; then again, perhaps there is something to Linette herself, though I do not personally fancy her."

"The gods perpetuate their worship by inciting the initiates to take on students."

Ejord reined Blackthorn abruptly and turned about in his saddle to face her.

"A man generally does not need prodding from the gods to take an interest in a willing wench."

Rifkind felt the warm prickly sensations of embarrassment on her face and neck. Linette had ceased being a child the moment she'd redesigned the gowns Anelda had given her, taking in the sides and slashing the necklines to reveal her well-developed breasts. Rifkind was unconcerned with Linette's obvious maturity, except that it was an unwelcome reminder that by either Dro Darian or Asheeran standards she was long past her own childhood, but not yet a woman. And Ejord was a man, just as Adijan was.

Fortunately, Ejord seemed to consider the con-into a compromise with yourself. You aren't the course along the trail. As it grew darker and colder, the ice runoff in the shadowed crevices froze. Ejord's shoulders settled into the fixed rigidity she had come to equate with worry and concern. They had covered far less ground than they had expected to. The sky had clouded over, and though she would not admit it, even to herself, Rifkind was more nervous than she had been in the Death-Wastes before the lightstorm.

"We've made it!" Ejord shouted back to her, springing down from Blackthorn's back. "And it's intact. I was afraid the Mountain Men would have gotten to all the shelters during the lean months."

Rifkind swallowed hard; until he had mentioned it, she had not considered the possibility that their shelter might be another ruined rampart. Ejord had shoved the door open by the time she had dismounted. A damp, fetid odor seeped out of the small shelter. The dim light of the twilight behind them was enough to reveal that the straw had already begun to rot and the stores of meal and water would be unusable. Her elation on seeing the shelter quickly faded.

"We're in luck," Ejord announced, to her disbelief.

"It is better than sleeping on the rocks, but no matter what you've heard of the clans, I'm not accustomed to living like this."

"Neither am I," he snapped back. "We're lucky because the cults haven't been down to restock the shelters. There's a good chance we'll meet them along the way. It will make things easier for us. I would sooner face their suspicion than the last sections of trail without a guide."

Rifkind nodded and began kicking the decayed straw out the door. They were traveling with adequate food for themselves for the three days Ejord had predicted their journey would take. They carried some grain for the horses, which they mixed with the best of the meal from the barrels. Neither Turin nor Blackthorn seemed to find it objectionable.

The idol in the corner was different from the ones

she had seen in the other shelter and in Adijan's underground sanctuary. A profoundly distorted female, it was giving birth to something even more grotesque than itself. Rifkind found the figure repellent and set it at an angle so that she did not face its blind grey eyes. She slept fitfully, alert and waiting for the spirit of the idol to investigate its visitors. But neither she nor Turin felt the ethereal presence and the ground-tingling power she had come to associate with the mountain gods.

A light freezing rain was falling when they opened the door at dawn. The surface of the trail glistened with its smooth, treacherous coating of ice. Had Ejord suggested they wait until the weather cleared, she would not have argued with him, even if they had to halve their rations. But he went out, and after kicking at the icy surface several times, announced they would proceed.

Rifkind led Turin a short distance along the trail until he was accustomed to the slick surface. The freezing rain formed hard rivulets on her oiled-leather cape. During the long wait for the thaw, Rifkind had prepared her Asheeran clothes for the journey. The rain steadily worsened; the sun never broke through the clouds, and the temperature dropped sharply. Ejord no longer sang the ribald songs of the gaming rooms to himself but led the way in utter grim silence punctuated only by soft curses.

Disaster struck and was over almost before Rifkind comprehended it had happened. Blackthorn, picking his way slowly across the glazed path, finally ran out of luck. The trail separated from the rock face of the mountain as the weight of his hindquarters struck a crack which was so like the others that he no longer took the time or energy to fear it.

Ejord leaned forward against their fall, but the stallion's hind hooves could find no purchase. The trail was crumbling faster than his front legs could pull him upward. His panicked struggles surged across the empathic sensibilities into Rifkind and Turin and had the effect of throwing them both into a numbing, time-slowing shock. She watched each chunk of rock fall away beneath the horse's churning legs, and saw with horrifying clarity the fatal course both horse and rider would take down the mountainside.

As it had done once before, her spirit flowed in one powerful direction.

"That shall not be!" she whispered.

Time hung heavy in the air, but Rifkind felt none of the surging mountain power she had felt in her battle against the Mountain Men. She had sought after no power but her own either time, but feared that now her own would not be enough. Then, without spectacle or miracle, Blackthorn's hooves scrabbled against solid rock and found purchase, and he hauled himself and Ejord to the other side of an eight-foot chasm in the trail.

Ejord was ashen-faced, immobile. Rifkind could readily imagine the twin shocks imposed on his mind—first that he was soon to be dead, and now that he was still alive. She did not expect her friend to answer when she called his name. Blackthorn stood with his head barely above the ground. His heavy black coat had withstood the ravages of the rain, but was now streaked and matted with sweat. He did not move. An experienced horsewoman, Rifkind knew, not by empathy but by sad ex-

perience, that the big black would not try to move.
He put no weight on his right forehoof—in his final
struggle, he had broken the leg.

"Ejord," she called again and again, until the
shock passed out of him and he turned to look at
her.

Movement brought sanity back to him and he slid
gently off Blackthorn's back and looked at the injured foreleg.

"He's crushed the pastern." His voice was flat and
barely audible across the chasm.

"I know," Rifkind confirmed.

"Witchery?"

"No, experience."

She had dismounted and moved to the edge of the
raw gash in the trail, walking carefully in front of
Turin who was himself calling nervously to his
companion.

Silently Ejord pulled his heavy hunting knife from
its belt-sheath. He ran his hand along Blackthorn's
neck. The horse raised its head to look at him—
neither understanding nor seeing the sharp knife.

"Wait!"

Ejord looked over his shoulder in surprise rather
than obedience.

"Wait," she repeated, edging back to Turin's saddle and fumbling with the many packs attached to
it.

"I will not stand here to see him suffer."

"Nor will I." She wrenched her leather sack free.

Tying one end of a rope to the saddle horn, she
advanced again to the brink of the chasm.

"Catch this."

She threw the coil of rope over to him. He missed.

She coiled it again; this time he caught it, and held it absently.

"I'm coming over; hold it tightly."

Whether out of curiosity or because he'd divined her intentions, Ejord braced himself while Rifkind hand-walked the length of the rope across the chasm.

"I shall need a fire."

She pointed to an overhang protecting a small portion of the trail.

"Witchery?" Ejord asked with unconcealed bitterness, picking up his knife as he spoke. "You won't use him for your tricks."

"I'm a healer, Ejord. I told you that when we met —I saved Linette from worse than this." She spoke with a tone of nervous desperation.

"I never heard of witches healing animals."

"There is no difference," she said firmly, adding under her breath that she hoped there wouldn't be. "Make me the fire; I'll prepare the herbs and oils."

She heard Ejord head toward the overhang, then directed all her attentions to her patient. The Old Tongue mnemonics came into her head—the start of a ritual which, since no two injuries or diseases were alike, had no fixed form. Guided by the questions Muroa had taught her, and the answers instinct, empathy and ethereal forces brought her, she studied Blackthorn. Her hands moved lightly over his body, nearing the site of the injury without the fearful, anxious beast's seeming to notice her presence. She did not notice Ejord's return to them after starting the fire.

She did not speak to him, lost in the Old Tongue and the ritual itself. The unfamiliar life-forces of the

Dro Darian horse became visible to her as she sought after them: different from those of men, but still life-forces. She knew she could mold and re-form them. Rarely moving her gaze from the stricken horse, she moved around the icy ledge with uncanny certainty, avoiding Ejord without ever looking at him.

Rifkind gathered miscellaneous herbs and oils from her ritual stores, carrying them to the brazier at the small fire Ejord had built her, carrying the liquid back to Blackthorn to see if she had found the proper mixture. She asked Ejord for his knife, un-aware that she spoke the Old Tongue. Her ritual sense told her the knife was necessary at all costs. She held out her hand; Ejord hesitated a moment, then reluctantly presented the hilt to her.

She stirred the boiling mixture with the knife, let-ting the viscous fluids coat the blade. She stared at it and saw not the hunting knife, or the rain beading upon it, but a shimmering spike of iridescent red and blue fire—the necessary and sufficient elements for this ritual. The tip of the flame traced down Blackthorn's injured leg, breaking the skin inches above the pulsing vortex of energy which marked the fracture. At the fracture point, she thrust the flame into the vortex.

Blackthorn screamed. Ejord fixed her with a look of raw hatred. She was oblivious to both, and neither was able to move against her. The flame burnt into her hand, feeding itself on her energies and will, emptying itself into the vortex. The life-forces realigned, covering the vortex and pushing the unneeded flame away. The flesh healed around the knife blade, excluding it from the now-healed wound. Rifkind fell back onto the ice in a dazed but familiar stupor as the normal parts of her mind absorbed the experiences of the ritual.

Ejord held out a square of cloth for her to dry her face; when she made no move to take it from him, he knelt beside her and dried the water from her face and the blood from her hands. A pinkish scald on her palms was the only reminder of the healing. She roused slowly, blinking her eyes, trying to restore coherence to her memory.

Blackthorn was already pawing the ground with his foreleg.

"You are truly a wonder to watch," Ejord said, smiling when her eyes finally focused on him.

"I am a healer."

After leading Blackthorn down the trail, Rifkind returned to the chasm to coax Turin into jumping it.

"Had we not best attempt to return?" Ejord interrupted.

"Yes, I'd rather be in the warm halls of Chatelgard listening to Anelda and dancing and I wish I'd never heard the name of Hanju or talked you into this trek. But while Turin can jump that gap—if I can convince him to—Blackthorn could not, no matter what I did. We can only go on and hope that Hanju—or someone—knows another way back."

Ejord mumbled that he had brought up the possibility only because he had thought she did know some way to get the heavy black horse over the chasm. He accepted her stated limitations and left her to convince the unhappy Turin that he wanted to jump over the abyss.

Turin finally leaped over the gap against his better judgment. Rifkind had to spend as much time talking to him and patting his neck in apology as she had spent cajoling him into making the leap. They were all thoroughly drenched and miserable by the time the brazier was cleaned and repacked and they were on their way. There was no question that they would not make the shelter by nightfall.

"We'll have to camp in the open here," Ejord called as darkness made the trail little more than invisible.

"We'll go ahead; I'll lead."

"We'll be killed for certain—both of us this time."

While they argued, the storm ended with disturbing suddenness and the Bright One shone with unseemly light on the trail.

"It's a bloody miracle!" Ejord grumbled with understandable exasperation.

Rifkind did not bother to deny the claim, nor did she direct any special thoughts to her patroness. Healing was exhausting work—if the Bright One expected her to keep on doing it, the least She could do was provide a reasonably warm and dry place for Her healer to recover in.

"There it is!"

Ejord stood in the stirrups, pointing at a section of trail and mountain which at first glance was no different from the rest. But by now Rifkind knew what to look for and sighed with relief. They approached it quickly, acknowledging their weariness out loud and lapsing into weakly hysterical laughter now that safety was in sight. Ejord jumped from Blackthorn and shoved the door open. Rifkind was off Turin as quickly and not more than two steps behind him.

The shelter was dark; ingrained caution told her never to stride into an unknown and dark room even as she realized that there was a commotion in front of her. There was no time—her last thoughts were bitter self-denunciations as a sack was dragged over her head. A thick, sweetish odor came out of its fibers, subduing her almost at once.

CHAPTER 18

The drug had worn off, but a clear mind was of no help in dealing with her new surroundings. Ejord was nowhere to be seen, Turin was beyond the range of her mental probes, and the eeriness of the translucent white walls which confined her kept Rifkind from exercising any of her tal abilities.

The room was bright; a gentle fresh breeze wafted across it, though she could see neither doors nor windows. Her clothes and weapons had been taken away and she was dressed in a robe not un-like the nightdresses Lady Anelda had supplied her with at Chatelgard. Several low tables furnished the room; when her strength had fully returned, she piled them on top of each other and explored the light-filled recesses at the tops of the walls.

"Surely it would be easier to use the doors?"

She looked down from her perch on the tables, since the voice seemed to arise from the floor. The intruder was tall, ebony-skinned, naked. There was no sign of any door he had used. Without her knives, Rifkind felt more naked than the stranger who was moving toward her.

He was unlike any other man she had ever encountered, enough so that she was unsure her knives would have been useful anyway. His skin was iridescent, as if it were covered with scales or feathers. Fear and discretion checked her curiosity about which one it was. His nostrils flared widely, making his nose into little more than two dark holes in the already black face. His eyes were bulging, golden hemispheres without pupils. When the initial shock passed, she realized that he was Hanju and that her previous tal-encounter with him had not revealed his true image because she had not imagined that one of the legendary Old Ones still lived.

"I cannot find them, Master," she replied, climbing down from the tables without once diverting her glance from his face.

"You have not looked for them. You have seen the semblance of walls and have accepted them without looking beyond."

He spoke the Old Tongue, of course, and confirmed her suspicions that the words were never intended for soft-skinned mouths to pronounce.

"I would not use my feeble powers in a place ruled by your presence, Master."

"I do not rule here, Rifkind; but if you feel that I

should, then I give you my permission. See the room as it truly is."

She had had to answer him in the language of men, since the intuitive phrases of the Old Tongue refused to come to her, even though she could understand him. The situation did not inspire her with confidence as she tentatively pushed into the tal-mind. From that vantage, the walls faded into lattice-work and arches leading to peaceful sheltered gardens beyond. She found a perspective which allowed her to see both the bare walls and the idyllic scene Hanju wished her to accept as reality.

"You have come a long way to talk to me. There must be much you want to say. Let's sit in the garden, it's more pleasant there."

Hanju walked through one of the arches to the garden. Rifkind attempted to follow him, but the portion of her mind which saw only the featureless wall triumphed, and she hesitated.

"Rifkind, it is for you to decide what is real."

Hanju's voice came clearly through the wall.

Rifkind concentrated; the garden reappeared. Suppressing her fears she stepped through the arch. The garden disappeared at once, and she stood in another white-walled room, differing from the first only in that it had carpets, a ewer of wine on one of the low tables, and the gold pin she had left at the first mountain shelter when they left the valley with Linette prominently displayed by the ewer. Hanju quickly poured the wine into two glasses which appeared as he lifted the ewer. He offered one glass to her.

"Yes. Now we will talk. I have been waiting for you also."

She took the goblet, but hesitated to drink from it. Hanju lifted his own, then sat on the carpet with a reptilian fluidity. The iridescence was definitely the result of tiny scales.

"I—I've come for new stones, Master," Rifkind said uncomfortably—not wanting to sit down, yet uneasy standing before him.

"Stones?"

His confusion seemed sincere, though she was scarcely about to count on anything actually being what it seemed.

"Moon-stones. I got mine from Muroa, but so much has happened. I thought I—" Rifkind put her hand to her neck and realized for the first time that the familiar pouch was no longer there. "My stones . . . the ruby!" She glanced around the room, which suddenly seemed very solid.

"Ah, the pebbles you kept with Leskayia's heart."

Hanju gestured with his hand. The pouch appeared suspended from his taloned forefinger. She took it.

"My ruby! You've taken my ruby!" She looked up after examining the plundered object, her features hardening to a cold hatred. "You are An-Soren!"

Rifkind yanked down on her braids, releasing a small poisoned spike. She leaped to him, only to be stopped short by a barrier which thrust her down, breathless, to the floor.

"If I were, my child, you would have been dead long before now—more dead than you can imagine. I am, as I have told you, Hanju." He smiled, revealing instead of teeth needle-sharp fangs which were set in hard, shiny black gums.

Rifkind recoiled from him, edging away without standing up. Her mind was translating the Old

Tongue consciously for the first time, though, and she did recognize that "Hanju" meant only "individual" or "life-force." He did not move toward her.

"I would like my ruby back. It is all I have from my mother, and though I don't remember her at all, I have always valued it above anything else."

"Gotten from your mother, who died in childbirth no doubt, as would her own mother, and her mother before that. Leskayia was like that."

He held out his hand again; it stretched to reach over her. The ruby appeared again when he opened his fingers, this time dangling from a heavy gold chain.

"You've taken the setting from Kerdal's clan!"

She exhaled with childish delight and reached for the stone. It disappeared.

"Kerdal? An Asheeran name, if I remember these things. You must know him? No, I have taken nothing from this Kerdal of yours. But now I see that despite your powers you know nothing about Leskayia's heart. This is remarkable, but also very dangerous for you."

"An-Soren spoke of an Eye of the Dark Moon. You've called it 'Leskayia's heart.' He would have killed me for my mother's gift, I think. Perhaps he did call it the heart of something or other. I don't remember it too well; it was right after a lightstorm."

"Cursed things, we have them here in the mountains too; only the air here is not so clear and the effect is not so general or predictable. He *would* call it the Eye of the Dark Moon. He knows rather little about these things. But that will not help you when you meet him. Come, sit here now. I will tell you the things you will need to know, since you do not know the questions to ask."

Rifkind sat up.

"Eyes, hearts—the legends you young races have picked up. They were the source of Leskayia's power. And when she was vanquished, they were separated and thrown into the sea. The one which has lately come into the hands of An-Soren was recovered from the sea long ago, though he was the first to guess its power. He draws his knowledge, I believe, from the Mountains of the West—they were never particularly reliable, so I did not worry, even when he found out that there was another one."

"Then the other one appeared. Yours. That changed things considerably. Each stone is powerful in its own right; we made them that way. But the pair—that was uncontrollable even for us, and completely unthinkable for your race."

Rifkind hesitated a moment before responding to his story. "Then there are now at least three of us who know where both stones are—stones you say are beyond your own imagination and control. It seems unlikely that the rubies will remain separate much longer. Were I you, Master, despite your venerable age and wisdom, I'd not dismiss An-Soren—or myself—so lightly."

"Oh, I don't dismiss you lightly. These are my mountains, given to me long ago, before your race was born. I've conserved and nurtured their power over the eons. I still survive because I have been so careful. I will not leave my mountains, but I am very concerned about the fate and movement of those stones!"

Hanju's eyes blazed with internal light. Powerful energies seethed around him, tingling at the soles of her bare feet. Rifkind suppressed any further curiosity about Hanju and his mountains.

"Will you bring An-Soren here—as you've brought me?"

"I would not have An-Soren here," Hanju stated with petulant finality. "And I have not brought you here—although I was not, of course, ignorant of Adijan's actions. Had he succeeded ... well, that would have been improbable at best. You are here of your own curiosity, if not your free will."

"Then what have you done with Ejord?" she demanded quickly.

"Your companion—that oddly transparent young man? He is here too, and well cared for, though I shall not talk to him. I have nothing to say to him. He could not hear me anyway, and I will not talk to someone I cannot see. There is not enough time in all eternity to solve all insignificant mysteries. They tell me he exists. I tell them to care for him as he appears to be. That is enough; I am concerned only with you."

"I won't give you the ruby."

"I don't want it; I've given it back to you. It does me no good."

Hanju drank deeply from the goblet, his eyes momentarily taking on the deep red color of the wine.

"Enough of this!" he announced when his eyes had regained their golden color. "I will take no direct part in your battles. My mountains will survive no matter what—I am careful to see to that. But I don't want An-Soren coming here to find you. You have come for my help—I understand now that you want stones to help you see the true nature of things."

He dropped five crystalline cubes onto the carpet.

Rifkind recognized them at once and knew that the pattern they displayed was "hanju," life-force at its simplest and strongest.

"Take them; they are a true guide, not biased toward one center or another—not even to my mountains here. You will need them; I sense you will do a lot of traveling. Stay with the Bright Moon, too. She is distant and slow to change, but she lacks ambition—you'll need that. And keep the ruby. Take it as far away from here as possible—bury it in the Death-Wastes if you've any sense at all. But since that is not common in your kind, and before I turn you loose with the necklace to focus it, learn what it is."

"I do not think it is something I would experiment with, Master. It is mine, like my sword and Turin, but I don't use it as I use them. I would wear it and let it be my talisman."

"Well, Rifkind, if you wear this ruby in the wrong place, you'll wish no one knew who, or what, you are. Even if you could fool An-Soren with that ridiculous attempt to hide the healer's mark, he will know that stone at once."

"I did not expect to fool An-Soren." She lifted her hand to her face to feel the waxlike scar covering the crescent. "I hope only to deceive the others at the court until it is time. If you have never left your mountains, Master, you know little of the disrepute and fear all the arts have fallen into—especially in Dro Daria."

"No doubt you know your own kind better than I do," Hanju replied. "I have never left these mountains. When the first of your kind began to appear, the others tried to exploit them. I did not think that was a wise course, and in the end I was right. The rest of my race destroyed itself in petty jealousies. In the end, even those who directly replaced us in the centers of power, like your Bright Moon, became involved. Now they are either gone, bound by their worshiping slaves, or shadows of their former power."

Hanju looked wistful for a moment—an expression Rifkind found disconcerting. She had begun to suspect that the effects of eternity and isolation had brought a special madness to the last of the Old Ones, by not having others around to base comparisons on. She was grateful for the crystal stones, and, contrary to her statement, fully intended to explore the powers of the ruby before they arrived in the capital. Rifkind waited silently while Hanju gradually returned to his apparently normal, impassive self.

"The stone is an energy focus; so is its companion. An-Soren has learned to use the one he possesses to channel and direct whatever inherent energy exists around him. He can mold that power to suit his own abilities and desires. He is by far the strongest of your kind. That is, unless your abilities and desires are the same as his. If you are truly the equal of each other, the stones will either destroy themselves and you, or supplement each other infinitely; I don't recall which."

"We really should never have made any of them. Little conveniences so we could travel about more easily. I never indulged myself. True, I do not leave my mountains—but so long as I am here, we are both safe. Not like what happened to the Death Wastes. . ."

Hanju lost himself in memories which flashed brightly across his golden eyes, convincing Rifkind that he had a special sort of madness.

"Even with both stones you would be powerless here, and I would not go elsewhere to meet you . . . remember that! But I like you—you can walk through my walls—no one else has done that. Leskayia could do that, long ago, before the rubies. Perhaps in time I would have a companion worthy of me again."

He stared at Rifkind, his eyes glowing with golden brilliance. Rifkind vowed to herself that with or without Leskayia's heart, she would resist becoming a companion worthy of Hanju. But she did accept his offer of assistance in controlling the stone and followed him through another series of walls to a chamber she swore to herself was the one they had left, but he insisted was the only place where he could safely show her Leskayia's powers.

Rifkind learned nothing from his demonstrations. Everything the Old One did was beyond her grasp— she saw no difference in materializations with or without the ruby's aid. His ability to create and destroy with utter casualness was testimony to the legends of the Old Ones and the Lost Gods. She doubted she would ever appeal to them again, lest they hear her.

Finally he put the stone in its setting and handed both to her, insisting it was her turn to try something. Still reluctant to extend her tal far from her body, and uncertain about the reality of anything Hanju presented, she proceeded cautiously to search for life-forces within the room. There were none except her own. Hanju was a seething tower of energy, but his essence was too simple to be a life-force, as she knew it. She had worked with other forces when she had called water from the air. Slowly, but with growing enthusiasm, she determined to make a real door in one of Hanju's perfect walls.

It was impossible.

Her mind could not imagine—much less shape—the forces Hanju had used to build his home. Rifkind hung the ruby around her neck, letting it slide beneath the fabric of the borrowed gown. There was a surge of power when the stone touched her skin. She tried her experiment again. The forces were accessible now; she could imagine spreading the wall apart, creating a thinness until the wall was truly translucent, then finally a glimpse of the rugged snow and ice mountains, the stormy grey sky and a blast of the raw mountain air she'd come to know so well. She had located her own reality.

Hanju wrested control again, without gesture or effort on his part. Her door simply vanished, and the garden reappeared behind the white lattice. Rifkind felt a thrill of victory. The Old One's eyes glistened with flashes of a thousand colors; his scales rippled with chromatic agitation. He reminded her of a lightstorm—and she stepped away from him.

"No, don't go yet. There is much you can learn—that I can teach you! You could be far stronger than An-Soren . . . not since Leskayia . . . you *can* learn—you *must* learn. You must be far stronger than An-Soren when you meet him. If you are not, only my mountains and I will survive."

"And if I am the stronger, and I take the two stones?" she said with a steadiness she did not truly feel.

"Then it will not matter that the others are gone; you and your kind will be ready, and I will go elsewhere with my mountains."

"I do not think you will have to leave your mountains, Master." She adopted a deferential tone as the

Old One's agitation increased.

"No, but I see now that it is time for you too."

He clapped his hands, though Rifkind felt rather than heard the concussive slap. She was swept up in a flash of disorientation and recovered an instant later to find herself fully dressed, seated astride Turin, next to Ejord and in sight of Chatelgard. They were all dazed.

"Are you all right?" she asked, checking an impulse to reach out and touch him to see if he were real.

"Huh?" He jumped, then snapped into awareness. "Witchery again. This is really getting out of hand, milady. One moment I'm eating roast meat and watching dancing girls, the next I'm here." He shook his head slowly, but did not seem particularly upset.

"How did your visit with Hanju go? Did you see him at all?"

"I think so."

"You *think* so?" Ejord leaned back in exasperation. "Three days sitting in a rock chair while very sincere, and utterly inept, people tried to keep me entertained, and the rest of them chanted at the largest, ugliest cult statue I've ever seen, while I was waiting for you, and you don't even know if you saw him or not!"

"Well, I was there with him—I'm sure of that. I just don't know whether anything I saw was real or not. Hanju is much less like other men than even I was expecting. I *did* get what I wanted though."

"I am relieved. Will you tell me just what it was you were so set on getting from him?"

Rifkind felt for her suede stone-pouch, found it, and drew out the carved rock crystals, carefully concealing the ruby pendant. Ejord took one from her and studied it in the late-afternoon sunlight before returning it to her.

"These will give you a substantial advantage, no doubt?"

Though she had been certain and comfortable with his bantering tone, this last question teetered delicately between sarcasm and sincerity. She decided it was sincerity and answered him in kind.

"I'd had the feeling for some time now that I needed to replace the stones Muroa gave me back in the Asheera. Hanju said something about these being unbiased. He said a lot of things—not three days' worth, though."

"I don't know how those things work, but all the others I've seen have a flaw in them—a crack which makes them fall in a certain way. That one doesn't have a crack in it," Ejord said.

Rifkind reached into the pouch again and held out one of her old stones.

"Is this one flawed?"

Ejord scanned it in her hand. "Yes. Not as badly as most I've seen, but it would not always fall true."

She put the stone back and stared at him in silence for several moments.

"Ejord, you say again and again that you know nothing of ritual, or what you call witchery, yet you see flaws in my stones and can tell me things about myself which I did not know—there is something in this I do not quite understand."

"It's as I've said. I'm immune to all your witcheries, and to everyone else's. Everyone else has some ability, or susceptibility; I don't. I see only what is, or at least what magic has done."

"Did you see Hanju?"

"Yes." He spoke with the certainty which had

been lacking in her own answer.

"What was he like?"

" 'Hanju is much less like other men'; he is not exactly like the cult idols either, but there is a resemblance. I didn't talk to him as you did. But then, what would we have said to each other—I doubt we'd even speak the same language."

Rifkind nodded. "A talent like yours, to see the nature of ritual and energy, would be very useful to someone like myself who was about to work 'witcheries' on a grand and likely permanent scale."

"Yes, I suppose it would be—except that I have no interest in it. I am not immune to poison or knives, regardless of the nature of the being using them. An-Soren is a person of many talents, just as you are."

"You'll leave me to deal with him alone?" she said, looking up at him through her eyelashes, a behavior pattern the other women of the castle used to considerable effect, and she found unpleasantly dishonest.

"Father seems to feel you can handle it. Hanju was certain you could last summer."

"But I'm not—and I'm not certain An-Soren is truly my enemy. He is the enemy of my Goddess, but you've told me now that the old stones won't always be true. I'll have to use the new stones. Your father —and who knows who else—has set me up to mold forces not likely to affect them with their undeveloped tals, but might destroy An-Soren and myself. The stones may now fall freely, but it's a risk I don't take lightly. Ejord, I will need your help."

"I'll think on it."

He turned Blackthorn, leading their way to the castle in silence.

CHAPTER 19

The closed carriage bounced along the rutted muddy inland road from Glascardy to the capital. Rifkind sat next to the small window, determined to see as much of the countryside as the narrow perspective would allow. She had reluctantly agreed with Lady Anelda that once they left the safety of Chatelgard no one must know she was anything but Lord Humphry's deceased wife's niece, and Ejord's intended bride. The continual jolting of the carriage on the road tired her as a journey astride Turin never did. She understood why both Lady Anelda and Linette disliked traveling as much as they did.

The small window gave her a view of two of the six-man mounted guard which accompanied them. Adijan rode at the head of the small group, nominally their leader, though Ejord, who rode at the rear, was in Rifkind's opinion more qualified for the task of moving them discreetly across the countryside. The two men she could see had been picked by Adijan; they were members of his cult, but also experienced men-at-arms, and conscientious in their duty. Insofar as she was able, Rifkind trusted them to be alert for dangers. She had greater faith in Turin, who walked or trotted freely with the entourage.

At Chatelgard, Lady Anelda had pointed out the obvious risks they took in traveling with a horned horse through lands where the Asheeran mounts were more legend than real. Rifkind had balked, refusing to leave the castle unless Turin accompanied her. The impasse existed until Ejord suggested the ploy of saying the war-horse was an intended gift for the king. The compromise did not entirely please anyone, but they had left Chatelgard on time with Turin content in position between the two back guards.

"Must you lean out like that?" Lady Anelda snarled. "One would think the carriage would overturn each time you do."

"There are men and women out working in the fields."

"They're planting grain—just as they've been doing in every field we've passed for the past three days. It's spring—what else would they be doing? Don't you ever get tired of looking out the windows?" Linette concluded.

Rifkind's eyes darkened. "Perhaps I would, if it were the same in every field we've passed for the past three days. But it isn't."

"Planting grain is planting grain," Linette answered with the weariness of familiarity; this was the first spring she was not out with the peasants in the fields herself.

"Most likely true, but if you chanced to look out the windows from time to time, you would notice that each field has at least one mounted and armed guard moving among the peasants. In some fields he watches the workers; in others he watches the road and rides over to watch us go by. And, for that matter, many of the fields are not being planted—some are scavenged as we would do when we'd come upon your fields during a migration—since we know nothing of planting nor harvesting, but only of feeding the herds now."

Both women looked at Rifkind with greater attentiveness, but her eyes were fixed on the passing countryside, and she did not notice the change in them.

Their conversations had been sharp or bitter almost since the trip had begun, driving Bainbrose from the carriage to the driver's seat after the first day. Lady Anelda was uncomfortable with what she presumed to be full responsibility for their safety, while Linette continued the war of wills which she and Rifkind had fought since before Rifkind's visit with Hanju.

"And some fields have been burned with the trees around them. In some places, the fires seem to have crossed the road itself. Not the planned harvest burnings you told me about, Linette." Rifkind thrust her head and shoulders out the window for a moment, causing Lady Anelda to gasp in civilized horror. Then she sat back and faced them. "I wasn't sure before, but now I am. There are corpses in these fields. Someone's been raiding these lands," she announced.

"You can't be sure at these distances and speeds," Lady Anelda said. "You could easily have been mistaken."

"I suspect, Lady Overnmont, I've had much more experience picking out a corpse on a horizon than you have, and I don't think I would make a mistake."

Lady Anelda put her handkerchief to her mouth, but craned her neck to see out the windows. She sat back pale and shaken.

"War," she stammered. "Hogarth is moving."

She rapped sharply on the wall behind her. A panel opened and Bainbrose's face appeared.

"Yes, milady?"

"Is this carnage the work of Hogarth's men?"

"Oh, we didn't think you'd have the windows open. Is it the smell? We don't really know who's to blame. It's not the nature of the army to burn the land it is conquering."

"It's no army. 'S An-Soren," Linette responded, her eyes tightly closed.

"Nonsense, child," Lady Anelda interrupted, but taking Linette's hand in hers. "An-Soren never leaves the palace, and we've still seven days' journey before we get there. May Malabar protect us," she added reflexively, imploring a god thought to have concern for unlucky travelers.

"It's him—I've seen it before. Nothin' grows. Don't need bother goin' out in th' fields 'cause 'tain't nothing'll come up."

Linette slipped back into the peasant dialect Lady Anelda had almost purged from her vocabulary.

Linette sat with her eyes tightly closed, recalling the horrors which had been her life until recently. Unable to reassure her young companion, Lady Anelda looked squarely into Bainbrose's face, hoping he would deny Linette's frightened assertions.

"It has been rumored that Hogarth's army is followed by men like the Mountain Men who wreak this havoc on the land. If this were true, then An-Soren might share responsibility. But the crops do seem to come up—although there is no one to tend them. I suspect some disaster which we did not hear about in Glascardy."

The carriage hit a rough section of road, bouncing and rattling so much that conversation became impossible; even Rifkind had to brace herself against the back of her bench.

"Well, what do *you* think is happening, Rifkind? You seem to know quite a bit about these things," Lady Anelda asked.

"I don't know, except I would prefer to be riding Turin than sitting in this box on wheels that's not fit to haul captives or cooking pots."

"Isn't it enough that we have your horned beast with us to attract attention, without you riding it, too? Great Mohandru knows what has happened to my brother, or what will greet us if we get to Daria at all."

Lady Anelda was appealing to the gods with increasing frequency and irritation, a habit Rifkind found distressing. Rifkind, on the other hand, was well acquainted with the powers of the various gods, and preferred to avoid most of them. She feared their intervention more than any misfortune which might have befallen Lord Humphry. With great deliberateness, she propped her feet upon the bench next to her, and, with a show of wedging herself into her bench-seat, settled into an uncomfortable rest.

For the rest of that afternoon she watched the road through Turin's eyes. The guard party was unsettled by the devastation they traveled through. There was none of the usual joking or grim humor. Each man rode with one hand on the hilt of his sword, and none appeared to look at the same spot for more than a moment. In time the blackened fields were left behind them and were replaced by more normal bucolic scenes.

A crow flew over their little band and followed them for a good distance, circling lazily and once even landing on the ground to watch them pass. In the carriage, Rifkind argued with herself over the suspicions the bird's behavior roused within her. The fact that she used Turin as extra senses when she could not easily use her own did not mean that the crow was anything more than a half-starved bird looking for a meal. Neither Adijan nor Ejord had noticed the bird, and she consoled herself with the idea that if they hadn't, then it was, hopefully, a normal crow.

The effort of remaining in Turin's mind tired her, and by sundown she had retreated back into her own mind. If the entourage followed its normal pattern, they would stop shortly before sundown.

"We've found an inn, milady," Bainbrose informed them through the sliding window to their compartment.

Lady Anelda shifted about in the carriage and looked out the window. "No, not that one—it's filthy. The sort of place soldiers or highwaymen frequent."

"We have seen no other inns recently, and it

doesn't seem likely we'll find another before night-fall."

"It still won't do. I can smell it from here. Go on, there will be another. Decent people must travel through this part of the country and they would have their own place to stay."

"You know how the roadway gets after dark, milady."

"Never matter. Mohandru watches over us."

Rifkind concealed a sigh, bracing even more firm-ly for the jolts which were certain to come. She could not reasonably expect anyone to believe that she would sleep through the punishment the driver subjected them to, not when she was also known to awaken at the sound of an unfamiliar footstep at the other end of the corridor.

"By Vitivar's useless tits—are they trying to kill us all. This carriage on this road is unsafe after sun-down!" Rifkind snarled—waking up in a bad mood gave an additional touch of authenticity to her feigned naps.

"The last inn we passed was not a proper place to stop. If we'd had Lord Humphry, it might have been all right, but we are ladies." Lady Anelda looked darkly at the dagger-sheath showing through the creases of Rifkind's gown. "And it would not be seemly for us to go to such a place alone."

"Is that to say that the addition of one more middle-aged, overfed nobleman who hasn't brawled since he was taught to talk is the true mea-sure of safety in Dro Daria, not the six healthy armed men who travel with us?"

The carriage bounced over a branch, skirted the side of the road for several bone-rattling moments, then came to a resounding, and to Rifkind's thoughts, permanent halt. They stayed steady for a moment; then the whole carriage listed to one side. A wheel was off and they were mired in the mud at the side of the road. Rifkind abandoned her role as a genteel lady and, forcing open the door of the carriage, jumped to the road to survey the damage with the mounted guard. Bainbrose had been thrown clear of the carriage by the final jolt and was shaken, but not seriously injured. The driver cursed with a colorful expertise, all of which Rifkind recorded in her memory. Everyone else was silent.

"We should have stopped at the inn," a chastened Lady Anelda called into the near darkness.

"We'll have to split up the party. Ejord'll take two men and the women back to the inn. The rest of us will stay with the carriage and fix that damned wheel," Adijan announced, pointing at the two men who would accompany Ejord.

Hitching her skirts over one arm Rifkind mounted Turin. While everyone else had been packing for the journey she had perfected her riding ability within the constraints of the attire of a proper Dro Darian lady. Lady Anelda took one look at her and the mounted guard and announced that she and Linette would wait with the carriage. Linette smiled and glanced over to Adijan, who would have nothing to do with the actual wheel repair. They had had little time together since the journey had begun. With Anelda remaining in the carriage, there was some doubt as to the necessity of splitting the party, but no one challenged Adijan's commands.

"Are you armed?" Ejord asked Rifkind as she took a position on his right.

"Save for my sword. I am always armed."

He relaxed. "I do not like following the back roads

like this. Even in supposed disguises, we are a prime
target for every bandit within miles, not to mention
Hogarth's men if there are any in these parts. Even
without the crest on the carriage, or the livery, it's
still fairly obvious that we've got people of some importance traveling. I'd rather we'd gotten an open
cart and traveled like peasants, if Father'd truly
wanted us to be inconspicuous."

"Peasants traveling toward Daria, wouldn't that
be rather unusual in itself?"

Ejord grunted a noncommittal agreement. "I
don't like the thought of an ambush. And if I were
planning an ambush, I couldn't ask for a better
target or cover."

Rifkind looked about at the forest and field as it
rapidly disappeared into darkness.

"Well, we'll just have to hope that the men that
Hogarth, or whoever, has in this area are inept.
Anelda says we're seven days out from Daria; we're
closer, aren't we?"

"Call it five. We've been covering territory at a fairly good pace. No offense to you ladies, but neither
Adijan nor I are that much concerned with your
comfort in there. But for once Anelda was right; under any other circumstances, I'd have avoided that
inn back there. It's the sort of place soldiers frequent;
for our purpose, we want a nice merchants' establishment."

"A place accustomed to secrets and intrigues? Following these back roads, we're lucky to find inns at
all," she retorted.

Again Ejord grumbled. "Granted it's been a
number of years since I came through here, and I
was younger, but I don't recall that the inland road
was this bad. Not as well-traveled as the coast route,

perhaps, but a lot of local trade used to go this way. And it's always cut the journey to Daria by three days."

There was a loud crackle in the trees to their right. Both drew weapons and mentally prepared for the worst, only to find themselves face-to-face with a stray cow who had stepped down to the roadside ditch for a drink.

"Ambush!" Rifkind muttered, thrusting her knife back into its sheath.

Ejord remained silent.

The low, rambling structure of the inn appeared at the next bend in the road. They approached it cautiously. There was the usual chaos of chickens, ducks, and pigs milling about in the courtyard, as well as goats and sheep in pens to one side. Before they had dismounted, Ejord had spotted a half-dozen well-fed and groomed horses tethered behind a rickety lean-to. Even unsaddled, there was no doubt that they were not the property of the inn, but a confirmation of the military guests inside.

With Rifkind a half-pace behind him as befitted custom, incidentally giving his back the best protection he could ask for, and the other two guards behind her, Ejord strode into the inn. Its foul odor and assortment of unpleasant or suspicious faces reminded Rifkind of her first contact with public hostelries back in Isinglas. Her back stiffened as she felt men's eyes focus on her. She wished for her sword, but kept her expression neutral and never moved her eyes from their focus on Ejord's back though her other senses absorbed every activity in the room.

"Innkeep!" Ejord demanded when the whole par-

ty was in the room, but still closer to the door than
anyone else.

'He's actually more commanding than anyone
gives him credit for,' Rifkind mused while the innkeeper scuttled forward to conduct his business. 'Because he is clean-shaven and lighter-built than his
brothers and cousins, it is easy to think Ejord is a
gawky youth without training or sense. But he is no
child; his voice is deep and strong, his tactics are
solid and well-thought-out. I would not care to cross
swords with him.'

The innkeeper raised his hands toward the skies
and invoked the power of the Lost Gods, immediately getting Rifkind's attention. He was only indicating
that he did not have the accommodations which
Ejord was demanding, but he would, for a price, see
what he could do. Grimly Rifkind realized that this
meant another evening with Lady Anelda and
Linette in a dark, infested room when she would
have been far more comfortable bedding down on
her cloak in front of the hearth with the rest of
the guard and taking her turn guarding the other
women.

She determined to avoid such exile at least until
Lady Anelda arrived at the inn. She sat down with
the men, enjoying the dark ale, fresh and tasty
sausage and cheese which the serving wench
brought them. The food was surprisingly good, and
she had almost put the upstairs bedrooms out of her
mind. There was little conversation among the men,
only enough to avoid the suspicion which total silence would have caused.

Someone noticed Turin in the courtyard, and for a
heartbeat Rifkind and the rest of the guard froze.
Ejord quickly recovered first, launching into a

lengthy tale of how the horned stallion had been captured in a border raid. Adijan had told a similar story at the other inns, making it into a dark, mysterious tale designed to discourage questions. As Ejord told of both the skirmish and the subsequent retraining of the war-horse, the soldiers from the other tables pulled benches and chairs around to hear.

A truce had been achieved which lasted until the rattle of the carriage in the courtyard signaled the arrival of Adijan, Lady Anelda, Linette, and the others.

"Ejord, the rest of you, take the lady's trunks to her rooms; we've done enough lifting for one day. And you, innkeep, prepare a meal for the ladies to take to their rooms. They'll not eat down here with the rest of the filth."

While everyone else watched Adijan, Rifkind studied the look of pure anger and hate which raced across Ejord's face, only to be quickly replaced by the familiar empty smile he wore whenever he dealt with his family. In terms of blood, age, and ability he should have been in charge of their party. Instead, Lady Anelda had ceded much of her authority to Adijan, who added the arrogance of a cult priest to the power she had given him. Rifkind wished that Ejord would confront his aunt and her old swordmaster, though she too quickly controlled her emotions, recognizing the far greater danger a family squabble would cause in their present circumstances.

Lady Anelda stared at her, making it very clear without using words that it was time for Rifkind to become a lady again. She left the men and the ale to follow the others up the creaking flight of stairs. Adijan was still snarling at the innkeeper and his wenches. The soldiers had retreated to their former tables while Ejord and the rest of the guard stood in grim silence.

'Adijan struts around as if he were Lord Humphry himself. Though I can't believe even the lord would use his rank to make such an unpleasant nuisance of himself. They will not need to know exactly who we are in order to develop a dangerous dislike for us.

'If any of these men are Hogarth's, there'll be a message flying back through the hills within the hour that something's happening here. If only they'd just shut up and let Ejord do things his way. He'd have had those other soldiers talking back to us in a little while, and we'd have found out something about what's been going on in the countryside instead of becoming targets.'

The innkeeper opened the door to a miserable room with two distasteful-looking beds in it.

"Best in the country! Turned two well-paying gentlemen out of here just for you fine ladies!"

'Liar! Those beds haven't had an intelligent body in them for months!'

Lady Anelda strode into the room, at once expressing her contempt for the innkeeper and his accommodations and her unquestionable authority now that she was forced to spend the night within his walls. She turned around, nodded, then pushed the innkeeper into the hallway, bolting the door behind him.

"We shall have to make the best of this," she announced to Rifkind and Linette.

"Fine. You two take the beds; I'll sleep on the floor

by the hearth," Rifkind said pleasantly while re-kindling the fire.

"That will never do; a lady can't sleep on the floor."

"With the door bolted shut like that, who will know if you don't tell them? These beds are narrow. I cannot imagine either of you sleeping next to me and my knives. And I am too much of a lady myself to suggest you leave me to a bed by myself."

Rifkind grinned through her teeth and spread her cloak before the fireplace.

CHAPTER 20

They had been on the road since midmorning. The final repairs to the broken wheel had delayed their departure, and now they traveled as fast as the weakened axle would allow. The soldiers had left just after sunup, and although none of the men could say precisely why, they had all been nervous since then.

Even without any particular empathic talents, Rifkind would have noticed the guards' malaise. There had been something about the soldiers' departure which had disturbed her also. More than on the other days, she wanted to be outside the carriage and prepared for any danger; her confinement was pure torture. Lady Anelda and Linette had each reacted to the tension in the same way; they'd bolted the carriage doors and windows, then settled down into a stiff silence that Rifkind supposed was an imitation of calm.

Turin, who was already excited by the emotional turmoil around him, contended with his mistress's constant need for information—information which she usually got simply by demanding that he watch or listen to some particular thing which had intrigued her.

"Isn't natural," the guard to Turin's left at the rear of the carriage muttered. "Fields all burnt over like this. If I was going to conquer a place, I'd make sure there was something to live on afterwards."

"Unless ya didn't plan to settle anywhere's near it," his companion on Turin's right replied.

"You don't believe these An-Soren stories, do you?" the first asked.

"Didn't used to. Then, well, first the lord fetches in a witch, an' he's not the sort to go believing in things that ain't so. An' now this . . . you said yourself 'tisn't natural, burnings like this."

"Oh, the burnin's not what's strange." The right-front guard turned in his saddle to join their conversation. "Makes a lot of sense to break the back of a people. What's odd's the way it stops and starts so sudden like. Fields charred on this side, an' stinkin' of death; an' on the other, they're out planting the crops like they can't see two fields distant."

"Lord Ejord." The one on Turin's left who had spoken first spoke again. "What do you think it is? Our witch in there—could her kind do somethin' like that?"

"Couldn't guess. Rifkind's a healer, not a 'witch.' She'd whip out her sword in a moment if she heard you call her a witch, but I don't know if healers can use their powers to kill."

"She's a tough little hellcat—that's for sure. Don't think the lord reckoned with what he'd get for bringin' her in like he did," the left guard said.

"Not our lord." The other rear guard spoke before Ejord could answer. "He's no fool like that. It's like buildin' a siege tower. You don't build one that's going to last until the next siege."

"Halloo! Off to the right!"

Rifkind was withdrawing from Turin's mind to consider the guards' conversation as the driver's shouts drew everyone's attention. Rifkind burst back into Turin's consciousness. Whatever the danger was, and Turin could not yet see it, the driver reined the horses sharply. The carriage bounced and jolted, throwing all of the women into disarray on the floor. Rifkind was forced to retreat from Turin's mind and take care of herself. She knew enough to settle her into a cold, efficient warrior even before she rose from the floor; they had been ambushed from the right.

The carriage had jerked into motion again, careering recklessly down the road. With her companions too frozen in shock to argue, Rifkind unbolted the door of the carriage and forced it open. Turin was already there—if the attack came from the right, he knew his Rider would want to mount from the left side of the box she'd been staying in. Rifkind gathered her skirts into an ungainly knot over one thigh and leapt from the carriage to Turin's back.

There had been two groups of ambushers. Archers, who had picked off the driver of the carriage and wounded the left-front guard, and a mounted band of easily twice their own number hurtling down the hillside at them. Bainbrose had taken the reins as the driver fell dead from the carriage. He stood up in the driver's box, the billowing of his dark scholar's robe threatening to lift his tall, thin frame out of the carriage altogether. But he kept his footing, and, amid archaic curses shouted at the top of his voice, kept the carriage on the road no worse than its regular driver had done.

The wounded guard slumped forward in his saddle—without checking further, Rifkind urged Turin forward and took the sword from the man's quickly weakening grip. She dropped back, taking a position beside Ejord at the rear where their pursuers would catch them first.

In the frenzy of a mounted melee, fighting with an unfamiliar and heavier sword, and wearing women's clothes, Rifkind lost track of anything that did not directly touch or threaten her. She heard her first attacker curse her as an Asheeran witch, and she took a perverse pride in knowing that her reputation had preceded her. But that did not deter her from the deadly business of killing him before he or his fellows killed her. The attackers wore no uniforms, any more than the men of the guard did themselves, but they were far too familiar with close-order cavalry melee to be a casual band of brigands.

Again and again her anonymous enemy used the brute weight of his mount to bear down on Turin and prevent Rifkind from using her superior sword-attack. The smaller war-horse stumbled and shuddered, but gamely held his footing while Rifkind met each sword-strike, deflecting it away from them both, but unable to score a telling blow of her own. She knew Turin was tiring, and in a small, but not unconscious, part of her mind felt a surge of sympathy for him. He had never fought with the size and weight handicap she had known all her life.

The massive Dro Darian beast crashed into his shoulder; he jumped sideways from the impact, then swung his horned head back in a vicious up-cutting arc which opened his tormentor's neck and fouled the other's reins in his horns. The Darian horse was not badly injured, though Turin's horns could have gored any attacker. The horns were a defensive weapon, and even in his anger, Turin had known better than to risk his own neck in gouging his enemy's.

The other rider had fallen forward when the reins had been ripped from his hands, and Rifkind brought the heavy sword down across the back of his neck before slashing through the fouled reins and cutting Turin free.

For a brief moment she was unharried—her other attackers had dropped back when Turin had begun to use his horns. Her eyes swept the battle around her. Of the ten or more who had attacked, only four remained; Bainbrose was still shouting above the noise of the fight, and except for the driver and the guard who had been cut down by the archers, their strength was intact.

Then they were at her again.

Her new opponent kept his own mount out of the range of Turin's horns, approaching her always from the rear or side. Rifkind had to twist around in the saddle and fight him with her back to the road ahead of them—but that was Turin's responsibility, and one he could handle well when unharassed.

Steel rang hard against steel, and Rifkind offered brief thanks to Lord Humphry that he issued blades of strong, tempered metal to his retainers. The man was good, and he chose a distance which was just beyond the strength of her sword-arm. Her cuts, which would have been serious threats were they closer, were instead easily parried. He smiled as he toyed with her. She could not guess what he was waiting for, but hoped only that he would wait long enough to become careless in his confidence.

Ejord had unhorsed his final attacker and closed quickly with the last of the ambush party who had focused all his attention on Rifkind. Blackthorn was more than the equal of any Darian horse she had seen for weight and brawn. The big black crashed into her enemy's beast, sending him off balance as the broad side of Ejord's sword smashed hard against the rider's head. Horse and rider went over. Rifkind raised her sword in salute.

"Halloo! Halloo!"

Bainbrose had been making so much noise all along that they had all almost discounted him. He was cracking his whip furiously over the foaming horses, and gesturing wildly at the woods to his right.

"Halloo! Halloo!"

Another flight of arrows came by, miraculously missing the obvious target of Bainbrose though two stuck into the carriage itself and screams could be heard from within it.

"They do not mean for us to get away!" Rifkind said, swinging her sword-arm and wheeling Turin about to face the new onslaught.

"Not us, fool—*you!*" Adijan called over his shoulder to her.

An arrow had caught him in the shoulder, blood already staining the front and back of his leather coat. Despite the ill-feelings and misunderstanding that had passed between them, the sight of the sword-master's blood roused Rifkind's battle lust as few things could have done. Turin surged forward almost before Rifkind could command him to do so.

"Go back, stay with the others! I'll take these. Get to safety!"

Adijan's voice was already thickening—the wound was more serious than she had first suspected. A flash of healer's insight in the midst of battle showed her that his life-force was running rapidly out from the holes the arrow had made. He took the sword in his good arm and dropped the reins of his horse, controlling him with tal-concentration which only sped the ebbing of his life's energy. He called the other front guard, and they plunged off the road toward the source of the arrows.

Rifkind took the lead guard position as they continued thundering down the road. Alone and in front of the others, with the wind and sweat to conceal her tears, she mourned the man who had been her friend and teacher—already forgetting the enigmatic priest of the mountain-cults who had tried to kill her. Her grief blended with the speed and recklessness of their course. She held them all at a gallop until Turin was tired and the other mounts lathered with weariness.

"Rifkind!" Ejord shouted to her, bringing Blackthorn as close as he dared. "There is no pursuit. The horses must rest—we've got to stop!"

She shook her head, but Ejord repeated his words. The second time, she listened and guided Turin to a halt. She remained mounted, her eyes focused on a small rock on the side of the road, while the others dismounted and tended to their horses.

"You were lucky," Ejord announced.

Rifkind turned, fixing him with a dark, angry stare. He pointed to her thigh. The knot she had made of her skirts had loosened considerably during the turmoil, but the fabric still remained in a large bunch over her leg. The shaft of a crossbolt protruded at an angle from the cloth, firmly affixed to the leather and wood of her saddle. She wrenched it loose and glared at it. The short, thick arrows of a crossbow were unfamiliar to her, but as a user of deadly weapons, she had only to look at it to know how such damage had been done to Adijan by a single arrow.

There was blood on the quarrel; she lifted the skirt cloth, half-expecting to find a deep, numbed wound in her own leg, half-fearing she had asked so much of Turin while he had been wounded. But even as she flexed her own muscles and felt the still-solid wood structure of the saddle, healer's insight told her that the blood was Adijan's.

"He was my teacher," she said simply, fingering the stubby feathers of the quarrel.

"Who, Adijan?"

She nodded.

"Then it was all true? All those years they wondered where he had been, and no one knew whether or not to believe the stories he told, especially the ones he told after you arrived." Ejord shook his head. "All I ever knew was that there had never been such a man with the horses."

"That is what we taught him—he taught me how to use this." She held up the sword, which she had carried at her side during the headlong escape.

Ejord's reply was cut short by a shrill scream within the carriage. Lady Anelda had fainted and remained unconscious for most, if not all, of the excitement—if the color of her face and the condition of her clothing was any measure. Bainbrose was already trying to calm her, with little success. There was real enough cause for her distress—Linette was missing and presumed to have fallen out somewhere along the road. Again Rifkind's memory conveniently ignored the difficult estrangement which had risen between them, and could envision only the injured young woman she had first seen on the road to Isinglas.

Silently and without conscious decision she abandoned herself to a trance and cast her mind recklessly back along the road, searching for the remains of both of those who had meant friendship or security at some time to her.

Adijan was dead. Her tal could find neither spirit nor body, only the emptiness left when a man's spirit had left his body for the last time. Linette was still alive, but lying in darkness not far from the spot where the second wave of arrows had hit them.

"I must get back to her."

She twisted about, expecting to feel Turin responding beneath her; instead, restraining hands held her firmly, and a bottle of strong spirits was opened before her lips.

"I must get to her."

"There'll be time for that. You rest now, milady. You've had a fall from your horse and hit your head." Bainbrose spoke as he poured some of the liquid into her mouth. His voice was infinitely gentler than the cordial.

"No. I've got to get to her now."

"We've sent one of the men back along the road a ways to see if she fell out on that last rocky stretch."

"She's back at the second ambush. I've got to get back to her."

Ejord and Bainbrose exchanged glances, which to her consternation she could not interpret. The embarrassing fall from Turin's back had fogged her mind and weakened all her abilities. Turin's frantic concern surrounded her and threatened to overcome what little coherent thought she could manage.

"When our man returns, we'll see about going back to get her," Ejord reassured her.

She knew enough to know they were lying; were she in charge of their expedition, she would not have gone back after the woman. She would have to go alone. That knowledge gave her back her strength, and she pushed her way to her feet.

"I said I must get back to her. She . . . she has used a ritual—she needs my help."

Turin was there at her side. She swung up onto his back, carefully concealing the dizziness her movement caused.

"Wait!" Ejord insisted. "We cannot split the party again. We're too few in number. I wouldn't allow you to leave us anyway. We need you, and Adijan was probably right that whoever attacked us was most likely after you. If you are going to insist on going back—then we'll all go back. We can't leave an injured woman lying by the road anyway."

Lady Anelda muttered, but Ejord had the loyalty of the men, and there was no one now who would challenge his orders. Rifkind waited while they turned the wagon, and the shrunken party made its

way toward the ambush site with Rifkind riding in
the lead. They had covered more ground in their
escape than she had imagined possible with the
cumbersome carriage. Late-afternoon rain clouds
had gathered to darken the sky by the time they
neared their destination. Adijan's horse had wandered back to the road. The beast recognized them
and trotted forward as they approached. Rifkind dismounted, and despite Ejord's stern warning disappeared into the woods.

Linette was crouched by a large tree. She was
pale and shaking, but not apparently hurt. Rifkind
was not surprised that the young woman did not
seem to notice her arrival. Rifkind didn't bother with
words, nor did she resort to healer's rituals at once.
Instead she tried to pick Linette up and carry her
back to the carriage. She was more wearied from
the ride and fall than she had thought, and Linette
was no longer the skinny girl she had carried
through the rain. Unable to lift her, Rifkind sat
beside her on the ground and held her hand.

"What's wrong with her?" Ejord demanded when
he caught up with them, Bainbrose puffing noisily
still further behind in the trees.

"She called upon powers she could not control,"
Rifkind answered, looking up at him.

"Witchery? Did she try to save Adijan with
witchery?" he asked without malice.

"I suppose you could put it that way. I'd given up
teaching her—you knew that. Adijan was her teacher; she tried to save him."

"He was also her priest and lover," Ejord said
calmly. "So, she tried to deal with the archers the
way you dealt with the Mountain Men back in the
passes?"

Rifkind nodded.

"Will you need anything special to heal her?"

"There's nothing to heal. I don't know what—or who—she called on. Doubtless she didn't know herself. But there is a price for calling such things before you learn to control them."

"Were you in that danger when you slew the Mountain Men? You've said you didn't control them."

"It is not quite the same. I am sworn to the Bright One . . . in a way, she is sworn to me. Had the powers of the mountain attempted to overwhelm me, she would have come to my aid. Of course, I endangered my oath to her even so, but it was different enough from what has happened to Linette. We'll have to carry her to the carriage."

As Rifkind stepped aside to let Ejord pick Linette up, the shocked woman opened her eyes and whimpered, reaching out toward Rifkind.

"I tried, Rifkind . . . I tried to save him . . . that's all," she said in a barely audible whisper.

"I know."

"I wanted to save him . . . I thought I could, but . . ." She pulled back her hand and covered her eyes. "I couldn't stop it . . . the ground just opened up and they all disappeared."

Rifkind looked around to see a spot of barren, broken soil, which could have been the passage point for whatever force Linette had summoned.

"He was dying from an arrow wound—he would have died no matter what you did. I had not taught you enough healing—I doubt I could have helped him myself. He understood that—he wanted us to go on ahead."

"I've done something awful," Linette wailed behind her covered eyes.

"Yes, but you saved all our lives, and we thank you for that."

Linette took little comfort in Rifkind's words, but allowed herself to be carried back to the road. Despite their diminished forces and Ejord's express desire to have her riding guard with them, Rifkind seated herself in the carriage and let Linette lean against her shoulder.

"Rifkind?" Linette whispered, long after Rifkind had hoped she'd dropped off to sleep. "I'll never be able to use the arts again."

"I know that."

"It's some sort of a punishment? I didn't mean any harm—don't they know that?"

"The gods care, but not about the things we care about. You have to pay the price for releasing something which should not have been released, and making the ones who have dominion here confine it again."

"I was only trying to save Adijan!"

"Things are as they would have been. From the first you did not see yourself marked as one of the ritualists—you said you would be a great lady and always yourself. The destiny you saw then is still yours."

The carriage rumbled through the night. Linette and Lady Anelda both slept soundly, and before dawn Rifkind herself fell into a dreamless sleep.

CHAPTER 21

The signs of war and An-Soren were more apparent and older as they approached the capital. Fields that had once been blackened now sprouted with sickly plants; trees at the edges of these unfortunate fields put forth misshapen leaves. There were no birds except the carrion hunters, nor game except for vermin. Travelers' inns were burned or abandoned, and the villages they could see from the road did not look to be places in which to seek hospitality. So they stayed in the carriage, eating roasted vermin and drinking water only after Rifkind had passed her hands over it and rendered it pure.

Rifkind rode Turin most of the time, retreating into the carriage only when Linette became upset. It was not in Rifkind's nature to analyze her own actions—she did what seemed necessary, and "necessary" had expanded to include the young woman who had lost her first love and her ritual abilities, and was passing through the wreckage of her homeland. Because Rifkind thought it was simply necessary behavior, she was oblivious to the whispered comments of the others that she had softened since Adijan's death, and displayed more affection than any of them had suspected she possessed.

Thus she was in the closed carriage when they first came in sight of the walls of Daria itself, and had to crane her neck to see the city through the tiny windows.

'Dear Bright One ... I had not imagined anything so big. We are farther away from it than I was from Isinglas when I first saw that place, and this is many times the size ... and behind it that blue-green which is not sky is the water of the oceans which Lord Humphry talked about at too-great length. I could almost believe that there is truly more water than there is land—but that it is all unfit to drink as Lord Humphry claims—that I cannot believe.'

"Does our capital impress you?" Lady Anelda asked with obvious pride.

Rifkind sat back before answering.

"I cannot imagine so many people living in one place for so long. Even at Chatelgard you had gardens to grow food, and sent hunters into the forests for game—but I don't understand how people can live in a place like that. It is not real."

"It's very real, my dear, and very comfortable, you'll find—at least at the palace where we are going. Can you see the palace atop the Seraline hill? Or are we still too far out?"

Rifkind returned to the window.

"Yes, that must be it... a mountain shaped by hands. Is that where we shall stay? I hope not, though from what you're saying we would not go anywhere else. Chatelgard itself is like a single tent to that—and it took half the winter for me to learn my way about that place."

Lady Anelda took her objections good-naturedly. Linette had been roused from her lethargy by the conversation and watched their approach with rapt attention and wonder. Rifkind let Linette have the vantage point of the one window, then sat and fidgeted. There was too much conversation for her to slip unnoticed into an apparent nap and watch the city from Turin's eyes. Now that she had seen the palace and reconciled herself to its size, she wanted to find the tower which was said to be An-Soren's private residence.

The sun set behind the city—a sight Linette reported to them in some detail—and lights began to flicker on in the palace and elsewhere. Linette said it was very pretty, and Rifkind restrained herself from pushing the other woman aside to see for herself. When the countryside was in full darkness, the carriage halted and they conferred.

"Father said to enter at morning, but I'm reluctant to spend the night out here in the fields," Ejord stated.

"My brother could be dead by now, it's so long since we've heard from him. If we approach Daria by night, we shall surely fall into some trap his enemies have set for us," Lady Anelda complained.

"Or be set upon by thieves," Bainbrose added.

"We've that risk if we camp right here. And moving slowly by night, we can approach the walls virtually unseen, which would be more difficult if we wait until morning," Ejord countered.

"Is the entire city walled?" Rifkind questioned.

"The part around the palace, anyway, though most of the gates have settlements outside them as I remember, unless the fighting has pushed everyone within the walls," Ejord answered.

"I wish we had some way of knowing if my brother was all right."

"Ejord could take the other guard, steal into the city and find out, then report back to us," Rifkind suggested.

"No, that would leave us without protection all night," Lady Anelda complained.

"Bainbrose and I would be here."

"No, I agree with Lady Anelda," Bainbrose averred. "We shouldn't separate—all together, no matter what."

Rifkind shook her head but remained quiet.

"Her idea is right. We will all approach the gate settlements and hear what is being said in the streets and taverns. It's sure to give us some idea of what's happening at the palace," Ejord finalized.

"We'll have to leave Turin out here. We'll attract too much attention if we take him into the settlements." Lady Anelda pointed to Turin, who shook his horns at her.

"Then you'll go without me," Rifkind cut in icily.

"No, our story that he is a gift is as good—or better —here by the capital—though Rifkind, I think you should stay out of sight. If people saw you and Turin together, we might not be able to counter their suspicions."

Rifkind nodded.

"A gift to whom?" Bainbrose asked.

"That will depend on who is asking, and how they ask. Perhaps I'll say we're taking him to Father, perhaps to Darius, or even to An-Soren himself—after all, he is rumored to be Asheeran, too, and we could always be coming to seek his aid rather than to destroy him."

"The lad has a devious streak in him after all—I believe we can make it work." Bainbrose cracked his first smile of the discussion.

Lady Anelda swallowed her objections, then stepped back into the carriage. They traveled slowly and as quietly as the carriage could manage. The three occupants retreated into their own thoughts or apprehensions as the dirt trail gave way to a cobbled roadway. Rifkind used Turin's eyes to watch their approach to a squalid settlement.

There were few people on the streets, none of whom looked particularly anxious to notice anyone else. It seemed they would have to go to the gate itself before they encountered anyone on the streets who could give them the information they desired.

"I'll go in there. It's the best of a poor choice, but I think I can do it."

Turin and Rifkind watched as Ejord led Blackthorn to an unsavory tavern from which two patrons were just then being tossed into the street. Rifkind could feel Turin's body tense and remembered the affection the war-horse felt for the young nobleman.

He shouldn't go in alone; someone should be at his back. No, not you, Turin.

The war-horse had responded to the concern in her thoughts and stepped forward to guard him. It gave her a better vantage point as she could now see through the open door and into the crowded room.

Once again we've underestimated Ejord, though I should have remembered how he handled the soldiers at the inn. Ejord is comfortable with those types. He laughs with them and slaps them on their shoulders yet never loses his dignity or control. With enough time, he could convince those fellows in there to follow us through the gate and up to the palace walls themselves.

Rifkind watched, noting his technique for gathering the patrons into an attentive group, then speaking to them just long enough to get them at ease and talking back to him. Though she could easily perceive the patterns he operated by, she did not expect to use them herself. She thought of Ejord as a clansman. His accomplishments were part of her own pride and, since she never thought of a clan without imagining herself to be a power within it, she took special note of his talents for use in future crises.

Lady Anelda, who sat opposite her, was growing anxious at the unexplained delay, forcing Rifkind to split her attention between the carriage and the tavern, an effort that left both her and the war-horse glassy-eyed and vaguely disoriented. But the older woman had enough sense of their position to remain silent, and when Ejord bade his new companions farewell, Rifkind was able to devote her whole attention to the outside scene.

Turin had begun to adapt to his role as Rifkind's extra eyes and ears. He had anticipated Blackthorn's walk back to the carriage and was already nibbling idly at some unappetizing grain which lay on the ground by the wheels when Rifkind slipped back into his mind.

"Well, what have you learned?" Bainbrose asked.

"Quite a bit. Father is alive and by all accounts still very evident and powerful. He was out reviewing the royal armies yesterday and haranguing them before they went off to meet with Hogarth's armies up the coast. No one has seen anything of An-Soren all winter, though no one thinks he's departed. Most of them have begun to suspect a link between the sorceror and Hogarth, and their stories seem convincing.

"There is civil war between Hogarth and Darius, but both armies have been swept by pox. There're reports of were-beasts stalking the fringes of both camps, but the only dead seem to be from the king's forces."

"Tavern rumors, Ejord. An-Soren will not need Hogarth after Darius is gone—mark that—but he'll give Hogarth any aid he needs until the rightful peerage is destroyed."

"For certain, Bainbrose, those men in there would not fight for An-Soren, though none of them seemed eager to be conscripted into Darius's armies either. There is the usual complaint of no food for the town while the palace gluts itself. No food for the army, so the officers rob the merchants, but give no money to the merchants whose goods are confiscated. If Darius didn't have civil war on his hands when Hogarth first raised the army, he's got it now from the mess his own people are making of the situation."

"But is it safe to go into the city?" Bainbrose asked

as he watched another tavern imbiber get tossed out.

"Safe as ever."

"There's little consolation in that. Tell the women-folk we're going in—the old bitch won't argue with you."

"That's only because she doesn't think I'm intelligent enough to understand her."

"Now, there is consolation in that, my boy."

Rifkind was centered within herself again when Ejord opened the door to say they would be going through the gates. Lady Anelda sighed, asked to speak to Bainbrose, and on being told that Ejord himself was making all their decisions, began to mutter unsubtle entreaties to all her favorite gods. Once the carriage had stopped moving, Linette had fallen asleep, and the slow pace at which they began to move along the relative smoothness of the street did not awaken her.

'They always fight and defend without moving,' Rifkind thought as they turned one sharp corner after another. 'No army could build a swift attack against the gates with all these twisted alleys. There would be guards posted on the walls, and they'd find it a simple task to harass and destroy the invaders while they were trapped in this maze. But if the walls could be breached, then the defenders have no place to go. The caravans fought the same way, using their wagons and animals to make a wall to hide behind; then it was only a question of slaying them one by one, because they had destroyed their own escape routes.'

She was completely absorbed in thoughts of the poor strategic planning of the Dro Darians, leaving Turin to negotiate the streets as he saw fit, though she would never have overriden his judgment in such things. Ejord had apparently picked up enough information at the tavern to know the best way to cajole the gate-watch into letting them into the city itself. The gate was set directly into the walls of the city, without the funneling barbican channel Rifkind had seen at Isinglas and thought typical of all Dro Darian cities. But Daria protected itself with two iron grates and doors half as thick as Rifkind was tall.

The scene changed only slightly when they emerged on the other side of the gates. The streets were possibly narrower and the buildings were more often of stone or brick than wood, but otherwise there was little in the darkened city to hold Rifkind's attention. They were too close to the palace to be able to see it. Except that her warrior's instincts forbade her to close her eyes in potentially dangerous terrain, she would have rested.

As it was, she was unaware of the man in the alleyway watching them while Ejord and Bainbrose discussed their route through Daria to the palace. Turin's concern burst through her consciousness. The shadowed figure was tall, lean, and almost completely concealed by a dark cloak pulled tightly around him. She could not perceive what it was that had originally drawn Turin's attention to him rather than any other half-hidden lurker who had watched their progress. When they chose a direction and thus passed the alley, the figure darted out behind them. But even that did not disturb her unduly.

He was there a short distance later, and from what she knew of Dro Darian cities and the twisted course they were following, Rifkind concluded that the second encounter could not be coincidental. She cracked open the window of the carriage and peered out. Turin could see movement in the dark shadows, but his vision was, in general, not as good as hers. The man was still veiled in the shadows, though she caught a glimpse of a black beard before they turned a corner and he disappeared.

'He knew I was watching him; that's peculiar,' she mused to herself as they bounced down the streets. 'I'm sure he didn't hear me open the window, and in the darkness he can hardly have seen into the carriage—yet I'm also certain that he knew I was watching him—he was watching for me.'

With that disquieting thought, Rifkind sat back in the carriage. The window was still open and she could watch the streets and alleys on her side, while Turin, who was also disturbed by the reappearance of the skulking figure, watched the other. The lights on the palace wall were visible now, looming high over them. The streets were all but deserted and gave the distinct impression of being abandoned.

At the palace gate, Ejord announced their identity. The gates creaked open and they entered.

To Rifkind's surprise, the palace was a collection of separate buildings within the high walls, a smaller city within a city. Lady Anelda started moving about, rearranging her dress and pulling her light fur cape around her. Linette awoke, and on discovering that they had arrived, stuck her head and shoulders out the window. Satisfied that everyone was actively absorbed in their own affairs, Rifkind opened the door of the carriage and stepped down to the large courtyard for her first survey of the palace compound.

There were more towers than she could count, and none of them seemed what she was looking for, though she had only intuition to guide her. Again it was Turin's mind which burst into hers with the knowledge and direction she needed. The lean, cloaked figure was standing at the top of one of the near towers. The distance was fairly great, but if Turin had spotted the man, Rifkind was fairly certain that it was the same one who had been trailing them through the city. Icy shivers raced up and down her spine, as she convinced herself that the man was An-Soren himself and that he was indeed watching her.

Turin walked to her side, thrusting his muzzle against her neck, filling her with his still-unshaken belief that she was invincible regardless of the odd habits of the Rider watching them. She noted with additional discomfort that Turin had placed the man in the exclusive category of strong personalities he considered capable of understanding a war-horse like himself.

The figure stepped back from the tower wall and did not return. Rifkind absently stroked Turin's neck and completely overlooked Lord Humphry bursting out of another nearby tower.

"Rifkind!"

He grasped her in a great embrace which startled her to near violence.

"I hardly recognize you. You're a lady!"

He embraced her again—she imitated the form of enthusiasm, with her eyes open and locked on the tower roof as she did so. Lord Humphry greeted Linette the same way, accorded his sister a polite handshake, and his son nothing at all. Servants in the familiar Overnmont livery approached from places unseen and quickly led the carriage and extra horses away.

Turin whickered in faint protest, realizing he would be separated from his Rider again. She patted his neck and reassured him with her mind that she would not be far or long from him. Then she hurried to join the group walking toward what she assumed were the Overnmont quarters within the compound.

Their path took them past An-Soren's tower. She found herself reflexively reaching for one of her throwing knives, though she knew that a knife would be useless against him if he was indeed a sorceror. She felt no measurable shock or surprise when he appeared, leaning against the entrance door of his tower. There was almost a sense of relief. Enough light fell upon him from the various torches and lanterns in the courtyard that she could see his face and take his measure.

He held still, allowing her the opportunity to see him. His dark eyes met hers directly but impassively. The black, well-groomed beard almost concealed the scar on his cheek, but she knew what she was looking for and could find it without difficulty. Her suspicions now completely confirmed, she felt a relaxed exhilaration at having finally seen him after all the winter of dreading him.

'An-Soren is as he should be—tall, proud, and intelligent. I had heard so much, I no longer knew whether to expect a man or something like Hanju—or worse. But he is a man—I have dealt with men before. Regardless of his betrayal of the Bright One, or whatever his patrons might be now, I can deal with a man.'

Rifkind settled into her confidence as An-Soren nodded at her and smiled. Carefully maintaining her composure—and disguise—she responded with the quick half-step curtsy Lady Anelda had drilled into her. An-Soren smiled again and opened his cloak slightly. Her eyes fixed on the heavy gold necklace hung around his neck and the great ruby suspended from it.

Rifkind berated herself for possibly revealing surprise when she should have experienced none. The weight of her identical necklace and ruby was still around her own neck; it was actually quite reasonable that An-Soren's should be the exact twin of her own.

"Well, tell me, my young country cousin," Lord Humphry stepped unwittingly between her and the sorceror and draped an arm around her shoulder. "What do you think of our capital and our palace?"

The masquerade was over before it had started, but she knew better than to tell the lord that. Rifkind swallowed hard and answered him.

"It is a wonderous place, milord, quite unlike anywhere else I have been before—and, I'm sure, full of surprises."

The slight quaver which had invaded her voice disconcerted her, but seemed to impress Lord Humphry as a mark of sincerity. He fairly swept her into the front door of their establishment and began regaling her with anecdotes about the history of the compound.

CHAPTER 22

"Rifkind. That's an odd name for someone from Glascardy, isn't it?"

The questioner was one of the queen's numerous (and to Rifkind's mind uniformly objectionable) handmaids. They were all about Linette's age, and their incessant questions made her long for Linette's quiet sullenness. Lord Humphry had introduced Linette to the king within a few days of their arrival, and the young woman now spent most of her time in Darius's private quarters, to the scandal of most of the court.

"It's an old family name," she replied with a

cheerfulness she did not feel.

"How did you live back there in the mountains?"

"I survived."

"You don't look like an Overnmont. They're all big and strong... what're your brothers like?"

Rifkind's mind wandered perversely to Halim's disfigured corpse. She hadn't thought of him in months, and the memory was not pleasant. Little that had happened since they had arrived at the palace was pleasant. She'd been impelled into a round of social activity which had worsened when the queen had taken a liking to her and would summon her to the royal apartments, then leave her waiting with the handmaids half the afternoon.

"They aren't."

"They aren't what?"

"I'm an orphan who has lived with Lord Humphry's household for several years." The vision of Halim refused to be banished from her thoughts and eroded her composure while she fielded the interminable questions which wove new intricacies into her basic deception.

"Then you aren't really an Overnmont anyway. You're probably common, judging from your color."

"Girls! That will be enough! Coraline is waiting for you. I expect my gown finished by nightfall!"

The girls muttered but filed out of the solarium past their mistress—Queen Gratielle was not a woman to be argued with.

"I'm sorry I was late. I don't know why you put up with them—insolent cats sent here to spy on me by my husband.

"That was the last fitting, thank the Lost Gods. I am a prisoner within these walls. Darius fears I'll

take another since I refuse him—yet I'm still supposed to be the beautiful queen, gracious and a
model for the court. Even now after all these years.
I want nothing more than to go back to my father's
castle and enjoy life again. You're lucky. No matter
what Humphry Overnmont does or says, nothing
will keep your Ejord in Daria."

Gratielle sat down in the window seat, hugging
her knees up to her chin. The queen had never had
a confidante before, and though Rifkind believed the
woman truly prized their time together it was a one-
sided arrangement.

"No, he loves the mountains of Glascardy as
much as he loves me."

The words came easily off her tongue; she had
adopted the masquerade of an impoverished, but
well-bred, young woman completely, occasionally
surprising herself by half-believing her own lies.
"Perhaps Darius will let you come and spend a
summer with us?"

"No, Darius would never allow that. I have not left
the palace in the ten years since I was brought here
to be his queen. Perhaps once, if someone had said
the mountains would improve the chance I'd have a
son. But now—I would not tolerate that even to escape these walls . . . but while you're here, you can
tell me about the mountains!"

"There's not really much to say," Rifkind said,
fidgeting about. "When you've lived in mountains all
your life, you get to taking them for granted—the
winters are too long, the summers too short. It's really more pleasant in the palace."

Rifkind attempted to steer the conversation from
the queen's seemingly obsessive homesickness. Lord
Humphry would be waiting for her at dinner back

at the Overnmont enclave, and in the three afternoon
visits she'd had with the queen, she'd yet to come
back to him with anything he found at all interesting. Rifkind had no great love of spying, though intrigue relieved the boredom of court life for her
much as it did for everyone else within the palace
walls. It was in her own interest to find out if Gratielle had indeed taken An-Soren as a lover, but the
queen invariably preferred to talk about the past
rather than any pleasures she might have in the
present.

"No, nothing happens here. I'm a prisoner within
these walls. There was plague all through the city
this winter—even my handmaids were taken by it—
but Darius would not let Hogarth take me back to
our father's lands for my health."

More than once Rifkind had wondered if
Gratielle's isolation were indeed so complete that
she did not know of the civil war which raged between her brother and the king's forces.

"We heard of this plague, even in Glascardy—a
most horrid and unnatural thing it was rumored to
be, with men running naked in the streets and
mothers killing their children. Some—at home—
think there was witchery involved."

The queen shuddered. "No, no witchery. There is
no witchery here, unless you be a witch yourself. It's
all rumors and false trails laid to discredit us!"

Rifkind's comment had sparked a profound
change in the auburn-haired woman, enough of a
change that she herself was a bit unnerved—it did
not seem possible that the queen knew or suspected
what her true identity was, but caution was going to
be necessary.

"To discredit whom?" Rifkind asked when the

queen's agitation had not subsided after a few moments of silence.

"Whom? Whom? An-Soren. They always blame An-Soren. The crops don't come up—they blame An-Soren. Darius whimpers he cannot prove his manhood, they suspect An-Soren, though I turned to him when I could not conceive a son in hopes he could do something. The army is swept with plague —it's his fault."

"But he is a powerful magician, isn't he?"

"Yes! . . . No. Without him there would be no Dro Daria. My foolish husband could not run the country alone. He can barely decide what clothing he will wear to dinner, or choose his own mistresses." The last was stressed more than the others, and Gratielle got up to pace the edges of the room like a caged animal. "Without An-Soren there would be only the peerage to guide the king—they hate me because I brought An-Soren here and he has broken their influence. Your father-in-law most of all, Rifkind; he would have Daria his way or crush it beneath his foot."

Rifkind tensed reflexively. Before, in their conversations the queen would lapse into these bouts of agitation for only a few seconds at a time, and never about anything specific. There was something vaguely menacing in Gratielle's movements about the room, yet Rifkind's healer's empathy told her that the woman was deeply tormented and sincere in her anguish. She held her peace while the queen's anxieties peaked and she gradually calmed down. It would have been much easier to understand Gratielle if they'd been able to meet in the stables, where Turin's more sensitive mind could have absorbed the complexities of the situation.

The queen was, in truth, a virtual prisoner within the palace—and within the royal apartments at that. There were guards on the stairways and halls, and although they had never challenged Rifkind as she wandered the palace, they were not the ordinary pensioned officers who staffed the rest of the palace security force.

"How do you celebrate arbortide in Glascardy?" Gratielle asked, suddenly her old self again.

"Much as everyone else does," Rifkind answered, cursing inwardly that with all her history and dancing lessons no one had bothered to teach her the things every peasant would know, such as the holiday festivals.

"Do you run garlands through the halls and make a great sweet cake in the center of the great hall?"

"Yes."

"That's odd—we do that at midwinter," Gratielle smiled.

Rifkind snapped to battle alertness.

'That smile. Just then, for an instant, as if she were trying to trap me. She is not always herself. There is so much in this place which baffles me. The presence of An-Soren is everywhere, but there is no focus. He keeps to the tower and is never in this room, so far as I know. The king is incompetent as everyone claims, and Gratielle is subject to these fits of agitation.'

"Well, in the mountains, arbortide is not much different from midwinter," Rifkind temporized.

The fleeting smile also signaled the end of Gratielle's agitated outbursts for the afternoon. She did not seem to remember that they had been talking about arbortide but launched into a dicussion of the day-to-day palace routine. Rifkind brought the subject up again to see if there would be another agitated response, but the queen talked only of the grand-scale preparation which she was responsible for and mentioned nothing about the tensions which Rifkind thought would be apparent to the most casual observer.

In her normal behavior, Gratielle revealed herself to be as much out of step with the court as Rifkind was herself, which accounted for the friendship of convenience which had sprung up between them. But ultimately they had little in common, and Rifkind was always relieved to see the inevitable messenger summon the queen away to other duties, though the queen never was. One of the armed guards would then escort Rifkind out of the royal apartments.

The time she had spent learning the secret ways of Chatelgard served Rifkind in good stead at the palace. In the seven days since their arrival in Daria, she had mastered the underground maze which connected the enclaves of the various high families and the royal complex itself. She had marked several dark passages in her mind for further exploration, but she had far less free time than she had had before. She emerged from the maze near the back staircase which wound upwards to the long-unused rooms she'd insisted on having for herself because they faced An-Soren's tower.

She had been in her room but a few moments when there was a knock at the door.

"May I come in?" Ejord called from behind the closed door.

Rifkind opened the door and stared past him down the empty hallway.

"Do you think it's wise? I'm not supposed to be

drawing attention to myself."

"We are supposed to be betrothed; it is expected that we'll be seen together."

Rifkind stepped aside and let him into the room.

"Actually, I expect there'll be more rumors about you living up here in the servants' quarters. I'd forgotten how many people Father has living here, but I'd thought he'd find you an apartment with the family."

"He tried—several times—but I wanted this set of rooms. I like being high up, this faces An-Soren's tower, and besides it makes it harder for your father to find me and ask questions."

Ejord chuckled softly. "Speaking of questions, though, I've got a few myself; that's the reason I came over here."

"What sort of questions?"

"Well, I've been down to the stables a couple of times since we got here. Most of the grooms and stableboys won't go near Turin, so I usually spend a little time with him—he seems to get lonely more easily than the others. I've got all the gear you had lashed to his saddle piled on a shelf above his manger. I figured he knew enough not to bother it, and he would probably protect it better than anyone else could."

Rifkind smiled and muttered a quiet thank-you.

"It's the least I can do. The stables are the one place that's off-limits for you, since we're still saying that Turin's a gift for Darius at arbortide ... but my question is—did you go down there last night and mess that shelf up?"

"What's missing?" she demanded, not bothering to answer his question.

"Nothing, so far as I can tell—and I straightened

everything up again. Turin was wild-eyed, so I didn't think it was you. He wasn't going to let me near the stuff, so I just stood there and thought at him for a while."

"Turin's very sensitive to all emotions; I can interpret his feelings. I'm sure he trusts you."

"He wasn't acting that way when I got down there."

"You wouldn't have come to me just because Turin was upset and that shelf was disordered..." Rifkind let her voice trail off, hoping Ejord would reveal his suspicions without further direct questions.

He shifted nervously on his feet, staring into the fireplace.

"It could have been the stableboys—a gang of them harassing Turin, one or two climbing over the walls while he was distracted. It could have been Turin himself who messed up the stuff—but it didn't seem that way. I thought you might know more."

Rifkind looked at the tapestries, the fireplace, her cloak thrown in a heap over the chaise while her mind sought a balanced interpretation of Ejord's visit. His eyes followed hers as she tried to avoid him, until at last she stared at her feet.

"An-Soren?" she asked in a whisper.

"I think he suspects something. Whatever he was looking for—"

She cut him off. "He knows I'm here, and who I am." She raised her eyes to meet his.

Surprise and shock registered on Ejord's face. Whatever he had thought, it was not what Rifkind had revealed.

"How, then? What went wrong?" He flopped down on the chaise and her cloak as he spoke.

"That's not important. He knew when I got here. He was waiting for me the night we got here, with a big smile." There was an edge of defiance in her voice.

"I don't understand. If he knows you're here—why doesn't he make his moves the way Father expects him to. Why rummage through the stable like that?"

"What is between An-Soren and me has nothing to do with Dro Daria or your silly wars, or your incompetent kings. You said it yourself—he and I are alike, Ejord, and I have something he wants very badly." Her eyes were hard and flashed with a hostility and irritation which focused on Ejord because he was the only Dro Darian and Overnmont present.

"What?" he asked, not responding to her anger.

She stopped short, checking the impulse to reveal the ruby.

"It's nothing you would want, or understand."

Ejord shrugged his shoulders. "Oh . . . well, then . . . can you at least assure me that he doesn't have it yet—and that you'll tell someone if he does get it away from you?"

"I still have it—and if I should lose it, you will not need me to tell you what has happened."

"Father will have to know that the disguise is useless."

"I never expected that it would fool An-Soren."

"Father will still have to know."

"Only if you tell him. It's been over a week now, and I haven't mentioned it to him. An-Soren and I would have had to reveal ourselves to each other sooner or later. Now there will be no waiting or deciding when is the best time. But the rest of the court

—and especially your father—is best off not knowing exactly what is going on between us. It never mattered to your father why or how I revenged myself on him, so long as the sorcerer was gone."

"That isn't true!"

There was a knock at the door; Ejord froze without completing his thought. Rifkind half-ran to the door. She jerked it open, using it as a shield between herself and whoever entered. A mirror strategically placed on the opposite wall gave her a clear sight of her caller.

Gratielle.

The queen wandered into the room, seeming not so much unfamiliar with her surroundings as unaware of them. Rifkind watched the queen but did not miss Ejord's sudden movement toward his knife. Something in the queen's entrance had made him respond as if a threat had been made.

"Your Majesty?" Rifkind's voice was barely above a whisper as she stepped out from behind the door.

"I thought I might find you here."

The queen's voice was vague and listless, as if she were speaking lines from a play which bored her. Rifkind attempted an empathic bond to the woman. The queen reacted as if a window had been opened and fresh air blown in on her. Her eyes cleared and focused on Rifkind. Extending her arms in front of her, she sprinted across the room to embrace her friend. Rifkind, as always, was discomforted by the impending physical contact—a combination of healer's and warrior's training made any touch she did not initiate a threat—yet she braced herself and was prepared to suffer the affections of the queen.

"Gratielle!" Ejord shouted when the two women were handspans apart.

The queen responded not so much to the sound of her name as to the discovery of another person in the room. She hesitated but continued to reach for Rifkind. Rifkind had been sufficiently aroused by Ejord's shout to realize that the queen's hands were not open for a friendly embrace, but ready to close about her own neck. She brought her hands up to protect herself but could only grapple with the queen, who, obsessed by an idea which was not of her own mind, was oblivious to the strains Rifkind inflicted upon her arms.

"Galieh An-Soren!"

The queen fell backward as if stunned by Ejord's soft-spoken words. Even Rifkind looked at him in surprise. He had used the Old Tongue—hardly a language she expected him to know. "I know you, An-Soren!" he had said, and broken the possession the magician had contrived upon the queen.

"Rifkind? Ejord?" Gratielle wound herself to her knees, rubbing her arms and staring at the bruises on them, her confusion seeming completely sincere.

"Yes, Your Majesty?" Rifkind stepped forward, offering to steady the woman.

Gratielle continued to stare at her hands and arms as if they did not belong to her.

"I—I—don't know where I am."

"You're in my apartment, in the Overnmont quarters."

The queen rushed to the door, brushing Rifkind aside. She continued to mumble to herself about being caught away from the royal compound until she had found the staircase and disappeared down it.

"Again my apologies—An-Soren *does* know who you are, and you do have something he wants—

something you wear or keep in that pouch around your neck?"

He stood beside her; she was shaking and for once welcomed the presence and touch of another person as she normally welcomed the moist touch of Turin's muzzle. An unpleasant suspicion flashed across her mind: Ejord himself was in a position to get the ruby, to act as An-Soren's unwitting agent. Then she told herself that she needed to trust someone, and that Ejord with his immunity, could never be possessed by the sorcerer. She held his hand tightly as if it were the hilt of her sword.

"It's true then. An-Soren can possess the queen."

Ejord nodded. Despite his easy comments, he was very definitely disturbed by what they had seen.

"This is the second time he has come for me."

"*Third*, if it was him in the stables. Should we post a sort of guard?"

"No. If there were a guard, he'd simply eliminate it, or find another way. I'm best off defending myself. I'm not without my own resources. But . . . I'm not as alert as I was in the Asheera. I've softened since coming here, and your dangers are more subtle than ours."

"I'll watch the queen for you—in case he tries again. You didn't seem to see her the way I did."

"There's no need—you called his name; he won't risk it again with you in sight. Anyway, how do you know the Old Tongue?"

"Old Tongue? I have enough trouble getting my tongue around Darian without sounding like a Glascardy woodman; I don't bother with ritual flower-speech."

"Ejord, you spoke Old Tongue to him. What else do you have besides immunity to us?" And her grasp on his wrist was a warning rather than a request for support.

"Hey, now!" he exclaimed, breaking away from her. "Whatever else you might think, I don't speak your Old Tongue. I called him out the same way I'd call out a thief in the marketplace."

Rifkind looked up at him. At this distance, and with the recent physical contact, there was no doubting his honesty. Shock and indignation poured out of him, and she was reassured that he did not know that he had used the Old Tongue to break An-Soren's possession ritual. She glanced out the window. Though it was only late afternoon, the Bright One was visible in her fullness. It was not unusual for Her to be visible during the day, especially at the height of her cycle. Rifkind thought she knew who had protected her, and that there were some powers which Ejord's immunity could not resist.

CHAPTER 23

Rifkind counted the number of flaws in the floor mosaic of Lord Humphry's study for the third time. She had learned to live with walls, long dresses, and forks, but Dro Darian politics remained beyond her comprehension. If there was going to be a war, then sitting in a room talking about who had started it was a waste of precious time. Raiding parties should be organized, women, children and wagons hidden away from the well, and the warriors should be out sharpening their weapons. The Dro Darians knew nothing about fighting—as an Asheeran she had always known this—the clans depended on the stupidity of the Wet-Land caravans to regularly bring them the materials the barren steppes could not provide.

Even Bainbrose, who could usually be counted on for some sort of logic, was swept up into the furor of blaming something or someone for the imminence of warfare and the royal unreadiness. It was only when they blamed An-Soren that Rifkind roused herself from daydreams and boredom, since a blame to An-Soren was likely to be followed by worried questions on what she was doing about this nemesis. She would reply to the questions that in the three weeks since their arrival in the capital, the king's sorcerer had been seen in public exactly four times—each time in the company of the king, queen, and Lord Humphry himself—and that if he was so eager for her to do something about the magician, then he could introduce her. Her current pose as a provincial bride-to-be left her little on which to base a conversation with the sorcerer.

Ejord was also present for these sessions, usually sitting quietly and appearing to be the model of an obedient son. As an empath, she had no trouble sensing his boredom, which bordered on disgust; but he had never contradicted her assertions that the only contacts she had had with An-Soren were the publicly verified ones. He never spoke of the stables, or of Gratielle's strange visit to the Overnmont compound—nor most especially of the failure of Rifkind's disguise. In return she had not spoken to him of the other incidents, of attacks on the invisible wards she'd mounted around herself and Turin. He might have guessed, but Ejord's discretion was faultless.

"The melting of the snows in Hallendol was the work of An-Soren!"

There was that name again. She hadn't registered who was speaking, and had no idea where Hallendol was.

"Rifkind, what's your opinion of that—An-Soren again?" Lord Humphry asked, skewing around in his chair to face her, since she usually sat as far from him as politeness would allow.

"I'm not sure. Without access to his tower, I cannot judge what rituals he performs."

"Can't you . . . flirt with him, do something? Look at Linette—half your experience, and she's living over with Darius now," Humphry said, his face turning a darker red with what Rifkind knew was false modesty and embarrassment.

For all his admitted imagination in political tactics, Lord Humphry had a deep conviction that the most successful way for a woman to find out anything from a man was to become his mistress. Rifkind wryly wondered what Lord Humphry's own private life was like, but did not bother to respond to his ideas.

"There has been an early thaw everywhere—even in Glascardy, Father. You had not expected us for another ten days when we arrived. Truly, if An-Soren has the power to end winter over all of Dro Daria, then we are wasting our time with armies composed of men," Ejord said coldly.

"My point entirely. Rifkind, you should be doing something with him, not spending your time with the queen; she's only sure to report everything you do and say to her brother Hogarth."

"I spend far more time listening to you worry out

loud than I do with the queen, who is at least interesting to talk to."

Rifkind slid a knife out of her sleeve-hem and deft-
ly removed a small splinter from her finger. The
splinter had been there since breakfast, but she
could not display a knife simply for effect—even
though she knew her weapons disturbed everyone
in the Overnmont household except Ejord.

"You are not here to talk to interesting people,
witch, you are in my service to eliminate An-Soren."

Again she did not answer him, but met his eyes
with projected anger only a warrior and healer
could manage. The Dro Darian lord barely flinched
from the perceptible emotion she forced against
him, but he let the matter drop quietly. Rifkind put
the knife back in her sleeve-hem and returned to her
thoughts.

His arguments had made her more uneasy than
she revealed—not because of some imagined debt to
Lord Humphry, but because her own instincts told
her time was running short. Whatever An-Soren's
connection to the impending civil war, his lust for
her ruby was a tangible presence in her life. She
had steeled herself for a foray into the windowless
tower, reconciled that she would have to leave her
body behind and risk being trapped in a tal-state
while she explored his secrets.

It was not as dangerous as she had once feared it
would be. In her need to preserve the ruby from An-
Soren, she had been forced to learn something of its
powers. The primitive words she had set up to keep
curious servants out of her possessions at Chatelgard
were now sturdy barriers. The ruby had built those
barriers, and though she did not understand the

spirits which strengthened them they withstood the
pure light of the Bright One, and she trusted them.
Her body, at least, would be safe.

And she could bring the power of the ruby with
her even when she transferred herself to her tal and
wandered through the night to learn An-Soren's secrets. The stone sharpened all her abilities. She had
traveled further and faster than Muroa had ever said
was possible for an initiate to do, and without the
ache of longing for her body. An-Soren's tower was
still unknown to her, but little else in the great palace was. She'd seen the queen writhing in
nightmare-ridden sleep, the king cavorting with a
more-than-willing Linette, Ejord sitting up until just
before dawn studying battle maps. The ruby gave
her new confidence in her powers, and in the Bright
One, whom she was sure had pre-destined that she
would be the one to use it against the ancient enemy—An-Soren.

It tingled slightly as she thought about it—a heavy
yet reassuring weight hung about her neck. Rifkind
let its warmth course through her, putting the petty
concerns of Lord Humphry far out of her mind. Her
mother's ruby and the destruction of An-Soren; she
reveled in her destiny.

The doors to the study burst open, jarring Rifkind
from her reverie but startling the others as well; no
one disturbed their meetings. Two men in the utilitarian gear of Lord Humphry's personal guard rather than the livery of his servants strode purposefully
into their midst—followed by two more of their fellows dragging one of the house servants between
them. The servant staggered with terror; saliva and
tears moistened his face and surcoat. Had the

guards not supported him he would have collapsed at once on the floor.

"A spy, milord," the soldier who wore a gold crest on his breastplate announced.

Rifkind fixed her attention on the servant once again, having felt Ejord tense as he always did in the presence of unsheathed magic or weaponry.

"Why, that's Garhad. He's not a spy," Bainbrose grumbled, not bothering to conceal his impatience with the military.

"We found him with this—leaving the compound." The first soldier stepped forward and handed Lord Humphry a paper.

While Lord Humphry read it, the servant Garhad dissolved into incoherent screams and wails. His knees buckled completely. He bit his tongue and raved as one who had become mad. Rifkind did not need to watch Ejord to sense the presence of something unnatural in the room with them. She whispered an entreaty to the Bright One, not caring if the soldiers heard her use the priestly language.

Lord Humphry crumpled the paper with one hand, throwing it quickly into the low fire. He watched it flare up and disappear before addressing the soldier.

"To whom was he taking the message?"

"We don't know for certain, milord. We caught him leaving through the kitchen door."

"Didn't you try to follow him? To get him to lead you to the others? Beat the answers out of him!" The shock had worn off, and Lord Humphry's anger surfaced in full swing.

The soldier brushed his hand against his thighs in a nervous gesture. He stammered before answering, but did not lower his eyes.

"The man saw us as we saw him. He made no effort to continue his mission, and has been like this since we approached him."

All eyes turned again to Garhad, but the man was oblivious to their attentions and aware only of some personal hell into which he had fallen. Rifkind was convinced the man had fallen under the domination of An-Soren and was about to use the ruby's focusing power to draw An-Soren out when Ejord caught her eye. He made a knife edge with his hand and slashed downward—a signal the players back in the gaming rooms had used to warn their friends of a dangerous player in their midst. Rifkind sat back in her chair, sliding her hand through the side slits of her dress to rest on the hilt of the heavier throwing knife instead.

"Make him talk!" Lord Humphry demanded, standing up and walking to Garhad himself. "Speak up, man. Explain yourself! How do you come to have such letters in your possession and to whom would you have taken them?"

Garhad tried to regain control; he braced his feet clumsily against his captors and struggled to support himself. He raised his face to meet Lord Humphry's accusations, but when their eyes met, an involuntary wail escaped him instead of coherent answers. He fell forward, sustained only by the alertness of his guards.

"Milord, I think the man is frightened beyond his wits. Have the men release him and he may return to his senses," Bainbrose suggested quietly.

"Stand by the door. He might attempt to escape, and madmen possess strength and speed beyond justice." Humphry ordered the officer and his companion to stand by the door, then signaled the guard to release Garhad, who immediately collapsed on the floor.

Rifkind had a gruding admiration for Lord Humphry. Despite his anger and threats of violence, he stepped away from the slobbering figure and waited patiently for the man's hysteria to pass. The vague sense of unnaturalness had congealed to an oppressive malignancy which affected the others as well as herself. Only Ejord might have had an inkling of the true situation; Lord Humphry, Bainbrose and the others were simply anxious and nervous far out of proportion to the apparent threat from Garhad, who was quieting down and drawing himself up to his knees.

"It doesn't matter. He knows now. He knows everything now!" Garhad crooned to the ceiling, his eyes still rolling wildly and his voice still hysterical for all that it was controlled and coherent now.

"Who knows?" Lord Humphry demanded.

"He knows!" Garhad smiled, then burst into maniacal laughter. "He knows everything!"

Rifkind had no doubts that the "he" to whom Garhad referred was An-Soren, and was strongly suspicious that An-Soren was as much in control of Garhad's mind and movements as she was when she used Turin as her eyes and ears. When Garhad's seemingly idiot eyes passed over her, she felt a coldness pass through her. She slid the knife out of its sheath, though she was not sure it would be at all useful against the possessed servant.

"Hogarth?" Lord Humphry demanded, fear rising over his patience as he approached his servant, "Is that who you mean? How long have you been spying for Hogarth?"

"Hogarth?" Garhad's voice rose to a childlike soprano, only emphasizing the eerie madness about the man. "What does Hogarth know but what he is told?"

"Rifkind!" Lord Humphry turned to her, as he began to understand that things were not as they had first seemed. "What is wrong with this man—you're a healer, you claim—do something with him—bring him back to his senses!"

Rifkind shuddered despite herself. "I can do nothing for him. I will not lay hands on him." She pulled her arms deeper into the folds of her dress, clutching the knife hilt tightly.

"You will not! I need information from this man—and you presume to tell me that you will not do what is necessary to bring him to his senses?" Lord Humphry stepped toward her, his anger suddenly finding a suitable focus.

"He has no senses. Another spirit controls his mind now. If I were to touch him, that spirit would attempt to displace me from my mind and body."

"Garhad ... possessed? ... What kind of spirit? Should we call for the priests?" Lord Humphry's anger again lost its focus as he grappled with Rifkind's logic.

"Perhaps we should send for An-Soren himself?" Bainbrose suggested softly.

Rifkind nodded. If An-Soren were in possession of Garhad's mind and body, then his own would, at best, be guarded by preset words—much as her own was at night. The others, except for Ejord, did not suspect that it was An-Soren who tormented the servant. And her use of the word "spirit" was well in line with the usual possession of unfortunate individuals by gods or demons who wished to travel the ways of their worshipers.

She was not surprised, though, that the mention of the sorcerer's name brought about a violent behavioral change in Garhad. The man began to rant again, and crawled toward the door. Rifkind noticed a spasmodic stiffness on the man's limits, Garhad, or the body of Garhad, was dying—the trauma of being forced to do An-Soren's bidding had cost the servant first his sanity and now himself. The sorceror would have to leave Garhad's body or drag it to the tower before it stiffened and rotted. Rifkind held her hand over her breastbone, covering the pouch which held the moon-stones and the ruby.

"What is happening?" Lord Humphry demanded of both Rifkind and Bainbrose.

"The offending spirit, having violated the natural order of life, must now leave the soul it has possessed and destroyed lest he be trapped in it—is this not so?" Rifkind answered Lord Humphry, but directed her final comment to Garhad/An-Soren.

The pathetic, still-weaving figure was reaching out his hands in supplication toward the soldiers; at once Rifkind realized that An-Soren could easily transfer his powers to any living being he could reach. She wanted to call out to the guard not to touch Garhad's body, but her voice was unnaturally still. With a soaring feeling of panic she watched the soldier reach out to his own doom.

"Garhad!"

Ejord leaped out of his chair and fell upon Garhad, knocking him away from the soldier's grasp. Lord Humphry sputtered in confusion while his son cradled the writhing servant—recalling how as a child he had watched Garhad carry his father's clothing down the halls each morning. Rifkind sighed as the spell broke. Ejord was no liar, and he had probably seen the incidents he described, and perhaps felt a profound grief for the man. But mostly he pinned the body and An-Soren within it to the floor and recklessly used his own immunity to ritual arts to protect the others from An-Soren.

Garhad let out a final shriek which filled the room with an unholy stench. Ejord fainted from the foul odor erupting so close to him, and for a heartbeat Rifkind feared for him and for them all. Then the fireplace blazed with a putrescent light, and she knew An-Soren was taking the quickest route back to his own endangered body. The corpse fell free of Ejord's limp arms. Its skin shriveled like ancient parchment and fell away from the bones like dust. Then the bones themselves dried until all that was left of Lord Humphry's personal valet was an irregularly shaped trail of dust within and beyond his clothing. The odor had intensified during the disintegration, and now they were all gagging.

Lord Humphry recovered enough to point to the window while holding one hand over his mouth. A soldier staggered to the window and opened it, vomiting into the garden below. Bainbrose made his way to the other window, and the fresh winds of late spring began to clear the horror from the air. When she was herself able, Rifkind went to Ejord's side and began to examine the young man, who had not yet stirred.

"Bring water—strong salts—herbs!" she commanded.

Ejord's skin was pale and damp, his breathing shallow, but there was nothing more seriously wrong with him than the air he had inhaled. An-Soren might have tried to enter his body—there was a burn mark on his hand she did not remember seeing before—but Ejord's ritual immunity was as strong as An-Soren's power had been. The guards hesitated to obey the order of someone known only as a poor relative of the family, but they also knew she was his bride-to-be, and one left the room in apparent pity for the distraught young woman he took Rifkind to be.

"You'll heal him no doubt, but not my servant Garhad. One could almost think you did care for that hapless lout of a son of mine—even the evil spirits would not take him!" Lord Humphry stepped back from the window.

Ejord's eyes fluttered open as his father spoke, and Rifkind saw anger bordering on hatred within them, but the strain of emotion was too much and he slumped back into a faint.

"Ejord has saved all of us. He risked his own life and soul to keep the spirit from invading one of the rest of us," Rifkind snarled as she sprinkled the pungent salts and herbs on a wet cloth the soldier had brought.

"At least he knows his worth. . . . Bainbrose, we'll go down to the garden to talk, until this room clears of foul air and witchery."

Bainbrose hesitated, wanting to stay with his friends, but the older man owed his comfort to Lord Humphry and with a worried glance over his shoulder followed the guard and Lord Humphry out of the room.

"Damned old bastard," Ejord murmured as Rifkind offered him the scented cloth again.

"I think he was more frightened than he was able to admit. There was real gratitude within him, Ejord. I could feel it—despite what he said."

Ejord pushed her aside, striding to the open window where he revived himself with gulps of pure air.

"You may be sure he was frightened, and that fright will extend to you, Rifkind. If my father cannot belittle what he does not control or understand —he destroys it."

CHAPTER 24

A thin crescent of silver light marked the emergence of the Bright One from her monthly slumber. Although Her light did not yet dwarf the stars as it would when She grew full at the end of the following week, in many ways the Goddess's powers were at their height immediately after Her cyclic darkness. The omens were further strengthened by the knowledge that Vitivar, the Dark One, was in his slumber phase now. Rifkind cast the crystal stones Hanju had given her carefully on the window ledge. The pattern was benign and gentle, a blessing on her endeavors. She shuttered the window and moved confidently through the darkened room.

First she renewed the permanent wards on the chest which contained her sword and her gold. She lifted the ruby pendant out of the pouch and placed it around her neck. The magically charged gold made her skin tingle slightly, and the ruby began to glow with a light of its own. Rifkind pressed the stone against her forehead, absorbing its power and wisdom.

Holding it tightly between her hands, she waited until the red glow oozed out from between her fingers like water and spread over the backs of her hands and up her arms. It was time. She touched the locks and hinges of the chest, then the metal and leather straps which bound the wood together. When the chest glowed with its own light, she stepped back a few paces. The glow quickly faded, but the chest was safe from any prying or destruction. Moving or burning it would result only in illusion; the chest itself and its contents were accessible only to Rifkind and her ruby.

She performed a similar ritual at the window and doors of her rooms, being especially careful at the fireplace since she would have to penetrate its wards herself when she entered the tal-state and began her wandering. Finally the wards were set and she could begin the night's work. Her hands shook as she traced a pentagram on the floor in front of the hearth.

It too began to glow with the same ruby color. The glow of the pentagram did not fade when she stepped back from it. Instead of stepping into its center as the ritual would require, she sat down at its cardinal point and covered her face with her hands.

"I am a healer. I restore health and ease pain. I do

not belong here," she whispered. "The mountain gods and the ruby give me powers Muroa and the others did not dream of, and I do not want them! The life-forces Muroa taught me to find and control are warm and vital. These new powers are hard, and their warmth is that of fire and not of life. I feel them creeping into me, robbing me of what always has been mine.

"Not even the Bright One can stop their movement. Even She has become cold and distant, as if this destiny I am to fulfill repulses even She who gave it to me. I long for the gentle, subtle feeling the arts had when I practiced them in the Asheera."

Rifkind's courage faded as she thought of the magnitude of the events she had endured since the previous summer. The roving styles of the clans were only a distantly remembered dream now. And memory had softened the image, making it more appealing than the reality had ever been.

'That was not the way of a warrior.'

Digging her fingers into her face, Rifkind could recall the acrid odors of the burnt-out camp that late-summer morning, the bitter taste of the water at their last well, and the gnawing ache of hunger after she had given her warrior's share of the scarce food to the women and children because she was also a healer and could not endure their suffering.

The pentagram flickered brightly in the otherwise dark room. The fire in the hearth had crumbled down to barely visible embers since the wards had sealed the chimney.

She stepped into the pentagram.

Energies swirled up around her feet even before she knelt; the red flow rose up until it was an open-ended cone surrounding her. Her breath came in shallow gasps; intelligence alone was not enough to convince her that the translucent wall of red flame was within her control and was in fact a magnification of her own tal.

As the flames rose higher, she was lifted up with them until the great throbbing ball of tal-energy was formed above her head. She had left her body and was fully contained within the ethereal presence.

She exhaled. The body beneath her relaxed.

'That, at least, is easier. Healers were meant to stay within their own bodies. We are not given the ability to project ourselves wildly all across the land or into different dimensions. Whoever made the ruby was not concerned with our limitations.'

The red glow faded when she willed herself to invisibility. She floated up the chimney, through her wards, and into the open night sky above the palace complex. From the tal-state, the Bright One was no longer a simple silvery crescent, but a constantly changing aura of intelligence and wisdom. Rifkind hung motionless in the air, feeling the warmth and compassion of the Goddess pass through her. None of the other stars—nor the ocean nor the mountains on the horizons—appeared to have the aura which surrounded the Bright One. It was a sign of the bond which had been made at the instant of her initiation.

'Forgive me for doubting you. I will not run from the destiny You have laid before me. I trust You to guide me. I'll use the ruby because You have given it to me—I will seek out An-Soren because he has offended and betrayed You, and the ideals which You taught me.'

Rifkind drifted over An-Soren's tower. If the Bright One had shone with a personal intelligence, An-Soren's tower had a multidimensional dark vortex surrounding it. Rifkind approached its warded precincts cautiously, mindful of the dangers of being detected, and the probable fate of anyone snared by the wards.

Rifkind had become the warrior rather than the healer. Her quarry was a creature similar to herself, but more powerful, and, by rumor, less constrained than the Bright One would allow Her initiates to be. The tower was guarded with wards from An-Soren's ruby and by the spirits and tals of some who had ventured to conquer the sorceror, and lost.

An-Soren protected his domain well; even with the aid of the ruby, she could not have gained entrance, any more than he would have penetrated her own wards. But like most of the other residents of the palace, An-Soren thought the walls of his tower were solid, and never thought of invasion or siege. The arrow slits chiseled carefully into the grey stone walls of the tower had been converted to narrow windows, except for one which faced a wall of later construction. Rifkind shrank down to the smallest point she could imagine and approached the narrow slit.

Rifkind expanded her consciousness slightly. The arrow slit opened out onto a dark, unused stairway. She followed that to a room with an open hearth, then probed through the hot, smoky flues until she found a cold hearth like her own.

Something large and irresistible surged around her, buffeting her like a single grain of sand in a storm. The presence of An-Soren was unmistakable. She no longer tried to conceal herself, but only to escape the ravening force which was drawing her out of the hearth and into a room.

She hung, contained and immobolized within her

own tal, above a large, glowing pentagram. An-Soren sat staring at her. She was still invisible within her imprisoned tal, yet equally certain that An-Soren had powers which allowed him to see her quite clearly.

"So you've finally come to spy on me?"

Sheer panic overcame her as she struggled to escape the bonds of the pentagram. Invisible ropes bound arms and legs she did not have, as she envisioned herself a beaten and confined animal.

"We have a stalemate. I have you, but you still have the Eye. Shall we arrange a trade?"

Rifkind looked down at him. He had the smooth confidence of one who clearly holds the superior position. His entire presence was one of competent power rather than evil. The mark on his face was not a scar but a still-open wound. Rifkind studied it with the reflexive compassion of a healer. An eon of searing pain shot through the pentagram.

"A token from your Goddess," An-Soren said with a bitter laugh.

"You are one of the Dark Brethren?"

"Dark Brethren! And what do you call yourselves, shunning daylight and casting bits of bone into the light of the moon!"

"You were a healer once?"

"And I saw things I could not heal with the feeble powers She gave me. So I looked farther. I learned things She had not taught me, things She did not know Herself. And this was my reward!"

"You perverted life-forces. Your knowledge corrupted you. I know what you've done to Gratielle, and Lord Humphry's man Garhad."

An-Soren's face paled with anger. "You speak of perversion, and you're here on the errands of Lord

Humphry and your dear, sweet Goddess."

Within the bonds of the pentagram, Rifkind backed as far away from him as she could. His eyes had the glazed intensity of one who had lived through a lightstorm but did not ever truly stop seeing it. But the agitation did not spread from his eyes, and his hands remained calm and steady on the arms of his chair.

"I do not serve Lord Humphry, only the Bright One whom you defied in the Asheera generations ago. I am here because of Her."

"And if you could outwit me, which you cannot, what would you accomplish? I protect the people of this land from their lords and kings. I care more for them than all their rulers and their gods. Do you think that a sniveling imbecile like Darius could govern his people, or a narrow-minded Goddess like the Bright One care for all of them?"

"The fates of Darius and his people do not concern me. I have come for you."

"Do not concern you? You do not care about them?" The sorcerer's voice grew violent. "You *must* care—you are a healer. That crescent you contrive to hide behind a disguise—doesn't that swear you to caring and feeling for every wretched creature who walks by day or night?" He stood and paced the length of the room. "Use your power, use my pentagram—take a look at the sufferings of these people. Take a look into the mind of Lord Humphry and the rest. Then cast judgment."

Rifkind refused to use her powers, so An-Soren flooded her mind with images of Dro Daria, the Asheera, Lord Humphry, and others until she could no longer distinguish one from the next but was swept up in the torment of confinement and despair.

Over all was the image of Lord Humphry smiling benevolently on the stagnation that weighted down the land and its people. She saw the Asheera, where survival itself was a brutal struggle. Still, the people fought for life and were proud and free despite their hunger.

In the subjective hideaways of her mind, Rifkind knew that An-Soren was manipulating the images flooding her brain—a skilled practitioner of the arts could have made the opposite seem equally convincing—but she held her peace and let him believe he had brought her around to his position.

"Hogarth will bring chaos to the land. He is young, filled with energy and bitter hatred for his fellow noblemen. They will destroy each other. Then I will use the Eyes of the Dark One and rule everywhere—even to the Asheera itself."

'He is mad,' she thought quietly to herself. 'No one could rule the Asheera. He could not guard all the wells, even with both rubies—not so long as healers like Muroa still roam free. And they will stop him again, as they did before, with or without the rubies —unless I stop him here first. What he says about Dro Daria might be true, but he is mad just the same.'

"You do not have the two rubies," she commented.

"I have you; it is all the same."

An-Soren pointed toward a cabinet-wardrobe which opened at his unspoken command. Rifkind watched in horror as her own self stepped out of it. The being moved slowly and was without apparent intelligence, but it made its way to the cardinal point of the pentagram where An-Soren made it stop.

"I do not completely understand the movements of a woman, but I do not think you will find anything to complain about."

"I am safe within my own wards."

"Until you enter your new body. I think you will find it something of an improvement over the one you had before; this one will not age. When you are comfortable, then you can bring me the ruby and we will rule together."

The same pressures which had drawn her into the pentagram now swirled around pulling her toward the new body. The pressures were more difficult to counter because An-Soren had known or guessed her vanities. The gown was black brocade richly embroidered with gold, but the skirt was slit into wide pants which would allow the wearer to ride comfortably. The sword-belt was finely wrought but left empty waiting for her own sword, as were the handsome sheaths for her knives. The thick black fur which trimmed the gown was gercat. The figure wore no jewelry, but An-Soren made it very clear that only the ruby, in its heavy gold chain, would be appropriate.

Rifkind backed away screaming.

"Why resist? You can tell that you will not succeed in outwitting me; I am too strong and powerful for you. Is what I offer so terrible? Together we can end the suffering of all the people."

She stared at her own face, now barely an arm's-length away. The face was unmarked. As she watched and resisted the impelling pressures, first a silver crescent appeared on the right cheekbone; then, with a burst of flame, an open black wound, a duplicate of An-Soren's own.

"I will not join you. I will not betray Her. Even if

you are right, I will not betray Her like that."

"Your petty fears!"

An-Soren's voice bore signs of strain for the first time, as if the effort of maintaining the pressure on her was taking its toll of even his immense energies.

"She cannot really hurt you. That is only a mark of Her impotence, a mark of freedom. From now on you will serve no greedy goddess—only yourself.

"Relent!"

The forces were crushing her as he poured himself into moving her into the waiting body. The empathic sense between the tal and the body was beginning to grow. She fought with her life-strength, and tears flowed down the face in front of her. That which might be her sobbed as the salt of the tears trickled over the black wound.

"Turin!"

The scarred face was in front of her. She fell into it, unable to resist any longer. For an instant, the agony of the Bright One's anger and her own betrayal was a part of her. An-Soren stood next to her, smiling. Then his smile stopped and he grabbed her. It was too late—she fell through the chimera he'd prepared for her.

"Turin! Turin!"

Rifkind was crying. Her face, her own healed face, was buried in the war-horse's mane. She could not remember having cried before, and now as she clung to Turin, timeless memories of every injury, insult, and nightmare clamored in her consciousness demanding catharsis. She tried not to think, but the emotional torrent was beyond her control. Amid her sobs, she appealed to the Bright One.

"Rifkind?"

Ejord stepped into Turin's stall and put his hands

on her shoulders. She paid no attention to him. She gently unwound her twisted clenched fingers from each other and released her hold on Turin's neck. Ejord turned her to face him. Pride forced her to get a measure of control over her behavior and emotions.

"What's wrong? What happened?" he asked with gentle urgency.

She shook her head.

"Something is wrong. You don't wander about crying like a madwoman. And the Bright Moon has never pointed a finger at me before . . . Your face!" He exclaimed as she looked up to answer him.

The panic returned, she reached anxiously to touch the place where the open scar had been. But Ejord grabbed her wrists and restrained her; she was too exhausted to overcome him.

"The crescent's back—that's all."

He held her hands tightly until she relaxed. Then he let her arms drop to her sides.

"He didn't think I could get away."

"To all appearances, I don't think you were all that sure yourself. What were you getting away from?"

She looked up at Ejord, suddenly ready to tell someone everything that had happened. He shook his head.

"It's almost dawn; you're a shivering, sweating wreck of a witch. I'll take you back to my rooms. You'll be safe there."

He picked her up and carried her out of the stall. She protested and writhed vigorously to get away from him. Both Turin and Ejord ordered her to be still and to relax. She weakly surrendered to the combined force of their concern and was asleep before Ejord had carried her up the stairs.

CHAPTER 25

For several days after her meeting with An-Soren, Rifkind remained in her rooms. The fall through the simulacrum mind and into her own had left her in a state of shock. She refused the overtures of both Ejord and Bainbrose to draw her back into the routines of the palace as all the residents prepared for the arbortide celebration. Even Lady Anelda made a rare visit to Rifkind's rooms, only to leave after a few minutes when Rifkind ignored or circumvented all her efforts at conversation.

She wore the same deep green gown that she had worn the night she had ventured into the tower, the ruby hung openly around her neck. Her hair had come unbraided and she left it that way, discovering that the heavy fullness of it could block much of the world. When Ejord was there alone, she would try to speak to him, but there was too much distance between her thoughts and her tongue and they would sit for hours staring at each other in candlelight, as Rifkind refused to open the windows.

"My father grows impatient to talk to you. Apparently I was not the only one to notice the behavior of the Bright Moon that night. He is convinced now that you are withholding things from him."

She shook her head, she did not wish to see Lord Humphry.

"If you do not go to him, he will come here. I have kept him away by saying you were ill, but you know my influence with him is very small."

"I don't know what to say to him, Ejord. I don't know what to say to anyone, for that matter."

She thought of the night, and of An-Soren, and lapsed into silence. The problem was that she did know what was wrong. Despite the Bright One, her destiny and the wishes of Lord Humphry, even despite his attempt to capture her with a soulless replica of herself, she could not hate An-Soren. The knowledge that he was mad and dangerous did not outweigh the suffering she had felt within him, nor within herself when for one instant she had felt the Goddess's anger. As Ejord had once pointed out the similarities between herself and An-Soren, she now drew parallels between Lord Humphry and An-Soren. And as Ejord had indicated before, there were more similarities than she had suspected, and

the differences were less significant than she had
wanted to believe.

The black-scarred double An-Soren had created
for her haunted her dreams and waking hours. She
had seen that image rather than her own when she
had glanced in a mirror. Its empty gaze had been
replaced with an unspeakable loneliness and
anguish. The other face continued to haunt her even
after she covered the mirror. It would have been easier to believe that An-Soren was working arcane
powerful rituals in his tower to torment her, but the
truth was simple. She had passed through the other
Rifkind, animating her with her soul, if only for an
instant. Her spirit was now divided, however in-
significantly, and the black-gowned woman in An-
Soren's tower, condemned to the dual torment of
separation from both the Bright One and Rifkind
herself, was capable only of yearning.

"You'll have to talk with someone," Ejord said
when she refused to continue the conversation.

"I would talk to you, Ejord, if there was anything
to say." She looked at him with an expression of
near-helplessness. "You would understand—but I
can't find the words to describe what has happened."

"Are you in love with An-Soren?" Ejord asked
with soldierly directness.

She stiffened, prepared to glare and shout at him
—she managed the glare, but that faded before she
could speak. Shrugging her shoulders first, she
looked down at her feet.

"You are to my guess, about nineteen, you've never loved a man—that is obvious—you never even
thought about yourself as a woman until Anelda

forced you to curtsy and hold your arm out from the elbow to show off the sleeves of your gowns. You've never met anyone before who you might consider worthy of your love."

"There's you," she said sincerely, after a pause while she adjusted to the idea that Ejord had supplied a piece to the pattern which tied much of its chaos into a coherent whole.

It was Ejord's turn to pull back in shock. He shook his head vigorously before mumbling that the idea was unthinkable.

Rifkind was happy to have successfully ended the conversation before it could progress to opinions not so easily circumvented. They sat in uncomfortable silence until Ejord got up to leave. When she was alone again, she got up and opened the window of her room which afforded a partial view of An-Soren's tower. Ejord had given a name to her discomfort—a name which fit, and a name she could fight. There was no room for love in the life of either warrior or healer—certainly not in the life of anyone who was both.

The crisis passed. She opened more windows, letting fresh air and light into her apartment. The reflection in the uncovered mirror was her own. Haggard from lack of sleep and food, disheveled, but the silver crescent bright from her still-recent tears.

'Thank you, oh Bright One, that the masquerade is over. I am glad to be myself again.'

Rifkind found combs in her wardrobe to take the snarls out of her hair, and threw her soiled gown into a heap by the fireplace for the servants to tend to. She was lacing a clean gown when there was a knock at the door.

'Lord Humphry!' She thought to herself. 'And I'm

ready not a moment too soon. If he had seen me before!'

Her thoughts formed with quick crystal clarity: how to deal with Lord Humphry—respectful, non-committal yet eager to complete her task. An-Soren—should she see him again—coolly deferential, but as if the night had never happened and under no circumstances to look at his face. Ejord . . .

There was a second knock, stronger and more forceful than the first. She accepted the interruption and unbolted the door for him. The visitor was not Lord Humphry, but one of his manservants accompanying a young woman Rifkind recognized as one of Gratielle's entourage. The woman carried a large bundle of cloth. Despite herself, Rifkind stepped back when she realized what the cloth was.

"My mistress, the queen, bids me bring you this gown, since you have been indisposed of late and unable to visit her. She hopes you will still attend the arbortide ball."

The maid recited her speech as if it had been memorized—a thought Rifkind considered likely. The girl then thrust the dress forward and waited expectantly for Rifkind to take it.

"It's not one of her used ones—it's just made for you, milady," she added.

"Oh, no, I can see that. It's quite lovely—thank her for me . . . no, I'll thank her myself tomorrow," Rifkind added the commonplaces of politeness, while taking the dress much as she would have accepted a still-bleeding corpse.

The two servants bowed quickly and left her standing in the open doorway. She examined the dress before stepping back into her room. With the knowledge the ruby had given her, she could have found a way to slip an object past An-Soren's carefully warded tower which would have burst into self-annihilating flames once An-Soren touched it. There was no sign that the sorcerer had tampered with the gown in any way. But it had been on the simulacrum in his tower; Rifkind could not bring herself to take the dress within her warded rooms. She thought of Ejord and resolved to take the dress to him for his examination.

Her luck ran thin. She found Lord Humphry with his son. She hesitated for a moment before entering the room, then lingered in the shadows longer to overhear more of the conversation.

"And you tell me not to worry . . . who are you to tell me not to worry? For four days this witch of ours locks herself in her room, talks to no one, all the while civil war's broken out, the capital is practically under siege from Hogarth's forces. And An-Soren's still working away night after night in his tower." Lord Humphry hit his fist solidly against a table; the discussion had apparently been going on for some time.

"It's certainly not Rifkind's fault. If Darius would stop doting over Linette—and I should have guessed from the start you had some design like that in your head, or you'd have sent her to the kitchens—then perhaps he could do something toward inspiring, if not leading, the army!"

Ejord was equally forceful. Rifkind noted his assertiveness with pleasure, until she realized he was challenging his father in defense of her. The pleasure was quickly replaced with discomfort, and the knowledge that if she were to fight her own battles now, as she always had, it would be at Ejord's expense.

"Darius is where he should be—if that bungling idiot got near the army, it would mutiny. Rifkind's the one who's not playing her role. She's not luring An-Soren. She's not distracting him. They've had one encounter, apparently, and he's crushed her like everyone else. Oh, gods, why did I put any faith in that madman in the mountains or listen to your tale about her fighting the Mountain Men?"

"Rifkind is neither crushed nor defeated, Father; she has tested his strength and is now planning her strategies."

"And just what are those strategies, since you seem to be the only one who knows what she's doing—why don't you tell me, since I provide for both of you." Lord Humphry's voice curled into a sneer her imagination could picture vividly.

Rifkind waited two heartbeats. Ejord had not replied. Arching her back to give the impression that she was looking down at everyone, she swept into the room with the commanding presence she'd seen both Lord Humphry and Lady Anelda use. Somewhat to her surprise, the strategem worked; Lord Humphry and Ejord both fell silent and she was assaulted with the perception of emotions ranging from fear to hatred and a fleeting sense of relief.

"The queen has sent me a dress for the arbortide ball." She shook the dress out and held it to her shoulders, forcing herself to breathe naturally, and watching Ejord carefully. "I think it will be most appropriate, don't you?"

Ejord was surprised, but not alarmed. Lord Humphry radiated suspicion to the point where it was a palpable force.

"It will certainly make you the most noticed woman there," Ejord answered to fill the silence.

"Your face ... your face. Witch, what have you done with your face?" Lord Humphry demanded, pointing his finger at the reapparent crescent.

"It is certainly no secret now that An-Soren has a rival for the position of king's adviser and sorcerer. I think it is time everyone knew who, and what, I am."

"That would be unthinkable," Lord Humphry raged. "The people—the court—are with me because I stand against An-Soren and magic. If they were to think that I—that I'd brought a witch into the court, they'd flock to Hogarth in an instant."

"Then you hold their allegiance with false pretenses. You brought me here—you have always intended to use me to defeat An-Soren." Rifkind folded the dress over her arm. "Perhaps you ought to explain to me again what you expected I would do for you, and why."

"An-Soren must be eliminated at any cost," Lord Humphry asserted.

"Then you must give me a free hand to deal with him."

It was rare that empathy could be so clear as to transmit actual thought—and Rifkind did not possess the empathetic sense to its greatest degree. Yet Lord Humphry's thoughts rose so clear in her own mind that she could not doubt their origin, only the deliberateness with which the florid nobleman assaulted her. Lord Humphry had no use for her, any more than he had for An-Soren. They were both individuals whom he could not control—and whom he hoped would destroy each other.

They stared at each other a long, intense moment. Then Lord Humphry shook his head and turned away from her. He went through the motions of conceding to her demands, but the force of his emotions remained constant.

"Whatever you do, it must be by the arbortide ball," Lord Humphry said finally.

"That is only seven days from now."

"It must be by then!"

"Why?"

"We can't hold Hogarth all summer—if we don't break him and An-Soren before the good weather starts, it will not matter what we do."

Rifkind nodded. There was a logic to the older man's plan—and using the ball as a pivot point was, in Dro Darian logic, no less reasonable than planning activities by the phases of the moon as the clans always did. Logical or not, however, there was nothing reassuring in Lord Humphry's manner; and to her mind, no reason to think that he was revealing all his plans, or even all his information. She returned the dress to her own rooms, then set out to find Ejord again.

"It is no longer a question of your father's distrusting me, Ejord; I no longer trust him," she said, upon finding Ejord studying maps in his rooms.

He hastily covered the maps. "You overheard our arguments?"

"Even if I hadn't, his emotions are very strong and unrestrained. And you—why are you studying maps—and hiding them from me when you know I could look at one and not understand at all what it means?"

Ejord looked down guiltily at the papers he had pulled over the maps, but did not move them. "All winter Father's been planning the counterattacks against Hogarth. I'm hoping to command one of his forces."

"That would be an honor. I would be pleased to ride with you."

"That cannot be."

All during the confrontation with Lord Humphry, she had been overwhelmed by the emotional duplicity and treachery in the room, but she had assumed it was all from Lord Humphry himself. Now, alone with Ejord, the same tensions crept toward her, albeit much weaker—but then Ejord's immunity always made it more difficult to sense his emotions.

"An affront to Dro Darian pride?" she asked, weighing her words carefully.

"No."

"Then what?"

Ejord punched his fist into the palm of his other hand. "Of course you'd suspect—even if you didn't know. I told him that as soon as we got here. The Darian line is weakened—the past two kings have been long-lived idiots—no, you don't care about our politics or history. We leave here after arbortide to join the army. Father has all his men in command; they follow him, not Darius. With the army he'll crush Hogarth, then return here to the capital to depose Darius. With the army on his side, and himself a heroic general, there'd be no furor. The only risk is An-Soren—there is no reason to believe the sorceror has given much aid to Hogarth as yet, but they are allies. Father does not want to leave the palace until An-Soren is safely disposed of. Protecting his back and flank, so to speak."

Rifkind thumbed through the papers on the table. She recognized occasional words on the papers, but her nomadic education had not provided her with measurable literacy.

"And me?" she asked.

"I do not know. He knows we are friends and will not speak to me of his plans for you—but I'm sure he would not allow you to ride with the armies—his war will be a crusade against the Ritual Arts."

"Then he will kill me, too."

"I would not allow that."

"How could you stop it?"

"It is enough to know that I could. I agree with Father in many things—not because of love for him, but because I have stayed back in Glascardy and seen chaos spread across the lands as the royal power weakens and the nobility gains the upper hand again. The Overnmonts have ruled well in Glascardy—they will do well in Dro Daria. But your path crosses ours only briefly, and for a moment our purposes are the same—the death of An-Soren. When that is done, our paths will not cross again."

"You seem overly sure of yourself, milord."

"I'm not. Father does not believe in gods or witchery—he thinks it's all fraud and deception. He believes he can use you as a tool to get rid of An-Soren for him—and I suppose he believes he can destroy or control you also. I think we should thank all the gods that your plans are the same as ours, but we should not force or constrain you at all."

Rifkind remembered her first arrival at Muroa's camp, hidden within the barren rocks which were avoided by the clans. Why live in such isolation and deprivation, she had wanted to know, especially when a wise healer who knew other ritual arts besides simple healing was an honored guest in every clan she visited. Muroa had laughed, but answered seriously that ritualists such as herself kept to themselves. It was only as Rifkind watched Ejord fidget nervously with the map corners that she fully understood why a cave among the rocks would be preferable to living with ordinary folk.

"The presence of An-Soren was all over that dress you said was from the queen," Ejord said, changing the subject but not the mood of their conversation.

"I brought it to you to see if there was anything more than his lingering presence on it."

"Then you knew it was from him?"

"Sometimes even I can see things for what they are."

"You will wear it to the arbortide ball then?"

"I will have to wear something—and at least that gown will allow me to wear my sword. Who knows. Perhaps it will start a new fashion," she said as she left the room. "It might even be a necessity before long."

CHAPTER 26

The neckline of the black dress had been designed to offset the heavy gold necklace which held the ruby. No other jewelry would have complemented it. None other was necessary. In the end, Rifkind had hung a long knife from the sword-belt rather than her grandfather's sword. As Adijan had always said, it was, in fact, too long for her to carry comfortably unless she was mounted on Turin. The rustle of the brocade and velvet was drowned out by the rhythmic clinking of gold coins and chain which decorated the bodice and sleeves of the dress. She liked the sound and strode resolutely down the cor-

ridors to the main hall of the Overnmont compound
where they were all gathering prior to the arbortide
ball.

'Let them call me a barbarian. I'd rather hear the
sound of gold on gold than all their pretty songs or
poetry. Their women have not taken a full stride
since they were children, and even the men cultivate
smallness and restraint as if it were a virtue.'

Rifkind met the politely shocked faces of the Overnmont household with a smile as bold as her walk.
It was raining, and servants stood waiting to carry
them across the palace courtyard to the royal quarters where the ball was to be held. Anelda was lifted
into a litter, but the bearers did not even offer to help
Rifkind as she stepped easily into hers; revealing, as
she did the hilt of one of her throwing knives protruding from the top of her boots.

When she was settled, and the impression she had
wanted to make firmly etched in their minds, she
relaxed enough to notice who else was attending the
ball. Lord Humphry, of course, in red velvet
trimmed with black fur. His knife was so crusted
with gems that it would have injured him to use it.
Bainbrose was there, in his scholar's robe as always
—his one concession to the grandness of the affair
the blue and purple sash of knowledge he usually
disdained. The servants of the household filled the
corners and sides of the great hall, watching the
pride of the family leave for a world which was
beyond their comprehension, even though it was little more than shouting distance away.

The various sons and nephews of Lord Humphry
were either with the army in the field, or attending
the ball in the company of ladies from other families
at court. For a moment Rifkind thought Ejord had

decided not to come to the ball; then he, too, came down the wide staircase. He'd shed the practical, comfortable clothes he'd always worn, and affected the formal court attire, with its barrel-chested brocade and velvet jacket, tight-laced pants and high, soft boots. Rifkind was fairly sure he had not selected the russets and greens which complimented the ruddy hair and complexion he'd inherited from his father—and yet she did not see Anelda's hand in the clothing either. It was an idle curiosity which amused her while the doors were opened and the litters carried one by one across the muddy courtyard to the ballroom vestibule.

"Do you think it is wise to wear that?" Ejord whispered to her as they waited to be announced.

"Though An-Soren's presence is obvious to you, most cannot detect that it was he who made the gown."

"Not that, the necklace."

"There are richer ornaments here."

"But none more powerful."

"An-Soren will not make his move here. And as he knows I have it with me at all times, it is unimportant who else knows."

"Lord Ejord Holvain Overnmont, his fiancée Rifkind, daughter of Rennier, brother of Lord Humphry Guelph Overnmont," the herald shouted past them and into the assembled nobility.

"If my true father had not died a dishonorable death, he would come and avenge me!" Rifkind hissed as they entered the main ballroom.

The list of Lord Humphry's titles droned on as they made their way to the fringes of the crowd. Propriety dictated that they spend a good deal of the evening in each other's company, despite the fact that since Ejord had revealed his ambition to command a part of his father's forces they had seen much less of each other. Few people in the hall had been deceived by the heritage the herald had assigned her; they looked at the shining crescent on her face, and the simple, utilitarian lines of the gold-handled knife at her waist, and realized that after a season of imitating the styles of the Asheeran clans they were finally seeing a true Barbarian.

"The king appears to be asleep," Rifkind whispered again.

"No, I'm told he snores when he's asleep. I think he's trying to look serious."

Darius XIII sat rigidly on a high-backed throne at the far end of the room. He was no more a fool and idiot than anyone else in the room—but the monarchy could no longer afford to reproduce itself in the preeminently average way that it had in the three generations that had passed since Darius X had united the feuding provinces into a centrally governed land. Linette sat on the floor at his feet, one hand placed indiscreetly in the king's lap. There was no resemblance to the bedraggled girl Rifkind had found on the roadside, nor even to the emotionally shocked young woman who'd been unable to prevent her first lover's death. With very little effort, Linette had become a consummate courtesan.

The smaller throne to Darius's left was empty—as soon as she realized that, Rifkind's eyes and mind wandered through the room to seek out both Gratielle and An-Soren. The queen was standing apart from the rest of the attendees, her face fixed in the same immobile stare she had had when she'd visited Rifkind.

"The queen," Rifkind whispered to Ejord, barely

moving one hand to indicate the direction he should look.

"Humph. Where's An-Soren?" he asked, stepping back into the crowd and beginning to move through it in the direction of Gratielle.

"He doesn't seem to be here."

Though Ejord wasn't overly tall by his society's standards, he could move through the crowd of people without difficulty or confusion, while Rifkind saw only a mass of shoulders and backs. The herald continued to announce names and titles as they made their way around the walls toward the queen.

"There he is." Ejord stopped and looked quickly at a tall, lean man standing in the shadows of one of the pillars not far from Gratielle.

Rifkind attempted to step in front of him, but was restrained by Ejord.

"Wait a moment. Close your eyes and look for him with your mind—or whatever it is that you do."

Rifkind's mind poked gently in the proper direction, but there was only emptiness where there should have been the intense vitality of the sorceror. She guessed that Ejord, who was used to avoiding An-Soren's powers, was sensing the lack of them. Then slowly, as she studied the emptiness where he should have been, the sense of An-Soren flowed into the space. She quickly retreated and opened her eyes.

"That's more what I expected. I could see him before, but he did not seem to be alive."

An-Soren looked at them, started to take a step forward, then apparently thought better of it and went back to Gratielle and the growing crowd. The candlelight and torches lit his face briefly when he turned—she recognized the man who had shadowed their carriage when they'd entered Daria. And realized that neither was An-Soren.

'Another chimera! Just like the one he sent to me in the Death-Wastes—perhaps they even look alike. But that is not the tormented man I saw in the tower. The scar is not real—I could never look on that again and not feel it—this must be only a simulation of his true self, just as the body he'd prepared for me was. It must be true then—that An-Soren does not dare to move in free air. He stays in the tower, seeing the world through these chimeras!'

"What did you say?" Ejord leaned over to her.

"I didn't say anything," Rifkind said, hoping that the excitement of her thoughts had not penetrated to Ejord's consciousness.

"Look at him—watch his hands!"

Rifkind stood on tiptoe and peered over his shoulder. The sorceror made small circular motions with his hands, occasionally adding other movements. They were too purposeful to be nervous gestures—and if she was right that she was watching a chimera of An-Soren, there was no reason for it to have nervous gestures. Imitating them herself behind Ejord's back, she tried to imagine what sort of ritual would require the movements.

"Ejord." She touched his shoulder. "He's taking over the mind of the queen!"

"With his hands?"

His voice was incredulous, but not entirely disbelieving.

"In a way."

"We'll stop him!"

Now it was Rifkind's turn to restrain him.

"Whatever it is that he's doing, it's either very innocent, or very serious—he knows both of us are here, and is ignoring us. Besides, there's not much we could do to stop him."

"I could peg a knife into him."

"It wouldn't affect him. Believe me—I know. I've tried with a sword."

She let a tone of grim knowledge pervade her voice, and Ejord did not press her for details or argue with her advice.

"So we stand here and watch?"

"For a while. He has something in mind for Gratielle—we'll do better to follow her."

The herald was finally quiet, and the musicians broke into a trumpet fanfare for the king. Gratielle moved forward stiffly; Rifkind guessed that An-Soren was either not in full control or unfamiliar with the movement patterns of a woman in a corseted and laced gown. She guessed it would be the custom for the king to begin the revelry by a dance with his wife, and that An-Soren was prepared to comply with that tradition.

The queen stood directly in front of the two thrones, staring at her husband. The assembled nobility which had moved forward stepped back again, leaving the queen very much alone in the center of the room. The fanfare ended. Darius stood up, still holding Linette's hand. With an appropriately regal gesture he signaled the musicians to begin—and led Linette down past the queen.

"That'll do it for certain!" Ejord said to himself with a tense sigh.

"Do what?"

"The king rejecting the queen in favor of the courtesan from Glascardy? Everyone will have to take sides now. By the Lost Gods, one would believe Father and An-Soren had planned this!"

"I'd rather you didn't refer to the Lost Gods like that."

Rifkind marveled at the powers of what Lady Anelda had called "proper society." There was no doubt in the emotional atmosphere of the room that there were few people present who were unaffected by the king's actions. Half were ready to declare a victory celebration; the others were possessed of an outraged anger that approached hatred. But they all found partners and fell in step behind Darius and Linette as if the rigid figure of Gratielle were not standing in their midst. Fortunately, Rifkind thought, as Ejord took her hand and they wedged into the line behind Lord Humphry and Lady Anelda, it was a very simple dance—little more than a dignified walk. Not even the Dro Darians could have divided their concentration between events and the whirling peasant dances Linette did so well.

They had moved far beyond Gratielle when the music stopped. Rifkind wanted to get into a position where she could watch the queen, who had finally moved and now sat on her small throne, and keep track of An-Soren, who had left the shadowed pillar and now eluded her.

"Let's assume you were right—An-Soren had something in mind for Gratielle—let's also assume that he's done it. Now let's all stick together. When the shock wears off, there's no telling what will happen. We may have to get Father out of here in a hurry."

"We?"

But she stayed near him. The conspicuousness of her dress and the crescent on her cheek began to bother her. Fewer couples followed Darius and Linette in the dances; the men left the ladies to clump in whispering knots, occasionally looking at the other groups forming in the shadows at the edges of the room. Groups like the one Lord Humphry seemed determined to collect, despite the combined efforts of Bainbrose, Lady Anelda, and Ejord to keep him from submerging into a conspiratorial huddle.

Rifkind leaned against a pillar. She was unconcerned with Lord Humphry's position behind her; she chose her place because An-Soren had appeared at a balcony curtain and was wringing his hands again. As long as she watched Gratielle and not the sorceror, he would not know she was alert to his actions. The chimera could appear and disappear at its creator's whim, but it was primarily an illusion. Through its eyes, An-Soren, seated in his tower, could observe and control the queen and perhaps others—but Rifkind was certain he was not able to absorb the variety of emotions and life-forces which flowed through the room.

The queen stood up; her head jerked briefly, but Rifkind observed that An-Soren had a surer and more complete control over the woman now. Gratielle smiled, then stepped down from the throne. At first Rifkind was puzzled that An-Soren would go to such trouble merely to get the queen out of the ballroom; then, as she roamed from group to group, Rifkind guessed that the sorcerer was making more blatant use of the queen's senses than ever she had made of Turin's.

But even spying wasn't enough to justify the risk of taking over the mind of another person: risks which were minimal in her actions with Turin, who was both an animal and therefore an inherently lower force, and attuned to her. Rifkind tensed into battle readiness as the queen approached the knot of people around Lord Humphry. It was her warrior's alertness, but her fingers grazed lightly over the ruby instead of a knife hilt.

"Lord Humphry. A word with you, please."

The voice was right, as was the slight tilt to her head which Gratielle habitually used when she was trying to sound regal. Lady Anelda, Bainbrose and the rest all stepped aside for her, leaving a clear path to Lord Humphry. Rifkind slipped around the back of the pillar and edged quickly toward the head of the Overnmont clan.

Ejord had been right, on both counts—An-Soren had something spectacular in mind for Gratielle, and they'd have to get Lord Humphry out in a hurry —or carry him out later. But Ejord had properly deferred to the queen, despite his knowledge of An-Soren's powers. The rogue sorcerer did not make the same mistake twice—Ejord could not sense the queen's possession.

Gratielle extended her hand to lead Lord Humphry to a quieter and more private spot. It was a proper gesture for the Dro Darian queen—

Then Rifkind saw her hand.

A golden coil fashioned to look like a snake wound around two fingers of the queen's extended hand. Though Rifkind favored the poisoned short knife she wore in her hair as her own final weapon, most women—even Muroa—preferred intimate devices like poisoned rings. The wearer broke the enamel seal on the underside, letting the poison coat several tiny, sharp prongs. It took only a slight touch if the right venom was on the ring, and Rifkind did not doubt that An-Soren's choice of poison would be precise and deadly. Of course, the ring-wearer died also—another reason Rifkind disdained the rings; no weapon was ever that much of a last resort to her. She slipped a knife into her palm.

She caught Gratielle's arm inches away from Lord Humphry's hand.

"My lady!" Rifkind weighted the words with all her mimic's ability, giving them concern, sympathy, and a sense of grief over the indignity her friend had suffered.

The poison ring pressed firmly into the knife blade, dooming the queen. While the others gasped at the social error Rifkind had committed in touching the queen, An-Soren's eyes blazed through the dying woman's and threatened Rifkind with a hatred that was not mortal. Rifkind drew on the power of the ruby to defend herself, but it was only the rapidly ebbing life-forces of Gratielle's body which protected her from An-Soren's vengeance. Then, as had happened with Garhad, the queen began to decay and disintegrate before the horrified eyes of everyone in the room.

"Witch!"

"Devil!"

"Sorceress!"

"She's killed the queen!"

The ruby produced the same sense of detachment that any ritual work did. Rifkind was scarcely aware that the crowd had focused on her as the murderer of Gratielle—and completely oblivious to the implications of such a conclusion.

"An-Soren," Bainbrose whispered with horror equal to those who blamed Rifkind—while Lady Anelda rushed toward the door covering her mouth.

Rifkind felt a tug on her arm; she turned slowly to gaze at Ejord.

"Ho, there! Come back to us! You've got to get out of here."

She let him lead her a few steps. The movement brought her proper mind back into focus and she knew her own danger—and that of everyone else who had crowded around Lord Humphry.

"I can get back myself—you get the others out. I'll give you time."

The ruby flashed with its own light as she poured her concentration into it. She had the power, as An-Soren and Hanju did, to move herself away from danger with her tal alone. There were other pressures—the other ruby pulled her toward it, and for one frozen instant she was falling toward the now naked and chained chimera An-Soren had made of her. Then horror wrenched her head, and she was within her own wards.

CHAPTER 27

"Rifkind? Are you in there? It's me—Ejord. I must talk to you."

Rifkind looked up. The steel blade of the sword reflected the bright red glow of the ruby and the strengthened wards she had placed around her room.

"Are you alone?"

"Yes."

"Then you may come in."

"But the door ... everyone's said it's bolted."

He gave the lie to his own statement by easily opening the door and stepping into her sanctum.

"Warded. Not bolted. Won't keep you out since you're immune. I'd prefer you closed it, though. No one else could get in, but I'm not sure whether they could see through the warding or not."

She'd bent back down over the blade, rubbing it with a soft cloth which was oiled and coated with fine emery particles. A pentagram was marked before the hearth with charcoal; in its center lay the crystal stones Hanju had given her.

"It's not safe—even Darius is against us now. Father has opened the old passageways out of here and we'll ride to the army, with any luck. I'd like you to come with us."

"Your father won't hear of it. He'd throw me to that mob down there." She gestured at the shuttered window, which despite heavy wood and the wards still admitted the angry noises of the mixed crowd of nobility and townsfolk who had kept vigil in front of the Overnmont complex since the abortive celebration four nights before. "*If* he could think of a way."

"You do him an injustice. So long as he is here, no one will reach this room except through Overnmont blood. And if you do not come with us and they find you here, it will not be because we have told anyone you are here. Turin is gone, and we have said you are also."

"Turin is still there; I have simply hidden him for his own protection. He is a noble fighter, but no match for a Dro Darian horde."

"Your abilities grow quite impressive."

"It appears I grow more attuned to the ruby talisman as I use it."

"Um . . . I would scarcely think you'd need the sword."

Rifkind looked again at the pentagram, with the crystal stones lying in pattern within it. In her usual cautious way, she had cast the stones several times, in different moods and with different attitudes toward the Bright One and the other gods who had seemed uncomfortably close to her. The stones were unbiased; they showed the same pattern with insignificant variations each time. They revealed nothing of her fate or of the fates of those close to her, only a persistent counsel to find safety in the past. For three days she had pondered their meaning in anxious silence, neither eating nor sleeping. Then she had engendered a juicy roast of meat, charred and spiced in the Asheeran style, and begun sharpening her sword.

"I do not think I will need it either. I know I must have it with me, and it would be supremely foolish to carry it without putting a fine edge on it first."

Ejord nodded. "I would still feel better if you'd come with us."

"Even if it were just you alone, I would refuse." She put the sword down on the fur carpet. "These wards are strong. They will keep An-Soren out as well as the rabble, but I can't move them—even with the ruby. They take their power from the stones of the walls themselves. I would be vulnerable if I were to leave them; more than that, An-Soren could follow me and bring disaster to you to force me to meet him on his terms and on his grounds. No, I'm going to stay here. As you said, our destinies have only crossed, not joined."

"Then I would stay here with you."

She looked at him with both surprise and anger.

"There is no reason for you to stay; there is nothing for you to do here."

"There's nothing for me to do anywhere."

A door to Ejord's deeper emotions and frustrations had cracked open, then shut tightly again. Unlike Adijan, who had left when she needed him, Ejord was stepping forward, asking to help her. She hesitated a moment and felt the impetus of his desire—perhaps even need—to be with her ebb away. The timing she had trained and cultivated as a warrior failed her utterly as a woman, or even as a person. The possibility of confronting An-Soren with a strong friend at her back had flared briefly in the sky, then begun to dim away. Rifkind saw no way to rekindle it, and silently, almost unconsciously, resigned herself to isolation.

"Should I have anything brought to you, or will you provide for yourself? Do you know how you will deal with An-Soren?"

"I know I shall go to meet him when I'm strong enough."

"I have sudden visions of this palace turning into a legend-haunted battleground, with you and he locked off in your towers, fighting each other with weapons no one else can see."

As if to emphasize his point, the room reverberated from an unseen blow. Rifkind was used to the multidimensional nature of the wards. They protected her rooms from asaults from any direction, forward and backward in time, as well as from direct attack and invasions from dimensions the ruby itself only hinted at. An-Soren had blocked their time-progression forward, but the wards had deflected him; that was the shock, and the time dimension shook violently. She had grown used to it. Ejord, who had not experienced dimensional on-slaught before, reeled under the sensory shock as his eyes and ears reported no impact or change, but his mind staggered from the shock wave.

"You see how difficult it would be for you to stay."

"What was—is—happening?" he asked, putting his hands over his ears in a futile effort to avoid the worst effects of the vibrations.

A woman's scream penetrated the wards—a scream Rifkind heard, but Ejord could sense only dimly. He closed his eyes as if in pain.

"An-Soren has tried again to shatter my wards. He throws the energy of his talisman against mine, and they both grow stronger."

"Gratielle!" Ejord said through clenched teeth. "I can see her!"

Rifkind paused. "The scream? An-Soren must have set her spirit up to block us. And that failed, so now we are passing through her," she said with calm dispassion.

"Can't you stop it? Can't you set her free? By the Lost Gods, she's in torment."

Rifkind shook her head in puzzlement. Ejord was a sturdy, capable fighter, but he lacked a proper un-derstanding of survival. Even as a healer, she knew when to dissociate herself from the impossible. The queen's spirit was locked at that instant of time—it was in torment—but she couldn't release it without unacceptably jeopardizing her own safety. The queen's spirit was not the queen; and even if Rifkind did release it, Gratielle would not be returned to the world of the living.

"Do something for her!" Ejord shouted as another scream rent the room, and the compound.

"I think it will be over soon, and An-Soren will not leave her spirit here while there is still such strength in it."

"Don't you care at all—she was your friend."

"And my friend is dead. There is no intelligence or consciousness in those screams. Gratielle is gone. She died horribly, and I'm certain she felt the agony of her death. But that is not Gratielle, however much it sounds like her and without denying that its torment is real. What was the queen has now become a tool for An-Soren. I must not be deceived into false pity which would only destroy me."

Before Ejord could respond, there was a wild pounding on her door. From the shouts, she and Ejord quickly surmised that the screams were perceptible—if not audible—to everyone in the compound. And panic was quickly taking over. Had the door not been reinforced by the wards, it would have splintered off its hinges; as it was, Rifkind opened it, letting the frantic household see her through the red aura of the wards.

"What are you doing to us?" Lord Humphry asked in a tone more questioning than commanding.

Rifkind stood up and walked to the doorway, staying carefully on her side of the wards, though like Ejord she could have walked through them.

"An-Soren has attempted to trap me in this room; his attempt has failed, and you are hearing the screams of the forces he sent to hold me, as the room moves through them."

They all looked at the red glow in the doorway,

heard the screams, and were not at all reassured. The household looked to Lord Humphry, who was as shaken as they were, but accepted the responsibility they gave to him.

"Moves through them? I see no forces, no movement."

"The forces are invisible to you, and to me as well. You perceive no movement because you are all moving with it—moving with time."

Only Bainbrose, standing at the back of the group, seemed to understand her reference to time and appreciate it. The others were confused. The screaming stopped, and though it had not been continuous, the pervading tension and agony subsided. Without Rifkind telling them how or why, they knew that the noise would not start again.

"But the glow?" Lord Humphry asked, cocking his head to one side and reaching forward slightly to touch it.

Rifkind raised her hand in a curt motion, signaling him to desist. "They are my protection—to keep my enemies away from me."

As the words left her mouth, Rifkind knew that Lord Humphry was already suspicious enough of her to readily interpret her remark to mean that he was also an enemy. But there was no ritual to recall words once said. She berated herself in silence while Lord Humphry stared back at her, then farther into the room where Ejord stood.

"Ejord, my son, how do you come to be on the inside of this barrier?"

"I had come to persuade Rifkind to leave the palace with us."

"It seems unlikely that she would want to travel

with us," he replied, without concealing his own dislike of the idea.

"When we leave, there will no longer be a guard at the door. The partisans out in the courtyard will ransack our quarters, as you have realized, and Rifkind will be trapped in her apartment."

"She claims that An-Soren and his sorcery cannot trap her; what would she fear then from unarmed rabble?"

"I don't fear them. Ejord came here in friendship and concern. I explained to him that I could not accompany you for fear that I might draw An-Soren's retribution on your party; though in truth, my Lord Overnmont, I would be as happy to see you and An-Soren confront each other as you have been to see An-Soren and me. Your battles are far from over."

"Don't think you can frighten me with your curses and second sight. All you witches and sorcerers have power because the ignorant believe in you and your gods. You can't affect my fate any more than any other mortal unless I believe in you."

"There are flaws in your logic, Lord Humphry, but it takes no second sight to guess that you have not fought your last battle or plotted your final intrigue. It would be an affront to the gods if I asked them for wisdom so apparent to mortals," Rifkind said, placing her hand on the door with the thought of slamming it in his face.

"Ejord, we leave at once!"

Ejord hesitated; Rifkind saw that he would not leave the warded room.

"Go with him," she insisted. "I cannot protect you, and I don't know how long it will be before I can face An-Soren. Immunity cannot protect you from everything."

"It will protect me from enough," Ejord answered, looking at the sword rather than at her.

"Ejord, you're my friend; I would like to think I will see you again . . ."

She could not comprehend the expression on his face when he strode past her and out the warded entrance to the room. The crowd stepped back with a collective gasp, and even Lord Humphry was too awed by Ejord's unprecedented feat of walking through the eerie glow to stop him when he walked down the corridor and out of sight. Bainbrose scuttled off in the other direction, but Rifkind knew the layout of the stairways and corridors well enough to guess that the old scholar was going to intercept Ejord.

"You've taken my son away!" Lord Humphry roared with sudden injured affection for his youngest offspring.

Rifkind's hand shook as she gripped the door. None of her knowledge and training could tell her how to cope with her own sense of despair and failure in dealing with her few friends, but she was not about to acquiesce to the condemnation Lord Humphry offered. Despite her anger, she took her time in answering, noting that Anelda and some of the servants she had come to know slightly were almost as surprised as she was by Lord Humphry's paternal outburst.

"You never gave Ejord enough room or time to be himself. Now, to be his own man, he must be completely alone."

They stared at each other. Then Rifkind slammed the door shut. The peculiar tingle of the wards ran up her back as she leaned against the heavy wood panels. The household remained outside her door

for a few moments; then she could hear the sounds
of their feet as they dispersed in silence. She could
not project her tal beyond the limits of the wards
without compromising their effectiveness, even
though her topmost thoughts focused on Ejord rather than the dangers from An-Soren or the hostile
crowd below her window in the palace courtyard.

As there was nothing she could do to satisfy her
curiosity, she rejected it and poured herself into the
final stages of putting a proper edge on the sword
and mentally preparing herself for a death-duel
with An-Soren. He continued to test her strength and
preparations with varied assaults on her wards.
Each attack energized the ruby still more, as if it had
required exercise after long disuse to regain its effi-
ciency and power. She felt the burning vibrations of
the pendant against her breast and wondered if the
sorcerer knew exactly what he was doing.

The mobs outside the Overnmont compound let
out a shout that aroused her more than any of An-
Soren's ritually created onslaught. The heavy bolted
outside doors had been breached; hopefully, the
family and their retainers were far enough along in
the secret passages to escape detection. She wondered a moment if Ejord had joined them or if he
were by some chance still in the compound. She
could not protect him if he were, and so did not
allow herself to worry about him.

The light of the Bright One flowed undistorted
through the red aura of the wards, bathing the center of her pentagram in silvery light. With the sounds
of rampage growing closer, she cast the crystal
stones one last time. The deviations were insignificant; there were many ways of advising caution and

reliance on what was known, but the message was still the same. She snapped the scabbard into the hasps of the leather and gold sword-belt, reaching out with her left arm to its fullest extension to slip the sword into it without damaging the edge she had put on it, settling into her self-image as warrior first over all other roles as the sword settled into place. A hideous shriek came from the other side of her door; the mob had found her quarters and discovered the invulnerability of the wards. She closed her imagination to the smoldering wreck of a man who had touched the door, and stepped into the pentagram.

'We are as attuned now as we can safely be,' Rifkind thought as the power of the ruby surrounded her and carried her out of the room. 'Even now, my thoughts are involved by it almost before I am certain of my course. Hanju may not have been exaggerating when he claimed the two stones were beyond any control.'

She floated above the palace, looking down at it. Many sections of the surrounding city, as well as the Overnmont complex, were being put to the torch by townsfolk and partisans whose enraged confusion rose in whirling eddies. The civil war Lord Humphry, Hogarth, An-Soren, and others whose names she could only guess had begun, was already beyond their control. The mindless destruction intrigued her for a moment, but did not draw her down into it. An-Soren's tower was shimmering in the darkness below her.

An-Soren had guessed or known of her departure from the safety of her wards, for the tendrils of his power groped up toward her. She concentrated

herself and began to fall toward the hidden pentagram in his study—easily avoiding the apparent
dangers they both knew were token hostilities compared to the powers they could wield through the
ruby talismans.

CHAPTER 28

There should have been more difficulty from the wards. An-Soren had been unable to penetrate hers; she had expected his to be equally strong and was not at all pleased to find she had passed through them as easily as Ejord had breached her own. There was a chance that had he come himself, her own carefully constructed defenses would have been similarly powerless, which was disquieting in retrospect. Or, there was the possibility that she was measurably stronger than her adversary—a thought she dismissed as poor battle-tactics. And a third consideration; that she had not passed through the wards at all, but had been trapped and deceived by them.

This third consideration appealed most to her, since it required action to be proved or disproved. The ruby functioned in ways she could not understand, flooding her mind with the reality that she was within the tower precincts, a few unguarded walls from An-Soren's private rooms, suspected but undetected by the sorcerer's wards. She passed through the walls as if they were the same as the ones in Hanju's sanctuary, and hovered, still undetected, over An-Soren's pentagram.

It glowed with the same red charges as her own, though its center was filled with a thick black column of smoke rather than with the silvery light of the Bright One. She decided for surprise rather than subtlety and brought herself into material visibility through the column of malignant air in the pentagram. An-Soren was bent over a large brazier and did not seem to notice her at first. Her simulacrum hung limply from heavy chains driven into the wall of his tower.

Whatever else would happen, Rifkind had determined to destroy the cursed imitation of herself. There were no free energies in An-Soren's rooms, any more than there had been in her own once she had fully set up the wards. But the ruby gave her access to all the willful force she needed. She extended her hand from the black smoke column.

"Begone from my sight and my world!"

A spark darted across the room, grounding out in the chained figure, making it vanish at once. An-Soren looked up from his brazier. He gestured with one hand, and the figure began to reappear in its chains.

"I said you were no more!"

Another spark flew from her hands, this one filling the room with the acrid odor of ozone and burnt flesh.

An-Soren gestured again. This time the chains rose away from the wall and tried to contain a rapidly expanding amorphous slime which groped toward her.

"Your illusions bore me," Rifkind shouted, sitting down in his fur-covered chair while the monster passed over her and dissipated.

"I have found what you fear most." An-Soren chuckled, lifting the brazier with his bare hands and heaving the scalding contents into the pentagram.

The room was filled with a blinding light. Then the light refracted into garish pulsating colors and discordant noises fighting for ascendancy. A lightstorm! Not a simulation, but a true lightstorm created during the night in the heavy acrid coastal lands. The ruby absorbed it all and burned with a hellish intensity against her. Almost desperately, she focused its intense power against the walls of the room and blasted a hole in one of them to let the light of the Bright One into the chamber.

Twisting inward in agony, An-Soren fell to his knees. He covered his face with his hands, but could not stop or conceal the expanding blackness of the scar. The rampant power of the rubies was matched by the depth of his torment. Through rigid, crooked fingers their eyes met. Rifkind found herself drawn again into his agonies. She faltered for an instant in her resolve to kill him—he staggered back to the confines of his pentagram and called forth the smoky darkness to seal the hole Rifkind had made in the walls.

Now the darkness writhed higher and stronger. It was no more an illusion than the Bright One had been and was equally intent on destroying its enemies. She pounded another hole in the walls, readmitting the silver light. The brightness and shadow twined around each other without mixing as the distant forces of the Bright One and the Dark One used the prepared battlefield to continue an ancient feud.

Rifkind watched An-Soren skulk back toward his book-covered desk. He began chanting in the Old Tongue, though without using any of the ritual forms she had learned. More shadow-being materialized out of the air behind him, advancing slowly on her.

The Bright One had no such controllable subalterns she could summon. She thought of calling the Lost Gods, then caught sight of the rapidly swirling vortex which marked the presence of two deities in the small room already. The black forms oozed forward, blocking An-Soren from her sight. She had a reflexive-training pattern which predated any ritual Muroa had taught her, the instinct to reach for a knife to throw. Her fingers closed on the slender, balanced knife in the top of her boot. She snapped it into the shadow's heart—if such beings had hearts.

A searing pain tore through her chest; she fell forward, catching herself on her hands and knees, unable to stand again. The ruby burned her fingers when she touched it, as it was burning into her breast. It funneled the energy of the summoned shadows into her own being and burrowed toward her own heart. The shadows were fading, and her own sense of mastery soared to heights never before thought of by her race and shared only by An-Soren, whom she glimpsed through the smoke.

Even the battle of the light and dark forces over her head was displaced by her newfound strength. She could easily have separated her Goddess and Her enemy, but the rising presence of An-Soren distracted her. The scarred ritualist stood firmly erect. The black horror of his ruined face glistened in the shimmering red light of the ruby talisman.

An-Soren's pain was gone. The Bright One was engaged in a duel with Her rival, but Rifkind knew her Patroness was not so ardently pressed in the battle not to be able to affect the last of the Dark Brethren who had betrayed her laws. Either An-Soren had used the power of the ruby to heal himself, or the power of the rubies had grown so strong that the gods no longer had any power over their initiates. And again, a third possibility crept into Rifkind's mind as another burning pain shot through her; perhaps the ruby had found in An-Soren a more valuable host than it had yet found in her.

Gathering all her own strength and resolve and calling on the Bright One, Rifkind split her tal from her body and sent it to the high ceiling of the room to study the conflicts beneath. It was as she suspected. The Bright One and Vitivar the Dark One were so evenly matched that their conflict was little more than a game and their emotional structure such that she suspected they conceived of their battle as eternal amusement. Her own self—and An-Soren, to a greater degree—had become suffused with a different sort of energy—an energy which as she studied its painfully dazzling structure seemed to drive toward some annihilating unity. Flames licked upward from the two of them, arcing higher and closer to each other.

'I cannot get back.'

Her thoughts were calm and coherent despite the danger in her bodiless state.

'The ruby has taken possession of my body; I cannot get past those flames, and they are going to consume my home.'

A bolt of silver light shot by her, followed by a blackened streak; she ducked to avoid them, and realized that the lessons she had learned from the ruby were not entirely in vain. Her consciousness was whole, and her powers fully intact though not located in any tangible place. She had an idea.

Her hands were little more than flaming brands, but she knew her body better than any hell-spawned gemstone. The fingers of flame reached up toward the seething inferno where the ruby itself burned.

'I shall need a fair amount of healing myself, my Goddess, if this notion you've given me works.'

The intense redness was transferred to her hands. One arm drew back. She cocked and released the necklace as if it had been one of her knives, deadly accurate, toward An-Soren's chest. There was an explosion; she had anticipated that. Even as her arm had begun its effortless, reflexive, snap release of the ruby, she had brought her tal down as close to the flames as she dared.

Body and mind joined in the instant the two rubies met. She experienced all the sensation of her airborne body compacting against the opposite wall, sliding down it to land on her feet, shaken, sore, but alert. The blissful silvered coolness of the

Bright One soothed over the ravages of the ruby. Her attentions were divided between thanking the Goddess, looking for An-Soren, and watching the combined energies of the rubies evaporate through the high ceiling of the tower room.

The Bright One was gone, and An-Soren's patron also. It was too much to hope that An-Soren himself was gone, too. The sorcerer was on his feet; his wounds, including the scars on his face, were healed. Rifkind had no time to consider how it had been accomplished; he was searching the smoldering ruin of his study for a weapon to use against her.

"You'd best look for a sword, Asheeran," she shouted, drawing her own from its scorched scabbard.

An-Soren turned to look at her. His eyes were no longer haunted with pain, but the agony had left its mark in an insane hatred that did not end when his torment was over. However it had been accomplished, the Bright One's curse had been removed from him. Rifkind was no longer under a compulsion to kill him, but there was no way she could have explained that to him.

"A sword? You were smart, little witch. I saw what you intended to do, and I separated myself from the ruby, too. But it was only that stone which made you my equal! Now you'll see the destiny of a weak-jawed chanter."

He swirled a copper censer over his head. It left a faint trail of smoke and odor, but nothing more.

"All that will matter is the strength of your arm. There are no free energies left here."

He turned his back to her, still seeking a weapon. She switched her sword to her left hand and extracted a throwing knife from the sheath at her

wrist. There would be little honor in slaying him
from behind, but there was little honor in simple
survival—and no survival in stupidity. The knife
spun slowly, smoothly on target until the last moment—Despite the small size of the room, An-Soren
had ample time to sidestep the knife. He had expected her throw and knew to avoid it without signaling apprehension. Rifkind took the sword with
her right hand again as he turned from a wooden
cabinet holding a heavy, wickedly curving assassin's
sword skillfully over his shoulder.

Madness blazed in his eyes. A low, almost
animal-like growl rumbled up from his throat. She
took the measure of her opponent to be soulless insanity—though depravity had not made the once-
powerful sorcerer into an easily defeated creature as
the Mountain Men had been.

She had fixed the layout of the room in her mind.
Loosened bricks and chunks of mortar littered the
floor; the furniture was mostly overturned or broken, and several liquids and powders of dubious
purpose lay in pools on the floor. She backstepped
and feinted over the rubble as if the room were her
own, more easily than her opponent, who was hampered by memories of how the room had once been.

Rifkind feinted. An-Soren charged, dropping his
arm in an arc that sang through the air. She dodged
the uppercut of his movement and met the downward arc of his figure-eight with the full strength of
her blade, her legs and back buttressed against the
floor to take the impact. An-Soren's arms collapsed
inward, and their faces were a hand-span apart,
separated only by their sword-blades. Rifkind took
an uncomfortable two-handed grip on her sword
without breaking his stare and snapped her body

forward without warning him. The sudden sharp movement overcame the downward inertia of his weight, and he was propelled upward and away from her.

He attacked. She deflected him with the same trick. The fight would not be a long one. Rifkind was surprised that she'd been able to use the same defensive gambit twice. Her path was relatively clear; she chanced the footing and leaped forward at him, arm extended, as he was regaining his balance and the powerful sword was in a poor position at his side. He dropped to his knees; the lethal thrust was absorbed by his off shoulder.

A wound—even a serious one—but not enough to stop the fight. Still it was a relief to know he bled the same red blood she did. His style did not require the now-useless arm, and she withdrew quickly before he could counterattack. They circled the room, testing each other's balance and willingness to fully attack. Rifkind changed her guard stance, trying to draw him into an attack, but the sword never moved from its chambered position finger-widths away from his ears.

Rifkind needed surprise. She tensed her lungs and diaphragm to emit a single piercing shriek which broke and tore at her own vocal chords. An-Soren hesitated a moment, and she surged past the strong defensive perimeters of his circular style. She did not dare a fatal cut even at this distance but hoped for another disabling jab, this time at his good shoulder. He brought his sword up, using his greater weight and leverage to bolster an inherently weak defensive stance. She braced for disengagement and saw out of the corner of her eye his weakened left hand coming at her with a short dagger.

Rifkind broke free but they were both wounded now, she with a painful hole in her thigh. It was not serious compared to the viciousness of their battle, and she forced herself to ignore the pain and to move the leg as if it were sound. She drove forward with an intensity which would send her crashing into the wall behind him if she missed her mark.

An-Soren hated her and reveled in the wound he'd given her, his guard was late—too late this time. He met her lunge, but deflected the point a bare rib higher before it skewered through his heart and back to the cabinet behind him. Rifkind let go of her own sword and used all the strength in her arms to keep from falling on the still-deadly blade he held in his hand. She scrabbled to her feet, unsheathing her long knife, in case An-Soren had been either more or less than mortal in the manner of other men, and could survive her attack.

An-Soren's eyes were unfocused. He uttered no final curses as he died. His features were fixed in the gloating sneer he'd worn when she'd begun her lunge, and stayed that way until death relaxed his face subtly and revealed his great age, power, and madness. She stood motionless until she was satisfied he was dead.

"He never knew. He didn't even see me coming at him," she mused as she peeled back the blood-soaked cloth from the wound in her leg.

The wound was shallow but well-placed. It bled freely. She loosened the cloth belt of his tunic and wrapped it snugly over the wound. Already it ached and throbbed; she grimaced as she tested the leg's ability to bear her weight. Without the ruby or other aid, she'd have to walk—or limp—the distance from the tower to her own rooms which were, she realized bleakly, now unguarded.

A sucking gasp of air, but little blood, followed her sword when she pulled it out of An-Soren. The tip was blunted slightly from its collision with the hard table, but that was the fate of even the best swords. She would regrind it at leisure. There was nothing else in the room she wanted, so she made her way slowly to the door.

There were other bodies in the tower—some freshly dead, others moldering and decaying. An-Soren's retainers had been freed to whatever fate awaited them with their master's death. Heads emerged from the stones in which they'd been imprisoned to strengthen the sorcerer's wards and power. One was Garhad, another Gratielle. Rifkind noticed them as she limped down the long spiral staircase. There was nothing potent left in the tower, and she'd never been one to gasp at past or future horror.

The courtyard was deserted, though a few flames licked at the windows of the Overnmont complex. She looked at the stars and the Bright One; it had all been over quickly. Picking up a little speed, she dog-trotted across the bare courtyard and through the battered open doors.

CHAPTER 29

The tapestries were slashed or pulled down from the walls, the furniture overturned and broke. Sounds and smells of fire filled the Overnmont quarters. Yet to Rifkind's experienced eyes, as she hauled herself up the stairways, little serious looting had been done. There was always the possibility that the Dro Darian mobs were so ignorant that they did not know gold from more colorful but less valuable ornaments. And there was the chance that the pyrotechnics in An-Soren's tower had frightened everyone away.

She had to stop frequently to tighten the bandage

on her wound, as her exertions kept reopening it.
The threat of fire forced her to push harder and
longer than she knew she should. But when the tents
burned, even though there were seldom injuries, a
clan was doomed. Most of her belongings had been
hidden away in Turin's stall, but a few remained in
her rooms: specifically, the crystal stones Hanju had
given her, and her hoard of gold coins. The looters
had not raided her quarters, which were in the area
more properly belonging to the chief household
servants than to the family, but smoke was rapidly
filling all the corridors on the upper stories of the
complex.

'Too much blood, too little air.'

Rifkind slumped against the wall at the top of the
last staircase. The door to her room was still closed,
though without the wards holding it. The sash was
soaked with blood; she grimly tightened it again,
wiping her hands on a frayed tapestry which hung
behind her.

'I can't think clearly—only that I've got to get out
of this place. Oh, Bright One, how quickly I was
spoiled by the powers of the ruby talisman, to be
able to lift myself over any obstacle and arrive gently
at my destination! Instead of staggering around like
this . . .

'I'll find my way to the stables and free Turin.
Turin! If the wards are down, then there's nothing
protecting him. He's shut up there in that stall. I
should never have relied so on that damned
stone . . . no, it was all I had, and it served me well
—though my sword served me better. I wonder if
Hanju knows what happened. The disruptions were
great enough that the dead themselves should
know.'

Rifkind had reached her own door and shoved it open. The smoke had not penetrated much into the room; some of the wards were fired with her own strengths and intuitions and had deterred the fire. She shut the door and leaned against it, breathing deeply of the still air of her rooms.

Her leg demanded first attention; after throwing the now-useless sash into the smoldering fireplace, she ripped linen strips from her bed and bound the wound with careful speed. Her herbs and oils were in the stables, but the fresh clean bandage eased her mind if not the actual pain. The gold was slung on her sword-belt; she reached for the suede pouch to put the crystal stones in. The suede was scorched and brittle; she discarded it and hastily improvised a new one from the strips of linen.

'Safety in the familiar. I guess that is about as clear as they ever are, though I wonder what would have happened if I'd brought the brazier instead?'

She made a final cursory glance over the room; she wore the clothes she had come in, the clothes of an Asheeran warrior, not those of a Dro Darian lady. If it had been possible, she would have left her entire Overnmont identity to burn in the palace.

There was a small ripple in the tapestry behind her bed; she tensed and waited for another. Since she had used protective wards since arriving in the palace, it had never occurred to her to check the walls for hidden passageways, though she knew the entire compound was riddled with devious and direct ways for getting to other places unseen. Whoever was behind the tapestry was unprepared for the obstacle of the hardwood bedstead butted up against it. The tapestry rippled several more times, then fell down onto the head of the trespasser. She recognized Bainbrose's sleeves before she saw his face.

"What were you doing in the wall?" she demanded sharply.

The old man looked surprised and somewhat panicked; she quickly guessed that he had not expected her to react to him as a threat, which could mean only that there was another threat which he had in mind to warn her about.

"Can you give me a lift over this? Oh, no, you're wounded! Have they been here already? Ejord told me about this passage, but I've been lost for hours."

"You talk too much," Rifkind grumbled, extending her arm to him. "Has *who* been here? The looters left."

"No. Humphry's soldiers. He had them in the passages. The family's out now, and Ejord with them, but Ejord suspected treachery on Humphry's part and sent me up here to wait for you. May I congratulate you on a successful conquest?"

Rifkind nodded. "What sort of treachery? Did Ejord say?"

"No, we had only a few moments in the halls ... but he wants you out of the palace, out of Daria, and away from all of us as soon as possible."

"Treachery? That can mean only that Lord Humphry has some plan to eliminate An-Soren or me, whoever survived the duel. I'd like to know more, but I think for once I'll take Ejord's advice and leave."

Bainbrose hesitated, shuffling the ample fabric of his sleeves through his hands. "Rifkind, milady ... I'm an old man, amusing at a dinner table, but not much use to anyone. For several years now I've stayed with Lord Humphry because of Ejord; now even he seems to be caught up in the lord's designs and ambitions. Let me come with you?"

A thousand cutting retorts came into her mind. She shut each off.

"Can you ride?"

"I do not fall off."

"Can you follow me now to the stables?"

"If not, I'm certain to be marked a traitor to someone's cause if I'm found in your empty chambers."

Rifkind hesitated; the scholar had identified his immediate personal danger without whining or pleading; she was not about to leave him behind. She opened the door to find heavy smoke billowing in the corridor with flames visible despite the blackness. They both slammed the door shut.

"The passageway! Can you find your way back?"

"I think so, but I would not advise it. Lord Humphry met his men in the passages. If there is treachery in the air, the winds will blow strong in these tunnels."

"Then what?"

"The windows?"

Rifkind opened the window and stared down to a roof, two stories below and separated from the wall of her own room by twice an average man's height. She studied it for long, hard moments ... healthy, she would have tried it at once, but with only one strong leg, and a frail scholar, the chasm seemed insurmountable.

"Go quickly!" Bainbrose shouted urgently.

She turned around, aware now of the sounds of footfalls in the dark passage behind her bed.

"It's too far ... we'll make a stand here. Douse the candles!"

"No, milady, there will be too many of them. I'd forgotten the fires when I asked you . . ."

"If it is as you say, you face certain death or capture," she said, fighting her own mounting desire to be gone from the place, no longer concerned with the distances to be covered or the soundness of her leg.

"I'll die quickly, an unarmed old man . . . but you —go quickly."

"I said I would take you." Loyalty to her own word if nothing else was winning out over the survival instincts of an Asheeran warrior.

"And you've made me happier than all Lord Humphry's gold. Take this, and remember me."

He untied the sash of his robe and wrapped it quickly around her; the weighted ends thumped against her wound, but she said nothing. He embraced her tightly, and rather than let him sense her discomfort, she returned the gesture. The sounds were close now, with breathing and whispers to go with the bootshod footsteps.

"And you take this—defend yourself. No clansman of mine ever went quietly to his death."

She closed his fingers over the hilt of her long knife. Bainbrose's eyes brightened, his back straightened, and he took a few tentative swings with the knife. Rifkind stepped back to avoid his awkwardness, the window ledge now squarely at her back. She saluted him and climbed onto the ledge.

It was too far—a death as certain as the one which waited for her in her room if she stayed. There were shouts behind her, Bainbrose distracting the vanguard's attention, giving her precious seconds more to procrastinate. He was a friend, and his death would not be in vain, though she screamed silently as she plummeted from the window at the curse which showed her friendship only after it was doomed.

It was not too far, it was too hard. The landing jarred her knees all the way into her back teeth. She rolled forward, biting her lips to avoid screaming in pain. The Bright One shone dispassionately on the roof, but it was no longer Her battle and Rifkind did not appeal to Her. She rolled behind a gargoyle and waited until the pain subsided enough to make it possible for her to determine her own injuries.

She was bruised, jolted, and certainly a closed hand shorter than she'd been earlier that evening—but no bones had been broken or dislocated. The wound had bled, but the compression bandage held, and she could stand with little difficulty.

'I think I'd best make the rest of my escape now. My body has not realized the extent of that fall; when it does, I'll be lucky if I move for a month unless I can get to my herbs and oils quickly. I'll be as old as the Lost Gods by tomorrow morning.'

It made no difference how fast she moved, so she ran across the rooftop, following the smell of the stables to the proper portion of the palace. There were voices in the courtyards below her; she could hear her name mentioned as the object of a massive search. But no one had mentioned Bainbrose, or anyone else being found in her rooms, and no one spotted the black-cloaked figure scurrying among the roof gardens and gargoyles of the palace.

Turin?

She sent her mind down into what was hopefully the stables, and was met by a rampant enthusiasm which overwhelmed her.

Not now! I'm hurt, I'm exhausted. Just show me where you are.

The war-horse's enthusiasm retreated and cowered before her. He let her into his mind to show her the stall he was in and the men milling around outside it. All men tended to look alike to Turin, and Rifkind was too tired to exert her own discriminating powers in his mind to see the actual features of the soldiers. If Ejord had been there, Turin would have known it; she could safely assume she had no friends in the stables except Turin.

The Bright One had shielded Herself behind stray clouds, enabling Rifkind to lift one of the heavy panels which let light and air down into the stables in the warmer days of the summer without alerting the men beneath. She landed heavily in a pile of hay, but with any number of horses milling restlessly in their stalls, a little more noise in the straw did not arouse enough suspicion to start an investigation.

The tack shelves and mangers ran continuously along the backs of all the stalls. There were many stalls between Turin and her; she had jumped down from the roof a bit impulsively. The muscles in her legs and back protested each slow length she crept through the manger. Several of the more spirited mounts did not take kindly to a stranger crawling in their food, and she called upon her reserves of endurance to calm them. Fortunately, those animals had reputations for being skittish or vicious, and they attacked the soldiers who came to investigate their antics with far more vigor than they displayed toward her.

Rifkind lost count of the number of stalls she'd invaded, and even the location of Turin. He had to nip her shoulder gently to keep her from wriggling on out the opposite side of his stall. The men were, of course, thickest outside his stall, but none expressed any desire to face the war-horse directly. She had fairly free movement in the stall to get the ritual gear loaded into sacks and the saddle on his back.

'Even with the most generous estimates of my ability to handle this sword right now, there is no way, by the Lost Gods, that I'm going to mount Turin and go riding out of here free and easy. Damn! Even if I were with the Lost Gods, there's no way I'd get out of here without a fight. Hanju walking down the aisle out there rolling his eyes and licking his teeth might be enough of a diversion, but even at that there's going to be at least one of those men whose devotion to duty overrides every other thought he's ever had and who will sound the alarm against me. I really need a party of allies, but a diversion will have to do.'

Rifkind sat in the shadows of the stalls, chewing on a handful of herbs to ease the pain and restore her strength while plotting her diversion. Her plots were not at their best, but in the end she decided to go with a riot from the horses in the stables. She would creep through the stalls unbolting the doors, and then give Turin a signal to rouse the other beasts. Even war-horses were herd creatures, and subject to contagious panic when not with their Riders. A few deliberate actions on Turin's part, and the few men in the stables would quickly be overwhelmed by frantic horses.

Stealing through the stalls and unbolting them took longer than she'd expected. The first light of dawn had begun to appear on the horizon when she slumped down in the last stall to give Turin the signal. She was near the tunnel entrance the soldiers had used to get into the palace—she hoped that Turin could reach her there and they could escape down the tunnels unnoticed.

There was no mistaking his piercing scream of danger. Even the men were affected by it, adding their own confusion to that of the animals. Rifkind stayed with Turin, making sure he got out of his own stall and battered the doors open on the other nearby stalls. The anonymous soldier whose presence she had dreaded noticed that Turin was saddled and sounded an alarm. The horses were loose and wandering frantically through the aisles, but the soldiers were beginning a difficult search, with a good handful following Turin.

Rifkind had taken off her sword and given the long knife to Bainbrose; her own defenses were minimal. She stayed quiet and hidden in the stall of a near-blind mare, waiting until Turin was close enough to assist her. There were shouts of men in the tunnel; her heart sank.

"Where is she?" a voice demanded, a voice she thought was uncomfortably similar to Lord Humphry's.

"Somewhere's in the stables, sir. The witch's panicked the horses but we've guarded the doors and the men are starting a search—she can't get out."

"Take her alive if you can; a thousand gold korli to the man who brings her to me."

She identified the voice as definitely Lord Humphry's. He was leaning against the door to the stall she was hiding in.

"The witch will be taken to the king to suffer the rightful punishment for killing the queen," another voice countermanded.

'Oh, Gods, they're going to fight over the honor of capturing me,' Rifkind thought with bleak humor. 'Now all I need is a party of Hogarth's men and the whole mad lot of them will be looking for me.'

The protective darkness was fast disappearing. Turin had eluded his pursuers, but had only a few minutes to find a way through the crowd of nobles gathered by the tunnel. Rifkind climbed in the mangers again and began edging closer to him.

CHAPTER 30

Rifkind closed her eyes against the pain and fatigue. The herbs she had hastily applied to the wound had worn off; alternate spasms of chills and sweat wracked through her. There was an unwritten law that made healers themselves more vulnerable to the ravages of injury than those who were normally their patients. She slowed her breathing and pulse; the pain began to subside to bearable levels. If she had not been in danger, she would have allowed herself to sink into unconsciousness and let her subconscious knowledge of healing care for her; but with soldiers still searching the stables, she dared not.

Sharp pieces of straw jabbed into her eyes; in her rest, she had slumped far forward. Her time sense was distorted beyond reliability, but there were men sweeping down the aisles looking for her, and she judged that only a few moments had passed since she closed her eyes. With the rough-hewn wall for support, she struggled to her feet. The pain had been reduced to a dull ache, but her entire body trembled with exhaustion. Turin waited in the shadows if she could reach him.

Grim determination got her to his side unnoticed; the open tunnel which hopefully would take her to freedom lay before them. She gripped the saddle, bit her tongue, and tried to haul herself to his back— without success.

"She's escaping! Call the others, the witch is at the tunnel!"

Rifkind turned around to glare at him with an expression of pure hatred which earlier in the evening would have doomed the soldier. Even weakened as she was, the soldier stepped back until his two companions joined him, unwilling to face her anger alone. The three soldiers held their weapons stiffly and advanced as if they faced an army rather than a sweat-soaked young woman.

'There's nothing left. My legs don't want to support me. I can't even jump to Turin's back, and now this.'

Her hand rested on her sword-hilt; she yanked it out of the saddle scabbard and turned to fight to the death. Turin pawed at the ground. His battle preenings were diminished by the absence of the coins on his horns, but long before his kind had been trained by the clans, the steppes-horses had been proud and feared fighters. The soldiers took an uneven half-step back, then continued their advance.

Without Turin, Rifkind would have been cut down almost at the start. She had neither speed, agility, nor strength, only experience and the insistence that she would die honorably or not at all. Turin gored one soldier and sent the second racing back to the main stables for reinforcements. Rifkind dodged and parried the awkward sword-work of the third until Turin all but drove him onto her sword. The one who had escaped would bring others, but for the moment they were free. Turin gently rubbed his head against her limp-hanging sword-arm. She was leaning against the wall, panting; the pain had all returned. Turin dropped, unbidden, to his front knees; to mount him, all she needed to do was fall forward. Shaking off a spasm, she lurched toward him.

A single figure appeared with the light behind him, then a bank of archers with their arrows nocked: Lord Humphry, his sword drawn and bloody, with invincible reinforcements. He had killed the officer of the king's guard in his determination to take her himself. Rifkind knew of this without understanding how she could read his thoughts so clearly. The knowledge roused enough fury within her to make the pain less encompassing and life worth living for a little while longer.

"Step away from the horse, if you please." Lord Humphry wagged his sword to indicate she and Turin should separate. Neither moved.

"Get the horse!" Lord Humphry ordered his archer. They checked their aim. Rifkind ordered Turin to stand aside from her; he refused, and she had to resort to unsubtle measures to shove him some distance from her in the tunnel. His trust was shattered, his eyes mirroring the internal shock, but he was safe in the tunnel and she ordered him to stay there.

"Now her."

They raised their bows again.

"I'll see each of you fed whole to Vitivar's priests and your spirits in the stomach of hell itself."

The men had likely seen the great red flames leaping out of An-Soren's tower, or some of the other manifestations of sorcery she and An-Soren had created. Their fear of Lord Humphry was manifestly not as great as their fear of a witch's death curse. They lowered their bows and would not face her despite Lord Humphry's threats.

In the unreal moments while the lord screamed at his archers Rifkind had the ironic notion that a man of his temperament and coloring might easily burst his heart with such outrage. She also thought of bolting for Turin's back; but though her own anger at Lord Humphry was enough to give new strength to her arms and legs, she did not trust the archers not to shoot if she ran from them—and no death by arrows was honorable—especially not one from an arrow in the back.

When his men refused his commands despite a threat of death Lord Humphry advanced on her himself, holding his sword like a cleaver. Rifkind did not mean for him to get so close, but injury had dulled her timing even more than she had thought. She blocked the full-force swing with a belated parry that spared her life but broke her sword a third of the way along its length. The snap pushed her backward out of harm's way, but the sudden motion was too much for her and she fell onto her back. Lord Humphry smiled with his teeth and raised his sword again.

Rifkind planned to roll violently away when he was committed to his slicing arc; she might avoid a fatal blow, but had no way to gain her feet while he possessed the advantage, and no way to wrest that from him. The sword moved. She waited a fraction of a heartbeat, then spun away toward Turin. Her strategy worked and she heard the sound of the sword striking stone.

"Leave it there!"

A familiar voice filled the tunnel entrance as Ejord strode out of the darkness, his sword drawn. The angers and frustrations which had flared briefly in him against his father were now fully in control of him. Even the muscles of his face were knotted, giving him the expression of a man in death agony—but a man nonetheless, and from her position sprawled on the floor, Rifkind judged she had never seen a warrior look so fierce.

Lord Humphry was father to the son, and she was not surprised that the two Overnmonts confronted each other over the fallen sword with unflinching blood lust.

"Stand aside! This has to be finished. With her gone, nothing will stand in our way."

There was still a glimmer of the court diplomat in Lord Humphry's voice—enough to make her stomach turn. Ejord hesitated; she thought he seriously considered his father's insinuations and despised him more than she had ever despised her brother for his weakness and opportunism. But Ejord was only testing his father's confidence, and when the old man's hand dropped toward the hilt, he kicked it away with such force that Rifkind had to dodge the flying weapon lest it inadvertently strike home.

'Before the Bright One, I recall the doubts I had of you, Ejord. Your survival and destiny was never linked to mine—except that you made it so. I would not have confronted my father, though my clan died because of it; you are risking everything for me. Even if I do not survive this, my Goddess, do not forget him!'

Her back was against Turin's hind leg. He would not disobey her command to remain motionless, though she could feel his flesh quivering with emotions that threatened to overwhelm and destroy him. She touched him gently with her mind and was forgiven of all the things he could only barely imagine and had fought not to believe. He held firm while she slowly rose to a standing position by leaning against his leg.

"Then slay her yourself, and we'll forget this has happened."

Lord Humphry's tone did not acknowledge that without a sword he did not have the commanding advantage in the situation.

"You have gone mad with killing. First Roubleard, and the captain ... your sword is stained with blood. I heard your words to the archers there."

"They disobeyed me—they all refused my commands!"

The sword twitched in Ejord's hand; he was not accustomed to rage or confrontation. Where Rifkind could have found many gestures of word or action, Ejord groped uncomfortably. He did what he thought was right and stopped those things he thought were wrong, but too many years of silence had passed for him to be able to express himself clearly under pressure.

"I give you one more chance, Ejord. Slay her yourself. Rid yourself of her. You've taken this witch far too seriously; she was never more than a carefully chosen weapon."

They both looked at her; she was standing and holding the point of one of her short throwing knives.

"No, Rifkind. No more killing. Get on Turin and ride out of here now."

His voice had the same intense flatness in it when he talked to her as it did when he talked to his father. She slipped the knife back into its wrist harness. At her whispered command, Turin dropped to his front knees again. She sat back down into the saddle, grateful that chance had her lifting her good leg over its high horn.

"A thousand gold korli to the man who rids me of this witch." Lord Humphry called to the archers behind him without turning his eyes from Ejord. "A thousand korli!"

Slowly one of the archers raised his bow and renocked his arrow. Rifkind yanked the poisoned spike out of her hair, scratching its waxy surface as she did to activate the poison. It was rock-snake venom, fast-acting and always fatal, with the added horror of turning its victims blue. There was no antidote. It was a long throw, but fortune shone on her. He screamed when it nicked his face. The spike fell to the floor, unnoticed in the confusion as her would-be killer fell to the floor.

Lord Humphry turned around to watch with thinly concealed horror; only Ejord looked at

Rifkind. She shrugged her shoulders, and as she did, the coil of her brain came down around her neck. Ejord looked at her another moment, then smiled and raised the sword a fraction toward her. She accepted the salute, but her attention was more closely drawn to the suffering of the archer. The spike was one of her oldest weapons, but she'd never used it before. Poison as a weapon—even a last weapon—was distasteful to her as a healer, though the gruesome spectacle of the cyanotic man with his bulging eyes and protruding tongue had probably saved her life, as it had always been intended to do.

She flicked Turin's reins slightly and began guiding him into the dark tunnel.

"You killed him without touching him," Lord Humphry said softly.

"What is the point of being a witch if you can't do things?"

"Strike me down, too," he demanded.

"Your fate is spoken for."

Unlike Ejord, she was seldom at a loss for words. She despised the diplomatic arts as devious and weak, but Lord Humphry himself had completed the training she had begun with the clans in the Asheera. She turned her back to him, a brazen but diplomatic thing to do, and let Turin continue into the tunnel at a slow, deliberate pace.

"Stop her!" Lord Humphry shouted.

There was a scuffle and the sound of swords scraping along stone. Diplomacy or not, she glanced back over her shoulder.

Lord Humphry had lunged for Ejord's sword, falling over with his son wrestling for the blade. It seemed for a moment that Lord Humphry's surprise move had overwhelmed his son; then Ejord's youthful strength regained the advantage. As they rolled on the floor, Ejord brought his foot up for a hard kick into his father's stomach. The older man released his hold on Ejord's sword.

Ejord waited, every muscle tensed, for his father's next move. It was another lunge, this time at the fallen sword which Ejord had kicked over to Rifkind. She cursed herself that she had not grabbed the weapon—she needed a sword now herself—but mostly that her shortsightedness had endangered Ejord. She needn't have worried; the young man grabbed Lord Humphry's brocaded tunic and redirected the lunge so that his father crashed headlong into the stone walls of the tunnel passage.

Wobbling, his eyes unfocused, Lord Humphry tried to stand. Ejord hit him in the solar plexus with a single cleanly thrown punch. Lord Humphry spiraled backward, his head again taking the full impact of the fall. He did not move again, even when a still-wary Ejord nudged his foot with the sword point. He looked up to face the nervous archers at the stable entrance to the tunnel.

Rifkind turned Turin and approached Ejord. He didn't turn to face them, though Turin's unshod feet rang loud enough in the tunnel. Lord Humphry was unconscious from hitting his head on the floor; she knew that because she was a healer, but Ejord, without her special talents, could not guess whether he'd killed or seriously injured his father.

"I think I might need a guide to get myself out of here, out of the city and to some place safe and quiet."

"I've killed him. I came to stop the killing, Rifkind, and I've killed him."

She lowered her voice so the archers, murmuring

among themselves, could not hear her.

"You'd have more luck killing the stones themselves; men like Humphry die in their beds from overeating. But don't tell our friends up there, or they're likely to take us prisoner to save their own necks."

Ejord shoved his sword into its scabbard.

"You're sure he's alive?"

"I wouldn't mourn his death, but I won't lie to you either. He'll rouse in a little while, giving us just enough time to get out of reach and those archers there enough time to loot his body and desert."

"Blackthorn's just down the way."

Before starting down the tunnel, Ejord stopped to retrieve the heavy sword his father had been carrying.

"This one'd be too heavy and cumbersome for you, but I've always admired it." He turned to her, drawing his own sword from its scabbard and offering it to her hilt first. "At least until you find an armorer who can make one more to your tastes?"

"I can tell from here—it's too long."

Rifkind hesitated, feeling weak not from her wound or the exhaustion of the duel with An-Soren, but from nervousness at accepting the gift Ejord offered. To accept the sword, to accept his friendship and perhaps more—as a healer or warrior Rifkind had never bound herself to anything but herself and her oath to the Bright One.

He held it out closer to her, his face an unreadable mask.

'I need a sword. I know that to be a fine blade . . . but I could get a sword anywhere—I have the gold. Gold, and Turin, and little else—no clan, no home, no ruby . . . no destiny? Have I completed everything that was set out for me?'

She reached out, placing her fingers just below his on the hilt.

'My father outlived his destiny . . . I'll outlive mine, but not the way he did. Without destiny to confine me, I'll live the way I want to.'

She met his eyes and smiled as he released the sword into her grasp. She took the proffered blade and slid it into the wide saddle sheath with a small flourish.

They headed down the tunnel to Blackthorn and freedom. In the pool of light they could see the archers looting Humphry's body as Rifkind predicted . . . Then everything was silent except for the hoofbeats of the horses.

CHAPTER 31

A strong light shone on her closed eyelids. Rifkind shifted uncomfortably to evade it, raised an arm to block the light; the movement brought the stiff muscles of her back into use. She grimaced and opened her eyes.

"Decided to return to the land of the living?" Ejord was silhouetted by the light of the setting sun.

She was lying on her cloak which was spread on the ground. Turin's saddle supported her head and shoulders; Ejord had used Blackthorn's larger saddle to support her leg. Memories of the night with An-Soren and the final confrontation with Lord

Humphry in the stables came to her. They seemed very vague and distant.

"Where are we? How long have I been in this trance? What's happened?"

"First things first. We're about a day's ride outside of Daria, headed in the general direction of Glascardy. You sat on Turin the whole time yesterday, but I'm not surprised you don't remember anything. You're a damnably proud woman, Rifkind, but there are times you'd do us all a favor if you'd admit you're not always stronger and more determined than the rest of us."

"I wouldn't have survived this long if all I did was sit back and expect others to do my work for me."

"I didn't say you should. But you refused to rest yesterday, so this morning there was no way I could rouse you. I could watch you heal yourself, but if we'd stopped yesterday when I first suggested it, you would have worn yourself out that much less, had less to heal, and could have traveled today."

"Then we are still in danger here?" She pulled herself into a sitting position and reached for her boots.

Ejord gave her a sharp tap on the shoulder which sent her backward into the saddle.

"If we'd been in any sort of trouble here, I'd have strapped you to Turin's back like a sack of grain, and we'd have traveled that way."

"I'm sorry. I should have realized you wouldn't have let me lie here like this if there were any real danger."

"Thank you. But to your original questions—I missed the first one—what happened: no one followed us out of the palace. An-Soren's tower had fallen, and ours was in flames by the time we got to the walls of the city. There were soldiers all over the place; they were ready to fight anything that moved, so we spent a lot of time going slow.

"Once we'd gotten outside the walls—and that was easy with the masses moving out now that the war's come home to the capital—there was no problem. I left the roads as soon as it was safe; we're traveling by the stars—I get nervous when there are that many people I don't know traveling with me."

Rifkind sat up again. "You said we're going back to Glascardy?"

"*I* am. I'm not about to go back to Father's armies, and regardless of what's happened between us, I would never offer my services to Hogarth."

"Don't you think it's a bit risky going back there?"

Ejord shrugged his shoulders. "I'll give it a try. Those are my mountains. I don't feel comfortable away from them, and if I can get back there, I'm sure I'll be able to do whatever I have to."

"I've heard that before." She shook her head with the memory of Hanju. "I think myself I'll go back to the Asheera."

"The Bright Moon rises directly over the Asheera from here. Just ride toward moonrise."

"I've heard that before, too."

"You're welcome to come back to Glascardy with me."

Rifkind stood up, going through the motions of testing the muscles in her leg. Everything that had been torn or sprained was healed, but ached from both the abuses of the past two days and the efforts of self-healing. Her eyes fell on the sword Ejord had given her.

'The Asheera is far away now—in time and experience, not just distance. I don't think I could endure the thirst and hunger. I'd have to live alone. I'm too young to take pupils—Linette proved that. I could never find the old Gathering place again—not that they would have me.

'I'm different now. I'll never be Dro Darian, but I cannot go back to the Asheera. But going to Glascardy with Ejord would mean winters, walls, and wars. . . . Still, there would be a lot for me to do . . . Ejord is more intelligent and able than Halim ever dreamed of being. He is not my brother; he must rule his own lands. His clan is not my clan!'

Rifkind shook the thoughts of creating a comfortable place for herself in Glascardy from her head, though the seeds of desire and the paths to compromise were already clear enough for her to see. Ejord was friendship and mutual respect; she could not yet conceive of love or trust, but even friendship was a powerful lure away from the life of exile she saw for herself if she did not join with him.

The aches were beginning to subside.

She tightened the sash of her tunic; they both eyed the frayed blue and purple embroidery on it.

"I was going to ask you about that."

"Bainbrose came to my room to warn me, but with the fire and the men in the tunnel, there was only one way out of my rooms. I jumped to the roof below; he stayed behind. He was just going to surrender and die. I gave him my long knife—he gave me this."

Rifkind lifted one end. It was uncommonly heavy for a knotted sash. She undid the knot; a shower of gold coins and small gemstones fell onto her cloak.

"That must be about everything he had." Ejord exclaimed looking at the sparkling stones and coins.

"I'm honored that he gave it to me."

Ejord reached down and picked up a small copper coin, the only one of its type on the cloak. "I gave him this when he first came to Chatelgard to tutor us—I gave him this so he wouldn't tell my father that I'd spend lesson times out hunting. He never did." He tried to laugh, but his efforts fell flat.

"He was your friend?"

Ejord nodded.

The sun set while they sat in silence, remembering. Ejord relived his own memories of his friend and tutor. Rifkind thought of the eccentric old man who'd taught her table manners, driven the carriage through the ambush, and in the end offered his life for hers. Feelings of love and trust, always alien and forbidden to her way of life, surfaced in safe grief for the elderly scholar. She struggled with the contradiction that if she had acknowledged the feelings she had for Bainbrose, she would not have left him to his death in her room, but if she had stayed to fight at his side, she would never have learned how much she valued the old man. She took it as a part of her education; knowledge bought at a very dear price that she would never forget.

Ejord was still lost in his own thoughts; she stared uncomfortably around him. A reddish glow remained on the horizon back toward the capital.

"They're burning Daria," Rifkind said flatly.

"All day—the flames appeared before dawn this morning."

She thought first of fire—one of the few things she truly feared—then of the people who would be trapped or fleeing in panic, and finally, narrowing the focus of her thought the final degree, of Linette, Darius and any others who might have been trapped back in the palace compound. She asked Ejord if he knew of the fate of the rest of his family and of Linette.

He shook his head. "My brothers head their own men—Roubleard's dead; he wanted to bring his wife—she's related to Hogarth—Father refused. Anelda took the rest out the tunnels to the royal field quarters. Darius was supposed to make his way there, probably with Linette and his flunkeys, but with Hogarth and Father against them, there's no telling if they made it or what the reception there was if they did."

"Will your father proclaim himself king?"

"Not in Glascardy."

The set tone of Ejord's answer answered any questions Rifkind had about his plans for the future. Interfamily wars were nothing new to her; it was only when they were unnecessarily prolonged that she raised any questions at all about their propriety. Mentally she assessed Ejord's chances, weighing his abilities to deal with the people against his tenseness in dealing with his father. The younger Overnmont certainly knew the lands of his ancestors better than his father, but he sadly lacked the ponderous experience of the older man. He would be outnumbered, and, unless he was very lucky at Chatelgard, without a strong base of operations.

He sensed her thoughts.

"You don't think I have much of a chance; 'friendly, dumb Ejord . . . what would he know about ruling or commanding?' "

"You're going to need help."

"And where do I look for that?"

"Well, with An-Soren dead, I could wait until the

dust settles and offer my services to the last survivor
—but without the ruby I'm no more than an ordinary healer. Of course I could wander the countryside healing—there's always a lot to do after a
battle. But Muroa always said to stay out of feuds
and their aftermaths—vengeance takes strange
forms. So I was going to go back to the Asheera—but
you once said you'd go to Daria with me, because
you thought I'd need help.

"I can adapt to mountains and those cursed winters of yours . . . if you don't have dances and deadly
dull minstrels every night."

"I don't want a witch."

"For the last time, Ejord, I'm a healer . . . I'm offering you my sword, my knives, my tongue, and only
incidentally my other talents."

"Like the poison you had on that dart."

Despite her dark complexion Rifkind colored with
shame and embarrassment.

"I didn't want to get killed by an arrow like an
animal . . . if my aim had been better the spike alone
would have killed him."

The Bright One rose over the place Ejord said was
the Asheera. Rifkind stared back at her homeland,
not really wanting to go back, and at the Bright One,
trying to clear her own thoughts and motives for
going with Ejord to Glascardy. She looked down at
the cloak—it had not been apparent before, but
Bainbrose's treasures had fallen in five roughly concentrated bunches. The groupings, if she looked at
them properly, formed a line, and to her immense
relief the line ran between her and Ejord—not back
toward moonrise, or moonset.

'But I'm not going on to Chatelgard because of
Bainbrose, or the stones, or even You Yourself, my

Goddess. It is where I want to go. I'm glad to know
that You approve, that I still travel with You, but I
have made your vengeance, now I'm going to live
my life—and I think I'll enjoy living at Chatelgard
and holding it against Lord Humphry, Hogarth, and
the rest of Dro Daria if they're foolish enough to try
to wrest it from Ejord. I might even find out more
about Hanju, but only in *my* reality.'

She swept the items into one handful and redid
the knot in the sash. Ejord had begun gathering their
belongings, in unspoken confirmation of their destination and their decision to travel by night. She
knotted the sash—the other end was also weighted,
and in impulsive curiosity she undid that side.

A heavy piece of black glass fell into her hand. It
burned and tingled; she let it fall on the cloak where
it virtually disappeared against the black cloth.

"What's this?" she asked, groping for it.

Ejord stooped over just as she grasped it again.
The tingling started at once, and she dropped it.

Ejord picked it up.

"Are you sure you're better?"

"I'm sure. What is that thing?"

"It's a piece of stone from Lowenrat. Bainbrose
tutored there for a while. He said holding it soothed
his nerves."

Ejord dropped it into her outstretched hand. She
was prepared for the tingling, but did not find it at
all soothing. She forced herself to hold onto it and
got it knotted into the sash before dropping it again.
The palm of her hand stayed numb during the
whole time she saddled Turin.

'Bainbrose had better nerves than I . . .'

She rubbed her palm against the coarse fabric of
her breeches, and sensation began to return to it.

Turin nuzzled the sash, drawing back with a loud snort when his nose encountered the knot which contained the stone.

You too, eh?

Rifkind swung up onto his back, settling into the saddle with more effort than usual. Ejord was already heading off down the hillside. She pulled the cloak tighter and set off after him.